Praise for the Novels of
Patricia Sprinkle

Hold Up the Sky

"Deftly handled by a writer who understands the secrets we keep and the truths we discover as women, *Hold Up the Sky* is a heartfelt story of losing the things that only seem to matter and finding the ones that truly do."
——Lisa Wingate, national bestselling author of *The Summer Kitchen*

"Patricia Sprinkle takes us deep into the thoughts and feelings of four women who realize the only way to true strength is to share their faith, their hearts, and each other's lives. A beautiful and thoroughly Southern story of the enduring bond of women's friendships through the seasons of the year and the seasons of life. Sprinkle knows this world and we are lucky that in her lyrical language she shares it with us!"
——Patti Callahan Henry, national bestselling author of *Driftwood Summer*

Carley's Song

Finalist for the 2002 Christy Award

"Sprinkle is adept at crafting memorable settings that feel historically authentic, and she portrays Carley's first crush . . . in sweet, nostalgic ways. . . . The writing is superb, the murder is resolved in a surprising way, and there's plenty of redemption and hope laced throughout to please Christian fiction buffs."
——*Publishers Weekly*

continued . . .

"Sprinkle entertains and enchants her readers. Her characters are so real you'll find yourself believing you grew up with them. . . . This is a book you'll find hard to put down and sorry to see end. You'll want to curl up with a hot cup of tea or an ice-cold glass of lemonade while reading *Carley's Song*—or maybe an RC Cola."   *—Christian Retailing*

"Sprinkle brings life to a dusty little town with many secrets and the reader is completely drawn into Carley's world, from beginning to end."
—Romantic Times

The Remember Box

"Deftly addresses racial tensions in the segregated South of 1949. . . . Readers will enjoy Sprinkle's memorable cast of characters and unexpected plot twists, and be challenged by her message of racial equality."   *—Publishers Weekly*

"Mystery maven Sprinkle lends her unique voice to the Christian market with this part whodunit, part black comedy, and part coming-of-age novel. For all collections."   *—Library Journal*

"Mixes prejudice and poverty with love and understanding . . . *The Remember Box* is a moving story, uniquely and carefully crafted between past and present."   *—Romantic Times*

"The kind of book that anybody would love to have as a present."
—The Spartanburg Herald-Journal (SC)

Hold Up the Sky

PATRICIA SPRINKLE

NAL
ACCENT

NAL ACCENT
Published by New American Library, a division of
Penguin Group (USA) Inc., 375 Hudson Street,
New York, New York 10014, USA
Penguin Group (Canada), 90 Eglinton Avenue East, Suite 700, Toronto,
Ontario M4P 2Y3, Canada (a division of Pearson Penguin Canada Inc.)
Penguin Books Ltd., 80 Strand, London WC2R 0RL, England
Penguin Ireland, 25 St. Stephen's Green, Dublin 2,
Ireland (a division of Penguin Books Ltd.)
Penguin Group (Australia), 250 Camberwell Road, Camberwell, Victoria 3124,
Australia (a division of Pearson Australia Group Pty. Ltd.)
Penguin Books India Pvt. Ltd., 11 Community Centre, Panchsheel Park,
New Delhi - 110 017, India
Penguin Group (NZ), 67 Apollo Drive, Rosedale, North Shore 0632,
New Zealand (a division of Pearson New Zealand Ltd.)
Penguin Books (South Africa) (Pty.) Ltd., 24 Sturdee Avenue,
Rosebank, Johannesburg 2196, South Africa

Penguin Books Ltd., Registered Offices:
80 Strand, London WC2R 0RL, England

First published by NAL Accent, an imprint of New American Library,
a division of Penguin Group (USA) Inc.

First Printing, March 2010
10 9 8 7 6 5 4 3 2 1

Copyright © Patricia Sprinkle, 2010
Conversation Guide copyright © Penguin Group (USA) Inc., 2010
All rights reserved

LIBRARY OF CONGRESS CATALOGING-IN-PUBLICATION DATA:

Sprinkle, Patricia Houck.
  Hold up the sky/Patricia Sprinkle.
    p. cm.
  ISBN 978-0-451-22914-4
  1. Life change events—Fiction. 2. Female friendship—Fiction. 3. Georgia—Fiction. 4. Domestic fiction.
I. Title.
  PS3569.P687H65 2010
  813'.54—dc22   2009039628

Set in Granjon
Designed by Ginger Legato

Printed in the United States of America

In memory of Gerard Van Lier,
whose insight inspired this story
and whose friendship still warms our lives

Hold Up the Sky

Some people keep memories in scrapbooks or diaries. Mine are preserved in quart Ball jars. They sit on my pantry shelves in shining rows. As autumn sunlight glances off their bright faces, they gleam like stained glass: scarlet tomatoes, emerald beans, golden peaches, and blueberries the color of my sister's eyes.

I need to be getting ready. We have a busy day. But first I tiptoe to the pantry to touch the jars. Like Dorothy's ruby slippers they have magic to take me home—to Daddy's steaming kitchen, where I worked last summer with three other women through drought-stricken weeks. Outside, it was so hot that the children's plastic pool softened and sagged. The kitchen was a sauna. We were not friends, though two of us were sisters. Conversation flared in irate outbursts or limped out in reluctant confessions. But if a holy place is where God is, then these jars are sacred relics.

I brush away a tear as I stroke a jar of beans.

"What are you doing?" my daughter demands from the pantry door.

Cerebral palsy bends Michelle almost double and freezes her fingers into improbable positions, like twigs on a tree. Her feet turn in, her tongue lolls, her head is twisted into a slant of permanent inquiry. But she has her daddy's golden eyes and my dimples, and I think her beautiful. I wish others saw her as I do.

She is saucy, funny, and smart. She has learned to operate a power chair by moving her head. She is learning to use a computer to keep up in kindergarten. However, at five going on fifteen, she has started making frequent spot checks on my behavior to make sure her mother remains somewhere on the fringes of normal.

Her sensors are fine-tuned this morning. When she catches me touching jars in the pantry, she knows I'm not checking to see if we have enough food to last through the winter.

"Mama! We need to get ready. What are you *doing?*"

"Looking at these jars." My finger traces a jar of tomatoes, lingering on a spot where sunlight shoots sparks off the glass. "It was tomatoes we canned first," I murmur.

"Mama!" Michelle packs whole paragraphs into that one word.

"Sorry, honey. I was thinking about Mamie, Emerita, and Aunt Margaret. Stuff we talked about while we put up these jars."

I see a flicker of interest in her eyes. Yesterday she would have begged, "Tell me a story." This morning she quenches the flicker to take charge of the family. "Bo-o-ring. You need to hurry."

Don't hurry, Michelle! Don't grow up so fast! Don't lose the wonder you have as a child. When you have passed through stormy years to become whoever you will be, I cannot promise you will find wonder waiting on the other side.

"I hate it when you say 'bo-o-ring' like that," I remind her.

Her golden eyes flash with mischief. "I know. That's why I said it."

I pinch her nose lightly. "You little devil." When she teases, she is my imp child again.

Having jerked my chain to get a smile, she shifts her head to make her chair turn. "Come on. Help me get dressed."

"I'll be there in a second."

As she rolls toward her bedroom, I see her rolling through years to come. Before I know it she, too, will be a woman. Will she have an easier time learning what I learned in that sweltering kitchen?

I press a cool jar of beans to my cheek. For Michelle's sake I will preserve on paper what I first preserved in jars.

PART ONE

Storm Warnings

"A storm was gathering out of the darkness, and already there was lightning in the sky."

—Lytton Strachey

One

Our story began not last summer, but a week before Easter—
the week, Mamie Fountain would say, when the great weaver
began collecting threads for his tapestry.

On Saturday, Mamie got a brand-new secondhand PT Cruiser the
color of eggplant. She had never owned such a magnificent car.

She had never owned a car radio that worked, either. "Oh happy
day!" she caroled with a gospel quartet as she rolled along. She switched
off the radio when the weather report came on. She didn't need some
white man telling her Georgia was having a drought. Anybody with
two eyes could see how cracked the earth was, like some old woman
showing her age. But God was capable of running the universe. Mamie
was free to devote herself to enjoying her new car.

Mamie's first car was an old Chevy an employer gave her. Her second was a rusted-out Dodge she paid five hundred dollars for when she
started working at the textile mill. It wasn't pretty, but it ran. Since the
death of her husband, Earl, eight years before, she had driven his old
green Ford—which had a number of peculiarities arising from Earl's
conviction that he could fix with copper wire or duct tape anything that
ailed a car. But on the previous Thursday, Earl's Ford had died.

"It's fitting for us to go to church on our first trip," she told the

Cruiser, patting the dashboard with a hand like soft brown cocoa. "The good Lord helped me get you." Already she knew that little car was going to be a friend she could tell anything.

She rolled slowly through downtown Solace, disappointed nobody was around to admire her. "Back when I was a girl," she told the car, "this place was *lively*. See those train tracks across from the stores? They only carry freight trains now, but a passenger train used to run between Solace and Atlanta every day. I'll bet if they'd kept all the trains, this country wouldn't be in that global-warning fix. I know Solace would be livelier."

It pained Mamie that Solace had shriveled to little more than three blocks of thrift stores, insurance offices, antique emporiums, and empty storefronts that drowsed behind mud-spattered plate glass windows.

"We had a growth spurt a few years back," she continued as she headed out of town. "Folks from Atlanta started moving out to escape the crowds. See that subdivision over there? For a while, they sprouted in pastures like dandelions. New folks bragged about living near a charming little town with no traffic, small schools, and great mountain views. They never seemed to notice they were filling up the schools, adding to the traffic, and messing up the view. You know what I'd bet?"

The car gave an inquisitive lurch.

"I'd bet Atlanta was a charming little place before all the people moved in. But when gas prices went up and folks started losing their jobs, Solace slid downhill again. Those new subdivisions are plumb dotted with For sale signs. A lot of them read Foreclosure." She paused for a moment, contemplating the worlds of pain contained in that word. But Mamie was seldom downhearted for long. "Some developers still have money," she assured the little car. "Thanks to one of them, I got you." She patted the dashboard again. Chatting to that little car, she could forget for a time the tests she'd had on Tuesday past and what the doctor might be going to say to her and her daughter, Lurleen, on Monday.

MAMIE WASN'T SURE SHE SHOULD take seriously anything said by a doctor so young he looked like he needed a hall pass to be out of class, but Lurleen would take every word he said for gospel truth. Mamie would never have invited Lurleen along if Dr. Hodges hadn't insisted when he had called on Friday.

She sighed. As soon as Dr. Hodges finished talking, Lurleen would start. All the way home Mamie would be subjected to the same old song, second verse: "You are past seventy, Mama, and you have a bad heart. You need to go to a place where people can take care of you."

"I can take care of myself," Mamie announced to her car, "and the good Lord wouldn't have given you to me if he wasn't gonna let me live long enough to get pleasure out of you." She clutched the wheel defiantly, hoping it was true.

Outside the city limits she stepped on the gas. Sun-bleached asphalt rushed toward the pointed hood. "I am so happy to have you, I could kiss both the good Lord and Mr. Landiss. I'm not sure Mr. Landiss believes in God," she admitted, feeling she and the car ought to start out with strict honesty between them, "but God uses all sorts of instruments to do his will."

Mamie had no doubt God had willed her to buy that car. She had been wanting a PT Cruiser ever since she saw her first one on the highway. It reminded her of her uncle Gene's '41 Plymouth, the first car she could remember. When she saw a picture of a Cruiser in a magazine, she taped it to her refrigerator and started squeezing a few dollars from each Social Security check. But Mamie did not buy things until she could afford them.

"I was lower than a worm's belly when Earl's old green Ford died on Thursday," she confided. "I hadn't saved up enough for even a beat-up jalopy. I worried all night, wondering how I would get around. Just before dawn the train blew for the downtown crossing, and I swear to you, that whistle played the first three notes of Mama's favorite hymn." Mamie's rich alto rolled out the open window.

What a friend we have in Jesus,
All our sins and griefs to bear.
What a privilege to carry
Everything to God in prayer.

"That whistle was a rebuke straight from God. I asked him to forgive me for worrying. I reminded him I was a poor widow in need of transportation; then I slept like a baby—although I don't know why we say that. None of the babies I ever had anything to do with slept particularly well. But God sure answered my prayers. I don't know why it takes me so long sometimes to remember to pray."

She had said the same thing to Lurleen on the phone late Friday evening.

Lurleen—visiting her own daughter, Janeika, in San Antonio—had called Mamie immediately after Skeeter, her husband, phoned to tell her what her mama had done. "What's this Skeeter's telling me about you're gonna sell some land for some old shopping center? Don't you sign a thing until I get home—you hear me? I fly in on Sunday evening. We'll discuss it then."

"Nothing to discuss. I asked the good Lord for help, and five hours later I got a sure-nuff miracle. A man showed up on my front porch— Mr. Landiss, his name is—looking to buy land for a shopping center. I sold him that strip up by the road."

"Don't you sign anything until I get home," Lurleen warned.

"Already did. Mr. Landiss carried me to town this morning and we signed all the papers."

"Mama! That was supposed to be for your old age! Or for my inheritance."

"I'm in my old age," Mamie pointed out, "and you and Skeeter both have good jobs with the post office. You all will be taken care of. Besides, this was an answer to prayer. God knew I needed a car. With what Mr. Landiss gave me for that land, I have enough for a car *and* a bit left over for catastrophes. I've asked Skeeter to come over in the morning to carry me to some car dealers. I'll appreciate his help in picking one out."

Mamie didn't believe in coincidence. She gave credit where credit was due. "Thank you, thank you, Jesus!" she shouted Sunday morning as she rolled along.

"Jesus even picked your color," she told the little car. "I thought I wanted black. Those black ones look so *elegant*! But the car lots we went to had only blue ones, silver ones, and you. Skeeter leaned toward one of the blue ones, but when the salesman said your color is called ober-*gene*, I could hear my uncle Gene saying, *Sugah, that's your car!*

"Thank, you, Jesus," she shouted again. She stroked the seat beside her. "You be good, now. You gotta last me the rest of my life."

ON HER WAY TO CHURCH, Mamie passed my place. I was out in the yard adjusting the carburetor in my truck while Lucky, my old black tom, chased chipmunks around the azaleas. Michelle sat on the porch counting birds. She had just sung out, "Fifty-leven," when Mamie pulled into the drive. "Hey, Chellie. Hey, Billie! How's the Waits family doing?"

"Uu-in oooh," Michelle called back. *Doing good.*

Mamie was one of the few people who understood Michelle's grating words. They were almost all vowels, for her tongue had trouble with consonants.

"That's good, honey. I'm gonna bring you some chocolate pudding one of these days."

Chellie bounced in her chair. She adored chocolate pudding.

I strolled over to the car so we wouldn't have to shout. Mamie transferred her attention to me. "Don't you wish it would rain so we can get rid of this—" She started coughing so bad, she couldn't finish.

"Pollen?" I finished for her. Every April oaks and pines blanket Georgia in soft golden dust. Usually spring rains wash it away, but in that second year of drought the state was deep in the stuff. My front walk looked like the yellow brick road. The 1976 Ford truck Daddy and I had totally rebuilt when I was in high school—and which I loved almost as much as I loved Michelle—was streaked like a tiger. My nose had been blown so often, I looked like a clown.

When Mamie could speak again, she rasped, "Everything goin' all right with you?"

Mamie was the closest thing I had to a second mother. She had taken care of me until I started first grade because Mama taught school. She was my first supervisor at the textile mill when I started there after I got married. In the year since Mama died, she'd dropped in often to be sure I was okay. I wished I could lay my cheek on her broad shoulder and confess that my present troubles were a heck of a lot bigger than pollen.

However, Daddy made it clear when I insisted on marrying Porter Waits the week I finished high school that if I was adult enough to make that decision, I was adult enough to live with the consequences. In the past ten years, I'd gotten accustomed to carrying my own burdens.

"We're keeping on keeping on," I told her, "considering this drought and the state of the economy."

Mamie flapped one hand to dismiss drought and the economy. "It's all part of God's tapestry, honey. A light thread here, a dark thread there. This thing they're calling 'an economic downturn' is just one of God's darker threads. He'll use it for his own good purposes."

Daddy always said Mamie could find theology in a stop sign.

"Speaking of God"—her disapproving eyes took in my oil-stained overalls—"what you doing fixing that truck on Palm Sunday morning? You ought to be getting ready for church."

God and I had not been on cordial speaking terms for five years. After Porter left, every night for months I filled the darkness with prayers, but God must have put me on his Do Not Call list. I hadn't noticed any heavenly blessings falling my way since then.

Even so, as long as Mama was alive, I went to church every Sunday. When she got cancer I poured out more prayers than I had in my whole life. After she died, I decided making Daddy happy wasn't reason enough to get myself and Chellie dressed up every Sunday.

After all, Daddy and I weren't on real cordial terms, either. He'd said a lot of hurtful things back when I married Porter—things about how I was throwing away a college education and a chance to become somebody in order to waste myself on a man who would never amount to a hill of squash. He hadn't even come to our little wedding. After Porter left, Daddy rubbed it in that a lot of the things he'd prophesied had come true. That didn't make me feel one bit better. So, feeling none too charitable toward either God or Daddy, I saw no reason to go to church.

I wasn't about to tell Mamie any of that, of course. She'd have been all over me like flies on molasses. I gave her my standard reply: "Our church doesn't have a ramp and Chellie is getting too heavy for me to carry up the steps. Nice car," I added, to distract her.

"Isn't it wonderful?" She patted the gleaming purple door. "Even got a radio and electric windows." She rolled her window up and down to demonstrate. "Well, I better be getting to church to give proper thanks for it. See you later." As she backed out, she called, "You could ask one of the men to carry Chellie up them steps."

"I know."

She tooted as she drove away.

A MILE DOWN THE ROAD Mamie spied Daddy and his dog, Jimbo, out in front of his hay barn, studying the sky. Mamie tooted. Daddy waved. You did that in the country.

"A good man, Bill Anderson," she told the car, "but persnickety. Likes things done just right. Makes a good dairy farmer, but it made him strict with his girls. He worked them hard growing up, and I think he stopped showing them much affection once they started turning from little girls into women. He probably didn't know how. He's real reserved around women. I've always thought he may be shy. The only woman he was ever comfortable around was his wife, Grace. She brought out the softness in him. Since she died last year, he's gotten skinny as a rail. That old dog looks like it's doing all the eating in that house."

Wanting the car to know a bit more of her history, Mamie explained, "I worked for Grace Anderson off and on for twelve years. The girls were eight years apart and I kept both of them until they started all-day school. I didn't know Bill well—he was generally out and about while I was there—but I've always felt beholden to him, because when Grace didn't need me anymore, Bill suggested I try for a job at the mill—said they paid well and gave good benefits. He wrote me a real good recommendation, and around here, his word carries a lot of weight. After I got on at the mill, I rose to supervisor. Now I've got a paid-up brick house, a little land, and Social Security. Who woulda thought I'd have all that plus you?"

Her chuckle died half-born. "Poor Bill, he looks pitiful. I'll make him a cobbler from some of those blackberries I froze last summer. He was always partial to my blackberry cobbler. I'll take it over this evening. His girls aren't likely to come by." Her voice was thick with disgust. "I'd like to spank them both for the way they neglect their daddy. I don't care how hard he was on them growing up, or how much he yelled when they got married."

Mamie turned into the unpaved parking lot of the Holy Comfort and Praise Baptist Church. "Billie's got a lot on her hands, raising Chellie alone, but tell me, Lord, what's Margaret got to do that's so all-fired important she can't drive out fifty miles now and then to visit her daddy?"

Before God had time to answer, Mamie saw two friends heading her way, pointing and grinning. They spent so much time admiring her car—sitting in the seats, stroking its soft plush upholstery—they missed the first hymn. After church a friend needed help, so Mamie postponed making Daddy's cobbler until the following afternoon.

Two

I wasn't a total heathen. Every Sunday morning after I stopped going to church, I turned on the televised broadcast of a big church in Marietta, where my sister's family went. Chellie sat glued to the screen watching for Margaret, Ben, Jason, and Andy. She had a crush on Jason, who was fifteen, and adored Andy, who was six. I watched because I nursed a secret conviction that if I could meet a man like Wallace Harison, their handsome preacher, I could turn from a sloppy, uninteresting mom into a woman of poise and purpose.

Like my sister.

If I was on God's blocked-callers list, Margaret was one of his pets. When she was in the womb, he gave her the best our family had to offer: Daddy's long, lean body and black curls, Mama's pretty face, and Grandmother Baker's blue-violet eyes. I got eyes the color of faded denim, frizzy curls somewhere between yellow and orange, a pointed chin, a too-wide mouth, and the genes for short and sturdy. After her third year of college, Margaret married a wonderful man, Ben Baxter. They'd been happily married for sixteen years. Their two sons could have been poster children for healthy, happy, and smart. Their business—landscaping and maintaining the grounds of office parks—was so successful, they'd been able build their dream home on a lot nestled against the shoulder of Kennesaw Mountain. The yard Margaret had created around that house was in demand for Marietta garden club tours. No wonder Margaret took her family to church every week. God deserved it, after all he'd given her.

Margaret told me once she also went to church to rest. She liked to sink into a velvet cushion and let the organ, like a hot bath, draw out all her weariness. She loved the bright jewels of light flung by stained-glass windows against the high creamy walls. She basked in the blended scents of flowers, expensive perfumes, lemon polish, and that musty scent of holiness peculiar to churches. She enjoyed having one blessed hour each week when her phone didn't ring and nobody asked her to do a thing.

A week of Margaret's life would have killed me. She kept her own house except for a maid twice a month. She took care of her yard except for mowing—Ben sent a crew to do that. She spent afternoons driving Andy to activities or playdates and picking up Jason from track. She cooked for huge parties she and Ben loved to host. For recreation, she and her best friend, Katrinka Smith, played killer tennis for the Atlanta Lawn Tennis Association.

She loved everything she did. She told new friends, "My life is my family, my house, and tennis."

Margaret was also so danged nice (to everybody but Daddy and me) and so incredibly capable that she got asked to do a lot more than keep house and play tennis. That year she was Andy's first-grade room mother, secretary of Jason's high school PTA, treasurer of her garden club, and chair of her church landscape committee.

I once warned, "Watch the traffic, Maggie. You are going to meet yourself one day."

She frowned. "Don't call me Maggie. You know I hate it."

Don't think I envied my sister her big house, her busy life, or even her perfect sons. I was content in a cocoon of my own making: a small house and a small life. When I wasn't busy with Chellie, I worked on my truck, kept up our yard, or tended my garden and little two-acre orchard. One thing we sisters had in common was that we both loved digging in the dirt. Daddy worked us hard growing up, but he taught us reverence for growing things.

No, I didn't envy Margaret, but I wouldn't have minded having someone like Ben to share my life with. I also wondered sometimes why God loved Margaret more than me.

MARGARET WASN'T THINKING ABOUT ME as church started that Sunday morning. She was doing a quick check to make sure nobody was picking his nose before the television cameras rolled. Jason, on her right, slumped on his tailbone. He was a handsome boy with her looks and Ben's easygoing nature. His posture, though, proclaimed to the world what he thought of having to sit with his family instead of with his buddies in the balcony, where they could spend the hour text messaging each other. Margaret gave him a warning nudge. He huffed, but slid back up. Margaret sent up a silent prayer of thanks that Jason wasn't rude to his parents like so many of his friends.

Andy, on her left, was a miniature Ben—sky blue eyes, short white hair, and a face full of freckles. His tongue peeked out of one side of his mouth as he industriously colored Jesus' robe purple on his children's bulletin. Purple was Andy's favorite color.

Ben, beyond Andy, sat with his arms folded on his chest, his eyes half-closed in an attitude of prayer. Attitude was all it was. Ben's pre-church grumbling was as much a part of their Sunday ritual as attending church or going out for pizza with the crowd after Margaret's afternoon tennis match. Margaret had long accepted the fact that Ben went to church for the same reason he belonged to the Marietta Country Club: to meet potential customers. That week, she suspected he was planning the landscaping for Rick Landiss's next office park. Business was all he seemed to think about anymore.

When did we stop talking?

They used to hatch ideas for building the business or improving their property, and plan extravagant vacations they would take when they got enough money. Lately, they had been so busy with the boys, her meetings, his business . . .

As if he sensed her gaze, Ben gave her the lazy smile he used to in American lit class, when those blue eyes could drive all thoughts of Hemingway out of her head. Even after seventeen years it made her heart flutter.

How long has it been since we made love?

The question seemed to blare from her pew across the congregation. Her cheeks burned. Margaret glanced up to be sure the television cameras weren't aimed on her. How could she be thinking about sex in church?

Don't be silly, said common sense. *Marriages are made and babies dedicated here.*

This is still no place to be thinking about sex.

She was glad to hear the opening notes of the first hymn. As the congregation stood, an acolyte carried a candle lighter toward the altar. Andy tugged her elbow. "Mama?" he whispered. "When can I be an acolyte?"

She made the familiar shift from wife to mother. "When you are in fifth grade."

He sighed. "That's a long time. Were you an acolyte?"

"No, my church didn't have them. Katrinka was, though. In this very church."

"As we sat down after the hymn," Margaret would tell me later, *"I was transported in an instant from the sanctuary to a damp cabin with gritty floors, a rattling air conditioner, and the smell of a disinfectant used to clean the bathroom."*

Here's how she would tell the story:

I WENT TO SUMMER CAMP when I was eleven. Daddy took me, so I arrived early, the only camper from our church. I was excited about meeting girls from other places.

The first four girls arrived at the cabin giggling about boys they'd already met. I wasn't interested in boys, but I wished I had friends to giggle with. Those girls, though, could have come from another planet. Their sneakers were the colors of sherbet. Their legs were shaved. Every one of them wore a cute top with matching shorts. Their duffel bags were hot pink, turquoise, purple, or lime green. I kicked my black duffel under my bunk with a grubby sneaker, dreading the time I'd have to pull out my cutoffs and faded T-shirts.

The girls ignored me as they chose bunks across the cabin, grumbling about having to make their own beds.

"Leave that for later," urged a skinny girl with a red ponytail and freckles. "Let's swim!"

They pulled out bathing suits in rainbow colors, squealing like baby pigs.

"Can you believe they make us wear one-piece suits? It's like the Dark Ages!"

"Which suit do you think I ought to wear first?"

"The blue. Those flowers around the neck are darling."

Next thing I knew, they were stripping to the skin. I had never seen a naked girl my own age. I looked down at my lap, red as a beet, but not before I noticed two of them had breasts.

One pranced toward my end of the cabin to fling a sales tag toward a wastebasket. It missed, but she didn't care. I picked it up to throw it away. Her swimsuit had cost more than my entire Easter outfit.

Not until they were ready to leave did anybody notice me. "Who are you?" asked a girl with long white hair. She was one of the girls with breasts. When I grew up, I wanted to look just like her.

I slid to my feet. "Maggie Anderson, from Solace."

"We're from Marietta. I'm Esther Sue Barkley."

Esther Sue. It sounded like a movie star's name.

"This"—Esther Sue pointed to a short girl with shining hair the same brown as pine bark—"is Sissy Woodside, who is a fantastic artist. This"—a girl with a large mouth full of braces—"is Nadra Landiss, the world's best tennis player. And this"—the skinny girl with a red pony-tail—"is Katrinka Cheney, also known as the Brain. Aren't you coming to the lake?"

"I don't swim." Mama had bought me a red suit on sale at Wal-Mart, but after seeing the other girls' suits, I had no intention of putting it on.

They couldn't have looked more astonished if I had said, "I don't breathe." They surrounded me in a scented cloud of floral shampoo.

"So how'd you get that great tan?" Sissy asked.

"Working outside."

She squinted in bewilderment. "Doing what?"

"Weeding the garden and picking vegetables. I live on a farm." I said it with pride. Daddy was always talking about how, without farmers, the world would starve.

"You live on a farm?" repeated Nadra, the one with the mouth full of braces.

"You mean, like, with horses? I have a horse." Esther Sue swung her long hair off her shoulders. "I love to ride, don't you? Do you ride dressage?"

I wished I could say, "Sure—every day," but I had no idea what dressage was. Besides, "We have a dairy farm," I admitted. "We don't keep horses. We do have chickens and pigs."

Nadra screwed up her nose. "Pigs? *Eewww!* Don't they stink?"

Esther Sue gave a delicate sniff, like she was checking to be sure I hadn't brought pig stink along.

I felt like hitting them. "We don't keep pigs near the house."

Sissy giggled. "I didn't know anybody really lived on a *farm*."

Nobody had ever made fun of me before. A cold lump of misery filled my middle. I had wanted to be friends with those girls! Still, being Daddy's daughter, I felt a duty to defend farmers. "Don't you all eat? Where do you think food comes from?"

Esther Sue tossed her hair. "*Ours* comes from the grocery store, silly."

"You're the silly one. Where do you think the grocery store gets it? Without farmers, you wouldn't have milk, meat, eggs, bread, fruit, or vegetables. You'd starve. If developers don't stop buying up farmland, we may all starve."

Nadra bared her braces. "My daddy's a developer."

"Tell him not to develop farmland. We have to have farms if we are to eat."

Esther Sue gave a careless shrug. "Whatever." With that one uncaring word, she reduced me and the whole issue of farming to something not worth her time. "Come on." She glided toward the door. "The lake's waiting!"

As they clattered down the steps in colorful rubber flip-flops, Nadra called, "Bye-bye, Farmer Maggie." The others giggled. I knew that name would stick all week, just below the radar of the counselors.

I wanted to kill them. I wanted to run all the way home. I certainly didn't think I could survive the week. I was swiping away furious tears when the girl with the red ponytail called through the screen door, "Don't mind them. They are brainless. I'm Katrinka Cheney, remember?" She came inside. "What's your name again?"

"Maggie Anderson."

"I am delighted to meet a girl who thinks about something besides boys or her next haircut." Katrinka stuck out one hand. I wiped my tear-damp hand on my shorts and gave it to her. We shook as solemnly as world leaders sealing a treaty.

"Do you really not swim?" She sounded surprised but not critical.

"No. We don't have a pool in Solace and the only water on the farm is cattle ponds."

"Want me to teach you? We can go down to the lake before the others get up."

"We aren't allowed in the lake without a lifeguard."

"It's okay. I teach swimming to little kids at our club pool, so I have my lifesaving badge. I'm a pretty good teacher, if I do say so myself."

She didn't mention that she was also a swimming champion, but she won every meet at camp that week. And we crept down to the lake at six every morning. By the end of the week, I could swim.

In exchange, I helped her with crafts. Katrinka was hopeless when it came to braiding lariats. When my beaded leather bag won a blue ribbon on the last day, Katrinka warned, "Watch out for Sissy. She expected to sweep the arts-and-crafts competitions." Sure enough, I found my ribbon cut to pieces when I unpacked back home.

I took more away from camp than a ruined ribbon. I took home a fierce determination to show the Sissies, Nadras, and Esther Sues of the world that I was as good as they were.

MARGARET WAS STARTLED TO HEAR the congregation murmur in unison, "And with you." Was it already time for the pastoral prayer? She had thought about summer camp all the way through the service, including the sermon. She hoped the television cameras hadn't caught her with a blank look on her face.

Dr. Harison began to pray, his voice as silver as the hair that waved back from his high forehead. That week he was taking seriously the Governor's Call to Prayer for Rain. "We beseech Thee, O Lord, to pour out Thy blessings upon us. Send rain for our parched state."

But not until after our match this afternoon, Margaret amended his prayer. Then, feeling guilty for a selfish petition when the state was desperate for rain, she sent up another addendum: "But do send rain to farmers. Especially Daddy. Amen."

WHEN MARGARET TOOK ANDY UP for a short nap that afternoon, he demanded, "Tell me about Katrinka being an acolyte. Did you ever see her carry the light?"

"Sometimes, when I'd come spend a weekend with her in Marietta."

"Did Katrinka ever go to Papa's farm?"

"Oh, yes. She loved it out there. She watched me milk, helped feed the chickens and pigs, and sometimes she picked vegetables to take home to her mother. At night, we slept on a pile of quilts on the living room floor, because Aunt Billie was little and we shared a room. Katrinka and I couldn't talk if she was asleep."

"I wish I could go to the farm. I *never* got to sleep there."

Margaret was startled to realize it was true. She had taken Jason for a week every summer until Andy was born, but by the time Andy was old enough to enjoy the farm, her mother had been too ill for overnight guests.

How long has it been since I spent a night there?

"Maybe we can go for a weekend this summer," she said.

"Promise?"

"We'll see."

"What did you do at Katrinka's?"

"We went to the club to swim—"

"Like our club?"

"The same club. Sometimes we shopped at a mall or went to a movie. I loved going to her house, because at my house I had to work hard on weekends. Besides, Katrinka's house was beautiful." She thought of something she knew would tickle his funny bone. "The first time Papa took me there, he told me not to get too big for my britches."

As she had expected, that earned a snicker. "Why?"

"Because the Cheneys' house was big, with grass all around it, and inside it had carpet on all the floors, polished furniture—"

"We have those things."

"Yeah, but we didn't at the farm. Katrinka had her own room, too, with twin beds and a bathroom she only had to share with her sister."

"Me and Jason have that."

"I know, but at the farm, remember, there's only the upstairs bathroom for the whole family. I thought Katrinka's house was a mansion. I promised myself that one day I would live in a beautiful house exactly like hers."

Andy's eyes were drifting shut. "And now you do."

She pulled his covers to his chin. "Now I do."

She mulled that over as she went downstairs. She was startled to realize how much Mrs. Cheney's taste had influenced the way she had decorated her home.

TWO HOURS LATER MARGARET STUMBLED off the court, hot, sweaty, and elated. She looked for Ben, but didn't see him.

"Good game!" said Nadra Binnings—the same Nadra who had dubbed Margaret "Farmer Maggie" at church camp. If she had recognized Margaret when they met again years later, she had never said so.

"Way to go, Mags! Those Dunwoody girls will cry all the way home." Rick Landiss, Nadra's brother, smiled down at her. Rick's face was lean like a wolf's. His wife, Louise, used to play on the team before she hurled a vase at Rick and went home to Memphis, and he still showed up for a lot of their matches. Ben joked that Rick liked watching legs more than matches.

Margaret wanted to snap, "Don't call me Mags and they aren't girls," but she shaped her lips into a smile. Rick helped his father run Landiss Construction Company, one of the large office park developers in Cobb County and Ben's biggest customer. "You're sweet to say so. What did you do to your hand?"

He held up the cast with a rueful smile. "Broke it in a freak golf accident a week or so ago. Want to kiss it and make it better?"

"No, but I'll sign it and make you famous. Have you all seen Ben?"

Nadra jerked one thumb behind her. "He's over near the parking lot, consoling Bayonne for losing her match."

Bayonne Bradshaw, the newest team member, had replaced Louise Landiss. Twenty-six and divorced, Bayonne had wide blue eyes and honey hair that swung six inches above her seat. When Margaret found Ben, he and Bayonne were clicking bottles of beer. Bayonne had shaken her hair out of the ponytail she'd worn to play and changed into pink slacks and a white cotton top that hugged her high little breasts. Margaret was acutely aware of a dirt smear across the front of her shirt.

Ben raised his bottle in a salute. "Great match!"

Bayonne wrinkled her pert nose. "I wish I had your backhand. We lost."

Margaret wiped one cold wet hand across her forehead. "I'd trade my backhand for a Coke, but I don't have energy to walk back to the food table."

Ben handed Margaret his bottle. "Take my beer. I've had a couple. It's a thirsty kind of day."

Margaret didn't like beer, but she let a swallow wash her throat before she handed it back. "That's enough. Thanks. Ready to go?" Short sentences were all she could trust not to catch in her throat. If Ben had been out near the parking lot with Bayonne long enough to drink two beers, he hadn't been watching her game. You couldn't see the court from where they stood.

He read her thoughts. "You were good, hon. I caught most of it. She's great, isn't she, Andy?" He rumpled their son's stiff bristle. Beneath the hair, Andy's scalp was bright pink. Why hadn't Ben made him wear his cap? He knew how easily Andy burned.

Margaret bit back the question and looked around. "Where's Jason?"

"He ran into some buddies. They've gone to a movie."

"Who were they?"

"I don't know them, but they said he'll be home by ten thirty."

"Ten thirty?" Ben himself had come up with Jason's rules until he could drive, and he had insisted they keep them simple: be home by nine on school nights and only go out with people your parents know or have met.

But Ben was notorious about breaking rules, even ones he had set.

Margaret had a rule, too. She never quarreled with Ben in public. She turned to Bayonne with a smile. "Coming for pizza with the team?"

"Not this evening." She touched Ben's arm lightly. "Thanks for the beer." As she swung down the walk toward the parking lot, that pendulum of honey hair marked time to her walk.

Three

At nine thirty Monday morning, Mamie watched the pencil held between Dr. Hodges's fingers swing over his desk.

"I tried to listen to what he was saying," she would tell us later. "He used phrases like 'long-standing hypertension,' 'heart seriously damaged,' 'years longer, with care,' but I kept getting distracted by watching that pencil. It was like a clock pendulum ticking away seconds of my life. My hands grew cold; then my whole body was cold—like I had already died but my brain hadn't been notified. I hate to admit it, but I was terrified. I tried to pray, but I couldn't. Dr. Hodges was talking about my life and I wasn't ready to let it go."

She stood up in the middle of a sentence. "Thank you, Doctor. Let's go, Lurleen. We've heard what we came to hear."

She walked slowly to the car on ankles that were so swollen they looked like small tree trunks. Lurleen's car was locked, so she leaned against it to wait. She tried to pray, but words failed her. In the end, she spent the time until Lurleen came watching a flock of robins pulling worms from the grass. Mamie identified with the worms.

Lurleen arrived with a prescription in one hand. "You were rude, Mama," she fussed as they got in the car. "He was saying—"

Mamie held up a hand. "I don't want to talk about it, and I don't want you talking about it. Not one word to anybody except Skeeter— you hear me?"

"We have to talk about it, Mama. There's things we have to decide."

"Not right this minute, we don't. For now, promise me. Not a word to anybody. I don't want people looking at me with pity eyes, wondering when I'm gonna drop dead."

"I've told you for years that high blood pressure is nothing to be messed with, that you ought to take better care of yourself. Stop doing so much. Get more rest. Take your pills. But would you listen?"

"Mother Teresa had a bad heart. She didn't let it slow her down."

Lurleen heaved a sigh from her toes. "You are not Mother Teresa. You are a Baptist who does far too much for other people."

Mamie glowered.

"All right, Mama. We won't talk about it right now. But if I promise not to say a word about this to anybody but Skeeter, I want you to promise to think about moving into a place where you can take it easy, where somebody else will fix your meals and be there if you feel sick in the night. Okay?"

Mamie closed her eyes. "Okay. I promise."

To think about it, she added mentally.

Lurleen didn't say another word on their way home. Without voices to drown them out, three words ran around in Mamie's head like a squirrel on a wheel. *I am dying. I am dying.* The way her heart was thudding, it would fail from fear.

Mamie was no stranger to death. She had sat by Earl's bed while he coughed his way into heaven. She'd been with her mama when she gave one last groan of pain and rested in the arms of Jesus. She'd stood beside her grandmother's bed the afternoon she slipped peacefully into her final sleep. Friends often called Mamie to sit with them while somebody died. Mamie knew how to offer comfort.

But, O Jesus, I'm not ready yet! I have things to do. Janeika's not even married. I want to see her children. How could this be happening to me?

Around noon on Monday I stared down the empty road in front of my house and hoped to goodness I wasn't seeing the rest of my life. Porter's check was late. For a week I had been haunting my dented mailbox like my cat, Lucky, haunted chipmunk holes. My only reward had been a handful of junk mail and a telephone bill.

I have a fertile imagination. In seven days I had conjured up any number of scenarios. We'd had a substitute mail carrier the past week who wasn't the brightest bulb in the porch light. He could have delivered my check to the wrong house. Porter might have scrawled the address so poorly the envelope was still looking for *Solace, CA*, instead of *Solace, GA*. Or maybe he'd been laid off. Porter always slid out from imparting bad news when he could. But what if he was in a hospital somewhere without any idea who he was? He could even be d—

I refused to think that word.

Maybe he's finally gotten tired of sending money to the wife and child he abandoned.

That wasn't my imagination—it was Margaret's voice. She might have made my wedding dress with her own two hands, but she never approved of the man her baby sister had married.

"He didn't abandon us!" I muttered. "Abandon" was too harsh a word for Porter's anguished cry and heartbroken bolt once he'd heard the doctor's diagnosis of what ailed the child we'd managed to produce after five years of trying. "He's real sensitive."

Margaret wasn't there, of course. She was probably sitting in her charming breakfast room admiring her perfect yard, drinking gourmet coffee from a china cup. But I often talked to people who weren't there. It gave me the illusion of adult conversation. Lurleen Banks, my regular mail carrier, was the only grown-up I saw a lot of weeks except for Daddy, who came on Tuesday and Friday evenings to bring us milk.

A train whistled for a crossing a mile away. It sounded as lonesome as I felt.

"Shoo! Shoo!" Frantic shouts yanked me from the threshold of my pity party.

Michelle jerked her arms toward the sky. We were having those warm, lovely days that come before the Easter cold snap, so I'd wheeled her out onto the porch. However, Lucky must have left part of a dead critter somewhere in the grass. Three buzzards lazily circled the yard.

Imprisoned in her chair, Michelle was terrified of buzzards. "Shoo! Shoo!"

"We're alive and well down here!" I called up. I did a few jumping jacks to demonstrate the fact. The buzzards left but Michelle was sobbing. I sprinted to the porch to reassure her.

I ran on a red dirt path. Our old house sat back a good sixty yards from the road, but the front walk, for some unfathomable reason, extended only fifteen yards from the porch. Previous owners had worn one path through the grass to the mailbox and another to the rutted drive at the side of the house, but nobody had extended the walk.

The loose sole of my right loafer flapped like a tongue. When I reached the front steps I shook my foot to make the sole jiggle. "Good morning, Miss Michelle."

Michelle swallowed her last sob. "Good morning." She giggled. Michelle had a marvelous giggle. It lit up my heart.

"Watch this. Three points." I grabbed my basketball from under the azaleas, backed down the walk, and shot into a rim attached to the peak of my porch. "Swish!"

"Yay!" Chellie cheered. She was my biggest—my only—fan.

I carried her with me to the porch swing. She loved to swing on my lap. "Sorry the mail is so late today, baby."

"Maybe Daddy's hurt."

Her fears echoed my own, but I refused to let her know that. "I think he's just late this month. The check will probably come today."

"With a present?"

"I doubt it. You got a present last week."

Because I couldn't bear for Michelle to know her father never mentioned her in his infrequent notes, I occasionally bought something—a bottle of bubbles, a barrette for her hair—and pretended Porter had sent it. So far she hadn't figured out that mailed packages customarily arrived wrapped, with stamps.

"Eh—ee—a—ory," she commanded, rubbing her hair on the underside of my chin. *Tell me a story.* "You and Daddy."

I had gotten heartily sick of that story, but it was her favorite. "All the time I was growing up, Porter Waits lived a mile down the road from me, in this very house. He was a year ahead of me in school, though, so I never really noticed him until my junior year. One day I was standing in front of the school with the football player I was dating at the time when a tall senior dashed into traffic to rescue a bedraggled kitten."

"Aak itn." Michelle would not tolerate condensed versions.

"Right. A bedraggled *black* kitten. My football player—"

"*Cretin* football player."

Lordy, the child was bright. Put a new word in the story once, she'd insist on it every time. Heaven only knew what she thought that word meant.

"My *cretin* football player hadn't noticed the kitten. He was too busy repeating every boring detail of his most recent touchdown. But Porter carried the kitten straight to me, put it in my cupped hands with a smile, and said—" I stopped.

Chellie bounced in my arms. "'Call him Lucky!'"

Lucky, prowling azaleas in search of prey, backed out at the sound of his name. "Go back to hunting," I told him. "We weren't talking to you."

"You looked . . . ," Michelle prompted.

"I looked into that boy's golden eyes and I saw my future. I didn't see you, though. You were the very best part." I nuzzled her soft hair.

She butted my chest with her head. "You are the best part, too."

WHEN I TOLD MICHELLE'S FAVORITE story, I never included what I failed to notice about the future I saw in Porter's eyes: he wasn't in it.

Cerebral palsy often isn't diagnosed for months, but our doctor knew what was wrong with Michelle by the time she was a couple of days old. The day I was to bring her home from the hospital, Porter called to ask Daddy to fetch us. "Something has come up," he said vaguely.

He explained more fully in a note he left on the kitchen table.

Billie, I can't stand to watch that baby grow up. It would tare my heart out to see other people stareing at her like she's a freek. I hate that you have to rase her alone, but a mother is stronger. I'll send money. I'm a good worker and I take care of my own. Porter.

His clothes and guitar were gone. He'd left the cat.

In the next week I was so exhausted, caring for my newborn, that I didn't put Porter's note away. When Margaret brought her two boys to meet their new cousin, it was lying on the counter for her to read.

"How could you marry a man who can't spell?" she demanded.

I hated it when Margaret treated me like I was still a kid. She left home when I was nine, so maybe she'd never noticed that I'd grown up. By the time I had Chellie, though, I was twenty-three and felt like I had earned my adulthood stripes. I wanted a sister like those I read about in books—a friend I could share things with and who would cover my back as I'd cover hers. Instead I had a big sister who tried not to wrinkle her nose at my house, pitied me for my child, and constantly insulted my husband.

I snatched the note. "Spelling doesn't count as much as providing. Porter's a good provider."

I could tell she was forcing herself not to look around my pitiful house. "Well, if you need money or anything. . ."

I could have used sympathy but I would not tolerate pity. "Porter will send money. Even if he doesn't, I earn enough at the mill to support us. We'll be fine."

Those next weeks were my personal crash course in economics. Our county didn't have a single day-care provider trained to care for an infant with cerebral palsy. I couldn't go back to work. My savings melted at an alarming rate. I am here to tell you that somebody is making a fortune off paper diapers.

When Porter's first check came, I wept with gratitude. Five years later, I was still grateful. "Porter's been dependable," I reminded Margaret in absentia—she was probably planning an elegant dinner party for ten, not thinking of me at all. "He has sent us a check every single month. When he got on with Landiss Construction over in Cobb County, he even put us on his health insurance. Porter is real dependable."

Which was the reason I'd gone out every day that past week to try to drag the mail carrier to my place by the sheer force of my eyeballs. Porter would never stop sending us checks if he had money.

I hauled myself to my feet, unable to sit still any longer. "I'm going back out to the box," I told Chellie. "Lurleen ought to be here any minute. If Daddy's check comes, we'll go to Wal-Mart—if somebody comes along to start the truck."

Wal-Mart was down by the interstate, a good twenty miles away and at the moment I was at the mercy of an unreliable truck battery. Still, I considered inconvenient shopping a small price to pay for privacy, six acres of my own, and the view. In our part of West Georgia, the Appalachians were worn down to small mountains that rose like bumps on a dragon's tail, curling toward Birmingham. My land was in a valley surrounded by Daddy's dairy farm, so pastures rose on both sides of the road. Soft brown Jersey cows grazed the pastures and dark pines lined the crest of the hills. I could not imagine a prettier place to live.

"I'm hungry," Chellie complained. "Feed me!"

I didn't fault her when she had a short fuse. Cerebral palsy—"shaky brain" I called it when I was trying to make her laugh over some frustrating new endeavor—is a devastating handicap. While it can affect the mind, its twitching limbs and uncontrolled tongue can also mask an unimpaired, even brilliant intellect. Michelle was at least as smart as any other five-year-old, but she couldn't control her spastic movements or her tongue, so people treated her like she was repulsive and mentally retarded. Between her fury with what she could not do and her yearning to be liked, no wonder she was an angry little girl at times.

Some days I was an angry mother, too, but I tried not to take out my frustration on my child. I cuddled her as I put her back in her chair. "I know you're hungry, sweetie. Why don't we go in so I can make your lunch? You can eat while I'm out here waiting." She could manage puréed soup in a sippy cup on her own.

I checked my watch as we went in. Lurleen always came by noon. It was almost one.

Four

When I finally saw Lurleen approaching my mailbox, I sprinted to meet her.

"What happened to that box?" she demanded. It sat at a sixty-degree angle to the ground.

"Some kid missed the curve last weekend and knocked it over. He said he'll be back to set it up again, but so far he hasn't come. Can you reach it?"

"You know the postal worker's creed: *Neither rain nor sleet nor falling-down mailboxes shall deter us from our appointed rounds.* But since you're out here, I'll hand it to you."

A stocky woman in her fifties with thick arms, a round face, and short grizzled hair, Lurleen was generally so cheerful that every move seemed like a bounce. That afternoon she was glum as she slapped my mail against her door. I itched to grab the pile, but since she had been gone a week, getting mail was going to cost me a conversation.

"You've been to San Antonio to visit Janeika, right? Did you all party so hard you couldn't get up this morning?"

"No, I had to carry Mama to the doctor."

"I saw her yesterday. She looks good."

Lurleen got real busy checking her tray to be sure she hadn't missed anything. "She's got a few health problems. She's getting old."

The way she wouldn't look at me made anxiety crawl up my spine like a spider. I forgot the mail. "She's all right, isn't she?"

Lurleen thumped my mail on her steering wheel, staring at the curve between my house and Daddy's. "The doctor told her to take it easy, but you think she's gonna listen? Why should she listen to a doctor when she won't listen to me? I keep reminding her that she is retired, that all she has to do on a given day is turn on the television, heat up some food, and eat it, but she's always finding things she thinks God wants her to do." Lurleen blew a raspberry. "She uses God as an excuse to do anything she dang well pleases."

If somebody came by my place taking nominations for sainthood, I'd put Mamie's name at the top of my list. "You know she has a direct pipeline to heaven."

"You think so? Then how about this. She's old, right? We know that and *God* knows that. But yesterday she claims God wanted her over at a friend's house helping her clean out a spare room so her grandbaby can come live with her. Mama swears she never lifted anything heavier than a quilt, but if you believe that, I have some nice land in the ninth ward of New Orleans I'd like to sell you."

"Mamie loves helping people."

"She could help me by listening for a change. I've found a lovely place—a woman who takes people in and treats them like family. It's even affordable. But do you think Mamie Fountain will consider it?" Lurleen thrust my mail at me, her voice still tinged with temper. "You don't need to go through that before you throw it away. Nothing but ads today."

I clutched the slender pile. My lips trembled. "No check? I haven't gotten it yet."

Lurleen's face mirrored my own. "For real? Child, it was due a week ago. Are you sure he's working? Construction is down."

"Yeah, but he wrote last month that he's on a job in Marietta that should keep him busy for the foreseeable future."

That got a snort of disbelief. "The foreseeable future? Porter Waits said that?"

"Well, no, what he said was 'a right long spell.'" I riffled through the junk so I didn't have to face her pity. I hoped I wouldn't cry until she'd left.

But Lurleen had nothing but a long string of mailboxes in her immediate future. "Speaking of May-retta"—she drew the word out in a parody of the way folks who lived there said it—"what do you hear from Maggie? Have you seen her lately?"

Margaret hadn't been out to Solace since Christmas, but I didn't have enough family to trash it in public. "Sure. I saw her yesterday. She had on a gorgeous yellow suit." I didn't bother to mention that I'd only had a couple of glimpses on TV. "She probably made the suit. She got all the talent in our family, you know—as well as the looks."

"You didn't do too bad in the looks department. You've got those great dimples, and Mama always said your smile can light up a room. Besides, men like curvy women."

"I'm not interested in men. I'm married, remember?"

"The question is, does *he* remember?"

I didn't rise to that bait, so Lurleen went back to our former subject. "Are you serious that Maggie is still sewing? Couldn't she pretty much buy anything she wants by now?"

"Oh, yeah, but sewing is her secret vice. Don't let it get around. She'd be mortified if any of her friends found out."

"I remember how proud your folks used to be of her in high school, winning all those sewing awards."

"While I wasn't winning a dadgum thing for sloshing around in mud and manure, raising calves."

"If you hadn't always picked the most pitiful beasts in God's creation, you might have won a few prizes. Your daddy used to get so put out with you! He claimed that once you saw a runt, you never looked any farther."

It was true. The need of those pitiful little animals seemed to grab my heart until I could hardly breathe.

"Remember that little Hereford you raised, the one you named Beau?" Lurleen pressed. "Hair in a hundred cowlicks?"

"Yeah, but he had a sweet face, and he used to rub his head against me the whole time I brushed him. He thought I was his mama. Too bad the judges couldn't see past his defects to the gold underneath."

Lurleen was more interested in Margaret than in calves. "I remember how proud your daddy was when Margaret won that home ec scholarship to college. When she quit to put Ben through, it like to killed your daddy."

"Daddy like to killed Margaret. She promised she'd go back once Ben was done, but then they had Jason, and after that, she got busy helping Ben start their business. I sometimes wonder if Daddy would have gotten so mad at me for marrying Porter if he hadn't already suffered such a great disappointment in Margaret."

"Oh, yeah," Lurleen assured me. "He would have. Daddies are real protective of their daughters. You should have heard Skeeter when Janeika told him she was joining the army. Besides, Porter—" She screwed her lips around like she was thinking over whether to say something or not. "Mama always said it was your liking for underdogs that made you fall for Porter." She watched to see how I would take that.

"Don't talk about me when I'm not there."

"Mama talks because she cares. You know that."

"Well, she's wrong about Porter. I fell for him because he has principles. He's a lot like Daddy in that. They both get mad when people do sloppy work, are dishonest, or don't take care of the earth. You'd think Daddy would adore Porter. They agree on almost everything."

"Honey, don't confuse opinions with principles. Your daddy has principles. He stands up for what he believes in, but he gets along with people who don't agree with him. Porter never learned that. All he's got is hothead opinions."

I hadn't seen it that way before, but Lurleen could be right. For years Daddy had played poker with a group of men who argued all the time, but they liked one another. Porter couldn't stand to be around anybody who didn't agree with him. As he saw it, they were wrong, so his mission was to change them. Within a month after we got married, I didn't have a single friend who would come to our home.

I'd think that over later, but I wasn't going to discuss Porter's short-comings with Lurleen. "Tell Mamie the real reason I fell for Porter was that he's so darned good-looking. Being seen with him improved my image."

"Porter is a handsome cuss," she admitted. "Good build, too. I can see how—"

Chellie pounded on the window.

I held up my mail in salute. "I'd better go. She wants a book before her nap."

"She's old enough to start kindergarten in the fall, right? When she goes to school, you can go back to work and not have to depend on Porter."

"I'd have to drive us back and forth."

"The county's supposed to provide transportation."

"They only own one bus equipped for wheelchairs. As far out as we live, she'd be picked up early and wouldn't get home until late. I'd rather take her. However, at the moment my battery's shot. Every time I need to go somewhere, I have to wait until somebody comes up the road to give me a jump. I can't see doing that every morning, can you? So I can't work until I get a battery and I can't buy a battery until I go to work— one of those chicken-and-egg things. I think I'll homeschool a while, anyway. We're already doing a little reading and math."

I didn't mention my real reasons for keeping Chellie at home. *They won't recognize how bright she is and will treat her like she's slow. They won't see how sweet she is and will treat her like a sack of potatoes. We haven't been apart an hour since she was born. Could I stand being away from her all day long?*

Lurleen looked toward my truck, parked under an oak in the side yard. "Your truck is how much older than God?"

"Hey!" I smacked her hood. "Don't insult that truck. I keep it running real sweet. All it needs is a new battery."

"If you don't have a battery, it doesn't run. Mama's car died last Thursday—did you hear? She up and bought herself a used PT Cruiser. A purple one."

"I saw it yesterday. It looks great."

A spurt of disgust came from Lurleen's lips. "Easy for you to say. She isn't spending your inheritance on cars. I was so put out, I told Skeeter not to help her pick one. 'Let her make the biggest mistake of her sorry life,' I told him. But you know Skeeter. He carried her Saturday while I was in Texas. I swear that man loves Mama more'n he loves me."

I smiled at the joke, but my smile wobbled. I missed my own mama terribly. As long as she was able, she ran over to my house a few times each week to exchange recipes, play with Michelle, or bring cookies. Daddy seldom came inside, and while he liked to joke around with Chellie, he didn't have much to say to me. I didn't have much to say to him, either. When was the last time I'd gone to his house? I frowned, trying to remember.

Misunderstanding, Lurleen laid a hand on my arm. "That check will come tomorrow, honey. I know it. I'll say a little prayer for your check. You say one for Mama."

As she pulled away, I thought I heard her say, "Bravest young woman in God's green creation." But maybe that was the wind.

I PUT ON MY HAPPY Face in case Chellie was still looking out the window, pivoted like I used to on my high school basketball team, and trotted toward the house.

Basketball was one thing I excelled at in high school. I was short, but I could shoot a basket from almost any position on the court. I made the girls' varsity team my junior year and was captain my senior year of a team that went to state finals. Those were—

I caught myself before I finished that thought. Twenty-eight seemed a mite young to be thinking about the Good Old Days.

Still, since I had so much ground to cover before I reached the porch, I permitted myself a few seconds of wistful thinking. What if I'd gone to college instead of marrying the week I finished high school? Daddy wouldn't have gotten disgusted with me for throwing away all my chances (whatever they might have been). Mama wouldn't have had to pretend she liked Porter when she didn't. Margaret wouldn't have spent the past ten years going all pruny-lipped at the mention of my husband's name.

Or what if God had given me a husband like Ben—a funny, gentle man and a good father—instead of a volatile, opinionated man who took off because he couldn't stand to have people feel sorry for his less-than-perfect child? I wish somebody had been able to make me understand, back when I was eighteen, how much a married woman's life is shaped by the kind of man she marries.

As I approached our house, my mind backed up in time. What if, instead of Porter, it had been somebody else who rescued Lucky? Somebody like—what was the name of that boy I'd had a crush on freshman year?

Auburn curls. Twinkly blue eyes. I could picture him, but I couldn't recall his name.

I had literally run into him hurrying to English one morning. As usual, I had my nose in a book. I thought I had hit a wall, but it was the captain of the boys' varsity basketball team. He was what Daddy called "a long drink of water," so he looked down from a great height at me sprawled on the floor. I wanted to die.

"You all right?" He hauled me up. "Sorry I hit you. You're so short, I didn't see you."

"It was my fault. I was reading." *You are red as a beet, Billie!*

He was very cool. "Halls between classes aren't generally good for reading." He picked up my book and looked at the cover. "I remember this. Do you like it?"

"Yeah." *Brilliant reply, Billie!*

I poised on my toes, ready to leave, but he didn't seem to hear the bell. Maybe he didn't get in trouble for being late like mere mortals did. "What's your name?"

"Billie Anderson."

"Billie? Your mother named you Billie?" His smile was so wide, I smiled back.

"No, she named me Wilhelmina after her mother, but everybody calls me Billie."

"I think you should go by Mina. It suits you. Short, cute, and different. But the bell's rung. You'd better run. Good-bye, Mina." He flashed me a smile as he strode away, a god on his way to Mount Olympus.

The next day I passed him in the hall. "Hey, Mina," he called. I blushed and waved, but I couldn't think of a single clever thing to say.

Freshmen didn't take classes with seniors, and he lived across the county, so I never ran into him outside of school. I lived for our infrequent meetings in the hall. I plotted my way to class so I could pass him. I planned exactly how brilliant I would be the next time we spoke. But although he always called, "Hey, Mina," my tongue refused to work. He probably thought I was a mute with permanent sunburn.

I went to every basketball game and cheered myself hoarse when he scored. I wrote his name in the backs of notebooks even though he was going steady with the homecoming queen. I joined the chorus so I could sing at his graduation. After he left for the army, I spent the summer dreaming how he would come back in a few years to find me grown-up, beautiful, and articulate. A couple of years later I heard he had married his homecoming queen and was stationed in Germany.

What was his name? It was lost in the recesses of my freshman composition books.

Sophomore year I started dating football players. The year after that, I met Porter.

Where was Porter's check?

I started shaking all over. Lurleen was right. I was brave. I had been brave for years. But that afternoon I stood on my cracked front walk and realized courage might not be enough. I could be brave from there to kingdom come and still not be able to support my child.

I grabbed the basketball and shot three angry baskets in succession. The only good thing that came from running into that basketball player was that I practiced shooting baskets until I was good, because it was his game.

"The past is past," I reminded myself. I took a deep breath of courage and got fetid air instead. "And the present stinks. Literally." Daddy had informed me Friday night that my septic tank needed pumping out.

THERE'S ALWAYS SOMETHING THAT NEEDS doing when you own a house, even a four-room box with a chimney on one side and a porch across the front—a house a kid could draw. Mine needed paint so bad that a pressure washing would reduce it to bare wood. Still, I owned it free and clear. Porter had sent a second note with his first check:

> *I want you to have Mama's house so you don't wory about*
> *haveing a roof over your head. Send the papers and I'll*
> *sine them. Love to you and our little girl.*

I suspected he was glad to be rid of that ugly place, but I sent the papers. Within a month I had the deed, made out in my name.

At the time, I hated the house. Its only claim to fame was that Porter grew up there while his mama supported them by working at the mill and selling land to Daddy. All she kept were six acres along the road that included the house and yard, a pitiful peach orchard, and a stand of pines at the other end. When Porter and I got married, Mrs. Waits was determined I would not take away her son, so she told Daddy she'd give us an acre of pines if he'd give us a mobile home. For four years she and I had butted heads over things like where Porter and I would eat dinner (she favored us eating with her every night, with me doing the cooking) and whether we needed a washing machine (she favored me using hers so she could complain about the way I sorted clothes). The only victory I ever won was that she let me take over the orchard. All it needed was fertilizer, pruning, spraying, and love. I handled everything but the spraying. Daddy did that.

Mrs. Waits died soon after I got pregnant. I figured the notion of sharing her son with yet another person did the old bat in.

Since Porter worked construction, I begged him to get some friends to bulldoze the house and help us build a brick ranch. He refused. "We can fix this place up nice, and remodeling won't cost much if we do it ourselves." The whole time I was pregnant we poured hours, sweat, and most of what we earned into that house. Daddy helped, which meant I spent half my time keeping them on separate projects so they didn't kill each other. Between us, we updated the wiring and plumbing, tuck-pointed the chimney, put on a new roof, and shored up the porch. I learned skills I never expected to possess.

A month before the baby was due, Porter announced we were moving in, even though we hadn't put on a lick of paint, refinished the floors, or done one thing to modernize his mama's awful kitchen. I told him, "I won't move until you paint and carpet the nursery. I want our baby to come home to a pretty room." After the nursery was done, I planned to ask him to start on the kitchen.

Porter painted the nursery on a Saturday. A friend of mine laid the carpet that evening. Moving on Sunday afternoon didn't take long, since Porter said, "We don't need to move all our furniture. We have Mama's right here." I looked at the saggy springs, the chipped Formica coffee table, and the wobbly kitchen table and I bit my tongue. I was feeling lousy. I would fight that battle later. "All I ask is that you swap her bedroom set for our own." He did. Neither of us wanted to sleep in his mother's bed.

I spent Sunday evening putting tiny clothes in drawers while Porter started painting the living room. In the middle of the night, I woke up in labor. Three days later, Porter took off. Given that he left drop cloths and paint cans in a half-painted room, I was glad the baby hadn't come while we'd had the roof off.

I finished painting the living room in the rare times when Chellie slept. Over the years I bought bargain gallons of paint whenever I could, and created a multicolor effect in the other rooms. Michelle called it our Rainbow House.

Even I had come to appreciate it. It sheltered me and the most precious thing I possessed.

But if Porter's check didn't come soon, what were we going to do?

I could think of only one thing I could do. As soon as Michelle was down for her nap, I went to the phone.

Five

I n Marietta, Margaret's phone grew warm in her hand. "Jason?" she
repeated. She wasn't stalling. She was verifying that there was no
mistake. "Jason Baxter?"

"Yes, Miz Baxter." The voice of the clerk dripped disapproval. "Your
son has been suspended. For a week. For fighting." She chopped the
message into short, blunt fragments. "You need to come get him. He's
waiting here in the office."

"But . . . fighting?" Margaret hugged herself with one arm to keep
from trembling. MacTavish, their West Highland terrier, whined at her
ankles, sensing her distress.

If the elementary school had called, Margaret would have been embarrassed but not surprised. Andy would take on boys twice his size if
they seized a swing he had his eye on. But Jason? Jason poured all the
passion he possessed into track. He vaulted hurdles with a determination that caught Margaret's breath in her throat, but she suspected he
had chosen track because it was not a contact sport.

"He was fighting, sure enough. Hurt the other guy real bad."

"*Who* was he fighting?"

"Curtis Mays."

"Curtis? He's Jason's best friend."

"Come get Jason," the clerk repeated. "He is waiting. Oh, and the principal left a big envelope in your PTA box."

"What about Saturday's track meet? Jason's running." He'd been practicing like he was training for an Olympic event.

"He's not allowed back on school property until Monday."

She didn't bother to park in the visitors' lot, simply pulled alongside a NO PARKING sign at the front curb. She ran up three shallow steps, jerked open the door, and reached the office in five long strides. Jason sat slumped on a bench, hands fisted. He was studying grazed knuckles on his right hand with the concentration scientists devote to finding a cure for cancer.

Margaret hadn't realized she was holding her breath until she saw he was whole. She exhaled fury with her fright. "What on earth have you done?"

He slung his backpack over one shoulder. "Let's get out of here."

Curtis sat as far from Jason as he could get. A wet cloth dripped pink down his shirt.

"Is he suspended, too?" Margaret demanded of the clerk.

"No, ma'am. He didn't hit anybody. Jason hit him. Curtis is waiting for his mama to come take him to the doctor. Nurse thinks his nose is broke."

"Mom!" Jason was halfway across the hall.

Margaret remembered that she was illegally parked and that security guards in the school outnumbered counselors two to one. She followed Jason, automatically snatching a big white envelope from her box.

She would come see the principal after she heard Jason's story. They couldn't keep him from running Saturday. Track could mean a college scholarship. Whatever silly thing he had done shouldn't jeopardize his entire future.

Make me calm, she prayed as she climbed in beside a sullen Jason. *Help me listen to what he has to say.*

"What happened?" she asked as they pulled away.

"I don't want to talk about it." His voice was sullen, his shoulders hunched, as much of his head as possible hiding in an invisible shell.

"What were you fighting about?"

"Nothing."

"Don't give me that! It had to be *something.*" So much for staying calm.

"Let it go, Mom. I don't want to talk about it."

"You at least have to tell me what it was about."

"I don't have to tell you anything!"

She was so startled, she braked, causing a car behind her to blare its horn.

Boys do fight, Margaret reminded herself. Having no brothers, she had been shocked to discover that even as toddlers, boys and their friends punched, hit, kicked, and gleefully knocked one another down. Jason, quiet as he was, had wrestled preschool friends until they tumbled in a heap of writhing arms and legs. Maybe this was nothing more serious than that. She decided to trust him. What else could a mother do?

He blew on his knuckles and pressed them against his jeans.

"We'll put something on that when we get home. Will they let you make up the history test you were supposed to have sixth period?"

"Who cares? I don't want to talk. Let's have a silent trip."

Silent Trip was a game Margaret made up after Andy learned to talk, to keep his incessant chatter from distracting her while she drove. She and Jason had never played it without Andy in the car—or needed to.

"What are you going to tell your dad?"

"Drop it or I'll get out right here!" He reached for the door handle.

"Don't be a fool! We're going forty miles an hour."

"In a thirty-five-mile-an-hour zone." His nostrils flared with disapproval.

"You aren't even driving yet. When did you become an expert?"

At least he had taken his hand from the door handle. Margaret vowed not to say another word until they got home. She would fix them both a Coke and they would talk.

As soon as she stopped in the garage, he headed to his room. She heard his door slam. Music filled the stairwell. She collapsed into the chair beside her kitchen phone, feeling as if she had been pummeled.

Dazed, she called Ben. "Jason got suspended at school for fighting. Apparently he hit Curtis and broke his nose."

"Are Curtis's folks going to sue?"

Margaret blinked. Men's minds truly operated on a different plane. "I don't know or care. Jason's hurting and won't talk. Could you come home? It might be a guy thing."

Ben hesitated. Margaret was usually the one who solved the boys' problems. He was the one who took them out for fun. "Okay. I can come for a while, but we're busy out here."

While Margaret fixed a glass of tea, MacTavish trotted up the stairs. The music blared momentarily as Jason let MacTavish into his room. The dog, but not his mother.

She went out to the deck to wait for Ben, but the pollen was so thick, it drove her inside. She felt tension drain from her as she heard Ben's truck growl up the drive. She went to meet him gratefully. They were a good team. Between them, they could handle this.

"Where is he?" Ben asked.

She nodded toward the stairs. "Follow the music."

Ben climbed the stairs two at a time. "Jason?" she heard him call. "It's Dad." After several bars of music, Ben's voice grew firmer. "Jason? Unlock this door! That's an order, son."

The music swelled; then she heard silence as startling as the music.

She took a couple of chocolate chip cookies from the jar. Her body craved sugar like her mind craved reassurance. She was biting into one when she heard a shout. Jason's words were indistinguishable but his fury was clear. MacTavish joined the racket. Ben's voice was a reassuring rumble.

"Don't give me that!" Jason shouted.

Ben barked. Jason's voice dropped, but a few seconds later his voice rose on one sharp expletive.

She heard a cry, a crash, and a yelp from MacTavish.

Margaret ran to the foot of the stairs, straining to hear. The boys were not permitted to swear before their parents, but surely Ben wouldn't hit Jason for swearing. No, he was talking again, his voice urgent.

Jason shouted again.

She was startled to hear the door open above her, drew back as Ben clattered down the stairs. His face was red, his fists clenched. As he passed her, he snapped, "Leave him alone, okay? Don't bother him with questions."

"But what's the matter?"

He paused briefly. "I'm dealing with this. Don't worry about it."

Margaret hurried after him. "Did he fall? I heard a crash."

Ben spoke over one shoulder as she followed him out. "He's fine. But leave him alone. No questions. Let us work it out." He swung up into his truck.

"Dinner at the usual time?"

"I'll be late, so I'll grab something. Eat without me." He backed out without even a wave.

She carried a Coke upstairs. "Jason?" When he didn't answer, she tried the door. It was unlocked. Jason lay across his bed fully dressed, a forearm shielding his eyes, chest rising and falling in ragged sobs. She stepped closer and caught a quick breath. One cheek was bruised. Both cheeks were stained with tears. MacTavish lay on the rug by his bed.

She bent across the dog to wipe away the tears, but Jason dragged his pillow over his head.

"I love you," she said, touching his shoulder gently. "Rest. I need to answer the phone."

I WAS THE PERSON CALLING her. She was my last resort.

Earlier, I had tried Porter's cell. His voice in my ear sounded as cocky as ever. "You made the call, so spill your guts. I might call you back." It took me a second to realize I'd gotten voice mail.

"Hey. It's Billie. Are you all right? Your check didn't come, and I—I really need it." My bank balance floated before my eyes: twelve dollars and thirteen cents. "Give me a call."

I read while I waited. All my life people had teased me about having my nose in a book, but books took me to marvelous worlds. They taught me things I'd missed by giving up college. They helped me understand what I could do to make Chellie's life easier. I would rather read than eat.

However, the slip marking my place said our books were due in three days. If I didn't get to town soon, I'd be in debt even to the free public library.

When Porter hadn't called by two, I punched in Information for Landiss Construction's number. Given the state of my finances, the call felt like stealing from the phone company.

The breathy voice that answered would have intimidated any out-of-shape, stay-at-home mom with split ends and a hole in her jeans.

"I, uh, need to talk to somebody about one of your employees. I mean, I want—I need to know where he's working—"

"I'll connect you to human resources." Elevator music replaced the voice.

"Human resources." That voice was a razor.

"I, uh, I'm calling about one of your employees, Porter Waits. This is, uh, his wife. I need to know, uh, where he's working." I could not seem to form a coherent sentence.

"I'm sorry, Mrs. Waits."

Was it my imagination, or did the woman doubt I was Porter's wife? Before I could interrupt, she moved smoothly on. "I cannot give you that information. I suggest you ask him when he comes home." The voice implied lots of experience with so-called wives.

"He doesn't come home." That wasn't going to impress her. I back-pedaled. "I mean, we live too far out for him to commute, so he's staying in town. But I haven't heard from him for a week or so, and I need—"

"I'm sorry. I cannot give out information about our employees."

Anger jelled my syntax. "Look, ma'am, I am Porter's wife. I've got a certificate to prove it. And I've got a handicapped child out here. I need Porter's check real bad. He sends one every month, but this month's hasn't come. I can't reach him on his cell phone, so could you at least tell me if he's still working for you? I have to find him so I can feed my child."

Maybe it was the mention of a child that softened her granite heart. "I could give you that information, I suppose. What was the name again?"

"Waits. Porter Waits."

More canned music followed by a doubtful tone. "I'm sorry, but Mr. Waits is no longer with us. The last day he clocked in was March twenty-fifth."

"Did he leave or get fired?" My voice shook almost as much as I did.

"I cannot give out that information."

"Can't or won't?" She didn't deign to answer. "Did he leave a forwarding address?"

"I cannot—"

Rage steadied my vocal cords again. "So what information *can* you give me?"

"I've given you all I can."

"At least tell me one more thing. Did he come by to pick up his last check?"

Grudging every word, "No. We are holding a check for him."

"Any way I could get it?"

Ice was back in the voice. "Only Mr. Waits can collect his check."

"Could you at least tell me the site where he was working? Maybe one of the other fellows knows where he went."

"I'm sorry. We do not give out that information." She hung up.

After I dropped the phone into its cradle, I let out all my frustration in one long "Aaargh!"

I didn't know if I was more frustrated with Porter or with myself. In the years he'd been gone, I had gotten so accustomed to living on the checks he sent, I hadn't ever thought of making money beyond what I earned from our little peach orchard. I'd drifted along, content to shape our wants to match our resources. Porter's missing check was a flag in my face waking me to how thoroughly I—who considered myself very independent—had gotten used to depending on him.

"You are no dummy," I told myself. I fetched a pad and wrote: *Sources of Money.* There had to be some way I could pay bills. I started a list.

Garage sale? I laughed. Everything I had except Porter's mama's tacky furniture had come from another garage sale. *Bank loan?* Ridiculous. Who would give a loan to a woman with no means of support? If they did, how could I repay it? *Daddy—?* I scratched that out with fierce strokes. I had never asked him for money. I didn't intend to start. Not only could I not repay him any more than I could a bank, he'd probably say, "You made your bed, shug. Lie in it."

Margaret? I would never ask Margaret for money, but maybe she could think of a way for me to earn something at home. And maybe Ben would know somebody at Landiss Construction who could get me on the site to talk to Porter's coworkers. Porter would never take another job unless he thought it was better than the one he had. If that happened, he'd have bragged about the new job to anybody who would listen.

The thought that he might have changed jobs both cheered and depressed me. If he was working at a new place, he would eventually send a check, but I might not get it for another month. It was unlikely a new place would offer health benefits, either—especially to start. We'd been without insurance before, and no mother should have to look at her sick child and know she can't afford a doctor.

Still, if I could believe a check would be coming, we could manage for a few more weeks. Somehow.

If anybody could get Porter's current location, Margaret could.

Feeling better already, I went to the kitchen to call her.

MARGARET DIDN'T WASTE LUNG POWER on a greeting. "Has something happened to Daddy?" Given the way they picked at each other whenever they were together, I was surprised she sounded so upset.

The speech I'd rehearsed flew off my tongue. "How'd you know it was me?"

"Caller ID." Margaret sounded like it was something everybody had. "Is Daddy all right?" Her voice still sounded strained.

"Finer than frog's hair when I saw him Friday. He was here checking out my septic tank. Said it's got to be pumped. Living in the city, you've probably forgotten about septic tanks."

"I haven't given them much thought lately. I'm glad he's okay. I was afraid that's why you were calling."

"No, it's—uh—I wanted—uh— Are you busy?" Once I heard her voice, I needed time to climb back into adulthood from nine years old.

"I'm about to start dinner, but I can work while we talk."

Of course she could. She had a cordless phone in her kitchen. My only phone was attached to the kitchen wall and only reached as far as the sink. Margaret also had stainless-steel appliances, a beautiful bamboo floor, gray granite countertops, and canisters in the shape of cute little cottages. I had pressboard cabinets, a forty-year-old refrigerator, and the dimpled vinyl floor Porter's daddy had put down back in nineteen eighty-two. His mama had sponge mopped it weekly, swiping dirt into the dimples. The floor might look better if I got down on my knees with a stiff brush and hot soapy water, but who had time? Don't flooring manufactures realize that depressions in a kitchen floor are nothing but traps for filth?

When I got low, it was easy to covet Margaret's kitchen.

"Did you want something?" she asked when the silence stretched.

"Yeah. I've got a little problem here. A big problem, maybe, but maybe not." I was still having trouble coming to the point. "I wondered if you could, uh, give me a little help."

"*He'p?* You weren't raised to talk like a hick."

I gave my countertop one hard *swack*. "Working at the mill and staying home, I guess I've let my elocution slide. But I didn't call to get a grammar lesson."

"What do you need?"

How many times a week did Margaret ask that question in exactly that tone, which said, "Whatever it is, I can handle it"? Whenever I visited her, it seemed like everybody in Cobb County called Margaret with problems. Katrinka had once confided, "Margaret can deal with anything. Sometimes I think she ought to run for president." Before she won a national election, I hoped she had time to do her sister a favor.

My worries tumbled out. "Porter's disappeared and I'm scared something's happened to him. I can't reach him, he's not returning my calls, and nobody knows where he is. I thought maybe you could find out where he's gone." I ran down as abruptly as I had started.

"Why me?"

"He's been working in Cobb County for two years. You live in Cobb County."

"Which has as many people as the entire state of Alaska. I don't know all of them. Besides, you know how volatile he is. He probably got into a fight with somebody and took off."

"He wouldn't do that without letting me know. Porter's always been reliable."

So reliable he left you to raise Michelle alone.

She didn't say it, but I heard it in the silence streaming over the wires. I tried to make Porter's case one more time. "I know you think he was heartless to leave me to raise our child, but in a funny way, his leaving was a gift to me. He could not have stood to watch Michelle struggle every day. Raising her alone is hard, but it would have been harder if I'd had to watch him grieving as well. And he *has* sent checks, faithful as clockwork, until now. And he gave me his mama's house—"

Margaret's continued silence let me know what she thought of *that* gift.

"I know it's not much, but I don't have rent or a mortgage. These past two years he's kept us on his health insurance, too. That's a big help." I made sure to pronounce the word correctly. "He's been so responsible up to now, he's got me worried."

"Did you try his cell phone?"

"Of course, but all I got was voice mail. I even called Landiss Construction."

"Landiss Construction?" Margaret sounded surprised.

"Yeah. That's where he's been working. You know it?"

"I know the company." Margaret said it like she hated to admit it.

"You haven't heard they're going bankrupt or anything, have you?"

"No, they still have a lot of business—as far as I know."

"You reckon Ben knows anybody there? Maybe they'd tell him where Porter was working. They might even tell you. You're better at asking things over the phone than I am. I get flustered. All I could get out of a witch in human resources was that Porter hasn't been on the job since March twenty-fifth. Oh, and she admitted he hasn't picked up his last check, but she implied I have a better chance of winning the lottery than of getting it. But if you called. . ."

"I'll see what I can do tomorrow morning."

Margaret didn't sound half as urgent as I felt. "You'll let me know as soon as you find out anything?"

"I'll let you know. In the meantime, do you need food or money?"

I nearly fell off my chair. Margaret hadn't offered me money since that day she brought the boys out to see Michelle as a newborn. Maybe blood is thicker than memory.

I wouldn't take charity for myself, but I would for Michelle. "I am getting low on a few things. I get milk from Daddy, of course, and my hens are laying, and we've got vegetables and fruit left from last summer, but Chellie needs vitamins and we could use meat, flour, and sugar. And"—as long as I was poor-mouthing, I might as well go whole hog— "I have a hospital bill I'm paying off a little each month from when she got sick before we got health insurance, and my phone bill is a month overdue. I don't want them to cut me off, in case Chellie has an emergency. Once I get Porter's check, we'll be fine."

"Have you asked the church for assistance? The pastor probably has a fund to help members in crisis, and I'll bet they still have those bins where people put food each week."

Margaret wasn't offering money; she was offering advice. My goodwill evaporated like puddles on a hot Georgia sidewalk. I took a deep breath to steady my anger. "I guess so. I haven't been going lately. Chellie's getting heavy to carry up the steps."

"They'd probably give you assistance, though. Daddy still goes, doesn't he?"

"Oh, yeah, he goes. But if I could talk to guys on the site . . . Could you try to find out where Porter was working, Maggie?" The childhood name slipped out.

Maybe that convinced her how desperate I was. "I told you, I'll try. Meanwhile, how about if I send you a couple of hundred to tide you over? Would that help?"

Would it! I could see a bag of groceries on our table. "I hate to borrow."

"You aren't borrowing. It's a gift. I didn't send anything for your birthday."

We both knew my birthday was in January and we never exchanged gifts.

"Thanks. We can really use it." I felt more in charity with my big sister than I had in years. "You'll call me about Porter?"

"As soon as I find out something. Don't worry, Billie. You hear me? You are not to worry."

Easy for Margaret to say. Margaret didn't have a worry in the world.

I HAD FORGOTTEN TO ASK her for ideas about how I might earn money at home. I stood beside the sink, admiring my peach blossoms while I tried to think of something I could do.

Maybe I could mortgage the house, but it wasn't worth a lot. And how could I pay a mortgage if I could get one?

I could keep children, but I didn't have a lot of time to put into other people's children.

I could raise and sell a pig, but I'd need fencing, and hogs eat a lot.

I could buy more chickens and sell eggs by the road, but I didn't have money to buy more chickens. "Help!" I said aloud as I set the glass by the sink.

That was as close to praying as I ever got.

A bright red cardinal on the windowsill gave me a perky nod. I felt my heart lift a little. *We're gonna make it*, I reminded myself. *We have our health, a roof over our heads, and birds on the windowsill. And Margaret's check ought to tide me over until I can get hold of Porter.*

Six

While I was trying to figure out how to earn money, Mamie was putting together a blackberry cobbler for Daddy. When she figured he was done milking, she carried it to her car.

She pulled up the gravel drive, parked next to his truck, and sat a moment admiring the Anderson house and talking to her car. "Bill's granddaddy built this house," she told it, "and sold it to Bill when he and Grace got married. Those big oaks are some old Mr. Anderson planted. Bill painted the house—don't you like that white with black shutters?—and Grace transformed that old farmyard into one of the prettiest in the county. I notice that even in this drought, Bill is keeping up Grace's yard."

Fat boxwoods flanked the porch and scented the air. Dogwoods bloomed along the drive. Down at the far end of the drive, three magnolias partly blocked the view of the red hay barn, the metal silo, the white concrete milking barn and old Mr. Anderson's unpainted barn, where Bill kept farm equipment. Clumps of daffodils and irises dotted the lawn. Come summer, flowers would fill the beds and jasmine at the western end of the wide front porch would pour rich sweetness over everything.

The house itself had only a living room, dining room, kitchen, and a small utility room/pantry downstairs, and two bedrooms and a smaller sewing room upstairs plus the bath. But the rooms were large—the living room stretched across the whole front of the house—and Grace had made them charming.

The only drawback to the house was that it had been built close to the road for convenience back when people didn't have cars, so the front yard was scarcely more than a strip of grass above a red clay bank. Visitors always went to the back door. Mamie noted that since Grace had died, Bill had enclosed the front yard with a chain-link fence—probably to keep his big dog from running into the road when he was away.

Bill and the dog came to the back door together, curiosity in both sets of eyes. Bill must be sixty-five by now, she realized in surprise. His skin had weathered to tan leather and his short curls were more gray than black. The dog at his side was so huge that Bill could fondle its ears without bending. An assortment of ancestors had given it a thick body, wide shoulders, and rough tan hair.

Mamie held out the Pyrex dish. "I had some blackberries in the freezer and remembered how much you used to like a cobbler."

"That's mighty nice of you, Mamie. Mighty nice, indeed. I can't think of the last time I had blackberry cobbler. Will you come in and eat a bowl with me?" She was trying to decide whether he meant it when he added, in an uncertain tone, "You probably have things to do. I don't mean to keep you."

He sounded so wistful that she stepped past him into the kitchen. "I would be honored to eat a bowl with you. I hope it's . . ." She never got to the word "good."

"I nearly had a heart attack," she would tell us later. "Cobwebs drooped from the valance at the window like dirty lace. The kitchen table was stacked so high with plates and glasses that he had to be shoving one set out of the way to use the next. Every pot he owned was sitting on the countertop, dirty. Several plates were on the floor, licked shiny clean. I devoutly hoped Bill wouldn't pick up one of them and offer me cobbler on it."

As he shut the door behind them, Bill seemed to see the room through Mamie's eyes. "I've been working such long hours outside, I haven't gotten around to my housework this week."

He hadn't gotten around to housework in six months, from the size of the dust bunnies under three kitchen chairs. Mamie knew the inertia of grief when she saw it. She'd had a spell right after Earl died when she'd let things slide, but she hadn't let them slide that far. *If Grace Anderson could see this mess, she'd rise from her grave and haunt him.*

Jimbo padded at Bill's side as he opened a cupboard. He found no bowls there, so he went to the dining room. "Be right back."

He brought two of Grace's wedding china soup bowls and two tarnished silver spoons. "Ought to use the best dishes now and then. That's what Grace always said."

She never said it because she didn't have another clean dish in the house.

Mamie thought it, but she couldn't squeeze a single word past the lump in her throat. She rinsed and dried the dishes and reached into the sink for a greasy serving spoon. She squirted detergent on it, washed it in hot water, and spooned cobbler into the bowls. "I don't reckon you've got any ice cream to go on this, do you?"

He brightened. "I've always got ice cream, Mamie."

She had counted on it. She smiled as he loped to the freezer back in the utility room. "I figured you did." She added a couple of scoops to the still-warm cobbler.

While he returned the ice cream to the freezer, he called, "Could we eat out on the porch? It's such a nice evening." Mamie agreed, but she secretly hoped she wouldn't catch a chill. The wind had gotten sharp since morning. The Easter cold front must be coming in.

Bill was so eager to be a good host—and so incompetent at it—that she felt her smile sliding south into pity.

As they carried their bowls toward the porch, Mamie contemplated the wreck of the rest of the downstairs.

The large dining room held Bill's grandmother's oak table, buffet, and china cabinet and the desk where he kept his records. The girls had done homework on the dining room table while Grace graded papers. The television was in there, too. After the girls had left, Bill and Grace had replaced an old couch with matching recliners and added a computer desk.

Since Grace's death, Bill had added a considerable amount of debris.

A mound of catalogues covered the table and spilled onto the floor. Dog hair lay thick on Grace's recliner. Magazines toppled from stacks on the floor. A thigh-high stack of newspapers flanked Bill's recliner. Spiderwebs draped the corners of the ceiling.

Bill hurried her through to the living room. It was uncluttered, but dusty and unused. At one end was the daybed Bill had installed when Grace got too weak to climb stairs, where she had spent her last few months and died.

He unlocked the front door. "Let's eat." He waved her to a rocker and perched on the swing. Mamie resisted an impulse to wipe her chair, even though she suspected rusty dust would leave a mark on her beige pants. Bill dug into the cobbler like he hadn't eaten decent for days. Jimbo settled between them with a hopeful lift to his chin. Bill let one bite of ice cream slide off the spoon into Jimbo's mouth. "That's all for you, boy. You aren't supposed to have sugar."

Jimbo got up and ambled to the far end of the porch. As Bill's gaze followed him, he noticed the PT Cruiser. "Whose vehicle is that you're driving?"

"Mine. I got it Saturday." She hoped she didn't sound guilty of the sin of pride, but it was hard not to boast when you owned such a magnificent car.

"You blow your horn at me yesterday morning?"

"Sure did."

"I wondered who that was. Looks like a fine car, Mamie. You've done well for yourself."

That was when Mamie got a nudge from God. Lurleen might sniff at that idea, but Mamie had gotten enough of those nudges in her lifetime to know one when she felt it. They usually showed up as ideas she would never have thought up herself.

"So how come nobody else gets these nudges?" Lurleen wanted to know.

"Everybody gets them, but most folks don't pay attention. If everybody followed up on their nudges, some of us wouldn't have so much to do."

That afternoon, Mamie's nudge was telling her somebody needed to help Bill. The people who *ought* to help, of course, were his daughters. Mamie was pretty certain they'd gotten nudges in that direction, but they didn't seem to be listening.

So when Bill said, "You've done well for yourself," Mamie said, "The fact is, that's partly why I came over here this afternoon." She faltered a little, because she hated to lie, even in pursuit of a righteous goal. Hopefully Bill thought she was reluctant about what she was going to say. "I get Social Security and have a little land, but with a new car and all, I'm afraid what I've got won't cover all my expenses." She started tracing circles with her finger on the arm of her chair, unable to look him in the eye. "I was wondering whether you could, like, give me a couple of days each week. Even a couple of mornings would help out. If you can't, now . . ." She waved one hand to dismiss it from his thoughts.

He gave a sharp bark of laughter. Jimbo looked up, puzzled, but seeing nothing amiss, he went back to his nap. "You thinking I could use a little help, Mamie? You're right. I think we could work something out. Two days a week, you said? I doubt I'll need that much once you get me organized, but for now, that sounds real good."

She pressed while the iron was hot. "How about if I come over Tuesdays and Fridays? I'll come around eight, like I used to, and stay until two. That suit you? I'll cook you a good dinner in the middle of the day, and make enough so you can have leftovers at night."

She would also cook up extra so he could eat the rest of the week, but she wouldn't mention that.

He pushed the swing gently while he thought. "Would thirty dollars a day be about right?"

It had been a long time since she'd made that little for a hard day's work, but it had been at least that long since Bill had paid a maid. Besides, she wasn't doing this for the money, and heaven knew farmers didn't have money to throw away that year. "That would be fine."

"You want to start tomorrow? I'll try to clean up the kitchen a little tonight. . . ."

"You leave that kitchen to me. I'll come over tomorrow and get a good start on it."

She hoped she'd have the stamina to work two hard days a week.

As she got up to leave, she remembered something. "Please don't tell Lurleen I'm working here. She and Skeeter would think they ought to help me out a little, and they have enough on their own plates. I don't want them feeling like they gotta support me, too." She waited, holding her breath.

"It will be our secret," Bill promised.

"Can I park behind the barn so Lurleen won't see my car when she brings your mail?"

"Sure, and I'll pay cash. You won't even have to tell the government."

"It's Lurleen I don't want to find out. I'm not worried about the government."

The government hadn't talked to her doctor.

THAT NIGHT ARCTIC AIR COLLIDED with tropical air over Georgia in a battle of heroic proportions. Mamie woke and lay listening to wind shriek around her roof like a demented creature. Even though her house was warm, she dragged her comforter over her head, ashamed of her terror but helpless to fight it. Under the lash of a night storm she became five years old, living in a wooden shack with newspaper stuffed between cracks. Any minute the wind would yank off the roof and fling it into a cotton field while rain ruined every pitiful thing her family owned. She would find her baby sister, Emmaline, crushed beneath a rafter the wind had wrenched from its nails and dropped onto the box where the baby slept.

She relived it during every stormy night. The wet. The cold. The anguish. The way Emmaline felt—like a cold little doll—when Mamie found her. Mamie had pressed the baby to her own skinny chest, hoping to warm her to life, but she would not warm.

Mamie prayed in moans while memories of Emmaline's death blurred into anticipation of her own. "Oh, Jesus, I am not scared of what comes after death, but I am mortally afraid of the process." She grieved that she must leave Lurleen, Skeeter, Janeika, her church, her new car, and all the people she loved.

As she grieved, she felt her pain join a broad stream of grief that flowed above her bed, running before the storm. She did not know how long she was swept along in that stream before the storm blew away, but suddenly the world grew still. Exhausted, Mamie relaxed in the cocoon of her comforter.

She thought she would sleep. Instead she lay thinking about the place Lurleen wanted her to go—a place where she could sit down and let others take care of her. Mamie didn't like living at crossed sticks with Lurleen, and she knew Lurleen meant well, but Lurleen didn't understand the surge of life that comes with knowing you are going to die. Mamie wasn't ready to die. She wanted to see her granddaughter married with children. She wanted to enjoy her new car. But if she was going to die, she couldn't just wait for death to show up. Lurleen ought to know by now that her mama was born helping folks. She needed to help them as long as she could. "That's how God made me. You can't go against the way you were made." She was trying out the argument for later.

But she quaked to remember a grievance against her that Lurleen didn't even know about yet: Mamie had been so taken with her little car that she had spent more on it than she should have. She had little left of what Mr. Landiss gave her for the land—the money she'd planned to put by for emergencies.

"If I get sicker—*when* I get sicker, O Jesus, don't let me be a burden to my child. And please don't let me die in a hospital full of tubes." Until dawn, Mamie lay sleepless beneath a thick comforter that gave her no comfort.

ACROSS SOLACE, I WAKENED AT three fifteen to a clap of thunder. A chill snaked through my old wooden window frames. A couple of seconds later, my room lit with lightning. Thunder rumbled again. I pumped air in the dark. "Rain! Yes!"

Chellie needed more cover. I steeled myself to crawl from under my blankets.

Mrs. Waits had left us several ugly quilts pieced from mismatched remnants she'd gotten at the mill. I dragged two down from closet shelves, tucked one around Chellie, and wrapped the other around me. I wished I could go back to sleep, but have you ever noticed how worries swell at night? By day I might be halfway confident that I could handle all my problems. At night fear swelled to a crouching giant, whispering questions to torment me: *Where is Porter? Why did he leave Landiss Construction? Did he quarrel with somebody? Did he find a job he liked better? Why didn't he say so? What if he never sends another check?*

As I paced, I argued aloud, "Porter wouldn't do that. He will always take care of us."

Maybe "always" is only five years long.

I tried shoving fear down, but after being restrained by sheer willpower for a week, it fed on the manic wind and built muscle. *What if Porter is lying in his apartment sick or injured? He might not be able to reach his cell phone. The battery could have died. Who except you would care or even notice if he never showed up for work?*

I admitted what I had been trying to ignore for days: I needed to go look for him. Nobody else would. The problem was, I didn't know where he had been staying. Except for his checks, we had very little contact anymore.

"Stop worrying. You can't do a thing about it tonight," I admonished myself. But I wasn't going to be able to sleep with fear wailing around my roof.

I fixed myself a cup of hot tea and wrapped myself more tightly in Mrs. Waits's quilt. I found it oddly comforting. The only thing the old bat and I ever had in common was Porter. She seemed to be sharing my worry. But while I waited for the tea to steep, something flying past the window caught my eye. Snow?

It was a blizzard of peach blossoms. "Lord, not the peaches!" Since Porter had left, I had made extra money each summer by selling peaches in a little shed I'd built out by the road. The ones that didn't sell, I made into jam that sold well in boutiques. So far city folks hadn't discovered how simple jam was to make. Peach money provided the little bit of jam Chellie and I had on the white bread of our finances.

I ran to the back door. The blast of air that met me was so icy, it took my breath away. But I didn't feel any moisture. I held my hand out beyond the roof. Not a drop.

"What the heck is going on?" I shouted to the sky. "This weather is plumb crazy. Sunday it was nearly seventy. Now"—I checked the thermometer hanging on my back wall—"it's thirty-five?"

My only answer was a flash of lightning that lit the yard.

"If the rest of those blossoms freeze, Chellie and I might as well lie down under the trees and turn up our toes. How about some rain to go with this wind? We need a good crop to make ends come at least within shouting distance. Can we get some relief down here?" Mama probably whirled in her grave at my raging prayers, but if you can't be honest with God, who can you be honest with?

THE STORM ROARED INTO MARIETTA just before dawn. Margaret peered at the digital clock beside her bed. In a flash of lightning, she saw Ben squatting upright on the bed like a big square Buddha in a white T-shirt.

"Rain at last?" she asked drowsily.

"I don't hear any rain, but listen to that wind!"

As the gale flung debris against the windows, she hurried to the nearest window.

Lightning flickered like a strobe-light show. She felt the hair rise on her arms. In the dancing light she watched the wind strip away new leaves and rip off small branches. It whipped oaks to a frenzy, bent poplars like saplings. Margaret loved those trees, but that night, in the glow of the security light beside their driveway, the trees were long-armed monsters swaying hungrily toward the house. An invisible snake of frigid air curled into the room from a slightly open window. It smelled of sulfur.

Ben counted seconds between lightning and thunder. "It's getting close." He scratched his belly. "I ought to go see if everything's secure at work."

A wrought-iron chair scuttled weightlessly across the deck. MacTavish's outdoor water bowl sailed up into a dogwood. The wind swooped around the eaves like the big bad wolf, roaring that this time it would finally blow the brick house down.

"A tree could fall on your truck before you get down the drive. Why don't you wait until it blows out?" She pulled on her robe.

"Where are *you* going?" Ben didn't need to ask. He knew where she was going—where she would always go when danger threatened.

"Checking on the kids."

As she spoke, the digital clock went black. The driveway light sputtered and died. The tornado siren wailed.

"Get Andy to the basement. I'll call Jason." Ben could still move like a high school quarterback when he needed to. He hurried out, forgetting his robe.

"Bring the flashlight," she called after him. She snatched up his robe on her way to Andy's room.

She scooped Andy from beneath the covers, wrapped his comforter around him, grabbed his bathrobe, and headed through familiar blackness toward the stairs. Behind her, she heard MacTavish hit the floor with a thump.

She staggered downstairs inhaling the scent of sleepy boy. Andy's hair scratched her cheek. MacTavish gave a sharp bark as he scuttled past her ankles.

Andy's eyes flashed blue in a burst of lightning. "Where are we going? Why don't you turn on a light?"

"There's a big storm and the power has gone out. We're going down to the playroom, in case the wind blows a tree on the house."

"I want to see!" He struggled in the comforter. When she set him down, he stumbled ahead of her down the basement stairs like a small king trailing his royal mantle.

In a flash of lightning she saw Ben and Jason peering out the high basement windows. Both wore only T-shirts and boxers, although the basement was chilly. She wended her way through the shadowy room to hand Ben and Andy their robes. "Here. You can have mine, Jase." She fumbled with the tie.

"I'm all right, Mom. Let me do my own suffering." Still prickly from the incident at school, he sounded prepared to walk barefoot across the Arctic before he'd consent to wear his mother's robe. She noticed he kept his distance from Ben, as well.

"Where's the flashlight?" she asked.

"I forgot it," Ben admitted, "but we're okay. Your eyes will adjust pretty soon."

"Look!" Andy butted his head against Margaret's side. He pointed up at the windows. Across a deep black sky, jagged streaks of blue, green, and yellow coursed horizontally toward the east. "Isn't that absolutely beautiful?"

"Beautiful," she agreed. "A poet said that lightning writes God's autograph across the sky."

Ben's chuckle rumbled. "Trust you to remember that."

Even Jason was torn between fascination with the storm and maintaining his reputation as a jaded adolescent. When a flash was followed by a crash, his voice skated up an octave with excitement. "It took down a tree in the woods!"

MacTavish pranced about their feet with short, excited barks.

Andy started to say something else, but Ben rubbed his stubby hair. "Shhh. Let's just enjoy the show." Mac, sitting on Margaret's feet, subsided to uneasy whines.

Ben draped his arm around Andy's shoulders. Jason sidled close to Andy on the other side and didn't object when Andy snaked an arm around his waist. Margaret eased up behind to circle them all with her arms. They stood until the storm blew out as suddenly as it had come, leaving the sky as calm as a child after a tantrum.

Resting her cheek against Ben's broad back, Margaret murmured, "Nobody should have to go through a storm alone."

Ben dropped his arm from Andy's shoulders and pulled away from the family. "I need to check the business. You all get up to bed. You'll be warmer there until the heat comes back on."

As they trooped up the stairs, Andy said, "Wasn't that the greatest storm ever? I hope we have another one."

PART TWO

Cracks in the

Firmament

"The sky is falling! The sky is falling!"

—Chicken Little

Seven

I n spite of their broken sleep, Ben and Margaret got up before the sun. Ben was a morning person, and Margaret cherished the hour they spent together before the boys woke. Conscious that the deep maroon of her robe suited her, she put on blusher and lipstick before she went to fix their breakfast. She liked to look nice for Ben.

The power had returned, so the house was warm, but when she went out for the paper, a frigid wind made her clutch her robe around her. She decided to make oatmeal, which Ben loved.

He doused his with brown sugar and milk while she poured their coffee. "Garbage collection this morning," she reminded him.

"Sure." He studied her over his mug.

"I've got PTA this evening. Will you get home in time to feed the boys?"

"Sure." He sipped his coffee and looked at her like he was memorizing her face.

"You aren't eating your oatmeal. It's cold outside. You'll need the warmth."

He set down the mug. "Margaret, I've been thinking. . . ."

Her muscles tensed, beginning with a spot under her stomach and moving up her spine. It took all her self-control to ask casually, "Yes?"

In seventeen years, the only time Ben's "I've been thinking" had pref-
aced something she wanted to hear was the afternoon he'd suggested,
"Let's get married." His last "I've been thinking" had been about taking
out a home-equity loan to buy a larger truck for the business. She had
cosigned only because he assured her their other trucks weren't large
enough for Landiss Construction's needs, and the business Rick was
giving them would repay the loan in a couple of years.

He sat forward, elbows braced on the table, and took the deep breath
of a diver preparing to plunge into a pool. "I want a divorce."

The words took several seconds to reach her brain. "Where did that
come from?"

"It's been brewing for a while. I just needed time to line up some
things."

Margaret went numb. The only thing she felt were remnants of
brown sugar on her fingertips. "I need to wash my hands."

"Did you hear me? I said—"

"I heard you." Amazing how level her voice sounded when the room
had gone cockeyed. She listed as she walked to the sink. *Help me! Help
me! Help me!* She washed and dried her hands with extra care. *Give me
the right words to say!* She placed each foot just so as she returned to the
breakfast room. The world had become a fragile place. A sudden move
might shatter it.

The hard thing said, Ben was eating his oatmeal with gusto. *He has
always been impulsive,* she reminded herself. *He depends on me to hold
the reins while he careens all over the place.* If she could hold them for a
few days, he'd get over this. *Help me! Help me! Help me!* Detached, she
watched herself sit down across from a husband who had gone temporarily insane. "Okay, I'm ready to talk."

He reached for his orange juice. "I don't want to talk. I want out.
You know how it's been lately, not much going for either of us—"

"We need a vacation. Or maybe we need to see a counselor."

"I don't want a counselor or a vacation. I want out." He spoke in a stubborn tone she knew well. Ben hated conflict, but when crossed, he could dig in his heels.

"You . . ." She stopped. She had recently read you should use "I" sentences when dealing with conflict. They were less threatening. "I love you." She laid a hand on his thigh. "I need you. The boys need you." He pulled away his leg. Her hand hung suspended until she put it on top of the table. She leaned toward him. "Ben, you are my life!"

He gave a small snort. "Then get a life."

She was too startled to reply.

Even he seemed to recognize he had been not only flip but cruel. "Look, I can't stand it any longer, Margaret. It's all fake."

"What's fake?"

"You. Me. Us. On my way home every night, I try to think of things that happened so I'll have something to say when you ask, with that put-on little smile, 'How was your day?'"

"It's not a put-on smile. I'm glad to see you. I ask because I'm interested."

"You're programmed to *act* interested. If you were really interested, you'd ask things like, 'Did that load of sod come in?' 'How much money are you losing because of this drought?' But why *should* you be interested? Most of it is boring, even to me."

"Your coming home is the high point of my day."

"How much pressure is that? If I come in like a bear, I blow your day? Think how that feels. I come home all sweaty, and there you are, fresh and smiling, waiting to ask the perpetual question. Do you realize that not once, not *once in sixteen years*, have you greeted me in grungy clothes without makeup and snarled, 'Don't talk to me, Ben Baxter. I'm in a terrible mood'?"

"I can arrange that." She tried to smile, but her lips had frozen.

"I don't want you arranging things. I want— Look. In the end, this will be better for both of us. I'm thinking of you, as well as me."

He had rehearsed that line. She knew it. When he had a business proposition to make Ben always came up with a few clichés to hammer home his point. His voice droned on, explaining why divorce made sense for them both, dissecting sixteen years of marriage like a surgeon separating Siamese twins. She was following a question scuttling down corridors of the past. *What did I do wrong?* If she could only lay hold of that, maybe she could make it right.

Was she too strong? He relied on her strength. Still, she could let up a bit, let him handle more things around the house. Did she spend too much time with the boys, not enough with him? She could spend time with him. Had she neglected his interests? She had shaped her life around his interests. Sex had never been a problem—not until recently. Bewildered, she cried out at last, "What did I do wrong? What do you want me to change?"

His answer chilled and damned her. "I don't want you to change. You are fine as you are—a terrific woman. I just don't love you anymore."

"Is there somebody else?"

"No. Of course not." Had there been a slight pause before he spoke?

Fury choked her. "Am I an old shirt you can give to Goodwill when you're tired of me?"

Ben's face tightened. He hated scenes. In another minute, he'd leave. She willed her voice to be reasonable. "We aren't adolescents. Maybe we need to spice up our marriage. We've been busy lately, haven't spent time together. Why don't we take a cruise? We enjoyed the other one." They'd taken a Caribbean cruise to celebrate their fifteenth anniversary. It was the closest thing to a honeymoon they'd ever had.

"We can't afford a cruise."

"A weekend, then. Or why don't we talk to the preacher? We can't throw away all these years. I'll be glad to call—"

"I don't want your help!" His words exploded through the downstairs.

What right does he have to be angry? Her ears roared so with anger, she could barely hear what he was saying.

". . . run the boys' lives if you have to. I'm sick of you running mine!"

Her fury turned to ice. "What on earth are you talking about?"

Instead of answering he pulled himself heavily to his feet, lumbered to the kitchen, and returned with a beer.

"Beer this early? You'll get—"

"That's what I'm talking about." His voice rose to a feminine register. "'You'll get indigestion, Ben.' 'We're going to be late for church, Ben.' 'Why did you let Jase go out with those boys, Ben?' How do you have time to run your own life with all the time you spend running mine?"

Her rage spilled out in torrents. "Whose choice was that? When I met you, you had spent five years in college and still hadn't picked a major. You couldn't decide what tie to wear with your sports coat, much less what to do with your life. All you knew was how to party. Your parents were fed up, remember? No more money after this year, they said. Who believed in you, studied with you, edited your papers, figured out how all those crazy courses you had taken could be rolled into a degree in one more year? Who quit school after we got married to work a cash register to support us until you graduated? Who persuaded her parents to cosign a loan to start a business because your folks—who, I point out, were far more able to help—thought landscaping was too blue-collar for their son?"

"I paid back that loan."

"*We* paid back that loan. I ran the office with Jason playing around my feet. I sat up half the night after you both were in bed, keeping books because you couldn't be bothered to learn how to use a computer. Remember that? And it's not simply big things you don't deal with. You can't be bothered to deal with little things. 'I need some help here, Margaret.' How often do I hear that in a week? You can't remember to pick up your own dry cleaning. Don't tell me—"

"I am telling you one thing." His breath came in angry gasps. "I want a divorce. I want to come home when I feel like it without saying where I've been or what I've been doing. I want to come home without having to be nice to anybody—plop down, turn on the television, and chill. I want to eat what I want when I want it. Watch television all night if I want to."

"You want to be a teenager. No, a middle-school kid. Even Jason knows you have to accommodate yourself at times to other people."

"I'm tired of accommodating. I want to live my own life."

She willed panic to subside. Ben didn't want a divorce. He wanted space. She said in a mild voice, "You want more freedom? You've got it. Come home when you like. Fix your own meals. Pick up your dry cleaning. If you want to make decisions about your life, do it."

Ben rubbed one hand over his face, a sure sign he was thinking. When he spoke, it was clear he was ignoring the past few minutes and returning to his prepared script. "This isn't about you, Margaret—it's about me. About growing up. When we met, I was twenty-three. I needed a lot of help. I'll admit it. You gave it. I'm grateful. But I'm nearly forty. I need and want things now I did not need and want then, and I don't need and want some things I needed and wanted then. I'll take care of you and the boys, but I'm smothering in this marriage. I need space. I want *out*."

She didn't believe he'd go through with it, but she raised the bar on how easily he could leave. "You will have to tell the boys. Both of them. I won't do it. If you choose to go"—her voice faltered, but she willed it on—"you will have to tell them why."

"Mom? Why are you all yelling?" A rumpled Andy stood on the front stairs, calling between the banisters. MacTavish's bright black eyes peered out just above him.

"Get back to bed!"

Margaret winced at Ben's roar, but understood. He was terrified Andy had heard them.

Andy's hands clutched the banister. "Me 'n' Mac heard you shouting. . . ." His voice trailed off. Mac whimpered.

Margaret waved Andy back upstairs. "We were just having a discussion, honey. Now go back to bed. It's not time to get up yet. Shall I bring you up some warm milk?"

He nodded. "Okay."

With the feeling that she'd gained a reprieve, she went to heat a glass of milk. When she carried it up with a couple of dog treats for Mac, she said, "Daddy didn't mean to yell at you. He's got a lot on his mind." *He's lost his mind,* she wanted to say, but she would not mention this to the boys. Ben would never carry out his threat.

She waited until Andy finished his milk, then kissed him and carried his glass back downstairs. The only sign later that she had not been her usual self would be a milky glass sitting in the refrigerator.

Ben was at the coffeemaker, pouring himself a second cup. "It's not the end of the world, you know. It happens all the time. You want coffee?" He held up the pot.

She fetched her mug. *How domestic we look,* she marveled. *Nobody would guess he is shredding our lives like mulch.* "Not to couples like us, Ben. Not to *us.*"

"Maybe we could try a separation for a while, not do anything hasty."

Relief surged through her, followed at once by despair. "You're taking the easy way out, aren't you? You're saying that to avoid talking about it."

He drained his mug without a word. She had her answer. Good old Ben. No need to fight if he could waffle out of it.

"You will have to tell the boys," she repeated.

"Okay." He took his parka from the coat closet under the stairs. "It's cold today. Did you see the thermometer? Only thirty-three."

"You will have to tell the boys, Ben."

"I said okay. I'll tell them tonight after I've found a place."

She didn't feel the full impact of that until he was gone.

Tonight? He was already gone, and she was too numb to cry.

Still, as she rolled out the garbage—which Ben, predictably, had forgotten—she told herself, "It's a phase. He's going through a midlife crisis. I need to be patient. Understanding."

She didn't feel patient or understanding. She wanted to run around the yard screaming like a banshee. "Have all males gone crazy?" she asked a squirrel on the drive. "Jason, Porter, Ben—is the whole universe having a testosterone surge?"

The thought of Porter reminded her that she needed to call the construction company. She also needed to send Billie the check she'd promised. She was tempted to write the check for a thousand dollars, but recognized that as an impulse spawned not by generosity but by a desire to hurt Ben.

He wouldn't notice. He never checked their bank balance.

How will he ever get along without me?

That thought sustained her as she drove Andy to school, swung by the post office, and slid an envelope into the drive-by box. But by the time she got home, her own troubles—Ben, Jason—had so swamped her, she forgot about Porter Waits.

AT SIX THIRTY THAT EVENING, when Ben was still not home, Margaret stood in the den, where the boys were playing a computer game. "Please comb your hair and wash your hands. I have PTA tonight and can't reach your dad, so you're going to have to come with me. We'll grab a burger or something afterward." She had been calling since five, but Ben's office didn't know where he was. He didn't answer his cell phone.

"We're playing," Andy objected.

As Margaret watched, she saw Jason choose not to make points so his brother could. She gave him a quick hug. "Mom!" He pulled away, but looked pleased she knew what he'd done. "I can't go to school," he reminded her. "I'm not allowed on the grounds until Monday."

That was news to Andy. "Cool! What did you do?"

"None of your business. But I can't go. We'll stay here. We'll be fine."

She seldom left them home alone in the evening, but Jason was old enough, and good to Andy. "Okay. There's a pizza in the freezer. Tell your dad where I've gone."

She returned at nine to find the boys sprawled on the couch. Jason gave her a look of pure venom. Andy's cheeks were stained with tears. "Were you scared?" she asked, rubbing her hand over his stubble of hair. "Where's your dad?"

"As if you didn't know." When his lip curled, Jason looked much older than fifteen.

"Know what?" Bewildered, she met two pairs of eyes full of betrayal. A cold chill started at her knees and crept up her body.

Jason slammed his fist down on the table so hard a magazine slipped off. "That you two decided to get a divorce, but couldn't be bothered to let us in on the secret. That somehow *you* didn't get around to telling us, so Dad had to do it. How could you do this to us?" His voice cracked on the last sentence. His face contorted with the effort to keep back tears.

Margaret was too stunned to reply.

Andy started to sniffle. "If we're good, can Daddy come back? Why won't you let him live here anymore?"

When she didn't answer, Jason snarled, "Not only did he leave, he took the computer with my history paper on it. Not to mention my TV and some of our best DVDs."

Margaret looked wildly around the room. Sure enough, the computer was gone from the desk. The DVD shelf was gap-toothed where jewel cases were missing.

She dashed for the stairs. Ben's chest was empty except for an old pair of boxers draped over an open drawer. A note was propped on her pillow.

> *Margaret,*
> *I found a place, so I might as well clear out tonight like*
> *we planned. No point in prolonging things. I'll get back*

to you tomorrow or the next day to discuss what I'll need
from the house. Ben.

"Bastard!" she screamed. She flung his boxers to the floor. "You can't even move out without leaving me a mess to clean up!" Three messes. The bedroom and two boys who stood in the door with accusing eyes.

Eight

I waited all day Tuesday for Margaret's call. I didn't go out except for the mail and—during Chellie's nap—to pick up storm debris. It was so cold that the rest of the day, I kept her wrapped up in the living room with a fire going so we didn't need the furnace. We drank hot chocolate, read, and played games. As we played, I remembered chilly Sunday afternoons when Mama would make hot chocolate and clear off the dining room table to play games with Maggie and me. I learned addition by playing dominoes and how to spell from playing Jr. Scrabble. Even Daddy would join us for Old Maid and dominoes. When I was ten and Mama went out to church women's meetings, he taught me to play poker. We laughed a lot as a family back then, especially after Maggie went to college. Michelle and I laughed a lot that day, too. I forgot, for a time, how close we were to the precipice.

That evening Lucky went out for a ramble and didn't come in at his usual time. The temperature was dropping fast, so after Michelle was asleep, I pulled on my parka and boots and went looking for him. "Kitty, kitty," I called, tramping through the orchard with my flashlight. I got almost to the trailer before I heard an outraged mew. He was caught in blackberry bushes.

"Silly cat," I scolded as I untangled him. "Chase chipmunks closer to home." His only reply was an indignant growl. Once released he scampered back to the house, utterly ungrateful. I stood and stretched my back. My flashlight reflected off the trailer.

The trailer! Why hadn't I thought of that before? I could rent it out. I didn't relish close neighbors, but it wasn't in sight of the house when leaves were on the peaches, and it had been only three years old when we bought it. We'd been comfortable there. It was even furnished.

Furnished?

The trailer had a floral couch and chair and a solid table and chairs. Its guest room bed, chest, and mattress were much better than the ones Chellie had inherited from her father's childhood. I would have moved the trailer furniture to the house years before if I hadn't been too busy to remember it was there. If I was going to rent out the trailer, why not bring the best stuff home?

I pushed through the briars and shone my light around the small front yard I had wrested from the woods. When I saw that blackberry bushes had taken over the edges of the abandoned clearing, I was delighted. I could make blackberry jelly to sell.

But the yard was a mess. "Definitely a sign of humanity's fallen condition," I muttered. "Weeds where grass ought to grow, grass in the flower beds." Still, the air was scented with honeysuckle. A few daffodils and paperwhites bloomed like stars in the tall grass. Using the light and the toe of one sneaker, I found clumps of daylilies already two inches high, shoots of hosta pushing up around the empty birdbath, and daisies showing leaves near the door. "The hydrangea is even going to bloom!" I waded knee-deep through weeds to stroke tiny green flowerets. Whipping the yard into shape wouldn't take more than a day or two.

I seldom left Michelle alone so long, but knowing she slept deeply, I took a deep breath of cold air and enjoyed a few minutes of freedom. "Might as well check the inside while I'm here," I said. Knowing Porter, I was sure the door wasn't locked.

I strode up the steps and stepped into despair.

Porter had been so impatient to move, and I had been so sick that day, we hadn't bothered to clean. I had planned to use some of my maternity leave getting the trailer ready to sell. I had pictured myself bringing a fat, happy baby down to lie gurgling in a carrier while I worked. Since Chellie's birth, I hadn't given the trailer another thought.

As I shone my light inside, roaches skittered into hiding. The chilly air was stale. I flipped the switch before I remembered Porter would have turned off the electricity at the box. He wasn't good about locking doors, but he pinched pennies as tightly as his mother did.

I played the strong beam of my flashlight around the room. Dust lay over everything like a veil. Cobwebs draped from the lampshades. Scraps of debris littered the carpet. A mouse had chewed a hole in one corner of the chair cushion. Tears stung my eyes to recall the surge of hope I'd brought to that place as a bride. Its decline paralleled my own.

To stave off a pity party I clomped back out through the weeds to turn on water and power. The water ran. Lights, stove, and refrigerator worked. When I flicked on the heat and the fan purred, I gave an invisible partner a high five. "There's nothing I can't handle here," I told a little brown spider in the bathroom. I eased back out to let him live another day.

The furniture was definitely worth swapping with what I had. I hated to make tenants live with Mrs. Waits's awful stuff, but I would replace the furniture as soon as I could afford to.

Buoyed up by the thought of a monthly rent check plus Margaret's promised money, I went home and ate a bowlful of peaches I'd canned the summer before. Every bite reminded me of happier days when I had played with Michelle in the orchard, sold peaches beside the road, and canned through long twilight hours. "We will have happy days again," I promised Lucky. He curled himself at my feet, but he did not purr. He never did.

WEDNESDAY, I DECIDED BEFORE I opened my eyes that I'd call Margaret as early as was decent, to see if I had missed her call while I was at the trailer. But I hated to get out from under the covers. The room was so cold, I made dragon breath when I exhaled.

I pulled on a heavy sweater with my jeans and turned on the furnace before Michelle woke up. Heaven knew how I'd pay a heating bill on top of everything else, but I couldn't afford for either of us to get sick. When I dashed out to check my peaches, every blossom had frozen. I went from tree to tree touching the trunks as if I were comforting mothers who had lost their children. What would Chellie and I do for extra money come summertime?

I went inside, made hot tea—grateful I still had tea—and turned on a mindless television show so I wouldn't have to think. The TV woke Michelle an hour early.

I was glad of her company. We watched cartoons for an hour. Nothing takes your mind off worries like giggling with a child.

At eight, I called Margaret before she left to take Andy to school. Her voice sounded thick, like she was talking underwater.

"Hey, it's Billie. I don't like to bother you, but I wondered if you tried to call me last evening. I was out a little while, so I was afraid I might have missed you."

That overly polite way of asking "Why the heck didn't you call?" showed the pathetic state of our relationship.

Margaret didn't say a word.

"If this isn't a good time, I can call back. I was wondering if you'd found out anything about where Porter was working last."

More silence.

"Are you there? Can you talk?"

"I'm here." More silence.

If I hadn't known my sister, I'd have thought she was taking drugs. "I didn't wake you, did I?" Margaret and Ben were morning people, but maybe he had let her sleep in. I wished I had somebody to let me sleep in.

After what seemed an eternity, Margaret said, "Sorry. I'm a little distracted today."

"Did you get any of that bad storm Monday night?" Maybe her roof was off or all her trees were down.

"Yeah, we lost a couple of trees in the woods."

"You were lucky. It blew half my peach blossoms off. The rest froze last night."

"We had a freeze last night?"

"A hard one." Ben must have brought in their paper, too, if she didn't know.

"I'll bet my peach tree is gone, then, as well."

Sometimes I wanted to smack Margaret. Didn't she know the difference between losing fruit from one family tree and losing a chunk of your annual income? I reminded myself she had no idea how much I counted on those peaches. Might as well press on with my purpose for calling. "Did you have time to check on Porter?" I tried not to let my urgency show.

"No. Sorry. Yesterday— Let me drive Andy to school and I'll get right on it."

"Okay, but I sure hope you find out something soon. Give Ben and the boys my love."

Margaret took so long answering, I wondered if she'd heard me. I was about to say good-bye when she said, "I will. I'll call as soon as I know something."

I hung up, wondering if she was coming down with a cold. Her nose sounded stuffy. She sure didn't sound like Margaret.

She called back around ten. "I found out where Porter last worked."

Hope rose in me like helium. "What's the address?" It was a small combination of letters and numbers to mean so much. "This is great. I'll drive in as soon as I can fill up with gas, to see if any of the men Porter worked with might know something."

"Don't bother. The place isn't far from here, so I drove over."

"You didn't need to do that."

"I had nothing else to do."

Margaret had nothing else to do? I was so surprised I missed a few words.

". . . talked to the foreman, who reminded me of that black hog Daddy used to have—the one that bellowed at anybody who came near him."

"Caesar?"

"That's the one. The foreman is exactly like Caesar. Black bristly hair, a little snub nose, and his office looks like a sty. When I got there, he was on the phone. He even bellowed like Caesar."

"Maybe really bad hogs get reincarnated as people."

"Maybe so. I told him I was trying to locate Porter because he'd done some work for us and hadn't been paid. He said Porter doesn't work there any longer."

"Which we already knew."

"Yeah. He said Porter never clocked out one evening—he must have simply walked off the site. They haven't seen hide nor hair of him since. He did say he misses him—that Porter is a good worker when he isn't losing his temper, and he speaks more Spanish than the foreman does. I didn't know Porter speaks Spanish."

"He took it in high school and probably learned more working with Mexicans. He's quick to pick up new things." I wished I could talk about Porter to Margaret without feeling like I had to defend him. "That's all that the foreman said? He doesn't know where Porter might have gone?"

"No. I asked. He said, real impatient, 'Look, lady, I don't babysit these men. If you owe Porter money, he'll find you.'"

"Did you talk to any of the other workers on the site?"

"Of course not. I don't speak Spanish. Why don't these people learn English? Or stay in a country where they can be understood?"

Fortunately, she didn't expect an answer. I hadn't had time in the last few years to form an opinion on the national immigration crisis. "Maybe if I went over and talked to the men . . ."

"You can't go onto the site without permission. Besides, do you speak Spanish?"

"Maybe five words."

"I'm pretty sure I learned everything there is to learn. You need to accept it, Billie—Porter has taken off."

"He wouldn't do that to us! Would Ben take off and leave you and the boys?"

Margaret didn't deign to reply.

Nine

I was elated when her check arrived that morning to spice up my junk mail. "Aunt Margaret's sent us money! Let's eat a quick lunch and go to town!" I picked up Chellie, and we waltzed around the room. Breathless, I collapsed with her onto the couch. "We'll get clothes and groceries and cleaning supplies so Mama can clean up the trailer and rent it out."

I didn't tell her, but I also planned to drive to Marietta later, after we got gas in the truck. I wanted to see for myself that site where Porter had been working. If I dressed like a construction worker, I might get more out of the men than Margaret had in her Junior League clothes.

"Iii-eeem?" Chellie's face was alight.

"Definitely ice cream. Let's put on the outfits Aunt Margaret gave us for Christmas."

Margaret had made Chellie green corduroy pants and appliquéd a bear on the chest of a creamy sweatshirt. "Pretty!" She tried to stroke the bear. Margaret had even embroidered eyes, a nose, and a soft pink tongue. I remembered how special I used to feel when Mama dressed me up and brushed my hair, so I brushed her hair until it shone. "You are pretty, honey. Watch TV while I get pretty, too."

Margaret had made me a burnt orange pantsuit that was perfect for my coloring. When I put on my gold earrings—the only nice present Porter ever bought me—I almost didn't recognize the woman in the mirror. But what would I do for shoes? My black heels would look tacky with the outfit. My other choices were brown loafers with one flapping sole, tennis shoes with a hole in the toe, or red plastic flip-flops. I fetched glue and reattached my loafer sole. "Hold until we can get to Wal-Mart," I told it. "That's all I ask."

My old blue parka ruined my look, so I decided I could tough out the cold. I wouldn't be outside much if somebody came soon to recharge my battery. I zipped Chellie in her parka, wrapped her warmly in an afghan, and left her on the porch while I went to the road to wait.

I was turning into an ice cube before a truck rounded the curve. I flagged it down.

Dented and battered, it didn't look any more prosperous than we were. The driver didn't either. Black hair flopped in his eyes. His nails were filthy. He needed a shave. He seemed familiar, but I couldn't place him. "Could you give me a jump?" I tried to keep my teeth from chattering.

He looked me up and down. "I might manage that," he drawled like a movie cowboy. "Out here or inside your place?"

I glared. "My truck battery's dead. I'm asking for the use of your jumper cables."

"Where's your husband?"

"Not here at the moment, or he'd beat you to a pulp. But never mind. I'll get somebody else." I turned away. That, of course, was when my sole decided to come unglued. It ruined the effect of my grand exit.

"Don't get your britches in a wad," he called after me. "I'll give you a jump. But a pretty thing like you shouldn't be standing on the side of the road flagging down strange men."

"I didn't expect you to be quite so strange." All of a sudden I remembered where I'd seen him. "Aren't you Jennie McDougal's husband? We met at your wedding. She and I graduated from high school together." Being married to Jennie could explain his unkempt state. Jennie was one of those people who believed in taking a bath once a week whether you needed it or not.

He had the grace to look embarrassed. "I was just fooling with you, you know?"

"If Jennie finds out about your kind of fooling, you're going to be walking funny the rest of your life. But if you'll jump my truck, I'll let her find out some other way. I'd really appreciate it. I need to get my daughter to town." I nodded toward the porch.

He studied Chellie. "Go get in your truck." He pulled into my drive.

He soon had my truck humming. "Keep it running. I'll bring your little girl." He lifted Chellie into the cab with surprising gentleness. "There you go, love." He smiled at her and Chellie smiled back. "Shall I put her chair in back?"

"If you would. Thanks." I snapped Chellie's seat belt with fingers like icicles.

He came over to the driver's window and knocked gently. When I rolled it down, he held out his hand to shake. As we shook, I felt something in his palm. "Get her a treat of some kind."

"Thanks." My smile wobbled. "Tell Jennie that Billie Anderson Waits says hello." After he drove away, I looked at what I held. As an apology, a ten-dollar bill wasn't half bad.

ON THE WAY TO TOWN I made up funny songs to make Chellie laugh and keep us warm until the heater kicked in. My good mood lasted until we got to the bank. I filled out the deposit slip to deposit a hundred dollars and keep a hundred. The teller clicked busily on her terminal, added the check to a stack beside it, and shoved back a receipt. "I can't give you any cash. There's a hold on the check while it clears."

"Say what? I've banked here all my life. You've never put a hold on a check before."

"You don't have sufficient funds in your account to cover this if it doesn't clear. It's only for a couple of days, since it's a Georgia check."

"I need money *now*." I nearly held up my foot to show her how bad I needed shoes.

"You'll have to speak with the manager."

I hadn't met the new manager, but I recognized her instantly. Ashley Evans. She'd been a bushy blonde in high school with thick eyebrows and teenage acne. She hadn't matured into a flaming beauty, but she had tamed her hair and cut it short, reduced her brows to slender arches, and discovered pancake makeup. In a gray pinstripe suit, she looked professional.

She didn't look like she had ever sweated on a basketball court, but she had, briefly. Two years behind me in school, Ashley could have been a stellar player. Unfortunately she thought she ought to be allowed to dribble until she lined up a perfect shot and erupted in fury if a referee cited her for shoving. When the coach put her off the team, she came to me in tears. "You have to play by the rules," I told her, "or you can't play at all." Ashley decided not to play.

That morning, she greeted me like a long-lost friend. "Billie!" She stood as I pushed Chellie toward her desk. "How nice to see you." She gave Michelle a quick, dismissive glance as she offered me her hand. Her palm was soft, her nails dark red.

She motioned me to a chair in front of her desk. "What can I do for you?"

I explained about the check.

"What's your account number?" Ashley turned to her computer screen.

My cheeks burned as she called up my meager balance. "Like I said, I'm having a cash-flow problem."

"You don't have enough in the account to cover the check if it doesn't clear."

"It will clear. The check is from my big sister, Margaret. Remember her? She married a man who owns a landscaping business in Marietta. There's plenty of money in their account. You can call the Marietta bank to verify that if you need to."

"I'm sorry, Billie. That's not the way we do it. We have to transfer funds into your account before we can let you have them." She slid the checkbook back across her desk. "I'm real sorry, but there's nothing we can do."

"I guess I'll have to get the check back and find somebody else to cash it."

"Unfortunately, you have already deposited it. We can't give it back until it has cleared."

"You can't keep my money!"

"You deposited it."

I was certain if somebody with a big account was sitting in my chair, she would return their check in a minute. Of course, somebody with a big account wouldn't need to ask for a check back.

Ashley stood. "We have to play by the rules, Billie. I'm sure you understand." When I looked back from the door, her lips curved in triumph.

I WHEELED MICHELLE TO THE parking lot at a dangerous pace. I couldn't take my business to another bank. Solace didn't have another bank and I couldn't afford gas to bank somewhere else.

How far would ten dollars go toward essentials plus gas to get home? Not very far. I had planned to stop by Foxworthy's Garage to buy a used battery, but that would have to wait until Margaret's check cleared.

As I was lifting Michelle into the truck, I saw our church steeple two blocks away. If they'd let me have a few groceries, I could replace them in a few days.

I put Michelle back in her chair. "Iii-eeem?" she asked as I tucked her in warmly.

I'd have prefered hot chocolate with whipped cream, but we had a fat chance of getting either in the near future. "Not yet, honey. We've got another place to go."

I had never noticed how steep the hill was between the church and the bank. Chellie's chair was heavy, the wind icy. "Cold," Chellie complained. I was freezing, even with the exertion of pushing the chair. Icy wind whistled through my pants. The chill of the sidewalk seeped through my soles. I stopped long enough to pull up Chellie's hood and tuck her afghan more securely. "Hang in there, kid. It's only one more block." A very long block.

At the church entrance, I had ten steps to climb, for the sanctuary and church offices sat high above classrooms, the fellowship hall, and the kitchen. I carried Chellie up the steps, wrestled open the door, and deposited her on an old pew inside the door. By the time I'd hauled up her chair, I was damp with sweat.

As we went down the hall to the office, Chellie exclaimed, "God's house!"

"Yes, this is God's house," I agreed, surprised she remembered. "We're going to ask if they can give us a little food to tide us over until Aunt Margaret's check clears."

"Check clears," Chellie repeated, as if she understood. Maybe she did. She often got more out of adult conversation than I expected her to.

The church office was heated by a small oil-filled radiator. Miss Georgia Simpson, the church secretary, wore only a light jersey dress. My bones began to thaw.

"Billie! And Chellie! How nice!" Miss Georgia had been old when I was young, wearing the same curly perm. Since Solace was not a plum congregation, we got new pastors with discouraging regularity. Miss Georgia held us together. Many in the congregation called her Saint Georgia.

She reached into her bottom drawer for a Hershey kiss. "Can she have this?" When I nodded, Miss Georgia popped the candy into Chellie's open mouth like she was feeding a large chick. With a twinkle, she reached into the drawer and handed me one, too. "Can't neglect Mama." That chocolate was nectar from the gods.

"I'm so glad you stopped by." She beamed at us both like we were exactly what she had needed to complete her day. "I haven't seen you for a coon's age. I've missed you."

Chellie beamed. "God's mommy?"

Thank goodness Miss Georgia couldn't understand. I rested one hand on Chellie's shoulder to quiet her. "It's hard getting Chellie up those steps these days."

"I know. They really must build a ramp. You aren't the only ones who need it. I turned eighty last month. The steps are getting hard for me." Her eyes twinkled behind her glasses. "I told them that they're either going to have to build a ramp or find a new secretary. But you know that any man in this church would be glad to carry Chellie up, especially her granddaddy. You also know that while faith isn't a habit, Billie, churchgoing is—one it's easy to get out of if you let it happen. You need to start coming back on Sundays, for Chellie's sake as well as your own." Miss Georgia never minded lecturing people whose diapers she had changed.

"I know. We'll be back one day."

The lecture was over. Miss Georgia always preferred mercy to judgment. "What can I do for you? The pastor is away for the day."

I licked my lips. This was harder than I had imagined. Behind me a large round bin in the hall sported a sign: FEED MY SHEEP. Our family had contributed to that bin every week Mama was alive. I suspected Daddy still did. Chellie and I had brought something many weeks. She needed to learn that you don't have to be rich to give away. But asking for food out of that bin was like climbing a dirt mountain hanging on by my fingernails.

"God's house," Chellie prompted.

I took a deep breath. "The fact is, Miss Georgia, I've run into a cash-flow problem. We're almost out of groceries, so I wondered . . ."

"Oh, my dear!" In an instant Miss Georgia was reaching for a key in her drawer. "Come with me." She cast a dubious look at Michelle. "It's downstairs."

I wheeled Michelle to the window. "I won't be but a minute. Watch for birds. Okay?"

"Okay." Chellie leaned toward the window. I hoped birds were out in that cold.

Miss Georgia led the way down dim, steep stairs that had terrified me when I was in preschool. Margaret used to get annoyed because Mama insisted she hold my hand and deliver me to my classroom. "Baby," she would mutter, but I never let go of her hand.

At the back of the fellowship hall, Miss Georgia wrestled with a heavy padlock. "We didn't use to lock the closet until someone broke in. They took everything. Can you imagine?"

When I saw the shelves, I wondered if imperiling an immortal soul had been worth the haul. The pantry only held a few cans of soup, one large can of tuna, two cans of beef stew, three boxes of macaroni and cheese, two bags of grits, three boxes of cereal, one box of spaghetti, a small jar of sauce, and a couple of shelves of canned fruit and vegetables, some of which had probably come from my daddy's garden.

"We're low at the moment," Miss Georgia apologized. "We're having more visitors these days and people aren't bringing in food like they used to. But take enough for three days. Bags are over there. I need to check on something in the kitchen." I gave her high marks for tact.

I took two cans of soup, the smaller can of beef stew, one box of macaroni and cheese, and a bag of grits. I hesitated between tuna and spaghetti, but a larger family could make a casserole from the tuna and two boxes of macaroni and cheese. Besides, Michelle loved spaghetti, and we hadn't had it in a while. I could buy a little hamburger with my money. I was reaching for a box of Cheerios when Miss Georgia returned.

"I can also give you a twenty-dollar voucher to the grocery store for milk, eggs, cheese, and produce," she told me, "and a twenty-dollar voucher for gas."

"Between Daddy and what I put up last summer, we're okay for milk, eggs, fruit, and vegetables, but we sure could use flour, sugar, and meat." We hadn't had meat for weeks. I could almost taste bacon with eggs and grits for breakfast, a little ground beef in the spaghetti, maybe even one very small steak to share.

"Oh dear." Miss Georgia grew flustered. "You can get flour, but otherwise the vouchers only cover milk, eggs, cheese, and produce. We used to give cash, but found some people were likely to spend the money for things like cigarettes, beer—even steak."

I sure hoped she couldn't read thoughts.

"We could use cheese and fresh produce," I conceded. "Could I get a few cleaning supplies, as well? I want to clean up a mobile home on our property so I can rent it out."

"Not with the vouchers, but I can let you have a can of cleanser from under the sink." She hurried back toward the kitchen. "Go on upstairs. I'll meet you there."

I carried the sacks and deposited them beside Chellie. "Iii-eeem?" Chellie asked.

"Not yet, honey." I hoped Miss Georgia, coming in the door, couldn't understand. Ice cream might be on her list of luxuries poor people shouldn't waste money on. People who have enough don't realize how desperately people who eke out an existence need a luxury once in a while to remind them they are still members of the human race.

Miss Georgia handed me a can of cleanser and a bottle half-full of window cleaner. "That's all I can let you have, I'm afraid. That plus these vouchers."

I added the cleaning supplies to a bag and stuffed the vouchers into my purse. "Thank you so much. I'll repay all this when I can." My voice wobbled.

When Miss Georgia took out her purse and handed me a five-dollar bill, I bawled. She handed me a tissue. "It's all the cash I have with me, honey, but I want you and Michelle to have a little treat. Buy sugar and some ice cream for the child."

I still couldn't speak, but I gave her a hug. She had tears in her own eyes.

I slung the bags over the handles of Michelle's chair. "We'll see you later."

"In church?" She twinkled at me. "I hope so. I'll keep nagging them about that ramp, but remember—any of the men will be glad to help Chellie up the steps." She walked us out and waited with Michelle at the church pew while I lugged the chair to the bottom of the steps and again draped my bags over its handles.

She was holding the door for me to carry Michelle out when two young teens sashayed down the sidewalk. Both wore black parkas with jeans. One wore a black knitted hat, the other a blue Braves cap. They swaggered like they were thirty, but they couldn't have been more than fourteen. What were they doing out of school so early?

"Cool! A wheelchair!" said the boy in the black hat. His voice cracked on the last word. They exchanged a look. "Double dare you!" he told his friend.

"That's mine!" I yelled as the boy in the Braves cap sat in the chair. The other gave him a shove. He rolled down the block, grocery bags swinging from side to side. His friend dashed after him, hooting encouragement. Michelle screamed bloody murder.

"Stop! Stop!" I hurried down as fast as I dared with Michelle in my arms, but I couldn't run as fast as a chair going downhill. "Stop!" I yelled again, pounding after them.

Halfway down the block, the flapping sole on my loafer caught on a high place in the sidewalk. I pitched forward. Instinctively I whirled so Michelle landed on top of me, so I came down on one shoulder. I yelped with pain. She uttered shrill screams of terror.

The boy in the chair looked back, which threw him off balance. He swerved into a brick wall. His face hit the bricks. Grocery bags burst. Cans rolled downhill. Boxes careened under parked cars. He clutched his nose while blood poured through his fingers to mingle with spaghetti sauce, grits, and cleanser on the sidewalk.

His friend took off at double speed.

"That's our chair!" I yelled again, but only for show. I couldn't get up. Not pinned down by a child screaming in terror.

The hijacker gave me a scared look, jumped from the chair, and darted after his friend.

Michelle seemed unharmed, just hysterical. I lay on my back holding her, and talked softly until she subsided to a whimper. "It was scary, honey, but we're gonna be okay. Your chair is right down the street."

"Bad boys," Chellie moaned.

"The bad boys are gone."

"My dears, my dears, are you all right?" Miss Georgia panted up alongside us, curls fluttering like silver feathers in the wind. She shivered so hard she could hardly stand.

I sat up awkwardly, still cradling Michelle, and took stock of my injuries. My sleeve and the knee of my pants were torn. Blood oozed from a scrape on my hand. My shoulder would be painful the next day. Still, nothing was broken. Carrying Michelle, I limped down to check the chair for damage. One footrest was bent, but otherwise it seemed all right. I settled Michelle, then fished Cheerios and macaroni from under a blue truck. The cans had rolled farther down the block.

"Here's the window cleaner," Miss Georgia retrieved it from the gutter. She pulled the box of spaghetti from under Chellie's wheel and looked at the smashed jar of sauce with dismay. "The spaghetti seems all right, but we have no more sauce."

"That's okay," I comforted her. "I can get sauce with the money you gave me." I stacked the rescued items in Michelle's lap. "I've got cans to chase between here and the bank, but you get back to the church before you freeze." Her lips were blue with cold. As she gave me a parting hug, I tried not to wince.

AT THE FILLING STATION AND grocery store, I put up cards advertising my trailer to rent. Michelle whined as I put the few groceries we could afford in our cart. "Next stop is the library, honey," I promised as we left. "It's story-hour day."

I parked her chair in the story-hour circle and limped over to the magazine section. My swelling knee was painful and my spirits were lower than a teenager's jeans. But when I opened a *National Geographic*, I was soon lost in an article about penguins. When I finished that magazine, I read *Architectural Digest* and tried to decide which house I'd build when I made my first million. By the time I'd finished choosing an armload of books and a couple of movies, I felt much better. Chellie and I spent another happy half hour reading children's books and choosing some for her to take home. For lifting the spirits and providing good, clean entertainment, few places compare with a public library.

WE PASSED THE POLICE STATION on our way home. On impulse, I pulled in. Chief Veritee Hodson—Tee to anybody who wanted to live another day—had been one of Daddy's poker buddies longer than I'd been alive. I wanted him to find those boys and put the fear of God in them.

The dispatcher must have been on break, because Tee stood at the front counter shuffling papers. He grinned when I limped in pushing Chellie's chair. "Morning. You here to spoil my bluff?" Tee loved to embarrass me in public by telling how I climbed up on his lap when I was four, pointed at his cards, and proudly read, "A-K-Q-J-10!"

"If she'd been older," he always claimed, "I'd have locked her up."

"No, I'm here to report two teenagers who swiped Chellie's chair an hour ago."

"That right?" He looked down at Chellie. "Since she's got the chair and you are limping, am I to deduce you took them down?"

"No, I chased them and they ran away, leaving it behind. I fell running down the hill. One of the boys won't be hard to find. He was riding downhill in the chair and ran into the brick wall of the thrift store hard enough to make his nose bleed. May have broken it, for all I know. He took off too fast for me to find out."

Tee pulled a form from a drawer and picked up a pen. "Black or white boys?"

"White, both of them." I wished he hadn't asked. He would be more likely to consider it a prank if white kids did it. "I figure they're thirteen or fourteen. Both had on black parkas, one wore a black knit cap. The other had on a Braves cap. I didn't get a good look at their faces."

"Freckles. Red hair," Chellie said. "Braves cap had red hair and freckles."

"Really?" I asked. "How could you see that?"

She stuck out her bottom lip. "Red hair and freckles."

"Chellie says the one in the Braves cap had red hair and freckles."

A chair creaked in the back office. Probably the dispatcher, hiding out to eat.

"I'd look for a kid with a black and blue nose if I were you," I told Tee.

I doubted he'd follow up. Looking for kids would require leaving the office and checking all over town. If he found them, he'd have to book them and deal with their parents. That was a lot of work for one afternoon. Tee, a burly man, was getting old. He wasn't fond of exercise.

Too bad. I had another assignment for him. "That's not all I came in for. I want to file a missing-person report. My husband seems to have disappeared."

Tee threw back his head and laughed. "Billie, honey, your husband disappeared years ago. Did you just get around to missing him?" Again a chair creaked in the inner office. I got the impression that somebody was listening real good.

Tee's rotten humor made me mad. Michelle was listening, too, with both ears. "He didn't disappear. He always lets me know exactly where he is, and every month he sends a check—until now. This month's check hasn't come. I'm worried something must have happened to him."

Again I heard the chair in the inner office creak. Tee ought to oil that thing.

He threw an uneasy look over his shoulder, leaned across the counter, and lowered his voice. "He's probably decided not to send any more. It happens."

"Not to Porter it doesn't. He's real reliable. So let me have whatever form I have to fill out to report him missing."

"Honey, you can't report a grown man missing when everybody knows he left town years ago. He's an adult. If you want to report him for not paying child support, go to the county seat and talk to family services."

I lowered my voice, too, for Michelle's sake. "I'm scared he's hurt or . . . worse. He would never stop sending money otherwise."

"Where was he living lately?"

"Marietta."

"If he disappeared in Marietta, it's their jurisdiction."

"Could you call them?"

"Nope. I wish there was something I could do. But as his ex-wife you don't have—"

"I'm not his ex-wife. We never got a divorce."

"Well, if you want to report him missing, go over there and tell them about it." He got busy with the papers he'd been shuffling when we arrived.

I wanted to scream, but Tee would treat me like I was four. I took a deep breath and willed myself to stay calm. "Could you at least call to ask if they've had any unidentified people turn up sick or—you know?"

"I could, but it won't do any good. Atlanta and Marietta have dozens of unidentified"—he looked down at Michelle—"people. Besides, what would they use to identify him? Height, medium. Hair, brown. Eyes— what color were they?"

"Same as Chellie's. Gold. And he was real handsome."

"Any scars or identifying marks—a tattoo, for example?"

"No." I said it regretfully. Right after we were married, Porter wanted to put my name on his biceps, but I hadn't let him. For the first time, I wished I had.

The phone rang. Tee picked it up with obvious relief. I sure wasn't getting any help from the Solace Police Department in finding Porter.

Ten

Friday I called the bank to verify that Margaret's check had cleared. Ever since I'd heard where Porter had been working, I had been itching to get to the site and see if I couldn't find at least one person he'd talked to before he left. I dressed in jeans, boots, and my parka, and decided if the foreman seemed suspicious while I talked to the workers, I'd ask if he was hiring.

I flagged down a truck to jump my battery, but it was obvious the thing was on its last juice. If I didn't want to get stranded in Marietta, I'd better get one before I made the trip. I drove by the bank for some cash, then headed to Foxworthy's Garage to see what kind of deal Stamps Foxworthy could give me.

Stamps was a long, skinny man with an Adam's apple as big as a golf ball. More important, he was that rare phenomenon: an honest mechanic who fixed only what was wrong with your vehicle and charged you a fair price for doing it. As I wheeled Chellie into his office, one of his assistants was by the counter, saying, "I can give you another week, but I have to go to Alabama. My wife's the onliest one can look after her mama." He started to leave, then added, "You can call the man with the Toyota to tell him his car is ready. It wasn't his radiator. It was nothing but a faulty gauge." He gave me a small nod as he headed back to the shop.

Stamps reached for the telephone. "Be right with you, Billie." When he'd finished delivering good news to his customer, he asked, "What can I do for you?"

I opened my mouth to tell him he could find me a used battery. Instead I said, "You could give me a job."

Stamps was as surprised as I was. "Beg your pardon?"

"Give me a job. You're losing a mechanic, right? I can fix cars. Let me work for you."

He looked past me out the window. "You still keeping that old truck running all by yourself?"

"Working except for the battery. It's about to die, so I came in to replace it. But I've got more experience than working on that truck. People sometimes bring me vehicles to fix—people who can't afford to pay much." I didn't want him to think I took away his business. "I've sent some of them on to you."

He nodded. "Yeah, you have." He leaned his arms on the counter and thought it over. "I never hired a woman before. Don't know how the men would take to the idea. But from the way your daddy brags, you can fix any car or truck ever made."

Daddy bragged on me when I wasn't around? I didn't have time right that minute to think about it, but I tucked the knowledge away to savor later. Meanwhile, I had to be absolutely honest if I planned to work for Stamps. "I can't fix real new cars, but I'm a fast learner. Give me a week's trial and some manuals. If I can't hack it, you can find somebody else."

He looked at Chellie. "What will you do with your little girl?"

"I'll find somebody to keep her." At the moment I could leap garages in a single bound. Working on cars was something I genuinely enjoyed. If I could get a job with Stamps . . . I held my breath while he ruminated.

"Come in Monday and we'll see what you can do. Now let's see what I can do about finding you a battery."

I was so excited that while he put in my battery, I used his phone to call Mamie's cell phone. "Could you watch Chellie if I go back to work? Stamps Foxworth says I can work for him."

"I would if I could, honey, but I just can't."

"Are you sure? I can pay."

"I can't, Billie. I'm sorry. I can't lift her."

"Do you know anybody else who could?"

"How about the day-care place that's opened in that cute yellow house?"

The cute yellow house was on our way out of town, so I stopped by. Chellie was entranced by the view of children doing art in a room next to the office, but the manager shook her head as soon as I pushed the wheelchair up to her desk. "We aren't able to care for a child with serious handicaps. I'm sorry."

Chellie's face fell. She had been so excited about the idea of going to "school" with other children. Why couldn't people be more considerate? Did they think she couldn't hear?

"Could you suggest any place that does?" I asked.

"Not around here."

ON OUR WAY TO MARIETTA, Chellie and I sang along with a children's CD, and she giggled at funny verses I made up. I sometimes thought, though, that she was sunniest when she thought I needed cheering up.

I'd had no idea Porter was working on such large projects. This one had three buildings facing one another around a parking lot. I pulled my truck to the curb near the foreman's trailer and left Chellie listening to music. The wind was too cold for her to be out.

The exteriors of the buildings looked complete, and the grounds were already landscaped with sod, bushes, and small trees. The walk to the front entrance was barred by yellow tape while it cured, so I headed around one side. I walked directly across the grass, which was spongy underfoot. Builders didn't worry about the drought. Professional landscapers were permitted to water all they wanted.

Two men were unloading a truck at an entrance near the back. Their skin was tan, their hair black. I spoke slowly and clearly. "I am Billie Waits, Porter's wife. Do you all know Porter?"

The one wearing a blue jacket ducked behind the truck. Did I look like an immigration official? The other, in a yellow jacket, grinned, showing stained teeth beneath a black mustache. "Porter? *Sí.*" He added something in Spanish.

I made a circle to include the whole site. "Is Porter here?"

He shook his head. "No" was the only word I understood, but the way he waved two, then three fingers, I figured he was saying Porter had been gone two or three weeks.

"Where did he go?"

He lifted his shoulders in an elaborate shrug. "Luis?" He asked a question in Spanish. The other man muttered something I couldn't hear, even if I could have understood. But while yellow jacket was again pouring a torrent of Spanish over me, Luis sidled around the back of the truck. The whole time his friend spoke, he stood poised like he would speak if he had the words.

I asked him directly, "Have you seen Porter?" He ducked behind the truck again.

"We no can help." Yellow jacket turned his back to show the interview was over.

I headed to the foreman's trailer. Surely he spoke enough Spanish to translate if Luis would talk.

Margaret was right. The foreman looked exactly like Caesar the hog. Bristly hair. Flat nose with big nostrils. Fat, round cheeks. But maybe he was kinder than Caesar had been.

"Sir," I said, "I hate to bother you, but I'm Porter Waits's wife, and I'm trying to find him. I haven't heard from him for two weeks, and I'm worried. I believe one of your men might have some information, but I don't speak Spanish. Could you—?"

He set down his pen. "You're the second woman looking for him this week. Like I told her, I don't babysit these men."

"Yes, sir. I mean, no, sir. But it's not like Porter not to let me know when he leaves a job. If one of the men knows where he went, could you—?" I motioned to the door.

With a sigh that let me know I was interrupting work at least as important as that done in the Oval Office of the White House, he shoved back his chair and followed me. "Which man did you want to talk to?"

"I think his name is Luis. Over by that truck."

His gaze followed my pointing finger, but yellow jacket was now working with a man in a green sweatshirt. "Neither of those is Luis. One is Juan. The other is Diego."

"Luis was there a minute ago."

He strode across the site and spoke to the men. Yellow shirt pointed to the nearest door. The foreman strolled back to me, lord of his construction site and in no hurry—exactly like Caesar. "Luis is working inside. But Juan says nobody knows anything about Porter except that he's gone."

"I thought Luis wanted to tell me something."

"He probably wanted to tell you to get off the site. We don't allow trespassers. You'll have to look for Porter someplace else."

"Do you have the address of where he was living in Marietta?"

He narrowed his eyes, suddenly suspicious. "You don't know where he stays?"

"No. Our daughter and I live out in Solace, but he was staying somewhere in town."

"We don't give out information about our people. Look for your husband—if he is your husband—someplace else."

We didn't stop by Margaret's. We weren't dressed for visiting.

———

"WHERE'S DADDY GONE?" MICHELLE ASKED on our way home. Her eyes were anxious.

"I don't know, honey. He must have taken another job and not let me know. But he'll write soon, I'm sure. How about if we stop at Wal-Mart on our way home and get you some pink panties?" She was already feminine enough to enjoy pretty underwear.

While Chellie napped later that afternoon, I called every child-care place in the phone book. Not one of them would take her. I called Stamps to regretfully say I couldn't work after all. After I hung up, I went out into the orchard and took out my frustrations by pounding the trunk of a peach tree. When a train whistled in the distance, I wished I were on board.

OVER IN MARIETTA, MARGARET'S THURSDAY wasn't much better than mine. She had told nobody Ben had left. She didn't even tell Katrinka when they went out for lunch after tennis practice. She still believed Ben would eventually come home, so she didn't want to embarrass him by discussing his temporary absence.

It was her turn to pay for lunch, but the waitress brought back her credit card. "I'm sorry, ma'am. This card was declined."

"Declined?" Puzzled, Margaret paid with the debit card for their checking account. They had three credit cards: one for the business, one for big items, and the one she'd tried to use. It had a smaller credit limit because they used it for small items—clothing, entertainment, and im-pulse purchases. Still, they should have had five thousand dollars' avail-able credit on the card.

She went home and called the company. "I'm afraid somebody must have stolen my credit card number."

"You can see your charges online."

"My computer is, uh, away for repairs. Could you read me the last few charges?"

The first item explained the problem: Ben had maxed out the card buying merchandise at Ikea.

Furious, she tried him every half hour. He neither answered nor returned her calls. She finally reached him at midnight. Even in her current pain and anger, her treacherous heart surged with happiness when she heard his voice.

"I need to talk to you. I tried calling earlier," she said.

"I want to talk to you, too, but not now. Come to supper tomorrow. Just you—not the boys. I'll grill steaks. Seven suit you?" He named an apartment complex that gave her a jolt. He was living only half a mile away.

Eleven

F riday evening Margaret dressed in a peach cotton sundress with embroidered flowers around the bodice. Ben had bought it for her on their Caribbean cruise. "You look like an island princess," he had whispered as they danced. It had been a magical night. Maybe this would be, too. She dabbed on his favorite perfume and slipped on peach flats.

His apartment could have been an Ikea ad: birch couch with black cushions, birch chair with red cushions and matching ottoman, tasteful birch shelves holding two books and a few decorative items purchased to match the decor, birch dining table with four black chairs, and a bright accent rug. A large Mexican painting hung over the sofa, creamy houses with red tile roofs under a brilliant sky. A similar painting dwarfed a birch sideboard. A tall yellow vase held huge red silk poppies near the sliding doors. The table held black goblets, red napkins, and black-and-white plates. The effect was colorful, spare, and modern. Margaret thought of their own furniture in sedate beiges, browns, and greens.

He chose our furniture. It's not what I would have picked.

If she was honest, their furniture was not what either of them would have picked. It was what they settled for together. Who said that compromise is the art of nobody getting what they want?

"What do you think?" Ben hovered at her elbow.

She swallowed a lump in her throat. "It's—nice. No, it's beautiful. But—"

"Thanks." He beamed. "I really like the way it turned out."

She forced a teasing tone. "You know, don't you, that you maxed out our credit card setting it up?"

He winced. "I was afraid of that. It was a little more expensive than I expected. You know how it is. You add something here, another thing there . . ."

She kept her tone light. "And your wife gets real embarrassed when her card is declined at a restaurant. Yeah, I know how it is. You should have told me."

"I meant to." He glanced out toward the grill. "I need to check the steaks. Wander around. Make yourself at home." She recoiled as if he had slapped her, but he didn't notice.

Soft jazz came from the bedroom, music they used to listen to in college. They hadn't listened to jazz since Jason was born. Was Ben trying to go back to a time before the boys? Did he think he could erase his entire married life?

You want Ben to come home, Margaret reminded herself. *Don't sabotage this evening by being snide. Be pleasant—the kind of woman he'll want to come home to.*

In the bedroom, she found the Ben she once knew. A black entertainment unit held Jason's TV, a new DVD player, a new stereo system, and some of their family's favorite DVDs. A king-sized mattress filled most of the room. A black comforter had been pulled roughly over crumpled black sheets. *Black sheets?* Two suitcases and several cardboard boxes trailed boxers and undershirts. Dirty clothes were piled knee-high on the closet floor. The room could have been lifted from his fraternity house.

Ben circled her waist with his hands. "I think we're ready. Would you light the candles?"

Soft jazz, candlelight, steaks—he had thought of everything. Normally she only drank one glass of wine, but warmed by Ben's delight in playing host, she let him refill her glass without protest. As the level of the bottle dropped, she remembered how in college everything Ben did had seemed sophisticated and certain. She—younger, less experienced—had been glad to let him take the lead. He taught her to lie in the grass to watch meteor showers. Fly kites. Carry exotic picnics to secluded woodland streams. *Ben always had a gift for play. That was one thing I loved about him. We should never have gotten so serious we forgot to play.*

When the meal was finished, he stood and reached for her hand. "May I have this dance?" They melted into each other as they always had. When the music ended, he still held her close. "You really are gorgeous, Margaret. Do you know that?" She lifted her face. He kissed her.

It was the wine, she would tell herself later. *Wine and candlelight. I forgot why I came.*

Or maybe she didn't. She didn't protest when he danced her into the bedroom, pulled her down to the mattress, and made love to her like he used to. Spent and happy, she curled against him, her head in the crook of his shoulder. "I love you, Ben Baxter."

He stroked her hair with his big palm.

Because she was by nature a nester, in that quiet moment she found herself placing his new furniture in their home. His table and chairs would look great in the breakfast room. The black couch and bright rugs would be perfect in the basement playroom and would give Jason space to entertain his friends. The red armchair looked comfortable to read in beside their bedroom window, if they got a new comforter and curtains. Something happier. No more plaids, tans, and dark greens. She might even paint the room. From now on, their lives would be washed in color. She was mentally rearranging kitchen cabinets to accommodate the extra dishes when he asked, "Are you ready to talk?"

She snuggled closer. "Sure."

He took his arm from around her so abruptly that her head bumped on the mattress. "I think we ought to get dressed first." Clothes in hand, he headed to the bathroom. Startled, she picked up her clothes and followed him. The door was locked. "Just a minute," he called.

Standing naked in a strange bedroom clutching clothes to strategic places was an experience she did not like. "Come on, Ben, let me in."

He opened the door. "Your turn." Who was this man in business khakis and polo shirt who could go from passionate to brusque in five minutes? The only familiar thing about him was the shape of his bare feet. As she dressed, she felt out of balance between the two Bens. The passionate lover had morphed into—what? Not a stranger, but a casual acquaintance.

When she came out, he was in the kitchen pouring coffee into black mugs. "I've talked to our lawyer. He says it will be better if we can work out things between us."

"The sooner the better. Then you can come home." She sat on a dining room chair.

"What?" He stopped in the process of handing her a mug. "I don't mean work things out in the marriage. I filed for divorce yesterday. I'm talking about working out a property settlement we can agree on." He took another chair as if they were at a business meeting.

"You've filed for divorce? I don't understand. What happened"— she jerked one thumb toward the bedroom—"in there?"

He covered her free hand with his and gave it a squeeze. "We made marvelous love, like always. What do they call those things we've got? Phemerones?"

"Pheromones."

He grinned. "I'd never have passed biology without you. Ours still drive each other crazy, don't they? You'll turn me on when I'm ninety. But right now we need to talk about practical matters." He picked up his mug.

"You—you aren't coming home?" She hated that her voice sounded so small.

Ben set down his mug with a *thunk* of finality. "I am home. I've filed for divorce."

"I didn't agree to it. I don't want a divorce."

"That doesn't matter. One partner can file whether the other wants it or not."

"Are you serious? Two people have to agree to get married but either one of them can end it?"

"That's the way it works. They call it no-fault divorce."

"But there *is* a fault—your fault! You left me! You left all of us."

He gave the sigh of a man who was about to explain a simple truth one more time. "The marriage is over. I don't love you anymore."

Again she gestured toward the bedroom. "Then why—?"

He gave her an aw-shucks grin. "For old times' sake?"

"Old times' sake?" Margaret felt so frozen that if she thrust a finger into his eye, it would stab like an icicle. If she hit him with her fists, they would shatter. She stood and swiftly crossed to pick up her purse.

"Where are you going? We need to talk."

"If there's a word for you, Ben Baxter, it's not in my vocabulary. Something along the lines of 'low-down skunk' is close, but nowhere near strong enough."

"Hey, you wanted it as much as I did."

"No, you wanted *it*. I wanted *you*." She was so heavy with grief that her knees could not bear her weight. She sank into the bright red chair. It was as comfortable as it looked.

Ben carried his coffee to the sofa. "Our marriage is over. O-v-e-r. But we need to straighten out a few things. You can keep most of the furniture. All I want is my recliner and Jason's bedroom furniture— except for the mattresses. I don't need those. Sell them in a garage sale or give them away, but I need the frames and springs for my bed. Jason can take the extra bed from Andy's room and you can get him a chest to match."

If he had hit her with a sandbag, it couldn't have stunned her more. *You'd take your child's furniture?* She was no longer cold. Anger poured out in a scalding screech. "May I remind you we bought that furniture to give him when he sets up his own home? He knows it's his. You've already taken his TV and computer—now you want his furniture? No! Take ours. I can put the mattress on the floor."

She meant it for sarcasm. He took her seriously. "No need to do that. You can take Andy's extra bed and keep your chest."

"The fact that they don't match shouldn't matter in the least. Right? No, Ben, you are not going to decimate our house. Move out if you want. Divorce me if you must. But find your own furniture. If the boys no longer have a father, they at least deserve an intact home."

"The boys have a father. I'll see them. But like I said before, we've got a little problem." He went for more coffee, spoke with his back to her. "We've got to sell the house."

Surely she hadn't heard correctly. *"What?"*

"We have to sell the house. We can't afford it. You won't be able to keep it up on what you'll probably make, and I can't afford two places. Besides, I need the money."

"For what?" She paid the bills. They were up-to-date.

"To pay off the loan we took out to buy the new truck. It's killing me."

"You mean the loan *you* took out to buy the truck? I didn't want it."

"You cosigned."

"Because you assured me Rick's business would more than pay for it."

"It would have if the rest of the business hadn't slowed because of the drought. I've been paying the interest on the loan each month, but I'm using most of what I bring in from Rick to keep the business going. If things get much worse, I'll have to let people go."

She looked around at the room full of new furniture. "How many wages could you have paid with what you spent furnishing this place?"

She surprised them both. That question was never asked in Ben's circle—the circle they had both traveled in since their marriage. Their circle presumed that the owner of a company deserved the lion's share of the income. What the owner didn't want was doled out to other employees. *That's why they call it the trickle-down theory of economics,* she suddenly understood. In hard times, Ben's sort of people retained their lifestyles by reducing the trickle—lowering other people's wages or letting them go.

He ignored the question. "I've checked with a Realtor. Our house has lost value, but it's in a great location. The creek is a bonus in the drought. She said the place ought to sell pretty quickly. Still, with the drop in home values, we won't get a lot more than enough to pay off the mortgage and repay the loan. We won't either one get much cash."

Words couldn't get past the rage in her throat. They had moved into that house when Jason was a preschooler. Brought Andy to the house from the hospital nursery. Decorated Christmas trees there. Hunted Easter eggs. Enjoyed picnics on the deck, hot chocolate by the fire, family movies with popcorn. Held parties for countless friends. So many memories. So much love.

Ben went on shredding memories like a cat on lace curtains. "We can hope it sells for more than the Realtor thinks it will. She hasn't been inside, after all. We've done a lot to it."

"I've done a lot to it."

"Yeah, you did most of it. What you've done ought to help it sell faster. In terms of other financial arrangements, what our lawyer suggests is this: we'll split the equity in the house and other financial assets fifty-fifty. I'll pay child support until they are eighteen, and I'll give you a housing allowance until the place sells. I'll even give you alimony for up to six months, unless you find a job sooner. Does that sound fair?"

She was finally roused to battle. "No, it does not sound fair. For a start, there is no such person as *our* lawyer. You have a lawyer. I will get a lawyer Monday. Somebody who is able to put a fair value on what I've done to improve the house and help you build the business in the past sixteen years. I want my *fair* share"—she emphasized the word—"of our assets."

"Build the business?" he demanded, his face pink. "You never do anything about the business."

"We'll skip all those years I worked in the office and kept the books.

What about the medical center you landscaped for Dr. Graham two years ago after I talked to his wife, Myrtle, at garden club and invited them over for dinner? Or the three office parks you did for Sid Davis last year after his wife and I worked together on the PTA fund-raiser? Or Todd Walker's new shopping center—his wife, Sandy, and I taught Sunday school together, remember? What about Rick Landiss? Who was it who met him first through Louise on my tennis team, and suggested that Landiss Construction ought to let you bid on the first project you did for him? Don't you tell me I haven't done anything for the business!"

"I—I never thought . . ." He rubbed his chin in bemusement.

"It's time you did. For starters, think about this: until the house sells, you will continue to deposit exactly the same amount into the household account you always have. Our expenses will not go down because you aren't there, and the boys and I will not go without heat, lights, groceries, or personal items because you abandoned us."

He blinked. "I didn't abandon you! It's not like that!"

"It is exactly like that. Furthermore, don't you max out our other credit card or cancel a single bank account, and don't you sell any stock until our lawyers have talked. I have a complete list of what we own, so I'll know if you do." She stood. "There will be no more little dinners between us and no more sex. I have never felt so dirty, so—so *used* in my entire life."

She left with the final word, but she didn't taste the triumph. She still tasted Ben.

She wept all the way home, her vision so blurred she could hardly stay in her lane. Her tears of fury turned to sobs of grief. She loved Ben. Loved making love to him, but also loved sitting with him over a cup of coffee, laughing at his jokes, wrestling through a business problem together. She had loved making love to him that evening. She could not bear the thought of never holding him again. For sixteen years they'd had a good marriage. How could he throw it away?

She grieved not only for what he had done to her but also for what he was becoming—the kind of man who could use her that way. The kind of man who thought more of himself than of his sons. She ached for him to be his best self again. She ached to be with him, no matter what he became. A future without him looked like a long, dark tunnel with no lights ahead. "Oh, Ben," she wept, "I don't know if I can physically *live* without you."

She was crying so hard she nearly missed her driveway, swerved sharply, and drove straight over a bed of blue rug junipers. Frightened at how out of control she was, she braked just inside the driveway and laid her head on the wheel. "The boys mustn't see me like this," she sobbed. "I've got to stop crying." She could not stop. Tears soaked her hands as they clasped the wheel. "How could you?" she screamed. A moment later, she whispered, "I love you, Ben! I can't live without you! I can't! I can't!"

She saw a light go on in Jason's room, then go out. Checking her watch, she saw it was nearly eleven. How long had she sat there sobbing? Had Jason heard her car and wondered why she didn't come in?

Concern for her children slowed her tears to a trickle. She scrubbed her eyes with a tissue, took deep, heaving breaths, and tried to think what she would tell the boys if they were still awake to account for how she looked.

The boys' doors were closed, and neither came from his room. She tiptoed to her own room and stripped off her dress, wadded it into a ball, and hurled it to the far corner of her closet. She would never wear it again.

She stepped into the hottest shower she could bear and soaped vigorously, wanting to wash Ben from her skin. Then she cried again. She wished she had preserved one small circle of skin as a memorial to what they once had.

She didn't bother to get into bed. She couldn't sleep. In robe and pajamas she wandered around downstairs, mourning Ben and the loss of their home. "Endless death," she whispered, stroking the mantel a woodworker had made especially for the den. "If he'd died, it would be dreadful, but I could have gone on carrying him in my heart. With divorce, he's as good as dead, but he's still alive—I just can't have him. I cannot bear it!" Silent tears streamed down her cheeks as she moved from room to room, gently touching special things. Drapery she had sewn after the boys were in bed. Shelves they'd had built by the fireplace to house Ben's golf trophies. Granite countertops in the kitchen, which they had chosen at the quarry on a special day in the mountains of Georgia.

"They are only things," she reminded herself. But they were precious to her because they commemorated her life with Ben. How could another woman appreciate them as she did?

Ben was precious to her, too. Would another woman appreciate him as she had?

She fell onto the den couch, weeping.

Will you ever get a house like this again?

The question startled her. She had boasted to Ben that she had backed up all their financial data, but that was several weeks ago. Now he had the computer.

She stood, purpose stanching her tears. She had to get that information.

After checking to be sure Jason and Andy were asleep, she dressed and drove to Baxter's. She let herself in, disarmed the alarm, and went to Ben's office. She did not turn on a light until the door was firmly shut. She propped a chair under the knob. She didn't want to be surprised. In the next two hours, she backed up all their bank accounts and their stock portfolio, working through a blur of tears. She made printouts as well as copies on her flash drive. As she backed up the business accounts, she was frightened to see how poorly the business had been doing in the past year. Why hadn't Ben told her? She studied the figures in growing despair.

Twelve

Saturday morning I drove to the library to look up food-stamp and welfare-eligibility requirements on their computer. Margaret's check wasn't going to last forever. Who knew how soon I could rent the trailer? I found myself peering over my shoulder as I typed in the Web site, making sure nobody I knew was nearby. I had never imagined I'd get so far down.

To get welfare in Georgia, I would need to attend a thirty-hour-a-week training program. Heck, if I could get child care for Chellie thirty hours a week, I could work at the garage. I could only get food stamps if I could produce proof of income such as check stubs and "last month's rent receipt or mortgage payment book." Porter had never sent checks with stubs, and I didn't have a mortgage. That was what had made life manageable so far.

It was possible I could persuade them to help me if I drove to the county seat and sat there all day waiting to speak to a live caseworker, but that would be hard on Chellie and could be a waste of precious gas. I had better rent my trailer fast.

I carried Chellie down to the trailer, opened the windows to warm up the air inside, tuned her radio to peppy music, and set to work. Chellie polished the coffee table from her chair while I got rid of dust and cobwebs. Her jerky motions weren't predictable, but she worked that tabletop until it shone. I wiped down the refrigerator and sprayed the oven with cleaner. As I tackled the bathroom, I found Porter's hair in the shower drain. It was as dry and dead as our marriage.

"That's all I can do in here for now," I finally decided. "Let's go eat lunch. I want to tackle the yard this afternoon. I'll finish the oven tomorrow and bring down the vacuum. I'll wash the windows, too. I probably ought to clean the carpet, but I don't have anything to clean it with. I can promise to do that after the tenants have been here a month."

"What are tenants?" Chellie asked.

"People who will pay us to stay here. They'll help pay our bills."

She bounced in her chair. "Lots of ice cream!"

After lunch, because the day was sunny, I let Chellie skip her nap and sit outside while I started pruning and weeding the trailer yard. I piled large brush at the edge of the orchard and carried a plastic five-gallon bucket around for small weeds. As it filled, I dumped it next to the brush pile. Another day I'd mulch the brush and move the weeds to the compost pile behind my henhouse.

I was wiping sweat from my face when a police car pulled into the drive of our house. A man in uniform climbed out and headed for my front door. I didn't recognize him. He was too tall and thin for Tee. Had he come to tell me something about Porter? My heart thumped so hard I could hear blood rush behind my ears.

"I'll be right back," I told Chellie. I started running. Without thinking, I carried my half-full weed bucket with me. It bumped against my legs as I ran. "Over here!" I called.

He was knocking on the door, too far away to hear me.

"Yoo-hoo. Over here!" I arrived at the foot of the porch steps completely winded. "I'm here." I dropped the bucket on the walk behind me with a clatter.

He turned. "I've come about the complaint you lodged Wednes—" He broke off and pulled off his sunglasses. "Wilhelmina? Mina Anderson?" His face broke into a grin that took me back fourteen years.

I took a step backward, tripped over the bucket, and sat in it.

Getting out of a five-gallon bucket by yourself is well nigh impossible when the bucket and your backside are approximately the same size. In two long strides he was beside me, offering me a hand. "You *are* Mina Anderson! I'm Luke Braswell and I seem to have bowled you over again. Here—take my hand."

He tugged, I wiggled, and at last I stood beside him. In the process I turned over the bucket, littering my walk with weeds.

I wasn't thinking about weeds. I was thinking about hair that was frizzing around my face, where it had come loose from my ponytail, about holes in my grass-stained knees, about mud streaks that didn't improve my T-shirt, and the stink emanating from my septic tank. I hoped he didn't think that awful smell was me.

Luke looked as good as he had in high school. Better. His hair had darkened to a rich mahogany. His uniform molded shoulders that had filled out to fit his height. His blue eyes still twinkled as they looked down at me. "I see you've still got those terrific dimples. How the heck are you?" He was still holding my hand.

I began to chatter like a squirrel. "You're a policeman, now? In Solace? Last I heard you were in the army or something." I took my hand away from him before I got too used to the feel.

"I was. But Mama's husband died in February and she needed help with the kids, so I've come home." I remembered his mother used to come to his basketball games with an infant in a carrier and a small girl in tow.

He glanced back at the cruiser. "In fact, that's why I'm here."

"About my husband?" I was so scared, I nearly sat back in the bucket.

Before he could answer, a wail sounded beyond the orchard.

"Could we talk over there? I was clearing brush and left my little girl alone."

"Sure."

I scarcely heard him. Chellie was calling so loud, I was picturing everything from a bee to a bear. "I'll meet you over there." I started to trot.

"I was scared," Chellie told me when I wrapped her in my arms. "I thought the policeman was going to take you."

I heard Luke coming along the path. "He came to help us, honey. He's a friend."

She looked over my shoulder. "Bad boy! Bad boy! Bad boy!"

Luke wasn't alone. With him was a boy with red hair and a face full of freckles. They clashed with his green-and-purple nose. He wasn't looking at Michelle or me. He was studying his shoes.

"Bad boy!" Michelle called louder. "Bad, bad boy!"

The others probably couldn't understand her, but her tone was unmistakable. The boy's expression went from sullen to scared. He looked younger than I'd thought and heavier than he ought to be, but he should slim down when he got his growth. He winced as Luke clamped a hand on his shoulder. "Is this one of the boys who stole your chair?"

I didn't need to nod. Michelle was still repeating, "Bad boy!" while glaring at him.

Luke shook him none too gently. "Franklin?"

The boy studied his shoes.

"This is my brother," Luke told me. "He has something to say to you."

"Sorry." It was little more than a mutter.

Luke shook him again. "Loud enough for them to hear you."

"I'm sorry, okay? I didn't mean to hurt anybody."

He looked so young and Luke so stern, I took pity on him. "You didn't hurt us. It wasn't your fault I fell. I tripped. But you shouldn't have taken the chair. Michelle really needs it. Would you go over and tell *her* you're sorry?"

He glanced at Michelle with the anxious expression children often get when confronted with somebody who looks like God made a mistake. "What's the matter with her? Can I catch it?"

"No, you can't catch it. She has cerebral palsy. It makes her muscles tighten up and twitch, but she can understand you fine. She's as smart as you. She's almost as smart as me."

"Go on." Luke gave him a little shove.

Franklin slouched over to the chair.

Michelle frowned. "Bad boy."

"I'm sorry I took your chair," he mumbled. "I just wanted to ride in it a little."

Michelle thought that over. "Okay." She tried to touch his face. "Are you hurt bad?"

He didn't understand her, so I translated. He shrugged. "Not too bad. I'm glad you didn't get hurt."

"Me, too. Mama catched me." She smiled. He may not have understood her words, but when Michelle smiled, it was like sunshine coming out. A timid smile twitched Franklin's lips. When Michelle continued to beam at him, he slowly grinned.

"Did he break his nose?" I asked Luke softly.

"No, but he should have." Luke still looked stern. "I was in the back office when you came into the station. I thought one of the boys sounded like Franklin, especially when I went home and found he'd hurt his nose. He swore he did it running into some steps while playing with kids after school, though. It took me until today to get him to confess he's been skipping school on days when nobody's home to put him on the bus. Mama's a nurse, and works a seven-to-seven shift three days a week. Maybe this will be the lesson he needs. Do you want me to take him to the juvenile-detention center?" I could tell that wasn't what Luke wanted. In his place, I wouldn't have wanted it, either.

"Heavens no. How about if you let him stay today and work for me? As you can see, I've got a lot of weeding, pruning, and clearing to do here. He looks strong."

"You're sure?" When I nodded, he called, "Franklin, Mrs. Waits has offered not to file a complaint if you'll work for her the rest of the day."

Franklin shrugged. "I guess." Anybody could tell he was relieved.

I didn't let him off easy. I gave him stout work gloves and made him cut the heaviest branches, prune the blackberries, and pull the prickliest weeds. He was a good worker, and he didn't complain except when he disturbed a wasps' nest and got stung. By the time Luke came back at six, the yard and trailer were clean, and Franklin and I were filthy. He had that acrid smell peculiar to dirty boys. Seeing Luke in his crisp uniform, I hoped I didn't have a smell peculiar to dirty women. I had considered leaving Franklin to watch Michelle while I showered and changed, but Luke had already seen me at my worst. Besides, I was still a married woman.

I didn't know if he was a married man. Not all husbands wore wedding rings.

"I could not have finished in one day without him," I said honestly. Franklin flushed.

After they had gone, I stood near the steps of the trailer and pointed. "Look, Chellie! The first star. Let's wish somebody will call tomorrow to rent it. Star light, star bright, first star I've seen tonight . . ."

When we got to the end of the rhyme, Michelle said, "I wish somebody would come Sunday to rent the trailer."

For her it was a familiar ritual. For me that night, it was a prayer.

DADDY AND JIMBO CAME OVER later that evening, and Jimbo sat with Chellie while we swapped the furniture. After we'd placed the trailer furniture in my house, Daddy said, "I don't know why you didn't do this five years ago, shug. You didn't need to live with that junk."

His tone irked me. Why couldn't he just say, "That looks great," without criticizing me?

"Don't you think I'm smart to rent out the trailer?"

Why was I hoping for praise? Praise hadn't been bred into Daddy's bones. "You be careful who you let live over there. You don't want just anybody."

While I made up Michelle's bed, he lifted her onto his lap and read her a story. "New bed," Michelle told him happily as he laid her down gently.

"It's a beautiful bed, chickadee." Daddy lightly brushed the hair off her forehead. "Sleep tight, now." He bent and kissed her. As I watched his truck drive away, I remembered how he used to read to me, stroke the hair from my forehead, and kiss me good night. I wished that he could be as sweet to me again as he was when I was five.

AFTER MICHELLE WAS ASLEEP, I found myself restless and lonely. I prowled the house, wishing for somebody to sip drinks with and make grown-up talk. When I saw the full moon out the window, I wished I had somebody to put his arms around me and stand by the window looking at the moon. I wished—

With a start, I realized I wasn't thinking about standing in the window with Porter, although we used to do that. It was Luke Braswell I pictured behind me, breathing sweetly on my neck. It was Luke I pictured sitting across from me making grown-up talk. Luke—

"Enough about Luke Braswell," I told myself firmly. "You are a married woman."

To reinforce that fact, I searched my jewelry box for my wedding ring, which I hadn't worn for three years. "Until death do us part," I said as I shoved it on my finger. Back when I made my promises to love and cherish Porter as long as we both should live, I firmly intended to keep them. Maybe I'd better wear his ring to remind me of that.

But as I pulled the covers up to my chin, I again saw Luke, bending to haul me from the bucket with that twinkle in his eye. He sure did look good.

Thirteen

On a bright morning in early May, Mamie sat at her breakfast table contemplating four pillboxes sectioned for each day of the week. She had a yellow box for breakfast pills, a green box for lunch, a blue box for supper, and a white box for bedtime. Those pillboxes felt like inchworms measuring away her life.

She tried to forget them as she drove to Bill Anderson's. It was a beautiful day if you could ignore how brown the grass was in the pastures and how spindly the crops were in the fields. Mamie had been looking at drought too long to pay it much mind. Instead she rejoiced as a flock of birds rose like confetti into a sky as soft as blue organdy. She wondered if the big white cloud ahead of her was anything like the one God used to show the Israelites when to move across the wilderness. She wished God would send something as clear as a cloud to show the way across her particular wilderness.

"Should I quit working for Bill?" she asked her little car. She had grown accustomed to talking things over with it. "His house is in order, his freezer is full of enough meals to last him a while, and I'm finding it hard to walk to the house from behind the barn. By the time I get up the steps to his back porch, I'm as out of breath as if I'd run a mile. Not that I ever ran a mile, understand, but I sure am out of breath."

She got out of breath just from talking. The doctor said it was because fluid around her heart was filling her lungs, taking up space she needed for air. "The problem is, when I pray about leaving Bill's, I don't get any peace. Seems like I'm supposed to do something else there, but I don't know what. I guess I'll keep on keeping on until things get clear."

Things didn't get clearer that morning; they got muddier.

She was mopping Bill's kitchen floor when she heard something go *thump* on the back porch. She opened the door to find Lurleen standing there, a large package at her feet.

"Mama? What you doing here?"

"I—uh—I—" Mamie had never lied to her daughter. She didn't know how to start. "I've been giving Bill a few hours now and then to help him get his house in order."

Lurleen narrowed her eyes to slits. "Since when?"

"Since around the first of April."

"How many hours you been giving him?"

"Five or six, maybe, a couple of days a week."

"Mama! You know what the doctor said. You're not supposed to exert yourself. Look at the size of your ankles. They're big as logs!" She glanced past Mamie to the mop leaning against the stove. "You been *mopping*?"

When Mamie didn't answer, Lurleen pushed her aside. She looked around the kitchen, then sauntered over to peer through the dining room doorway. "This place looks like it gets a regular cleaning. Last time I saw in here, it looked like a sty. You do all that?"

Feeling like a five-year-old caught with her hand in the collection plate, Mamie hung her head.

Lurleen brought in the box. She dropped it onto Bill's kitchen table with a thud like Judgment Day. "How you been getting here? Your car's not out there."

"I park behind the barn. I—I didn't want you to see it."

Lurleen clenched her jaw. "So you walk all that way in this heat.

You do beat all. The doctor made it plain as he knows how that you are a very sick woman."

"I been taking some new medicine to drain my fluids. I think it's doing me some good." She didn't mention that it also made her dizzy.

"Even so, you need to conserve your strength or you could drop dead." Lurleen raised her voice. "Do you hear me? Dead. D-e-a-d. Is that what you want?"

Mamie leaned against the wall by the door, dizzy and ill. "Of course it's not what I want. But I can't sit down and just wait to die, Lurleen. I can't. You can't expect it of me. Besides, God sent me here. Bill needs me. Not just to clean. We talk. We talk a lot."

"Talk about what?"

"Grace. Earl. Good and bad times we've had. Losing somebody makes a bond between people. You don't know, honey." She hadn't married Earl until Lurleen was grown. The two of them had been civil to one another for her sake, but they'd never had what Mamie would call a real fondness for each other.

Lurleen reached the back door in two strides. "If you keep working like this, I'll know about losing somebody all right. But if you want to die, go on and die. I can't keep on worrying and worrying when you don't do your part." She gave her eyes a fierce swipe. "Leave my number by the phone. Tell Bill to call if you need me. But don't bother calling me yourself. I can't stand talking to you. I'd be wondering what other lies you're telling." She slammed the door behind her like she was announcing the end of the world.

Mamie pressed both hands to her cheeks. "I've done it now. I've made her mad. She won't speak to me until—maybe never. Oh, God, what am I gonna do?"

I'D BEEN PRAYING THAT SAME prayer for over two weeks—I just didn't know I was praying. Night after night I had asked the darkness, "What am I gonna do?" Nobody had called about the trailer. I had stretched Margaret's money so far, the pennies squealed and I still had unpaid bills. I gathered up my pride and threw it away twice to visit two more church food pantries. That didn't get any easier. I felt like I was dangling over a cliff held by a spiderweb.

"Don't turn up your nose at that food," I told Lucky one evening when I scraped leftovers into his bowl. "You're eating as good as we are." He growled. I felt like growling back.

It took all the energy I possessed to get creative with eggs, milk, and the canned fruits and vegetables we had left from last summer's crop. When Chellie complained about having too many canned tomatoes, I used her Elmo puppet to say, "Look on the bright side, honey. You sure won't get scurvy."

Mamie showed up one Monday evening with chocolate pudding. I left her eating with Chellie, went into my room, closed the door, and bawled, holding a pillow against my face to stifle my sobs. I washed my face to get the red out of my eyes, but when I got back, Chellie was saying, "Mommy's crying 'cause we got no food."

Mamie looked in my pantry and refrigerator and glared at me as she stomped out. An hour later she came back with three loaves of bread, a pound of butter, a gallon of vegetable soup she had probably planned to eat on all week, and a half gallon of orange juice. "Don't you go hungry again without telling me," she fussed. Chellie and I had soup and toast for our bed-night snack. The soup, made by Mamie's own hands, went down as smooth as love.

The next morning, Daddy showed up with a box of frozen steaks, hamburger, bacon, and pork chops. "Can you use any of this? I got a lot of meat left from a calf and a hog I slaughtered last year, and it ought to be eaten. I can't seem to get through it all."

I wanted to hug him, but he was already heading out the door. I suspected Mamie had phoned him when he called back from his truck. "You let me know if you get low on food—you hear me, girl?

No daughter of mine is going hungry while I've got food in my freezer."

HAVE YOU EVER NOTICED THAT God has a sense of humor? We'd prayed for a tenant to call on Sunday. At eleven fifteen on the Sunday morning three weeks after that prayer, the phone rang. I was surprised, since everybody I knew ought to have been in church. The voice sounded female and very young. "You got a trailer to rent?"

"Right." I tried not to sound eager, but I did a little dance by the phone.

"Is it private? We like our privacy."

"Very private. It's down at one corner of my lot, next to a hayfield, and there's an acre of orchard between it and my house. It's furnished, too. Two bedrooms, a living room, plus a kitchen table and chairs."

The girl consulted somebody behind her. "How much do you want?" she asked.

I was stumped. I had no idea what trailers were renting for. I didn't even remember what we had paid Porter's mama for utilities. Worried about charging too little or too much, I asked, "How much are you paying where you are?"

She named a figure that sounded like manna from heaven. I added fifty dollars a month and held my breath.

She consulted with the voice behind her. "That's good. When can we come see it?"

"This morning, if you like." I gave her directions.

There was another consultation. "We can be there in half an hour."

I hurried outside to cut grape hyacinths. I stuck them in a vase, said, "Be right back, baby," and set them on the trailer's coffee table.

Lazing in the swing while we waited for them, I tried to think of questions I ought to ask. Their names, where they worked, and the name and number for a reference in case they moved one night without paying rent. I also needed to get an extra month's rent up front as a deposit, in case they tore up the place. I felt very businesslike.

Practicality, though, couldn't diminish the bubbles of excitement in my stomach.

When a monster black Ford truck pulled into the yard, my heart sank. Nobody with a truck that expensive was going to live in my pitiful trailer.

It's not pitiful, I reminded myself. *It was three years old when we bought it and we took care of it. The furniture isn't the best, but the place is private. That's what they want. I'll get better furniture as soon as I can afford it.*

In the time it took me to put a little backbone in my spine, two people climbed out. The girl looked eighteen, the man a little older. His hair was so white it looked silver, and nicely trimmed. Hers was a deep chestnut brown and hung to her waist. Their jeans and T-shirts were clean. *Me and Porter ten years ago. Starting out and needing a cheap place to live. That truck was probably his graduation present.* I felt as old as Noah.

"Hey," I called, walking to join them. "You the folks wanting to look at my trailer?"

"Sure are." That boy was so handsome, he must have broken hearts when he married—if they *were* married. Should I ask? Did I care? Would they be a bad influence on Chellie? Heck, if their money was green, I'd take it. Chellie didn't go out much.

The girl wrinkled her nose as I approached. "What smells so bad?"

I hate to admit it, but I'd gotten used to the leaky septic tank. "Sorry. I'm having a little problem with my septic tank, but that won't bother you folks. The trailer is quite a distance from the house and has its own system."

"That's good." The guy stuck out his hand, real friendly. "I'm Kyle Kenley. This is Mo."

"I'm Billie Waits. Why don't you all follow me over? My little girl is in a wheelchair, so I need to drive, too. It's beyond the orchard and has its own driveway."

Over at the trailer, I went in to turn on all the lights. I got back to the yard to find them looking around at Daddy's pastures and hayfield, my orchard, and the private stand of pines.

"Looks real good to me," he was saying. Seeing me coming out, he said in a louder voice, "Let's see what it's like inside."

It was like a used trailer. Tacky couch and chair, scarred table, saggy mattresses. The flowers seemed like what they were—a pitiful attempt to make it look decent. But he stuck his head into both bedrooms, glanced around the living room, tried the blinds to be sure they worked, and said, "Looks fine, doesn't it, honey?" He gave me one of his blazing smiles. "How soon can we move in?"

I nearly said, "This afternoon," but common sense stepped up to remind me this was a business proposition. "As soon as your check clears for the first month's rent and a month's rent on deposit. You'll get the deposit back when you move out, if you don't damage anything."

The way the girl looked around, she was probably wondering what there was to damage.

He counted out cash from a roll as big as my fist. "This do you?"

The experience of holding that much money in my hand choked me up so I could scarcely speak. "That's fine. Come over to the house and I'll write you a receipt." I shoved the money into my pocket before he could change his mind.

He shrugged with one shoulder, which was infinitely sexier than using two. "Give it to us after we move in. This afternoon suit you?"

"That's fine. Electricity is included and water's on a well, so you can use all you want."

"Great." He put one hand at the girl's waist to help her down the steps. Not until they drove off did I realize I hadn't asked for references.

I refused to let that bother me. That afternoon after her nap, I took Michelle to Wal-Mart to buy me some new loafers. In the grocery section, I bought food for the month. I even splurged on ice cream and one twenty-ounce Coke.

Sunday night after Chellie went to sleep I made myself a tall Coke float and watched *You've Got Mail* on my old VCR for the five hundredth time. I wished I had a man like Joe Fox—cute, funny, thought-ful, and rich. Like I said, I've got a fertile imagination.

As I got ready for bed, I wondered when I'd run into Luke Bras-well again. Hopefully one day when I was clean, well-dressed, and articulate.

Fourteen

Margaret and I both loved May. The pollen was gone, the earth ripe to dig, and the weather balmy enough to work outside every evening. We both usually spent most daylight hours of the first weeks of May working in our yards.

Margaret's first weeks of May that year were a vast, barren landscape of grief on which certain boulder events cast long, knife-sharp shadows.

Every morning she woke to a moment of forgetting, but the other side of the bed—empty, cool, impersonal—jolted her into reality: Ben was gone. She piled laundry, library books, and her hair dryer on his side to provide bulk and weight.

Getting out of bed took so much energy that she had little left for other things. She didn't pick up, dust, or mop. What difference did it make? One night she caught herself shoving aside the previous night's spaghetti pot so she could make a salad.

"I didn't know I could be such a slob," she would confide to Mamie that summer.

"Honey, that wasn't you. It was grief. Your daddy's kitchen was like that when I came back. Show me a filthy kitchen, and I'll show you somebody too busy grieving to clean."

She had never known bottomless unhappiness before. Unanswered questions swarmed around her head like buzzards: "What did I do wrong?" "How can this be happening to me?" "Would he have stayed if I had . . . ?"

Even simple questions—what shall we have for breakfast?—were too much for her, so every morning she poured cereal. When she set a plastic milk jug on the table, the boys didn't notice. She wondered why she'd used pretty pitchers all those years. But they did complain, "We're tired of cereal," so one morning she scrambled eggs. She burned them so badly that she hurled the skillet far out into the woods for somebody else to find and wonder about.

Her body craved Ben's. She wept through interminable nights.

Deprived of sleep, she lost her manners. Raw, anxious, easily angered, she lashed out at a store clerk one day. She got as far as her car, then went back to apologize. "I am dreadfully sorry. I have a terrible headache."

Some nights when sleep eluded her, she roamed the house. The thought of leaving it made her double over with a gut-rending pain as sharp as menstrual cramps.

Leaving the yard would be harder. She had planted every flower, every shrub. Even if she must leave them, she could not let them die in drought. The county had decreed that watering could only be done between four and ten a.m. She dragged herself out of bed at four on the mornings she was permitted to water and until ten she dragged hoses from site to site, cursing Ben for never installing the automatic sprinklers he'd promised for years.

She prayed incessantly—*God, bring him home! God, help him see how much he's hurting us! God, punish him for this! God, help me get through this! Oh, God, I want to die!*—but she stopped going to church. She couldn't think up honest excuses for why Ben wasn't there, and she would not lie. She had still not told anybody he was gone. If people asked about him, she told the truth: "This is a busy time of year for him."

She began to distrust her judgment where the boys were concerned.

If she had been so wrong about her marriage, was she too hard on her children? She let them stay up late, get away with smart remarks, and eat in front of the television.

Notes arrived from teachers: "Andy is not completing his work." "Jason is not living up to his potential." When Jason's guidance counselor asked to see both parents, Ben grudgingly took time off to go.

"He is dropping behind in every subject," the counselor said. "Unless he improves drastically before the end of the year, he'll have to go to summer school for algebra."

"Algebra?" Margaret was baffled. "Math is his best subject."

"Is he having problems at home?"

Margaret opened her mouth to say he certainly was, but Ben spoke first. "Everything's fine at home. We'll talk to him. He'll be okay."

"Do you even know this is your fault?" Margaret demanded when they were outside.

"My fault? You're the one at home with them."

"Your leaving has upset them. They miss you. They need you."

"I see them every weekend and talk to them almost every day."

"That's not enough. They need you at home."

"I am at home—my home. They'll get used to it. This is nothing but a bump in the road."

"A bump in the road? If Jason has to go to summer school? If his grades are too bad to get into college?"

"He'll adjust. Parents get divorced every day."

"Some writers say children of divorce never really get over it." Margaret's bedside table was stacked with literature about the effects of divorce on children.

Ben's huff told her what he thought of the literature. "Our boys will adjust. Keep after them. They'll bring those grades up."

Keep after them? All she ever did anymore was keep after them. "Pick up your clothes. Finish your breakfast. Don't forget to feed Mac-Tavish. Hurry so you won't miss the bus." How long had it been since she and the boys had had any fun? She resented excursions Ben thought up for weekends he spent with the boys. Having fun had become his part of parenting. Nagging was hers.

The boys also began to lose things. Jason lost his history book, which Margaret had to replace. Andy lost his precious catcher's mitt. "I'll get you a new one," she promised.

"But Daddy gave it to me," he wept. His small face was so like Ben's that she wept, too.

SHE COULDN'T BUY ANDY A mitt. A lack of money stalked her by the hour. The household credit card was still maxed out, and Ben was erratic about depositing funds into the household bank account. When the due date loomed on several unpaid bills, Margaret called him. Her fingers shook as she dialed. Anger made her sharper than she intended to be, he became defensive, and the conversation ended in a fight. He made a deposit after she'd called, but she was exhausted by the effort it took to wring the money out of him.

"You need to find a job," he reminded her before he hung up. What job? She took that morning's want ads out to the deck with a cup of coffee, but she didn't know what most job descriptions meant and wasn't qualified for the ones she did understand. When a breeze snatched the paper from her fingers and scattered it across the lawn, she stood at the railing screaming obscenities she hadn't known she knew.

She tried writing a résumé—by hand, since Ben had the computer— but her only work experience was helping to build their business. She doubted most employers would be impressed by what she had done: *Cleaned toilets. Watered plants. Sold bushes. Recommended sod. Made friends with potential clients.* Even though she had kept the books for a number of years, she had taken no bookkeeping classes and was out-of-date on even the software she had used.

"I could do nothing!" she would tell us later through angry tears. "I should have listened to Daddy before I married Ben. 'Don't give up your education for that boy, Maggie,' he said. 'Finish college first. Make some-

thing of yourself. You need to be able to stand on your own two feet before you stand beside somebody else at the altar.' Why didn't I listen?"

WITH MONEY RUNNING DANGEROUSLY LOW and Ben unreliable about deposits, Margaret took some of her best clothes to a consignment store. "The labels are gone," the proprietor objected.

"I made the clothes," Margaret admitted.

"You're a heck of a seamstress, honey, but I doubt they'll sell. Women don't come in for clothes. They come in to get big-name labels cheap."

The next day she called Margaret. "A woman was in here looking at your clothes. She asked if you would be interested in making bridesmaids' dresses for her daughter's wedding. There would be five of them and she needs them by the end of May."

Margaret was elated. She met with the bride and her mother to discuss fabrics and style. She bought the material and sewed after the boys were in bed and while they were at school. But making five young women look beautiful in the same style of dress stretched her skills to the screaming point. One gained five pounds after she sent in her measurements. Another had too much bust for the draped style the bride wanted. A third never came to scheduled fittings and came when it was inconvenient.

When Margaret calculated how many hours she would eventually spend on the dresses, she was straining her eyes and her patience for less than minimum wage.

SATURDAY WAS HER FAVORITE DAY. She saw Ben at Andy's baseball games and Jason's track meets. They were pleasant to each other, laughing and joking with friends who didn't know they were separated. Ben stood with dads near the coaches, as he always had, and Margaret sat with moms, but she spent as much time watching him as she did the events. She drank up the sight of Ben the way she had in college, never getting enough to last until the next time she saw him. No matter how angry she got with him during the week, on Saturdays she knew she still loved him.

At baseball practice she sat with Bayonne Bradshaw, who transported a little nephew who played on Andy's team. Bayonne chattered about tennis, troubles her ex-husband was causing her, and how much she admired Margaret's boys. Margaret almost warmed up enough to confide her problems—until the Saturday Ben showed up at Jason's track meet with Bayonne.

Margaret could tell from the way Jason and Andy greeted them that her boys were used to seeing the two together. She could not watch the meet for looking their way. Ben smiled at Bayonne in the lazy, teasing way he used to smile at her. Bayonne reached out to stroke the golden hair on Ben's arm.

Margaret regretted all the precautions she had taken to protect his reputation. They made her look like a fool.

When the meet was over, Ben and Bayonne started toward her red Miata. Margaret closed her eyes. She didn't mind if fire streaming from her pupils incinerated Ben, but it might bounce back to turn her into a pillar of salt.

THE VERY NEXT MORNING, WHILE Margaret was outside watering, Ben drove in. "You don't have a FOR SALE sign out front yet," he called from the truck without getting out. "I gave you the Realtor's number. We need to sell this house."

She pulled down her sunglasses so he could see her glare. "What happened to 'Hello, Margaret. How are you?'"

"Hello, Margaret. How are you? Why don't you have a FOR SALE sign out front?"

"I don't want to sell. It's the only home the boys have ever known."

"Kids are resilient. They'll adjust to a new place."

"Did you learn that word from Bayonne? It's a little big for you, isn't it?"

He glowered. "Don't change the subject. Sell the house!"

"I think we ought to wait until the market improves."

"Price it to sell. We need whatever it can bring, and we need it fast. Be seeing you." With a little salute, he drove away. She hadn't had time to mention last week's money, which he again hadn't deposited into the household account.

Hate, she discovered that next week, was as good as a superpower. She listed what needed to be done to sell and whizzed through cleaning cabinets and closets. Cleaned the oven. Cleaned the refrigerator. Washed woodwork. Cleaned carpets. She even cleaned Ben's workshop—dragging boxes of plumbing parts, electrical equipment, jars of odd nails, nuts, and bolts, and bits of telephone and computer equipment off metal shelves so she could dust. She never got tired.

She never got hungry, either. Often when it was time to get Andy, she hadn't stopped for lunch. When she passed a mirror, she did not recognize the gaunt, hard-faced woman who glared back at her.

By mid-May she still had not told me or Daddy that Ben had left.

"Why?" I would demand in July.

"Pride," she would admit. "I didn't want Daddy or you to know I had failed at marriage. You both always expected so much of me. I also thought I needed to protect Ben, in case he ever wanted to return. I decided I would give him the summer to come to his senses."

She also still hadn't told Katrinka Smith—who had been on a three-week cruise with her CPA husband to celebrate the end of tax season.

"Are you all right?" Katrinka asked after tennis practice one morning. Her eyes held an unasked question: *Are you suffering from a terminal illness you haven't told me about?*

Margaret said, "I haven't been sleeping well lately. Otherwise, I'm fine."

"How about if we go to the French bakery for coffee and pastry?"

When the check came, Margaret reached for it. "You paid last time."

At her lawyer's suggestion, she had gotten a new credit card in her own name. The balance was mounting at an alarming rate, but she walked to the register with a nonchalance that amazed her. She handed over her card with a smile. Smiles were free.

Fifteen

Blissfully unaware of what Margaret was enduring and Mamie fearing, I contentedly weeded flower beds, divided perennials, and transplanted shrubs I'd rescued from a developer who was building an ugly brick office building where a charming Victoria house used to stand. He planned to clear the lot before building. If he wanted to pay for new plants instead of keeping the mature oak-leaf hydrangeas, tea olives, and camellias old Mrs. Pincer had devoted her life to tending, that was my gain.

The days were so lovely, I wanted to seal each one in a canning jar to preserve it. Chellie sat out under the maple tree counting butterflies. While I worked, I taught her the names of plants, convincing myself I could teach her as well as any school. When she napped, I went back out to the yard and spun crazy daydreams about high school—dreams in which Luke Braswell and I said all those things I'd wanted us to say back then. "You'd better stop," I warned myself, "or you'll never be able to look him in the eye again."

Not that I was likely to get a chance, unless I broke the law. One afternoon I amused myself with a fantasy in which I robbed Ashley's bank and he showed up looking dashing and romantic to arrest me, but he let me off for the sake of my little girl.

Money was still a worry, of course—my tenants' rent money wouldn't cover all my bills—but I had enough to pay those that came due early in the month. I decided to worry about the end of the month when it got there.

The tenants themselves were great. I hardly ever saw them. Since their truck was gone all night and most of the day, I figured one of them must work night shift and one during the day. From four until midnight their yard was full of cars, so their buddies weren't giving them the privacy they'd desired, but the kids weren't unruly and didn't party late. I considered myself very lucky.

ONE EVENING I WAS WASHING dishes while Chellie watched a video. "Pretty!" she exclaimed. "Come see, Mommy! Blue lights on pink sky."

I figured it was something on her video. Instead, down at the trailer, police lights flashed across the sunset. My first thought was that somebody had gotten injured. My second, I am ashamed to admit, was, "Will they try to sue me?"

"I'm going to run over to the trailer for a minute," I told Chellie. "You watch the video until I get back." Normally I didn't leave her alone, but surely the Department of Family and Children's Services wouldn't show up in the five minutes it took me to run to the trailer.

I found Tee Hodson standing by one of the cruisers. "What's going on?" I clutched my side where I'd gotten a stitch from running too fast.

He nodded toward the door. "Drug bust."

Luke came down the steps, thrusting Kyle before him. The boy's hands were cuffed. Luke didn't look dashing and romantic like he had in my bank-robbing fantasy. He looked grim. After them came Mo, also cuffed, escorted by another officer. None of the four glanced my way.

"They were using drugs?" I asked Tee, astonished. Sure, well-scrubbed kids, raised right, sometimes experimented with drugs. Some got hooked. But these two had seemed so clean, so fresh—I realized

I had mentally considered them the couple I wished Porter and I had been.

"Not using," Tee said grimly. "Selling. We've been looking for this pair for months. We knew there was a big supplier in the county, but had no idea where they were operating from."

Chills went up my spine. "Am I in trouble because they were on my property?"

"Not unless you were buying or selling."

Tee had known me since I was born. I glared. "You have a sick sense of humor."

I stepped in front Kyle as Luke frog-marched him to the cruiser. "You sold drugs on my property? With my child across that orchard?" I must have looked fierce, because Luke stepped between me and Kyle. Coming after them, Mo colored up when she saw me. "How could you?" I asked her. "I trusted you."

She shrugged, but I saw tear tracks down her cheeks. I wondered if she'd known what Kyle was doing when she hooked up with him, or if he had sucked her in.

Luke stowed both kids in a cruiser, slammed the door, and drove away. I could have been a hydrangea bush for all the attention he'd paid me.

I started toward the trailer. "Don't go in there," Tee warned. "It's a crime scene."

"How soon before I can advertise for new tenants?"

"I'll let you know." A policeman was winding yellow tape around my yard.

A black truck pulled into the drive. "What's going on here?"

Great. All I needed for the evening to be complete. "Hey, Daddy. Apparently my tenants were dealing drugs."

"Is that right?" He was asking Tee, not me.

"Afraid so."

"How could you be so dumb?" Now Daddy was talking to me. Jimbo gave an inquisitive "woof?"—supporting Daddy.

"They didn't carry signs saying WE ARE DRUG PUSHERS. They looked harmless."

"They give you any references?"

"I didn't think to ask for any."

"Next time, get references," Tee advised.

"Next time, rent to a Sunday school teacher," Daddy snapped. "You hear me?"

He backed up his truck and left.

LUKE'S CRUISER PULLED INTO MY drive the next afternoon. "I came to tell you we are done with your trailer," he called as he got out.

I was my usual glamorous self, out dividing iris in cutoff jeans.

"Thanks." I brushed soil from my knees and wondered why I didn't garden in nice clothes like Margaret did. Maybe because I didn't have any nice clothes?

Luke picked up my basketball from under the azaleas and shot toward the basket. He missed. "Out of practice," he muttered. "Your shot." I was so embarrassed at how I looked that I missed, too. We both improved on our next shots, but neither of us would have made a B team that day.

When he left, I sent his mother some iris. "Let me know if they bloom." As he drove away, I mentally kicked myself. What if he knew iris always bloom? He'd think I was trying to get him to come back to see me. Which, of course, I was.

As soon as Chellie was asleep, I took a flashlight through the orchard to inspect the trailer. Lucky came along. He had a field day chasing roaches.

Kyle wasn't getting his deposit back. They must not have cleaned the bathroom since they moved in. The furniture was filthy with grease, like folks had eaten fast food and wiped their hands on the upholstery. I concluded they hadn't lived there—merely used the place for drug dealing—because the bottom of the oven was as shiny as I'd left it.

It took me a full day to polish the trailer to my satisfaction. Cleaning the furniture turned my stomach. It took me another day to get up the nerve to drive into town to put ads in the filling station, library, and grocery store. This time I would be firm about references.

The next morning I called a man to clean my septic tank. That seemed an appropriate use for Kyle's deposit.

But what was I going to do until I got tenants? When I pulled out Chellie's summer clothes, she had grown out of all of them. Margaret came to mind again, but I hated making that call. I knew she thought I'd made a mess of my life. It probably embarrassed her to have a poverty-stricken sister. The only thing that drove me to the telephone was the thought of my child having nothing to wear.

As soon as Margaret answered her phone, I spoke without pausing. "Could you possibly make Chellie a few shorts and tops for this summer? She's grown like a weed and can't get into a thing she wore last summer, and I still haven't heard from Porter. I hate to ask, but I'm desperate."

If I thought Margaret—who helped everybody in Cobb County—would jump right in and say, "Sure, I can run up some shorts and a couple of dresses. No problem," I had another thought coming. "I don't know. I'm pretty busy right now." She sounded like she was dragging every word through thick mud.

What did she have to do that was more important than clothing a naked child? Hadn't she heard sermons about how Jesus said, "If you do it to the least of these, you do it to me"? Chellie certainly qualified.

"She doesn't need much," I pressed. "A couple of pairs of shorts and tops would do. She could use a couple of nightgowns if you had time to make them, but if you don't, she can sleep in my T-shirts. She really needs shorts and tops, though. I can't pay you for the fabric right now, but I will as soon as Porter sends a check."

Margaret was good in math. She knew as well as I did that Porter was now two checks behind. I figured that was why she took her own sweet time thinking it over. I fumed. How much time would it take her to run up a couple of pairs of shorts and tops? How much would she spend on fabric for a couple of outfits? Less than she probably spent at Starbucks in a week.

All of a sudden she said—like she'd just had an idea, "You know, I think I can. But I can't work on them until the weekend. I've got a lot going on right now."

Lucky Margaret.

A WEEK LATER LURLEEN SHOWED up on my porch with a box. I had been so busy working in the yard that I had only waved at her across the yard for several days when she brought the mail. I was shocked by her appearance. She had dark circles under her eyes. Her grizzled hair, which usually glittered like Christmas tinsel, was as lifeless as a Brillo pad. "Good morning," she muttered as she thrust the box at me.

"You don't seem very chipper this morning."

"I haven't been chipper for some time. Did you know Mama is working for your daddy?"

"Doing what?" I got a wild picture of Mamie high on a tractor, mowing the hayfield.

Lurleen looked grim. "Cleaning house, apparently, a couple of days a week."

"Why?" Mamie hadn't been a maid for decades. Why would she go back to that now? Besides, Daddy wasn't a man who spent money he didn't need to, and I couldn't imagine why he would need a maid. Daddy was an "everything in its place or I'll tan your backside" kind of guy.

Lurleen glared. "Have you seen his place lately?"

"I haven't been over there in a while. Probably not since Christmas. He brings me milk a couple of times a week, so I see him then. . . ."

The rebuke in Lurleen's eyes stopped me cold. "His house looked like a pigpen when I took him a package in March. Papers on the floor, dishes everywhere—but Mama doesn't need to be cleaning it. I told you, her doctor said she"—Lurleen paused, as if trying to remember exactly what he'd said—"has to avoid stress."

"You told me that. Have you talked to her about it?"

Lurleen looked at the floor. "I tried, but that woman's head is made out of Stone Mountain granite. She gave me some rigmarole about God sending her there and your daddy needing her. We had a few sharp words. Now we aren't speaking."

The way Mamie and Lurleen both loved to talk, that was serious. I couldn't think of a single thing to say.

"Maybe if you talked to her, Billie—she dotes on you. Tell her she shouldn't be mopping floors and carrying out trash. Or tell your daddy."

"I'll try but they may not listen to me, either. We can't really tell our parents what to do."

Lurleen sighed. "We can tell them, honey. We just can't make them listen."

I went inside and called Mamie before I even opened my box. "What's this Lurleen tells me about you working for Daddy?"

"I've been helping him out a couple of days a week. Keeping the place clean while he's busy outside. It gives me something to do."

"Lurleen said—" I walked over the next sentence as carefully as if it had been shattered glass. "She said you're not feeling real well."

"Pooh!" Mamie blew out a spurt of air. "Lurleen worries herself about every little thing. Of course, I'm not up to turning cartwheels." She laughed.

"This isn't funny if the doctor has told you to slow down. What's the matter?"

"Nothing much. He's a little worried about my heart. Nothing serious, mind, but he told me to take it easy. So I do. I work slow and rest when I need to. You tell Lurleen to keep her mind on post office business and stop worrying about mine."

"You tell her."

"I will, honey, just as soon as she starts speaking to me again. You tell her I'm here if she wants to give me a call."

MARGARET SENT CHELLIE FIVE PAIRS of shorts in beautiful plaids, five matching tops in knit material so soft I wanted to hug it, two knit nightgowns, and a beautiful little peach sundress with embroidered flowers around the neck. I went straight to the phone. "Oh, Margaret, the clothes are wonderful! Michelle and I both love them. That dress is so gorgeous, she's going to want to wear it every day."

"I'm glad." Margaret didn't sound particularly glad. She sounded like she was talking underwater. Not until midsummer would she tell me where she got the material to make those clothes:

While I was talking to you, I remembered how I had been telling Ben to come get his stuff out of the house, but he couldn't be bothered. I went to his closet and chose some of his nicest plaid shirts to make shorts. I chose soft polo shirts in matching colors to cut down for Chellie's tops, and a few others for nightgowns. Ben always had good taste in clothes, so they turned out real pretty. I loved every snip and slash. The hours I spent making those clothes were the high point of my month.

Sixteen

Mamie went to her doctor's the morning after Lurleen brought me Margaret's box. She sat across the desk and pleaded, "No difference? That new medicine that makes me so dizzy isn't taking away any fluid?" She trembled from head to toe.

Dr. Hodges ducked his head, concentrating on a silver letter opener he balanced between his fingers. "I'm sorry. Your kidneys are no longer functioning properly. That's another result of the hypertension that has messed up your heart. Discontinue the pills. At least you won't be dizzy anymore."

Mamie looked at her hands, thick brown fingers twisting in her lap like they had a life of their own. "But I won't be getting any better. Is that right?"

He nodded but he still didn't look at her. "I'm sorry."

She clutched her hands tightly together to still them. A woman of faith ought not get agitated at hearing bad news. But all she could think of was Lurleen's sad eyes, Skeeter's sweet smile, and the fact that her granddaughter, Janeika, still wasn't married with children of her own.

Mamie knew she was bound for glory, but when she thought of the process of getting there, she shuddered.

The movement caused the doctor to raise his eyes. He cleared his throat before he spoke. "Do—" He licked his lips "Do you have some-one in the waiting room? Someone who can drive you home?" His hands were shaking, too.

He's scared, she realized. *Scared half to death to have to tell me this, and angry that all his medical training can't do a thing to help either one of us.*

"I've got my car. I can drive my own self."

"You ought not be alone." He repeated it like a line he'd learned in class. His eyes, which Mamie's preacher called the windows of the soul, were utterly wretched.

She leaned forward to lay one hand on his wrist, and she spoke in the gentle voice she used to comfort children. "I'm not alone. Don't worry about me. I've got Jesus."

He blinked at her unexpected kindness.

"Do you have any idea how long I've got?" she asked.

He shook his head. "Not really, but research is telling us more all the time. Maybe a new treatment—"

She clutched his wrist. "Don't give me doctor talk. If I was your mother, how long would you expect to have me around?"

He sighed. "With care you might make it—oh, to Christmas." Tears glittered in his eyes. Young as he was, he probably hadn't had that conversation with too many patients.

But Christmas? Mamie had been thinking in terms of a year. Two, perhaps. It took all her energy to summon a smile. "Then I better get busy. Don't know if I can get done everything I need to do in that little bit of time."

As she trudged to her car, she thought, *A boy that young ought not have to tell people they are dying.*

WHILE SHE WAS AT THE doctor's office, I was talking to prospective ten-ants on the phone.

A woman called midmorning to ask, "You have a mobile home for rent?"

I gave her ten points for maturity. She sounded at least seventy. "Yes, ma'am."

"My name is Ethelyne Jackson. My sister, Verna Bullard, and I need a place to live. How many bedrooms does it have? We don't need a large place, but each of us wants her own room."

I gave her ten more points for good grammar. "It has two bedrooms."

"That sounds good. How much are you asking?" When I'd told her that, she asked, "Would it be convenient to see it around three this afternoon?"

Good manners, too? She'd hit the jackpot. "Whenever you can get here will be fine."

Ethelyne was tall and stout with bottle red hair permed into tight curls. Her brown eyes looked huge behind thick glasses. She wore dark red nail polish that looked like a professional job. Verna was shorter with a blue rinse on short straight hair, delicate silver-rimmed glasses, and a plain gold band on her wedding finger. Her nails were done in a pale, almost colorless pink. She looked familiar, but maybe that was because she looked like so many other elderly women. Both wore lace-up shoes and double-knit pantsuits that screamed "outlet mall."

Ethelyne talked for both. "My sister, here, has been living with her son for the past five years while I've been living at home, taking care of Mama. She made ninety-eight before she died last month. But she left the house to our half brother, Roy, who was hers by her first marriage. He wants to sell it. Verna's daughter-in-law is a real pill, so we've decided to live together. But we don't want much to clean and can't afford much. A mobile home sounds good."

"Real good." Verna's first two words were spoken in a soft, apologetic voice. I got the feeling she apologized for her very existence. "I love your yard."

I dreaded opening the trailer door. "I'm gonna replace the furniture as I'm able."

Ethelyne was first inside. She looked at Mrs. Waits's plaid couch and said, "We have Mama's furniture. Could you put this in storage or something?" I knew "something" was a polite way of saying "the county dump." I couldn't disagree.

"Would Saturday afternoon be all right to move in?" they asked when they'd checked out all the rooms.

Asking those two for references seemed as silly as it would be to ask Saint Georgia at church, but I did it. "Do you have references? Somebody I can contact in case of an emergency?"

Ethelyne's laugh was as hearty as she. "Of course, honey. Verna, give her Roy's number and your no-count son's." Verna wrote two phone numbers on a sheet she tore from a little notebook from her pocketbook. I shoved them into my pocket, embarrassed I'd had to ask.

"Saturday afternoon will be fine," I told them. That would give their check time to clear and give me time to move out my furniture and shampoo the carpet. The trailer would look good without the tacky furniture.

Verna wrote me a check on the spot for their first month's rent and deposit.

Who could help me move furniture? Daddy was busy putting in his garden.

Freckles topped by bright red hair came to mind.

I called right after Franklin got home from school. "You want to earn some money tomorrow afternoon?"

"Doing what?" He sounded wary.

I laughed. "No briars, no brush, and no wasps. I'm fixing to carry furniture to the dump and move more furniture into a shed. If you'll help, I'll come get you, bring you home, and pay you five bucks an hour. It might take us two."

"Okay. Let me ask Mama." A minute later he returned. "She says okay, but you don't have to come get me. Luke says he'll bring me. He wants to talk to you anyway."

I was indecently glad to hear that.

The next morning I deposited the renters' check and withdrew enough cash to pay Franklin, rent a carpet shampooer, and buy groceries. I took one bag of groceries by the church food pantry. It is far more blessed to give than to have to receive.

That afternoon I was giddy as a teenager waiting for Luke to bring Franklin. I wished I didn't have to put on a T-shirt and jeans, but what else was practical for moving furniture? At least I could wash my hair. Maybe I'd invest in a tube of lipstick one day.

Luke came in the cruiser again, with Franklin in the backseat and a girl in the passenger seat. So much for his noticing my shiny hair. I looked her over while he was parking. He had no business running around with a girl that age.

"Wilhelmina!" He sounded glad to see me as he climbed out and opened the back door for Franklin, but I willed myself, *Stay calm!*

"One delinquent delivered," Luke said as Franklin climbed out, "and"—he opened the passenger door with a flourish—"this is our sister, Bethany." She had Franklin's hair and freckles, but a look of maturity and determination in her chin.

I was so relieved, I started babbling. "Don't talk rude about my employee, Officer. Glad to meet you, Bethany. You ready to help me this afternoon, Franklin?"

"Yes, ma'am."

"Let me see your muscles."

He grinned and flexed his arm. "Feel."

I pressed his biceps. "Feels good."

Michelle called from the porch, "Me, too!" He and Bethany joined her on the porch. Franklin flexed his arm again. Chellie flopped her hand around trying to touch his muscles, but she couldn't get it coordinated. Bethany gently took Chellie's hand and put it on Franklin's arm.

"You're strong!" Michelle exclaimed.

"Like a rock." Franklin struck a strong-man pose.

Luke slouched over to me and spoke out of the side of his mouth. "Wanna feel my muscles, lady?"

The shiver that climbed my spine carried a blush up with it. "Heavens no." Trying to recover my cool, I said, "Franklin said you wanted to talk to me?" I aimed for casual, but it came out cold.

He became every inch a cop. "I wanted to report on investigations concerning your missing husband, ma'am. I've checked all hospitals in the Marietta area. None has treated Porter Waits or an unidentified man of his description in the past three months."

Did I thank him for going to all that trouble? No. I blurted the first thing that came to my mind. "Tee authorized a search?"

"I did it on my own time. Tee's—ah—busy with other things."

"Like sitting on his backside. But I really appreciate this. I've been scared Porter could be lying in a hospital somewhere not knowing who he is." I hated to ask, but had to. "Did you check the jails? He's never been in before, but you never know."

"I did, actually, in three counties. He's not in any of them." I didn't mention my other biggest fear, but he added, "I also checked funeral homes and morgues. Nothing on the radar."

He had lifted such a weight off my shoulders, I felt myself standing taller. But Luke's eyes were full of the same question I had: if Porter wasn't sick, in jail, or dead, where was he?

"I could go talk to the guys he was working with last," Luke said.

"I already tried that. Unless you speak Spanish, you won't get far. But he hasn't abandoned us. He hasn't. He's not like that."

"Then we'll find him. When I get a good mystery, I'm like a dog with a bone."

"Thanks. I appreciate what you've already done."

I wished I could hurry to my kitchen and bring out tea and cookies like Mama would have done, but I didn't have tea or cookies. "I guess Franklin and I ought to get to work."

"And I need to get back to the station. Some emergency may need me."

I grinned. "Like drug dealers in a respectable trailer?"

"Or a kid stealing a wheelchair." He shot my basketball cleanly through the hoop.

"I'm sure keeping you busy lately, aren't I?" I caught the ball on the bounce.

"You sure are." The look in his eyes made me miss my basket.

He shot another perfect hoop. "Try again."

I backed up and shot. "Three-pointer." It went through clean.

"You are a woman of unplumbed depths." He shot another basket and it bounced off the rim. "Drat. I've been practicing, too."

I didn't bother to retrieve the ball. "Franklin and I'd better get busy if we're going to get a load to the dump before it closes."

"Could Bethany stay with Michelle while you work with Franklin? She's going to college to become a special-ed teacher, and she worked at a camp for special-needs children last summer. When she heard about Michelle, she wanted to meet her."

Up on the porch, Michelle was laughing. "She'd be a big help," I admitted. Paying two workers would take a bite from my rent money, but Michelle saw almost nobody but me. To keep that laugh on her face for another hour, I'd go without lipstick. "I'll bring them home. I want to stop by the hardware store and rent a carpet shampooer to use this evening."

"How about if I get the carpet shampooer, since I'll be in town anyway, and pick the kids up when I bring it out? I'll be back around six."

FRANKLIN AND I HAULED UPHOLSTERED furniture and saggy mattresses to the county dump. I pictured Porter sitting in that chair as we hurled it into the Dumpster. I wasn't as confident as I used to be that he hadn't finally decided to walk out on me.

How dare he up and leave without a word?

On the way home from the dump, though, I remembered something I'd thought about before. If Porter had found a better job, he'd brag about it to somebody. Porter was like a rooster. He loved to crow. He might not mention it if he'd gotten fired, but he hadn't. Which meant either somebody at that site knew where he went, or something was wrong.

We stored the rest of the furniture in a shed behind my house. "They might bring a little money from a secondhand shop," I told Franklin as we relaxed with ice water.

"Talk to an antiques dealer," he advised. "Some of that stuff looks real old."

Granted, "real old" to Franklin could be something from the nineteen eighties, but I looked at him with new respect. "I hadn't realized I was employing an entrepreneur."

When Luke returned, he brought not only the carpet shampooer, but two pizzas and a big bottle of Sprite. "Mama's got choir practice tonight. Can you take in three orphans?"

I went to fetch plates and glasses so he wouldn't see how glad I looked.

After the pizza, he brought out a set of dominoes. "How about if you kids play while Mina and I clean a rug?"

"Who's Mina?" Chellie asked.

"Your mother. Her real name's Wilhelmina. Isn't that pretty? So I call her Mina."

"Her name is Billie," Chellie insisted, sounding jealous for the first time in her life.

"You have two names, Michelle and Chellie. Can't she have Billie and Mina?"

She thought it over. "Okay. I like Mina. Eenie mina mighty mo."

Luke laughed. "Come on, Eenie Mina Mighty Mo. We have a rug to clean."

I had never thought of carpet shampooing as fun, but Luke told so many funny stories about being in the army that we laughed the whole time. Eventually, though, I had to open my big mouth and ask, "Does your wife mind you being out this evening?"

"I don't think so. I haven't seen her for six years, but I could call and ask. We're divorced, in case you haven't guessed."

Oh, wow! "Do you have children?"

"She didn't want children. After she and her sisters were born, her mother gained a lot of weight. Mary Sue didn't want to lose her girlish figure."

I looked down at my own round figure—the same size it had been when I was a girl, but nothing to brag about—and couldn't think of a thing to say.

"You and Porter aren't divorced?" He tossed it out like a casual question, but when I looked up and saw him looking at me, something that scared me to death sizzled between us. No matter how much I fantasized about Luke, I wasn't ready to face the possibility of anything real. Maybe that was why I told him the same lie I'd been telling Chellie all those years.

"No, Porter's been working out of town because that's where the jobs are, but once we save up a bit, he'll come home again." I held up my left hand. "I'm very much married. See?"

"A ring doesn't make a marriage. A marriage is somebody being there for you."

"Are you such an expert? Yours didn't make it."

"No, but it taught me what to look for if I ever do it again. I sure won't be looking for somebody who works in one town while I live in another. It was while I was doing a tour in Iraq that Mary Sue decided to move on. I want a wife I can live with forever."

"We don't always get what we want." I positioned a fan to dry the carpet overnight.

"We get what we're willing to put up with." He picked up the shampooer and went outside to dump the filthy water.

"You have no idea what I'm willing to put up with, Mr. Righteous," I muttered as I headed to the bedroom with a second fan. I thought he couldn't hear me. But when I turned, he was standing in the doorway, his face taut and his eyes stormy.

"I have some idea of what. I just don't know why." He wrapped the cord around the shampooer and carried it to his car without another word.

After Chellie went to bed, I swung on the porch thinking of things I wished I'd said instead of what I had actually said. How could I have been so dumb? Would I ever see him again?

I also wondered why I hadn't ever divorced Porter. If I was honest with myself, the answer was straight from a high school textbook: *inertia—an indisposition to motion, exertion, or change.* How pathetic was that?

VERNA'S SON BROUGHT OVER THREE pickup truckloads of lovely furniture and boxes, but how the ladies were going to fit all that into the trailer wasn't my problem. *My* problem was that rent checks still weren't going to pay all our bills.

I had one idea how to solve that. I called Bethany to see if she could keep Michelle so I could go back to work. If I had any ulterior motive for that call, I will never admit it.

Bethany could start the following Wednesday, after her graduation. Stamps was more than willing for me to come to work. "Business is good. Folks are fixing up their cars these days instead of trading them in."

When I called Bethany back, she sounded less enthusiastic. "I forgot I told some girls I'd go down to Panama City with them the first week of June. Could I start after that?"

"How about if you start Wednesday, and I'll set up something else for that week?" Heaven only knew what I could set up, but I would cross that bridge if I ever got to it.

Daddy and Jimbo dropped by that evening with our milk. "I hear you rented the trailer again. Did you get references?"

"Sure did, and I got two older women who go to Pine Springs Baptist Church."

"Even Baptists need references."

"Heck, Daddy, these women *are* references. But I got them, so stop worrying. I would suggest you go down and welcome them to the neighborhood, except you're an eligible single man. They might not let you out of that trailer alive."

He left whistling.

WITH MY LIFE PICKING UP like that, I ought to have been turning cart-wheels on the lawn. Instead, the night before I was to start work, I was unable to sleep. How could I have been so rude to Luke? Especially after he'd been so nice. I ought to call and apologize, but would he read too much into the call? What would I *want* him to read into it? Why had I lied to him about Porter and me? Why was I wearing my wedding ring again? Because I was scared not to?

I turned over, pulled the sheet to my chin, and worried about Porter. Where was he? Why didn't he write? The last time I'd tried his cell phone, it had been disconnected.

I turned over again and worried about Michelle. How could I leave her to go off to work? How could I not, now that I had a job plus child care?

Chill, Billie. You can't do a thing about any of this tonight. Sleep!

I couldn't. All night long I worried about Luke. Worried about Porter. Worried about Michelle. Worry, worry, worry, and repeat.

At dawn I carried a cup of tea out onto the porch into a gorgeous day. The sky was gold, peach, and lavender. Birds sang their usual early-morning concert. Lucky jumped into the swing and curled up on my lap. I remembered something Mama used to quote: *Blessed are the pure in heart who leave everything to God as they did before they ever existed.*

I stroked Lucky with my free hand. "We are going to make it. No matter what it takes, we are going to make it." Lucky blinked slowly and began to purr.

LEAVING MICHELLE THAT FIRST DAY was the hardest thing I'd had to do since delivering her. I guess every event that separates a mother and her child is a form of childbirth. I drove away feeling like she was being physically ripped from my body.

The fact that I left her happily chatting with Bethany should have made me feel better. It didn't. When I heard them laugh as I closed the door, I had to fight an impulse to march in, fire Bethany, and tell Stamps I couldn't work for him because I already had a job.

All morning I worried. Was Chellie sitting in her chair staring at the door, waiting for me to come home? Had she thrown one of her rare tantrums over something? Was she crying silently, as she did when she was especially sad? Would she ever forgive me for leaving her?

I lasted until noon before I called.

"She's doing great," Bethany reported. "We went out to look at butterflies and read a book I got at the library about how caterpillars turn into butterflies. Then I filled a dishpan with rice I brought, and she played in it a while. It's really great for kids—feels soothing on their hands. We're watching a video now. When we finish, we'll have lunch."

"Can I talk to her?"

"Hey, Mommy," Michelle said. "We're watching a movie. Bye."

Her telephone skills were roughly equivalent to those of her father, but knowing my child was happy relieved my heart. I went back to work humming.

Seventeen

By the third week of May, Margaret was also beginning to find bright spots in her desolation. She went to bed when she wanted to and read without worrying about keeping Ben awake. She tuned to public radio instead of Ben's country station, to fill the house with classical music and in-depth news. She and the boys ate lighter meals without Ben there to want meat every night. She had more time to spend with Andy, time to really listen when he talked. She would have had more time for Jason, too, but he remained surly. The television went off when the boys went to bed, instead of filling the house with late-night sports. She threw out Ben's enormous collection of Styrofoam egg cartons and opaque plastic containers, but felt a pang as she remembered how she used to tease, "If there's ever a national shortage of this stuff, you are going to be prepared."

She still hadn't gotten around to calling the Realtor. She was too busy sewing bridesmaid dresses to keep the place clean enough to show. She also could not bear to sell her house. "If God wants it sold, he'll have to send a buyer," she told herself. Secretly she was waiting for a miracle so they wouldn't have to sell.

She held a garage sale the third weekend in May. She actually enjoyed going through her rooms applying a criterion she'd once read about: "Does this have meaning in my life?" Anything that didn't went into the sale. She was dismayed to discover how full her house was of items that did not meet that standard. She asked Ben to name anything he particularly wanted to keep. "You know my stuff," he said. "Sell any of the rest." She saved his tools, his golf clubs, and tennis racket, but she put all the boxes from the basement in the sale.

Katrinka brought over additional merchandise. They sat in tennis visors, sipping tea and cracking jokes. Watching your possessions disappear into other peoples' trucks could be hilarious, Margaret discovered, when shared with a friend.

Katrinka noticed that items put in a certain spot invariably sold. She named it "our sweet spot" and kept it full of things that were getting overlooked.

"How did you get Ben to agree to those?" she asked when she noticed the array of his boxes. "Hal has stuff like that, but if I tried to sell it, he'd divorce me."

"Ben already divorced me." That wasn't the way Margaret had planned to announce it, but Miss Manners didn't have a chapter on "How to Tell Your Best Friend Your Husband Has Left."

"He didn't!" Katrinka's shocked eyes were large as tennis balls.

"Yes, he did. Last month."

"Let's sell those babies." Katrinka lugged the boxes to the sweet spot. They left in the next truck.

Margaret put the folded bills in her pocket. "I'll keep this for Ben. They were his things."

"If he complains," Katrinka suggested, "say, 'So, divorce me!'" They laughed like teenagers.

Toward the end of the sale, a woman climbed out of a black Lexus. "Am I too late?"

"Oh, no," they assured her. "Everything's half price by now."

As she paid for a table lamp, she said, "You have a beautiful place here."

Margaret felt giddy from sunshine, the sweet release of laughter, and the growing pile of money in her cookie tin. "You don't want to buy it, do you?" she quipped.

"Are you serious? My daughter's husband is being transferred here from California, and they have two precious children. This looks like a wonderful place for children." She looked over the yard like she was picturing her grandchildren there.

Margaret's body went numb. She managed a wan smile. "Have her stop by when they come to town."

"They're in town, scouting places out. Could they come this evening?"

"This evening? The place is a mess. I've been getting ready for this sale. . . ."

"They won't care. Can they come around seven?" With no notion she was bludgeoning Margaret with a sandbag, the woman practically skipped to her car. "I cannot believe how lucky this was," she called as she left. "I almost didn't stop."

"You never said you were selling the house," whispered Katrinka, appalled.

Margaret crumpled onto the card table, weeping.

Katrinka was wise enough to hold her without saying another word.

THE COUPLE FROM CALIFORNIA LOVED the house and loved the yard. They immediately accepted the asking price. "When can we close?" the husband asked. "Soon, I hope. We have cash."

Margaret felt like a condemned prisoner discussing her execution date. "I need to stay until the boys finish school."

They reluctantly agreed she could remain in the house until the Friday after Memorial Day. As the couple walked down the front walk, she heard the husband boast, "Compared to housing prices in California, this place is a steal!"

Her boys were furious, and predictably, they blamed her. "You are selling our house?" Jason screeched.

"Where will we live?" Andy's face was pale with worry.

She wanted to tell them it was their father's fault—that she was hurting as much as they were—but she knew they would not believe her. What fairy dust had Ben spread over them to convince them she was the villain in their family drama?

"We'll find a place," she promised, hoping it was true.

After the mortgage and home-equity loan were paid, Ben and Margaret each received a check for five thousand dollars. In the past twelve years, Margaret had earned four hundred and sixteen dollars a year for pouring herself into her house, her yard, and her family.

When Ben came with a truck to remove things he was taking from the house, he loped down from the bedroom with his old helpless look. "I need some help here, Margaret. You didn't sell some of my summer clothes in that garage sale, did you?"

"I didn't sell any clothes."

"I'm missing some. Do you know where they are?"

She kept stirring spaghetti sauce for supper. "I don't wear your clothes, Ben."

He wrinkled his forehead. "Maybe I took them over to my place already."

Ten minutes later he yelled from the basement, "Where are the boxes that were on the shelves down here?"

"I did sell those," she called back. "You didn't say to keep them."

He stomped up the stairs, enraged. "I spent years collecting that stuff! Do you have any idea what it was worth?"

"As a matter of fact, I do." From a desk drawer she brought out an envelope. "Since they were yours, I kept the money separate for you." The envelope contained twelve dollars.

As she went back to her spaghetti sauce, she hoped he'd choke on rage.

But when Ben had taken his fury home, she grieved her way through the house, haunted by memories—except she was the ghost, trapped between her past and her future.

What future?

She and the boys had a week in which to move, and nowhere to go. She had used a library computer one afternoon to price three-bedroom apartments and houses in their school district. She couldn't afford them. When she'd tried to expand her search to neighborhoods she might be able to afford, she'd floundered through sites not knowing how to evaluate schools or surrounding communities. She would need weeks to find a place.

I ought to die, she thought. *If I died, none of this would matter.*

That was followed by a second thought. *I could go far, far away.*

Where could she go with so little money?

You could go to the farm.

Where did that come from?

It would never work. Daddy and I fight all the time, he'd work us all to death, and if he found out Ben's left, he'd start harping about how I ought to have finished college before I got married. Besides, after all the things I've said about Porter, I'd be ashamed for Billie to know I'm in the same fix she is.

But where else could she go? She found herself remembering Robert Frost's poem about the hired hand, and how home is the place where they have to take you in.

The idea started as a seed that evening, germinated overnight, and by morning had sprouted into a possibility. "Boys?" she asked as they ate their cereal. "How would you like to spend the summer on Papa's farm?"

"Bummer," said Jason.

Andy's eyes lit up. "Could I milk the cows and feed the chickens?"

"I'm sure you could." If she knew her daddy, both boys would do a lot more than that.

"Oh, boy!" Andy bent to fondle MacTavish. "Hear that, boy? We're going to a farm!"

"I'm sorry, but Mac will have to stay here with your dad. Papa has a big dog named Jimbo, remember? He might not like having a little one around."

That saddened Andy for a minute, but his big heart won out. "Daddy will be lonely without us. Mac can keep him company."

Margaret waited to call until after milking time, and she decided still not to say anything about Ben. She could not bear to listen all summer to her father saying, "I told you so."

"Dad, could the boys and I come spend the summer with you?"

"A bit sudden, isn't it?"

She couldn't afford to argue with him like she usually did. "Yeah, but Andy's been peaky lately. I think the fresh air would do him good." Silence filled the line. "He's looking forward to feeding chickens and the hogs. He's never spent a night out there, you know."

Her dad spoke slowly, testing each word. "I think that would be all right."

"I didn't expect enthusiasm," she muttered as she hung up, "but it would have been nice."

MARGARET DECIDED TO PUT EVERYTHING in storage for the summer except clothes she and the boys would need at the farm. She could come back to Marietta a day or two each week to look for a job and a place to live, and move before school started.

On the Tuesday before the movers were due on Friday, Ben took Andy and Jason to dinner. Margaret walked through the house with rising panic as she saw what still had to be done. Jason hadn't started on his room. "I will not do this for him," she said grimly. "It is time he grew up."

She woke him at nine Wednesday morning. "You need to start packing, Jase."

"I'm tired." He turned over, wearing what had become his usual balky face.

"We pack two more days; then we go to the farm. Shall I help you in here and you help me with books? Packing together might be fun."

"Fun? You think doing anything with you is *fun*?" He pulled the covers over his head.

She refused to let him get away with that. She picked up a pile of clothes from his desk chair (clean? dirty? she didn't ask) and held them on her lap as she sat. "Look, I know you are unhappy with what's happened between your dad and me—"

"Unhappy?" His voice was muffled by covers. "You ruin our lives and you think we're unhappy?"

"I did not ruin your lives." She spoke slowly, emphasizing every word. "I did not know your dad was leaving until he did. I never wanted him to go. As far as I knew, things were fine."

"As far as *you* knew." His voice cracked on the pronoun.

"What does that mean?"

"Only that Dad took some blonde—probably Bayonne—to dinner in downtown Atlanta a month before he left. You ought to have known."

Margaret was shocked speechless.

Jason took her silence for denial. "He *did*. Curtis was having dinner with his dad and saw Dad with her over in a corner. They were holding hands and kissing."

Margaret wanted to scream, throw something, pass a law that divorced blondes were not allowed to prowl the world looking for other women's husbands. With difficulty she controlled her voice. "Is that why you hit Curtis?"

She presumed the convulsion under the cover was Jason nodding.

"Did you tell your dad why you fought that afternoon when he came up here?"

Another nod.

"What did he say?"

"He started all innocent-like. 'Son, what's the matter?' And I went,

'Like you don't know.' And he went, 'Of course I don't know. What's the matter with you?' And I went, 'What's the matter with *me*? What's the matter with *you*? Curtis saw you, Dad. He saw you downtown having dinner with a blonde with boobs out to here.' Then Dad gave a fake laugh and went, "Oh, son—that was business.' Like I'm that dumb. So I went, 'Don't give me that. He saw you holding her hand and kissing her and everything.'"

Her child should never have heard that about his father. Margaret felt physically ill. She wanted to run to the bathroom and lose her breakfast, but Jason flopped over and showed Margaret a tearstained face for an instant before he pulled the covers back over his head.

"Oh, honey, I'm sorry you had to go through that," she said, laying a hand on his shoulder. "What did your daddy say then?"

"I called him a bastard and he hit me. Like *I'd* done something wrong. Then he started crying and he went, 'Oh, Jase, I am so sorry.' And I went, 'Sorry that you did it, or sorry that you got caught?' And he said a lot of stuff about how he knew it was wrong and it wouldn't happen again, but he'd been worried about the business and you wouldn't talk about it. You were too busy with all your stuff to have time for him." The hardness was back in Jason's voice.

"Me? He blamed me?"

He threw off the covers and glared at her. "Why not? I mean, it's not like you have a job or ever do anything interesting. All you talk about is kids, or tennis, or the yard." He looked at his bare toes rather than at his mother. "And you nag, nag, nag all the time. I'd leave, too, if my wife was that bossy and boring."

Margaret flung the lapful of clothes at him. "You wretch! You know good and well your father never did anything around here unless he was reminded three times. And I never had a job because *he* wanted his wife home with his children. I will not have you blaming me for his sins! Nothing I ever did to him equals the pain he is causing all of us."

His eyes smoldered. "Get out of my room, please."

Her rage spent, she stood. "No matter what he did or I did, you still have to pack this room today. Put what you want to take to the farm in a duffel bag and the rest in boxes. You'll find boxes in the den." She closed the door firmly as she left.

Andy stood in the hall, his face so white that his freckles stood out like little orange dots. "Is Jason leaving, too?"

She bent down and hugged him. "No, honey. Jason's mad, but he's not leaving. He's part of our family."

"Daddy was part of the family and he left."

"Jason's not going anywhere."

"Promise?"

"I promise. Let's get you some breakfast."

Some promises are hard to keep.

THE MOTHER OF ONE OF Andy's friends called to invite him to spend two days with them at their lake house. "We've moved several times, and believe me—you don't want a six-year-old underfoot these next two days."

Margaret was so grateful that she stammered her thanks. She was discovering that true friends were those who gave the help you needed most. Maybe when she and Jason were alone, they could regain some of the affection they used to have for each other.

She called upstairs to say she was driving Andy to a friend's. When she got back, she called up again. "Jase? I'm going out in the yard to work a while." She got no answer, but she hadn't expected one. She fed roses and clipped a few dead canes, saying good-bye to her beloved plants one by one.

She was kneeling on a mat, secateurs in hand, when a car drove in.

Shading her eyes, she saw it was a police cruiser. Her breath caught in her throat. Had something happened to Andy?

A burly officer climbed out. "Mrs. Baxter?"

"Yes."

He opened the back door. "Is this your son?"

Jason sat with his eyed fixed on his hands, which were clasped in his lap.

She rushed to him. "I thought you were upstairs packing!"

The officer answered for him. "No, ma'am, he and another perpetrator were spraying obscenities all over the walls of an unoccupied suite in that new office park down the road."

Ben had landscaped that park the previous month.

"Jason?"

He still didn't look at her.

The policeman shoved his hat back on his head. "They didn't realize, apparently, that when they came down through a skylight they triggered a silent alarm."

"Who was the other boy?" She peered at the empty seat beside Jason. "Where is he?"

"Jason, here, refuses to say. He ran out the back before we could catch him."

"It was probably Curtis Mays. He's Jason's best friend."

Jason shot her a hard, angry look that told her she was right.

The officer noticed. "Do you have contact information for this Curtis Mays?"

"I can get it for you."

Jason glowered at her betrayal. She glowered back. He had betrayed her as much as she had betrayed him.

"I'll ground him," she told the officer. "It won't happen again."

"It's not quite that easy, ma'am. Since it's a first offense, I'm releasing him to your custody, but he'll have to appear before a judge Thursday at two."

"I've got movers coming Friday morning!"

"I'm sorry, ma'am. Here's the information." He handed her a piece of paper. "You know where juvenile court is?"

She shoved the paper into a pocket. "No, I've never needed that information."

He gave directions as he reached a hand to help Jason out. "You stay home, son, until you've talked with the judge. And stay out of trouble. Your mama doesn't need this."

She certainly didn't. She ordered Jason to his room—a fruitless exercise since he was halfway up the stairs—and told him to start packing. Then she called Ben. "Jason's been arrested. The police just brought him home. He was painting foul words on the walls of that office park up the road that you landscaped last month."

Ben swore. "Where were you when it happened?"

"I guess he left while I was driving Andy over to Michael's. I thought he was upstairs packing when I got back. The point is, it happened, and he has to go to court tomorrow at two. We both need to be there."

"I don't know if I . . ."

"Be there, Ben!"

"Will you be civil?"

"I'm more civil than you are. I don't walk out on my responsibilities."

"It's remarks like that I'm talking about. We'll need to show a united front at court. I don't want any sniping or rude remarks."

She still held the secateurs. She slammed the points so hard on the granite countertop that they drew a small spark. "My days of caring what you want are over."

WHEN BEN SAT BESIDE HER in the courtroom, he looked smaller than he used to. *Unkindness and selfishness have diminished him*, she thought with sadness. Or was it immorality?

Jason was sullen and monosyllabic, but gradually the judge got the story: Ben's leaving, Jason's fury, his desire to hurt his father by vandalizing the building he'd landscaped.

"No matter how angry you are, you cannot destroy other people's property," the judge pointed out. He sentenced Jason to probation and community service.

Margaret was about to ask whether Jason could do his community service in her father's county when the judge asked, in a kinder tone, "Son, what could we do to help you not get into trouble again?"

"Send me to live with my dad. I don't want to live with her." Jason made the pronoun sound like one of the obscenities he had sprayed on the wall.

All eyes in court turned to stare. Margaret felt like she had been doused with ice water. *I am a fit mother! I have done nothing to hurt this child! It is his father he is furious with!*

Her throat was too tight to speak.

The judge addressed Ben. "Mr. Baxter, is that acceptable to you? Are you willing for him to live with you?"

"Uh—well, Your Honor—"

As Ben squirmed, Margaret wanted to cheer. No more love nest, Benny boy. No more king-sized bed with steamy black sheets. See how you like riding herd on an angry teenager for a while. But all the time her heart was shrieking, *Jason! Not Jason! Please, don't take my son!*

Jason didn't take his eyes off Ben until Ben nodded. "Sure, Your Honor. He can live with me. I'll move his things over today."

Margaret leaped to her feet. "You can't take my child! Please, Judge—"

Ben hauled her down as the judge said, "I'm sorry, Mrs. Baxter, but Jason is old enough to choose which parent he lives with." He called the next case.

Outside the courtroom, Margaret grabbed Jason's arm. "How could you?"

He jerked it away. "Come on, Dad. I need to pick up my things before we go home." The last word, spoken with deliberate intent and emphasis, ripped Margaret from head to toe. She forgot how to breathe.

She would never remember going to her car, starting the engine, or driving away. She had no idea how long she drove around. The next thing she knew it was twilight, and she lay on her living room couch in a fetal position, groaning, "Oh, God, oh, God, oh, God."

She pushed herself upright and shoved her fingers through her hair. "How can a judge take a child from his mother with no warning? How could Jason do this to me? How could Ben?"

She went upstairs to prove to herself that the whole nightmare was not true.

Jason's room had been stripped of clothes, track trophies, and music. One bed and his chest were gone. Bare walls gaped where posters once hung. But childhood books, dirty clothes and trash littered the floor.

Tears came in such a torrent that a distant part of her mind wondered how she had so many. "I cannot bear this," she gasped again and again. "I cannot. Help me. Help me." She fell to her knees.

She buried her nose in a discarded shirt, inhaling Jason's scent. It was musty, familiar, beloved. "I gave my life to him!" she wept. "And he left me!"

She sobbed until she had no tears left. She wanted to die, sink into oblivion where there was no love and no pain.

Exhausted, she slid from kneeling to sit cross-legged beside the window. Salt from her tears stretched the skin of her cheeks. "I could use a knife to slit my wrists," she thought. "I could take all the pills in the medicine cabinet and go to sleep. I could . . ."

The house was utterly still, filled with a silence that seemed bigger than the space inside the walls. It seeped into her spirit until she felt within her the stirring of that incomprehensible urge that wills people to choose life in the hardest of times. She spoke aloud, slowly, stating her case to that vast silence. "I gave my life to them both and they have left me."

The silence waited for more. Fumbling, she explored the thought. "What life do I have without them?"

Again the silence waited.

"Was Ben right? Did I smother them and call it love?"

Still the silence waited.

"Did I give them too much? Did I make them gods?"

That thought startled her, but in the mind's eye where memory dwells, Margaret saw her mother's face one morning when she, an eighth grader, asked Grace to drive her to Douglasville that afternoon to a one-day fabric sale. "I can't. I have math club after school." Grace spoke as if the matter was obvious.

"But I'm your daughter," Margaret had protested.

Grace gathered up her books. "Daughter doesn't equal center of the universe. I have a life, too, you know." She dropped a kiss on Margaret's forehead and left.

As Margaret had stomped off to catch her bus, she made a vow: "When I grow up, my family will come before anybody else."

Remembering that morning, she marveled aloud, "My entire grown-up life has been built on vows I made as a child. The way I furnished my house, the way I treated my family—I have lived a childish life."

And Ben? Had she loved him, or only what he represented?

I didn't marry him for money or status. I loved him! I still do.

That searing silence demanded honesty.

But I do not know if I would have loved him if he hadn't come from the kind of life I wanted.

She caught her reflection in the full-length mirror on Jason's closet door. "Who are you?" she asked herself, her voice hoarse with tears. "What do you really want?"

The silence waited.

"Who are *you*?" she asked it. "What do you want from me?"

The silence was as deep as ever, but a shaft from the sinking sun pierced a crack in Jason's blind and made a small bar of light on the dark carpet. To Margaret, it was a line drawn between her past and her future.

She climbed to her feet and stepped over the bar. "I am more than Ben Baxter's wife and Jason Baxter's mother. I don't know who I am or what I was made to be, but I am going to find out."

PART THREE

Barren Thunder

*"There is a special place in hell for women
who won't help other women."*

—Madeleine Albright

Eighteen

Whoever decided summer arrives on June twenty-first did not live in Georgia. Here, summer strides in hot on the heels of spring. May is warm, scented with honeysuckle. Yards exchange pansies for scarlet impatiens, hot pink petunias, and bronzed red begonias. By June, we are well into summer and air-conditioning bills have arrived.

That's what happens in normal years.

In that second summer of the worst drought on record, nothing was normal except the hum of air conditioners—for those who had them. I didn't. By late May the state sweltered under what meteorologists called a heat wave, but it was more like a tsunami—blast after blast of relentless hot air pounding us day after day. I had two fans that I moved to the living room each morning and to our bedrooms at night. They did little more than stir the heavy air like batter.

Outdoor watering was banned even for those of us with wells. Green grass alerted neighbors to call the water police. Water barrels that provident souls had stationed at downspouts were full of spiders. Pastures were tan, crops as sparse as an old woman's hair. Migrants roamed the state looking for farmwork, but nobody was hiring.

I was bone tired. After putting in eight hours at the garage, I worked in my garden, spent time with Chellie until she went to bed, and studied auto-repair manuals until my vision blurred. Instead of sleeping, I lay awake remembering what I'd said to Luke the last time I'd seen him, and playing out scenes in my head in which I said nicer things. I wasn't likely to get another chance. I ran into him one lunch hour, and after he said, "Hey, Mina," he turned away. My spirit felt as dry as my front yard. Drier, since I carried our bathwater and dishwater out to my flowers.

Legal or not, I got up before dawn once a week to give my vegetable garden a good soaking with the hose. Those vegetables needed water, and we needed the vegetables. Since I was not by nature a lawbreaker, I imagined I was speaking to Tee while I watered. "Please don't put me in jail. Chellie needs me."

Daddy stopped by on the Tuesday after Memorial Day, Jimbo at his heels. He looked drawn, his eyes in a permanent squint as if he'd been worrying over his pastures. "You suffering a lot with this drought?" I asked.

"No more than other fellahs." I should have known better than to ask—Daddy never complained. But the way he bent and fondled Jimbo's ears, I suspected he gave the dog an earful when Jimbo lay beside his recliner in the evenings. Daddy loved that ugly dog.

He handed me my milk. "I stopped by to welcome your new neighbors. The place looks real nice. What did you do with your old furniture?"

"I took the couch and chairs to the dump and stored the beds and chests in my shed. And don't tell me there was any good left in that couch and chairs, because there wasn't."

"Don't jump down my throat, girl. I wasn't telling you a dadgum thing. I was fixing to ask can I borrow a bed." I was trying to absorb that Daddy was asking a favor instead of criticizing me when he blew my socks off. "Maggie and the boys are coming Friday for a visit, so I need another one."

"They're spending the night?" I couldn't remember the last time she'd spent a night.

"Sure are. Gonna stay a while."

I blinked. Not only was Margaret coming for a visit, but Daddy sounded happy about it? As long as I could remember, they had been at loggerheads. When I was little, they had fought about how many chores Maggie had to do. When I was eight, they had fought about which boys she could date and how late she could stay out. They'd had a royal battle over where she'd go to college. Daddy wanted her to live at home her first two years and go to the nearby community college. Maggie was determined to get out of Solace. Their ultimate showdown had been over her marrying Ben and quitting school. Mama wore herself thin convincing Daddy to attend the ceremony. He flat-out refused to walk Margaret down the aisle. After Jason was born, when Margaret used to bring him out for a week, Daddy had played with Jason while Margaret spent her time with Mama and me. They had pretty much ignored each other. In the year since Mama had died, the only visit Margaret had made to Solace was when she, Jason, and Andy drove out for a couple of hours on Christmas Eve to bring us presents. Even that afternoon she and Daddy had sniped at each other. Now she was coming home for a visit? "To what do we owe this honor?"

"She said Andy's been peaky this spring, and he's begging to come. He's never been here much. I told her to bring him on so he can get some good fresh air." The way Daddy said "good fresh air," you'd have thought everybody in Marietta went around in gas masks. "I'll give the boys your room, and let her have the sewing room."

That would be a comedown from Princess Margaret's beautiful bedroom. So would sharing one bathroom with three other people.

"You can have Chellie's old bed," I told Daddy, "but I threw out the mattress."

"I'll get a new mattress."

"You'd better take the chest, too. Maggie will need it. How long will she be here?"

"She said Ben's so busy, she may stay most of the summer. I told her she can do my canning if she does."

I might have a good imagination, but I couldn't imagine Margaret staying in Solace for three months. I certainly couldn't see her doing Daddy's canning. She'd hated helping Mama can when she'd lived at home.

If I'd had anybody to bet with, I'd have fattened my wallet by wagering she wouldn't last three weeks. Instead I told Daddy, "Come get the furniture tomorrow after I get home from work, and I'll help you carry it upstairs. I can stay and make the beds, too. Stamps might even let me off early Friday so I can cook supper."

"I can carry a bed and a chest upstairs. I'm not decrepit. And Mamie will make the beds and bake a ham. All you and Chellie have to do is come eat with us around eight."

He didn't eat late because he was cultured. He ate late because he started his evening milking at five, and it took him that long to finish plus clean up the milking barn afterward. He ate breakfast at eight each morning for the same reason. A dairy farmer easily worked fifteen hour days.

Daddy's life was simpler now, because he only had fifty cows. When we were home, he'd had over a hundred, and nobody knew what time we'd have supper. Mama once said if she ever left Daddy, it would be because she never knew when he'd be in for a meal.

Instead, she left him because she got too sick to live. As he drove away, his elbow cocked out one window and Jimbo's head out the other, I watched him go with mixed feelings. We hadn't eaten together as a family since Mama had died. What would it be like to sit around the table without her?

I would let Michelle wear her pretty dress—the peach one Margaret had made. I'd wear my best jeans and try to get the motor oil from underneath my nails. Margaret was sure to be beautifully dressed. I wished I had at least one outfit nicer than jeans.

MARGARET ADMITTED TO ME LATER that her hands were shaking by the time she got within ten miles of Solace. *I was afraid of so many things. That Daddy and I would fight all summer. That I couldn't stand being in the country again. That you and Daddy would find out Ben had divorced me. I had warned Andy we were not to say anything about that, but the way he chatters, I wasn't sure I could trust him."*

Andy chattered the entire trip, asking so many questions about the farm and his granddaddy, whom he had seldom seen, that Margaret finally declared a Silent Trip. When they came over the last rise, though, she felt a physical pull to stop and get out.

She took deep breaths of air scented with cattle and fresh grass. "All this is Papa's farm," she told Andy when he joined her. She stretched her arms wide. "Everything you see."

He looked at grassy pastures rising to the tops of rounded hills. "Wow! He's rich!"

"He's not rich, he just has a lot of land and cows. Those are some of his cows over there." She pointed to twenty Jersey cows grazing up a hill. "And that is his hayfield, where he grows grass to feed them. The red hay barn down the hill there, way behind the house, is where he stores the hay, and the white building next to it, with the big truck outside it, is the milking barn."

"I know. I saw Papa milk on Christmas Eve. The cows don't live there, they just go in to be milked twelve at a time. Is that silver thing where Papa keeps the milk?"

"No, that's the silo, where he stores more food. The milk is pumped through hoses into a cooling tank in the milking barn. That truck you see with the big tank on its back comes twice a week to pick up the milk. Papa will show you how it works." It all came back to her in a rush—opening the gate to let cows come in under the shade roof while they waited to be milked, the soft feel of their sides brushing against her, watching a long line of cows stroll back to pasture after being milked. The warm smell of cow manure and the soft lowing of contented cows. *The cows were a lot more content than I was.*

Andy sighed. "It sure is beautiful."

She considered the view with surprise. "I guess so. I never noticed before."

FOR ME, PULLING INTO DADDY's gravel drive that evening seemed both odd and familiar. "For somebody who lives just down the road, you sure are a stranger here," I muttered to myself as I climbed down from the truck.

When I saw Andy fly out the back door to greet us, I knew that whatever reason Margaret had for coming, it wasn't because he was peaky. A healthier child would be hard to imagine. His face glowed as he hurled himself down the steps shouting, "Chellie!" Her chair was too hard for him to push on the gravel drive, but he walked alongside, chattering all the way. "Isn't Papa's farm beautiful? I got to watch him milk the cows. He puts funny things on them, and it pulls out the milk. He's got a big dog, too, named Jimbo. Did you know that?"

At the steps, he helped pull Chellie, chair and all, up the three steps. He carried more of the weight than I would have expected for a boy his age.

Margaret stood on the porch like she was welcoming us to a country club. She wore powder blue slacks, a white tank top, a white voile overshirt embroidered in colorful butterflies, and silver jewelry with blue stones. She even wore a powder blue belt with a butterfly buckle and powder blue sandals.

"Chellie!" She cooed like society women do over in "May-retta." She bent down and kissed Michelle in her chair. "And Billie!" We exchanged a quick, obligatory hug. Her cheek smelled expensive. "Can you believe we've finally come for a real visit?"

"Sure can't, but welcome. I like your sandals. I didn't know they made blue cows."

She stuck out a foot. "Yep, just for me." Her laugh was high and brittle.

Her cheeks were pink with blusher, her lipstick as bright as her fingernails, but she was pale under the makeup. She must have been dieting, too. I looked her up and down and said, "You are skinny as a fishing pole."

"You silly thing!" She held the screen door and waved me inside. "I've lost a couple of pounds, but I'll soon fatten up with Mamie's good cooking. It feels like heaven to get here."

"Close that door! You're letting in flies," Daddy called from his recliner in the den.

Margaret let the screen door slam. "Heaven forbid that having both daughters under his roof for the first time in six months should interfere with his evening news."

"I'm not gonna pick up Mama's role as peacemaker between you two," I warned. "If you're gonna snipe at each other the whole evening, Chellie and I will leave now." On the other hand, I smelled baked ham, sweet potatoes, and collard greens. Maybe supper would be worth the warfare.

"We'll be okay. I'd just forgotten what a fusspot he can be." She laughed again, but the laugh didn't reach her eyes.

Andy tugged my shirttail. "Aunt Billie, did you know that while we're on the farm I'm gonna feed chickens and pigs and learn to milk the cows?"

"You'll be a big help to Papa." I knelt to give him a hug. Andy was a very huggable child. He was also the spitting image of Ben. I'd always been surprised that Margaret had named him for Daddy—William Anderson Baxter.

Andy grabbed Chellie's chair handles. "Can Chellie play cars with me? We are cousins, you know." He sounded like it connoted a royal relationship. When I nodded, he wheeled her up to the kitchen table and produced two little cars from a pocket. Chellie had a hard time clutching one, but I saw he was patient about helping her.

"Hey, Daddy," I called toward the den. He was too busy watching TV to answer.

A fly buzzed over our heads. Margaret fetched the swatter from the pantry door, where it had hung all our lives. "Where's Jason?" I asked while she waited for the fly to land. I was surprised he hadn't come to greet us. I was only thirteen years older than he, so we'd been buddies since he could walk and talk.

The fly landed on the table. Margaret smacked it with enough force to kill ten flies before she answered. "He's going to summer school, so he had to stay home with Ben."

I huffed before I remembered to be polite. "I wish you'd told Daddy he wasn't coming. He didn't need to lug a bed and a chest up those steep stairs." I raised my voice again. "Daddy, did you get a mattress for the single bed? Do we need to carry it up?"

"I carried it up this morning. But we don't need it. Jason's not coming."

"So I heard."

I lowered my voice. "What did he have to make up? Or is he taking an extra class to impress college-admissions officers?"

Chasing another fly near the sink, she answered with her back to me, "He flunked math, but it wasn't his fault." The way she whacked that fly, I suspected she wished it was Jason's math teacher. She set the swatter on the table and asked with the ghost of her old smile, "Did you notice I haven't lost my champion fly-killing abilities?"

"I noticed those flies died horrible deaths."

She brushed the one off the table into her palm and looked at its mangled remains. "I did hit them hard, didn't I?"

"Too much competitive tennis."

"Must be." She let the fly roll off her palm into the trash and washed her hands before joining me at the kitchen table.

The dining room table was where we studied and played family games, but the kitchen table was where we always sat to chat—me and Mama, Maggie and Mama, Daddy and Mama, even occasionally me and Maggie. We sat down there as naturally as breathing. But the next few minutes could have served for a dialogue in an ESOL class on how to talk to strangers.

"Are you doing all right?" "Fine. You?" "I'm fine. Did your roses survive the drought?" "Bloomed better than ever, for some reason. How about your dogwoods?" "They were gorgeous. Did the boys play sports?" "Andy played ball and Jason ran track. What have you been doing with yourself?" "Same old same old. Therapy with Chellie. Working in the yard. Have you played much tennis?" "Oh, yes. Katrinka and I finally beat that Dunwoody team we've lost to the past couple of years."

I seized on a subject I was really interested in. "How is Katrinka?"

"She's fine. We had a garage sale together a few weeks ago. It was lots of fun."

I liked Katrinka. When she used to visit the farm, she brought me Cracker Jacks and toys her sister had outgrown. She read stories before my bedtime and played paper dolls. Even after she and Margaret went to college, she would call sometimes to see how I was doing, and she brought her new husband to watch my high school championship game. (Maggie and Ben had had something else to do that night.) She still sent me a big can of caramel corn every Christmas.

Margaret, on the other hand, had resented my tagging along after them. A story Daddy found hilarious and told anybody who would listen was that when he and Mama informed Margaret she was having a baby sister, she had replied, "I'd rather have a pony." But whenever Maggie got annoyed with me for tagging after her and Katrinka, she would mutter, just loud enough for me to hear, "I'd still rather have a pony." Given that I'd grown up to become a nonachiever who didn't fit her definition of success, she might still rather have a pony.

What I wished was that she would accept me as I was. I wasn't ever going to be like her, but I was a grown-up. I wished we could talk like sisters—she would tell me the real reason she came to Solace, and I would confide my mixed-up feelings for Luke when I was still married to Porter. That conversation was about as likely as the possibility that Chellie would step out of her chair and quote Shakespeare so everybody could understand her.

Margaret and I fell silent, having run out of chitchat.

"I ov I dess," Chellie contributed, trying to stroke her bodice.

I could tell Margaret didn't understand a word. "She sure *does* love that dress," I said, trying to tactfully translate. "She liked everything you sent, but she'd wear the dress every day if I'd let her. It is gorgeous. You didn't embroider those flowers, did you?"

Margaret's eyes flickered toward the dress, then looked away. "No. But I'm glad you like it, honey." She gave Chellie the ghost of her usual smile.

We seemed to have exhausted every other subject, so I asked, "What's Ben up to?"

Andy started to speak, but Margaret held up a hand. "Don't interrupt grown-ups, honey." To me, she said, "He's fine. Busy in the summer, of course."

We fell silent again.

When we all used to live at home, supper talk had been about homework, chores, and community affairs. Since I'd been married, we sisters had seldom talked without Mama there to steer the conversation. I sorely missed Mama. I suspected Margaret did, too.

"Shall I set the table?" I asked. Nobody else seemed to be doing it.

"We're eating in the dining room on Mama's wedding china. It was Daddy's idea."

Daddy kept the dining room blinds closed when he watched television, and the room was so dim, I had missed Mamie moving around the table, taking care not to step on Jimbo's tail.

"Hey, Mamie," I called in to her, "how you doing?"

"Keeping on keeping on."

"That's good."

She lumbered in and headed to the stove. "How you liking your new job?" She took out a pan of biscuits while I answered.

"Real good, so far."

"You have a job?" Margaret, swatter poised again, was keeping an eye on another fly.

"I sure do. I'm working for Stamps Foxworthy over at the garage."

"Doing what?" She abandoned the fly for a second to pretend to be interested.

I hated to tell her. Margaret the Fastidious was sure to wrinkle her nose. "Fixing cars. I did a brake job this afternoon." I waited for her to prick my balloon. Wait for it. . . . Wait for it. . . .

"You're lucky to have an employable skill in this economy." She sounded—what? Surely not envious. I was so surprised, I almost missed her question. "Who keeps Michelle?"

"A girl named Bethany. Which reminds me. Mamie?" I asked as she trudged back toward the dining room with the ham. "Could you possibly keep Chellie next week? Bethany is going to the beach to celebrate high school graduation. I wouldn't ask you, but I'm getting desperate."

"I can't, Billie. I told you, I can't lift her."

I sighed. "It was worth a try. Could you, Margaret? I hate to fill up your vacation, but it's just for a week."

Her eyes slid to Chellie and back. "Let's talk about it later."

Margaret demolished three flies while Mamie carried in supper. Mama would have made us help, but I was bone tired from work. Working steadily for hours took some getting used to.

Margaret excused herself to run upstairs before supper, which gave me time to sidle over to Mamie and murmur, "Are you and Lurleen speaking yet?"

"I called her a couple of times, but Skeeter said she was busy. She's mad at me, Billie, and there doesn't seem to be a thing I can do about it." She untied her apron as Margaret returned. "Supper's served. I'm gonna let you girls do the dishes."

MAMIE TRUDGED WHAT SEEMED LIKE the distance across Africa before she reached her car. Her ankles were swollen so tight they itched, and she was so tired she could hardly drag one foot in front of the other. Those girls! Sitting there like queens while she carried all that food.

After a hard day finishing up the cleaning. And cooking that enormous supper. Not to mention wrestling the mattress upstairs with Bill.

You should have told him you have a bad heart, her conscience reminded her.

I don't want him to know. He'd probably send me home for good.

Mamie didn't like sitting at home. Dark corners crept toward her. The closer she got to death, the more fiercely she wanted to live.

WE GROWN-UPS WERE SO QUIET at supper that the children caught the chill. After a few minutes of unimportant chatting, I don't think we said a word except "Please pass . . ." the rest of the meal until Daddy shoved back his chair. "Mamie forgot to put the syrup on the table. Can't eat biscuits without syrup." He headed for the kitchen.

"I'm gonna feed chickens and pigs and milk cows," Andy announced for the second time. "Mama promised."

"You're gonna do more than that if you're here a while," his granddaddy warned, setting a half-full bottle of cane syrup on the table. "I've got a garden needs some hoeing, young man."

"He's never used a hoe," Margaret objected.

"High time he learned." Daddy reached for a biscuit and covered it with syrup.

When supper was over, Daddy and the kids settled down to watch television again. I started to clear the table. Margaret went to the sink, looked around the lower cabinets, and demanded, "Hasn't Daddy gotten a dishwasher? Or central air-conditioning? This is ridiculous."

Daddy's place must seem primitive compared to hers. His whole downstairs was cooled—if you could call it that—by a unit in the dining room window. The kitchen got very little of the cool air.

I started stacking dishes by the sink. "You must have forgotten how thrifty Daddy is. He still never buys anything he can do without."

"We added baseboard heaters and wall air conditioners in the two bedrooms upstairs when your mama got sick," Daddy called from the dining room.

"Thank goodness for that," she snapped. "Maybe I'll be able to sleep." When we were growing up, our family had made do with window fans in summer and huddled under thick comforters in winter—like Chellie and I still did. Warm air from Daddy's furnace didn't reach the upstairs, and I couldn't afford to run mine at night.

"Nearly got air-conditioning downstairs last year," Daddy added, "but your mama died before summer arrived."

"You could have gotten it for yourself. And a dishwasher." Margaret started running water into the dishpan and wielded a bottle of Joy like a weapon.

I pushed her aside. "I'll wash. You put away food."

As she scraped leftovers into Jimbo's bowl, I asked softly, "Please, could you take Chellie next week? I hate to beg, but like I told Mamie, I'm desperate."

Margaret slid plates into my dishpan. "I don't know a thing about cerebral palsy. I wouldn't have any idea what to do with her."

That hurt. Margaret had taken on jobs a lot more complicated than watching a handicapped child for a week. "She's no trouble. She stays in her chair unless she's napping. Daddy has a DVD player. She can watch a movie every morning and afternoon. That's four hours. She naps in the afternoon for another two. She could sleep on the daybed in Daddy's front room. You'd only have to play with her a little bit, read her a few books, and give her snacks and lunch." Surely Margaret could help out that much.

"And carry her up to the bathroom?"

"Well, yes. Or you could come over to my house. We don't have an upstairs."

"And feed her?" She had seen me feed Michelle at the table. She knew that was included.

"She can eat some things on her own, but not many."

"I'm sorry, Billie, but no. I've been under a lot of strain lately and I'm plumb worn-out. I can't do it. I'm sorry."

"You sure are. A sorry sister, anyway." I washed a plate so hard I nearly took the flowers off the china.

Margaret grabbed a dish towel to dry with. We finished the dishes in silence.

Daddy called from the dining room again. "Don't throw out that water. There's a bucket on the back porch to put it in. I'll pour it on my garden in the morning. And don't let flies in when you carry out the water."

"I know. I know." I picked up the dishpan. "Would you please open the door, Princess Margaret?" Margaret held the door without a word.

Nineteen

When I woke Saturday morning, my room was still dark. Drowsily I looked at the clock. How could it be nearly eight with the sky so dark? Thunder rumbled in the distance. Thunder? I ran to the porch and met a breeze with a chilly edge to it. I smelled rain. Rain! I sat in the swing to await the storm.

The sky looked dark and bruised. Drumrolls of thunder sounded overhead. Across Daddy's pasture, lightning forked down the sky. The scent of ozone overlaid the scent of rain. As the storm drew nearer, my heart beat like a girl's hoping for her first kiss.

It passed overhead without spilling a drop.

I felt as empty as I used to after sex with Porter. He always finished so fast, I never learned what getting aroused was all about.

I shook my fist at the sky. "Can't you see we need rain down here?" The only answer I got was the mocking rumble of thunder miles away to the east.

Most of the day lived down to its inauspicious beginning. I spent it on the phone, trying to find somebody who could take care of Chellie the following week. I found nobody. If I couldn't find a sitter on Sunday, I'd have to tell Stamps I couldn't come in.

After Chellie went to bed, I needed fresh air, so I sauntered over to the trailer lot to pick blackberries before it got dark. One advantage of living in West Georgia is that we're so close to the central time zone that we have long, light evenings. I found my ladies sitting in lawn chairs, sipping drinks. Verna twisted her wedding ring as she greeted me. "Can I get you a glass of tea?"

"No, thanks. It must be nice to be retired."

"Boring, if you want the truth," Ethelyne told me. "I used to work with Mama all day. Now I hardly know what to do with myself."

Maybe God was finally paying me some attention. "Could you keep my daughter next week? My regular sitter is away, so I'll need somebody for five days. I'll pay you, of course." I didn't want her to think I was taking advantage.

"How about giving us half a month's rent?"

"I can give you a week. That's more than I pay my regular sitter, but you're more experienced than she is."

I expected her to calculate the hourly rate and turn me down. It wasn't minimum wage but I couldn't afford minimum wage. Bethany was giving me a good deal because she wanted me to write a letter of recommendation for her later.

Instead, Ethelyne broke into a smile that showed big white teeth so even they had to be false. "Why, honey, I'll be glad to." I suspected they wouldn't do much except watch television, but at least my child would be safe and fed. How many working mothers take comfort in that thought every night?

Verna smacked a mosquito on her arm. "Sissy, we'd better go in."

I went to pick berries, more worried about snakes than mosquitoes. I shouldn't have worried about either. There wasn't a berry left on the briars. Surely birds hadn't eaten them all. Bushes along the roadsides still had berries. My ladies must have figured blackberries were included in their rent.

DADDY STOPPED BY THE GARAGE Tuesday afternoon. "Mamie's cooking enough over at my place for an army. Come get your milk and stay to eat."

I knew I'd be exhausted, but he sounded like he really wanted us. "Is Princess Margaret's company wearing thin? Has she gotten around to redecorating your place yet or called the air-conditioning company?"

"Watch your mouth, girl." But he was smiling. "We'll see you around eight."

I dreaded seeing Margaret. I knew I'd been rude and ought to apologize, but I seethed that she'd been so quick to reject my child. We greeted each other like casual acquaintances, pretending Friday hadn't happened. I tried not to be jealous of the red sundress she wore. *She made it,* I told myself. It looked like it had cost more than I earned in a day.

As soon as we'd said, "Hello," she exclaimed, "Oh! Let me carry these up." As she grabbed some plastic bags and headed for the stairs, her cell phone rang in her pocket. "She went to Wal-Mart this afternoon," Mamie confided. She was finishing gravy over at the stove. The way her shoulders slumped, she was as tired as I.

I took the whisk and edged her away. "Margaret Baxter shopping at Wal-Mart? What is the world coming to?"

Mamie bumped me away from the stove with her hip. "Give me that whisk. You never could get lumps out of gravy. Set the kitchen table if you want to be useful."

"Let me run up to the bathroom first."

I did not intend to overhear Margaret, but Daddy's walls were thin, and she was in the sewing room next door. I thought she was talking to herself until I heard, "Don't pull that. You don't need my help, remember?" Pause. "I would love to talk to Jason, but I doubt he'd listen." She took a breath so sharp I heard it. "Has he said he'd like to?" Another pause. "I know he can be moody—he's a teenager. And I know how busy you are. But . . ." She must have been pacing, because I caught only snatches of the next sentence. ". . . expect me . . . all your problems." Her voice rose in irritation. "You asked for this, so deal with it!"

I hurried to get back downstairs before her so she wouldn't know I'd overheard. Their conversation disturbed me. I had never known Margaret and Ben to quarrel. Was that why she had come to the farm? To give them time to get over a fight? Given the mood she was in the day she arrived, I didn't blame Ben if he'd suggested she head to Solace for a while.

She didn't mention the call when she came down, but she rapidly dispatched five flies.

AFTER MAMIE TRUDGED TO HER car, I said to Margaret, "I don't know whether to tell you this or not—it was a confidence—but Lurleen says Mamie's doctor has told her to avoid stress."

"She's certainly doing that. She moves as slow as molasses, and she spent a couple of hours this afternoon watching soap operas—or dozing through them. Said she was taking 'a little break' before fixing supper. She's too old to work, Billie. I told Daddy I can do housework while I'm here, but he said Mamie needs the money."

"I can't imagine why. She gets Social Security."

Margaret shrugged. "Maybe she's maxed out her credit cards. That happens."

"Not to me it doesn't. I don't have a credit card. But I guess if Mamie's needing money, Daddy's being nice to her."

"Daddy nice? Some poor man came over this afternoon while I was getting Andy some summer clothes, and you ought to hear Daddy's version of how he treated *him*."

I slewed my eyes at her. "Mamie said you went to Wal-Mart."

"When in Solace, do as Solace does. At supper, ask Daddy about the visitor he had."

I didn't get a chance right away. As we sat down and Margaret started pouring milk for the children, Andy boasted, "Aunt Billie, did you know I'm learning to feed the chickens? Tomorrow I'm going to hoe the garden and help clean out the chicken house, and one day Papa is going to let me help him milk. Aren't you, Papa?"

"That's right." Daddy rumpled his hair. "We'll make a farmer of you yet, boy."

"I want to be a farmer," Chellie said. "I want to feed chickens and milk cows."

The grown-ups grew still. Poor little chick, she still hadn't discovered how many limitations she was going to face.

"Okay, Chellie. We'll make farmers out of you both." Daddy rumpled her hair, too.

He used to do that to me when I was small. I could almost feel his fingers in my hair.

My sister was cutting a chicken breast with her knife and fork, so I picked up the thigh on my plate and took a bite. "Margaret told me you had a visitor this afternoon, Daddy."

"One of those danged developers. Came by wanting to buy land to put up an industrial office park. I told him offices don't need parks, and parks don't have offices, last I heard." He fed a bite of chicken to Jimbo.

"If he wanted to buy land, take his money," Margaret advised. "Not many people are buying these days."

"I'm not selling land. But that fellah wouldn't take no for an answer. Pestered me and pestered me to set a price. Finally I did. I told him I'd settle for five million dollars an acre."

"Wow!" Andy exclaimed. "You'll be so rich!" We grown-ups laughed, but Margaret's laugh sounded hollow, like she'd dredged it up from a hidden drawer.

"The fellah was at least smart enough to say, 'That's ridiculous.' 'No more ridiculous than you wanting to pave over perfectly good pastures,' I told him. 'People gotta have milk, you know.' And he said, 'You're behind the times, sir. This whole area will be houses, businesses, and light industry soon after the economy picks up.' I told him, 'Look around you, son. I own every acre you can see in any direction. None of *this* area is going to be houses, businesses, or light industry while I'm breathing, and I plan to keep breathing for a very long time.'" Daddy slung his wadded paper napkin on the table. "Come on, Andy, let's take Chellie to shut up the chickens for the night and look at the garden."

I wasn't sure Chellie visiting the chickens or garden was a good idea. "Her chair is going to be hard to push out there."

"I'll carry her. We'll be fine."

Margaret grabbed Andy's shoulder to stop him from heading out the door. "You can't go out to the garden in those clothes!" He was clean and pressed in khaki shorts and a pale blue shirt with white sneakers.

Daddy frowned. "Run up and change, boy. Chellie and I will wait. But hurry. We need to show Chellie the chickens and plan how we'll clean their house."

Margaret looked exactly like Daddy when she frowned. "Andy doesn't have any clothes he can clean a chicken house in."

"Then take him to a thrift store for some. He can't wear la-di-dah clothes around here. Billie, tell your sister where the best thrift stores are."

He didn't need to make it sound like I bought all my clothes there, even if it was true.

He wheeled Chellie out on the back porch while Margaret and I stacked dishes. "I still wish Daddy had a dishwasher," she grumbled.

"I had two," Daddy called from the porch, "but they both grew up and left home."

Andy clattered downstairs wearing dirty shoes and jeans with grubby knees. He must have worn them earlier that day. Daddy spoke again through the screen door. "You girls get the dessert served up while we visit the barn. I think Mamie set out some of the last peaches your mama canned. Let's go, kids. Barn, here we come."

"Chellie's getting heavy," I worried, standing in the door to watch them go.

Margaret came up behind me. "Daddy's strong. He swung Andy up to the tractor seat this morning. But I can't believe he's still canning. Doesn't he know everybody freezes peaches these days? Or that he can go the grocery store and buy fresh produce all year round?"

"Ah, but that costs money. You know Daddy. Why pay premium prices for fresh produce or waste electricity to freeze stuff when you can stick it in boiling water for half an hour and keep it for years? Don't buck him, Margaret. He still likes things done his way."

"If he doesn't do something about that temper, he's going to have a stroke. I got back from Wal-Mart right after the developer left, and Daddy was pink as boiled lobster."

"I am not personally acquainted with boiled lobster, but Daddy thrives on fusses. I'm glad to see him feisty again. He's been like a robot this past year. While I'm thinking about it, let me write down how to get to a couple of good thrift stores."

As I reached for a pad Daddy used for grocery lists, a business card tucked underneath fluttered to the floor. "Maggie, look at this!" I was so startled, the old name slipped out.

The card was white with blue letters. It read:

RICK LANDISS, V. P. FOR COMMERCIAL DEVELOPMENT
LANDISS CONSTRUCTION

It listed a Solace address on Main Street.

I studied the card. "He must be the boss of the company Porter used to work for!"

"He's the son of the owner—or so I've heard."

"If I go see him and explain my situation, maybe he can find out something for me. I'll apologize for Daddy, too. I'll start with that."

"I doubt the bosses know a thing about who works on the sites." She stretched to put a bowl on the top shelf. I watched, envious. Height was another gene Margaret had snatched in the womb. She had gotten at least six more inches than I did.

"Do you realize I've never been able to reach a top shelf in my life? But it's worth a try—going to see Mr. Landiss, I mean. I'm going to stop by there after work tomorrow."

She plucked the card from my hand. "Let me go. Their office will probably be closed by the time you get off, and I've got to go to thrift stores anyway. What kind of clothes am I supposed to buy for a child to wear mucking out a chicken house?"

"Clothes you don't mind getting dirty."

I opened the quart of peaches and fell silent. Those golden slices had been cut by Mama's hands, sweetened by Mama's hands, and pressed into the jar by Mama's hands.

Margaret handed me a serving bowl. "Are you crying?"

I sniffed. "Not quite. But opening these peaches feels like bringing Mama back for a minute. She touched them, Maggie. She touched every one of them."

Margaret took the jar from me and poured its contents into the bowl. We stood silent, staring at the peaches like they were the Holy Grail, until Daddy and the kids got back.

Daddy came puffing, exaggerating to make Chellie giggle. "This child is getting big as an elephant." He settled her chair at the table.

Margaret fetched ice cream while I set out bowls. "I warned you," I said.

"It's high time we built a ramp up the back steps and laid some walks around here so she can get around." He sounded like Chellie practically lived at his house.

My peaches stuck in my throat, but Daddy ate peaches and ice cream with a thoughtful expression. "You need a ramp and walks at your place, too, don't you?" Without waiting for an answer, he turned to Andy. "Looks like you and me got a few projects, don't we, son?"

Andy grinned. "Sure do, Papa. We got lots to do."

After the kids and Daddy went in to watch TV, Margaret whispered, "Billie, call the police. Somebody has abducted our daddy and replaced him with a very nice man."

EVEN THOUGH MARGARET HAD TAKEN the card, I remembered the address of Mr. Landiss's office, and I wasn't sure she'd press him to look for Porter as hard as I would. I was making enough now to support us, so I didn't need Porter in my life, but it grieved me that he had nobody else to care whether he disappeared or not. If I didn't try to find out what had happened to him, who would?

I went on my lunch hour.

Landiss Construction had taken one of the old storefronts on Main Street and fancied it up. The plate-glass window shone and the front office had a receptionist's desk and two green chairs with a magazine table between them. I noticed, though, that the sign on the front door was the kind you could take down real easy.

When I saw their white Berber carpeting, I was glad I had changed out of my work shoes, but realized that coming in my coveralls had been a mistake. On the other hand, taking off the coveralls would have been worse. The shorts and T-shirt I wore underneath were damp with sweat.

The woman at the desk made me wait while she finished whatever she was typing, and the look she gave me was one she'd give something that had crawled up from the slime. "May I help you?" She obviously thought that a distant possibility.

"I hope so. I'm Wilhelmina Anderson, and I'd like to see Mr. Landiss for a minute."

All the way over I'd practiced saying, "Wilhelmina Waits," but when I opened my mouth, "Anderson" jumped out. I liked Wilhelmina Anderson better. It sounded like a film star. Julia Roberts, maybe, in *Runaway Bride*, beautiful in spite of her coveralls.

Miss Persimmon looked toward an office that had been built along one side of the back half of the space. "Mr. Landiss is engaged. You could make an appointment."

"Will he be long? If not, I can wait." I did a Julia Roberts long-legged stroll over to the chairs—which isn't easy when you are five foot two. I picked up a magazine and was reading *Money World* like I had millions to invest when I heard a familiar laugh.

I went back to the desk. "Is that Margaret Baxter in there with him? If it is, she's my sister, and I don't think they'd mind if I interrupted."

She pruned up her mouth and called to ask Mr. Landiss's permission to bring a peasant back. "He will see you now." I considered walking backward out of her presence.

Margaret and Mr. Landiss were drinking coffee like good buddies. I wondered how much she would have paid for that elegant black pantsuit if she hadn't made it. I also envied her for being able to get so comfortable with a stranger that fast. However, Mr. Landiss looked like he came from her world. He was at least forty, but tanned and fit. His nails were manicured, his brown hair well-cut, and his white shirt could have posed for a detergent ad. I might have found him handsome if he hadn't showed so many teeth when he smiled.

His office held a big walnut desk and matching credenza, a long green sofa along one wall, and two matching chairs. The rest of the decor consisted of a suggestive silver nude on his desk and a pinup screen saver. He was not a man I would buy a used car from.

If Margaret minded my arriving in the latest style from Foxworthy's Garage, she didn't show it, but she didn't give me a chance to introduce myself with my glamorous name. She said, "Hello, Billie. Rick, this is my sister, Billie Waits. She's a mechanic."

Mr. Landiss half-stood behind his desk and gave me a hand as soft and clean as a dentist's. "Billie! Good to meet you." When I gave him my usual handshake, he winced.

"Don't press hard," Margaret admonished. "He broke his hand back in April in a freak golf accident. It's still tender."

Mr. Landiss waved like it wasn't important. "Please have a seat."

"I'd better stand, sir. I'm a bit grubby." I looked at Margaret. "Did you ask him?"

She shook her head. "We were talking about something else."

"If you all were talking about Daddy, I hope you made it clear he's not going to sell his land. You'll be wasting your time barking down that hole, Mr. Landiss."

He stroked his chin. "Maybe so, but I hope you girls will keep my card. He may find he'd like to sell part of his farm in order to save the rest."

I didn't mind Daddy calling me a girl, but I once gut-punched another man who did. I reminded myself I needed something from Rick

Landiss. "You'll have to take that up with him. I came to ask about my husband."

"Your husband?"

"Yessir. He works—or used to work—for Landiss Construction on a project in Marietta, but back in March he didn't show up for work one morning, and nobody has heard from him since." Mr. Landiss started to speak, but I raised one hand. "I know you think he deserted me, but he's not like that. He's a good worker, and he's been real dependable about sending checks home. That's why I'm trying to find out what happened."

He reached for a pen. "What's his name?"

"Porter Waits."

He hesitated. "Waits—that's his last name?"

"Yessir. His first name's Porter. Having two last names has been hard on him all his life." I waited for him to write it down before I explained, "What I think is, wherever he went, he's likely to have told somebody on the site where he was going. I wondered if somebody who speaks Spanish could ask all the men on that site whether one of them knows where he's gone. I'd really appreciate it."

He thought that over. "I can ask around, but these men come and go all the time. They don't always leave forwarding information."

"I understand that, but Porter's not like that. I'd appreciate any information you can get."

"I'll do what I can. Should I pass any messages through Mags, here?"

Mags? I didn't dare look at Margaret. "That would be fine. Thanks for seeing me." As I left, I heard him say to her, "So do we have a deal?"

What kind of deal were Margaret and Mr. Landiss hatching between them?

THAT EVENING I DROPPED BY Daddy's with a couple of thrift-store outfits and a pair of shoes for Andy. Andy immediately wheeled Chellie into the dining room to watch television.

"You bought those because you thought I wouldn't go to the thrift store, didn't you?" Margaret said.

She was absolutely right, but I didn't want to admit it. "The thrift store is between Mr. Landiss's and the garage, so I popped in on my way back."

"I know where it is—I found it. But thanks. Andy now has outfits he can get filthy in every day of the week and two pairs of farmyard shoes."

I went to the fridge and helped myself to a glass of tea. "What were you and Mr. Landiss plotting when I left?"

She wiped the counter with her back to me. "He's not real happy with the woman in the front office—"

"I wasn't real happy with her, either. She treated me like fill dirt."

"That's the way she treats everybody. Rick says she's bad for business."

"Rick? I noticed you were on a first-name basis with that sleazeball."

"He's not a sleazeball. He's a very nice man."

"You could have fooled me. 'You girls hang on to my card.' Girls?"

"He's still a nice man, and he has offered me a job. I start Monday."

I couldn't have been more surprised if she'd said she was going with him on an Arctic expedition. "Why would you do that?"

"I get bored around here, and he needs my help."

"Have you told him you're just here on a visit?"

"No. Don't you tell him, either."

"I'm not planning to tell him anything. I hope he's planning to find out something to tell me."

Twenty

I missed Bethany the week she was gone. I missed her not only because she was a bright spot in our household whom Chellie loved, but also because Bethany's conversation was full of Luke. Luke had persuaded her to apply to a college that offered a degree in special education. Luke had helped her write such a good essay that she'd been offered a scholarship. Luke had gotten Franklin into Boy Scouts and become an assistant Scoutmaster for the troop. Luke was putting a roof on his mother's house, working without a shirt and getting a gorgeous tan. "You ought to see it," Bethany said. "Hey, why don't you ask him to paint your place? He'd be glad to."

"Right—like he doesn't have enough to do already, working plus helping your mom." I didn't add that we weren't speaking anymore.

"I mean it. He said your place could use a lick of paint."

How dare he say such a thing to somebody else? "My place could use a whole swallow of paint, but not right now. I'll get around to it."

On Thursday of Bethany's beach week, I came home so tired I could hardly move. Stamps and his men were letting me work without hassles, but they expected me to carry my weight—including parts that were almost more than I could lift.

"Could you stay an extra hour while I rest and take a shower?" I asked Ethelyne.

"Of course, honey. Chellie and I are in the middle of watching *Aladdin*."

Chellie pushed me away when I bent to kiss her. "Mama! I'm watching the movie."

I went for a glass of tea thinking, *Hooray for library movies.*

I took my tea and a novel to a porch rocker—barefoot and wearing the sweaty shorts and tank top I'd worn all day under my coveralls. In a few minutes I'd summon the energy to go inside and shower.

A red truck I didn't recognize drove in. Luke climbed down wearing jeans and a fresh white polo shirt that looked great with the tan he'd gotten on his mama's roof. My first impulse was to run inside and pretend I hadn't seen him, but he had already waved, so I dragged my sweat-damp hair behind my ears and wished that just once he'd come by when I looked good. Unfortunately, those windows of opportunity were rare.

As always, when nervous, I babbled. "Have you come to arrest my new tenants? Don't. They are model citizens. One of them is even watching Chellie this week."

"Keep an eye on them, then. Nice folks are the worst kind." He set a travel mug on the porch and picked up my basketball. "Five in a row. Watch for it." He backed up and shot a perfect basket. Numbers two, three, and four slid in like butter. Number five bumped off the rim.

"Four out of five isn't bad. You want a shot?" He retrieved the ball and held it out.

"Not today. I'm so tired I might not beat you." I looked at him warily. Should I apologize now or wait a while? "Uh—would you like to sit down?"

"I thought you'd never ask." He took the other rocker and hitched it around to face mine. "How's the car-repair business?"

I suspected that wasn't what he'd come about, but if he needed to work up to whatever it was, that was okay. It kept him around a little longer. "Pretty good, if I can survive."

"I'm impressed you can do it at all. I don't know a spark plug from a solenoid—whatever that is." He leaned across the space between our rockers. "Is that a new brand of makeup? Motor-oil blusher?" He used one thumb to swipe my cheek.

I drew back. No man had touched me since Porter left, and he hadn't been big on touching. He expended so much passion on politics, the environment, and other people's shortcomings, he didn't have much left for marriage. Luke's thumb sent waves through my body like I'd stuck my finger in a socket.

I was embarrassed to have jerked away. What must he have thought? I cleared my throat and tried to match his tone. "You like it? I haven't gotten around to doing the other cheek. Do you want some iced tea?"

He held up his travel mug. "I brought my own." He settled back into his chair. "How'd you turn out to be a mechanic? Back in high school, I expected you to become a lifelong scholar—reading in the hall and all."

"I never found anybody to pay me for reading, and I have a fondness for eating."

"So you trained as a mechanic."

"No, I grew up helping Daddy fix farm equipment. Before I got my driver's license, he said I ought to learn to do minor car repairs in case I broke down on a deserted road."

"Not a bad idea. Did he make your sister learn how, too?"

"Princess Margaret? Not likely. She hates to get her hands dirty." I tucked mine under my thighs. They were still grimy. "Sorry I'm so grubby. You arrived before I got cleaned up."

"You're kinda cute grubby."

I hoped I was cute blushing fiery red. "Look—I'm sorry about the other night. I was out of line."

"We were both out of line. Call it even?" He held out a hand. I shook, hoping he didn't notice how mine trembled. He seemed perfectly at ease, but he held my hand longer than he needed to. I took it back and tucked it underneath me again.

"If you only learned to do minor car repairs, how'd you wind up a mechanic?"

"Daddy didn't want me experimenting on his Buick, so he bought that truck out there for two hundred bucks." I waved at my pride and joy. "We had to completely rebuild the engine. It was a lot of fun, working with Daddy. He didn't talk much and he didn't laugh much, but whenever I did something right he would sort of hum with pleasure. 'Um-*mmm*.'"

I hadn't heard that sound of approval since I'd bucked him and married Porter.

Luke sat there looking like he enjoyed listening, so I kept talking. "After that, I made spending money fixing cars for other kids. Over the years I've kept doing jobs for some folks, so Stamps offered me a trial week at the garage. I must have passed. He's kept me on." Talking about myself was such a novel experience, I had gotten carried away. Time to hand the ball to the other team. "You never worked on cars in high school?"

"Nope. I learned enough to put in gas when the light comes on and to get the oil changed when the numbers on my speedometer match the numbers on that little doo-hickey on the windshield."

"Odometer," I corrected him.

"What?"

"Your mileage is on your odometer. The speedometer shows your speed."

"See? I told you I don't know squat about cars. I applied to learn mechanics in the army, but they put me in the military police. For once, the army got something right." He reached over and peeled a strip of dried paint from a board. "I also know how to paint. Bethany said you'd like me to paint your place in my spare time."

I was so startled, I spilled tea down my front. *Graceful, Billie!*

I pulled my tank out and fluttered it a bit to try to dry it. "I never said a word about you painting my house. It was Bethany's idea. She said you were talking about how much it needs it—which, by the way, I thought was highly rude. While I'm the first to admit it does—"

He grinned. "That little dickens! I never said your house needs painting. She loves to play matchmaker, and must not have gotten the message that you are a married woman awaiting your husband's return."

The day had grown awfully hot all of a sudden.

I fluttered the neck of my tank again to cool down. "Bethany needs to mind Michelle and her own business. I'm going to paint the house one day, but not until Chellie is older. I don't want to fall off a ladder when I'm out here by myself with her."

"Who put up your hoop, your husband? I vaguely remember Porter, but I don't remember him playing basketball."

"No, that was me. Daddy let me have the one from his house and I put it up while Chellie was napping one afternoon, praying the whole time I wouldn't fall."

"Not to be sexist, but why would a man with two daughters need a basketball hoop?"

"I played on the girls' varsity my last two years of high school."

"Varsity? As short as you are?"

"I may be short, but I'm fast. And good."

"Is that right?" He set down his tea. "Am I to understand you only missed a lot last time to spare my ego?" He leaped down the steps and dribbled the ball while he waited for my answer.

It had been a long time since I'd had anybody to shoot baskets with. "Absolutely. But now that you've practiced, no mercy."

We came out pretty even. "Enough," I said finally, panting. "I've been working hard all day while you rode around in a cruiser."

I didn't want him asking why I took up basketball, so as soon as he joined me on the porch, I went back to the subject of painting. "I'll paint the house when Chellie is older and can summon help."

He flicked off another scab of paint. "A good pressure washing would take off most of this. A little sanding in rough spots and you'd be ready to prime. I'll bet we could do the whole thing in three or four weekends, if Franklin helped. Bethany could watch Michelle."

He said it real casual-like, but the way he watched for my response, he seemed anxious that I accept. That puzzled me. "Why should you? I mean, you've got a job, and you've already got your mother and two kids to look after. And I can't pay you."

I saw a look in his eyes I'd never seen there before. He seemed worried. "I don't want to be paid. I need to find things for those kids to do on weekends. Weekdays are fine—Bethany's here and Franklin's in summer camp—but Saturdays and Sundays are a bummer. Mama got switched to weekends for the summer, and I have to work every second weekend. You know what can happen to kids left alone all day—and Franklin is particularly susceptible to the wrong kind of kids. He won't mind Bethany, won't do a thing she tells him. So, since the kids enjoy being with you all, I hoped I could dump them on you for a few weekends."

"They can come over anytime, but they don't have to paint my house."

"It would be good for Franklin. He came home from moving that furniture real proud of himself. He hasn't been proud of himself much lately. If I can get the project started this weekend, maybe you and Franklin could paint every weekend, and I could work with you on weekends I'm off. Bethany can watch Michelle. You don't have to pay them."

"I can't use free labor to get my house painted."

"Sure, you can. I'm getting free babysitting."

"Are you planning to tell Bethany she needs a babysitter?"

"Of course I'm not. I'm going to tell them we're doing a good deed. They need to learn to help other people for free."

I agreed with that, and my house could use a paint job, but I still didn't like it. "I don't accept charity, and I don't like being seen as somebody who needs it."

"How about this? Tell them that when the house is done, you will do something special with them—maybe take them to Six Flags one Saturday."

A day at Six Flags with two kids, plus paying somebody to watch Chellie, would wipe out my budget for a month, even if it was a cheap price to pay for having the house painted.

Not to mention a great way to spend weekends with Luke.

Still, I had to be practical. "How about a day at Red Top Mountain State Park instead? They have a good beach. Chellie likes to swim, so it would be fun for her, too."

"We'll both take all of them. Deal?" He put out a hand.

Next thing I knew, I had committed myself to painting my house, plus spending a day at the beach in the company of Luke Braswell. I was going to need a better bathing suit.

He stood. "I'm off tomorrow. Why don't I borrow a pressure washer from a friend and get that done? Then we can start sanding on Saturday."

"Won't that violate the water ban? I don't want you having to arrest yourself."

"People who make their living using pressure washers are exempt, and my friend is one of those. He'll come along and drink a few beers while he watches me work."

"Can I buy the beer?"

"That would be lovely."

I pulled a bill out of my pocket. It was great to have bills *in* my pocket.

He waved as he left. "See you Saturday. By then you ought to have a naked house."

I wished he hadn't used that word. It made me aware of the tight buns filling his jeans.

When he was out of sight, I sank ten baskets in a row.

BY THE TIME I GOT home Friday, the house was as bare as a plucked chicken. Not only that, a wooden ramp filled half of my front steps and forms had been laid to extend my front walk to my driveway. When Daddy and Jimbo brought our milk that evening, he said, "I came over today to start on your work, and I ran into that Braswell fellow—the one you used to have a crush on, who played basketball. He was washing your house." His voice had a question in it. You know how daddies are about daughters taking favors from men.

"His sister sits with Chellie, so she got Luke and their brother to come help me paint. It's partly a plot to help keep their little brother busy on weekends."

"I figured it must be something like that."

Not particularly flattering, when I thought about it later.

LUKE AND FRANKLIN ARRIVED SATURDAY at eight. Franklin wore the self-important look of somebody who had come to do a good deed. It didn't take many hours of sanding before he learned that doing good deeds isn't necessarily fun.

Luke sanded the high places while Franklin did what Luke called "the low-down work." Since Bethany was still at the beach, I put Chellie in her chair out under a tree where she could watch while I sanded window frames and sills. Within an hour I was covered in sawdust, my hair was sweaty tails stuck to my neck, and my nails didn't bear looking at, but had Luke ever seen me looking decent?

Around ten Daddy, Andy, and Jimbo showed up with concrete and a tub to mix it in. I pushed Chellie over to watch them mix and pour the walk to our driveway. Jimbo lay down beside her. Lucky hissed and disappeared.

Once the mixing was done, Daddy told Andy, "I can take it from here, Tiger. You and Chellie go play." I wondered what he thought they could play, but Andy devised all sorts of games. He reminded me of Ben, the way he made simple things fun. He pushed her up and down the gravel drive, collecting bugs and odd rocks. They played Go Fish, with Chellie's cards hidden behind a wall of library books. Whenever

Chellie had to give him a card, she would point and he'd reach over and take it without looking. If he made a mistake, she'd scold, they'd laugh, and Jimbo would wag his tail. When cards palled, he took cars from his pocket, and they raced them on the kitchen table. Michelle's laughter rang throughout the lot.

When Daddy finished smoothing the front walk, he carried Chellie out so she and Andy could press handprints into the end. I used a stick to add the date and helped Jimbo press his paw in the wet cement. I tried to press in Lucky's paw as well, but quit when it became clear that success would entail a trip for me to the emergency room. As soon as I put that old tom down, he jumped onto the soft walk and made an entire trail of prints, tail swishing in contempt.

At noon I spread a quilt under my biggest oak and invited Daddy and Andy to stay for lunch. Andy accepted before Daddy had time to refuse. I wheeled Chellie's chair up beside the quilt, and the rest of us sprawled on the quilt and ate. Our family had sandwiches, apricots, and milk. I'd cut carrot sticks for everybody except Chellie and had pureed carrots for her. Luke and Franklin had brought thick bologna sandwiches, chips, and Sprites. Jimbo had whatever anybody would give him and a few things he stole when he thought we weren't looking.

"Do you all want carrot sticks or apricots?" I asked Franklin and Luke. "We have plenty." I cannot tell you how good it felt to have something to share.

Franklin looked at me blankly. "Why?"

"To keep you healthy." Luke reached for the apricot on my plate.

"I don't eat rabbit food," said Franklin. Chellie laughed like a coquette. I wondered why I hadn't made opportunities for her to be with other children all those years. Once they got over their initial curiosity, children were a lot more natural around her than most grown-ups.

Luke held up his half-eaten apricot and looked over at me. "*That's* the color your hair is," he said, like we'd been discussing the subject. "Apricot. Sort of a pinkish gold."

"What color are you going to paint the house?" Daddy asked. I hardly heard him. I was still processing that Luke thought my hair looked like apricots.

"Pink," I heard Chellie say. "We are going to paint it pink."

I hadn't given the color a minute's thought, but I had to head that idea off before it got fixed in her head. Besides, I could see exactly what I wanted. "No, baby. It's going to be soft yellow with white trim and a Wedgwood blue door."

Franklin spoke through bologna. "Blue shutters would be pretty."

"Swallow before you speak," Luke commanded. Franklin glowered. Did Luke not realize he was acting more like a parent than a big brother—a daddy cop—and Franklin resented it?

I didn't have money to buy shutters, but because I wanted to treat Franklin like his opinion mattered I said, "Shutters sound like a good idea. They could give the place a touch of class."

"Definitely." Franklin bobbed his head so hard, his curls jounced. "Real class."

I looked at the house and realized he was right. Clear as anything I saw a yellow cottage trimmed in white with blue shutters, a perfect background for my flowers. "Good idea. We'll add shutters as soon as I can afford them."

"I've got shutters from Uncle Jerry's house down in my shed," Daddy informed me. "I saved them when they took his place down. If you can dig them out, you can have them."

"It's a deal. When we finish painting, Franklin can help me find them, clean them, paint them, and put them up."

"Sure." Franklin sat up straight and chomped another huge bite off his sandwich.

Daddy climbed to his feet. "Could I borrow your brother awhile, Luke? I want to get forms in place for a walk out to the mailbox before I quit today."

"You'd better," Luke agreed. "Billie's worn a rut in her grass checking her mail."

I wadded a paper napkin and threw it at him. "That rut was here before I moved in."

He threw it back, hitting me square in the face. "Swish."

"I'll be glad to help you, sir." Franklin followed Daddy to his truck for lumber.

Luke watched them go. "You and your dad handle him a lot better than I do."

"We don't treat him like a child. Remember thirteen? It's a dreadful age."

"A memory I have tried to repress."

"You'd better dredge it up unless you want constant war with Franklin. Treat him like you would my little brother instead of your own."

"That's worth a try." He stood and cupped his hand on top of my head like a benediction. He gently pushed my head back and forth, which felt great. But just as I was about to swoon from utter relaxation, he ran a forefinger through my hair. "If you plan on setting up as the successor to Dear Abby, wash the sawdust out of your hair before you pose for your professional picture."

Twenty-one

My June was as different from my April as cold sweet tea is different from lukewarm swamp water. I was making enough at the garage to more than pay our bills, so every week I added to an envelope marked *Chellie's school clothes and emergencies* that I kept between the pages of a paperback mystery on my shelf. Miss Ashley at the bank wasn't getting my hard-earned savings.

Ramps at front and back doors made it much easier to move Chellie inside and out, and my house was getting beautiful. I also had something to look forward to every weekend. Every Saturday I woke up thinking, "Today I get to see Luke." We joked, laughed, and got along so well, I could tell Daddy was reconsidering his earlier opinion about why Luke was painting the house. I couldn't tell what Daddy thought of that.

I also had model tenants. They were home most of the time except Sunday mornings and Wednesday evenings, but they didn't have visitors. They were enthusiastic about my home-beautification projects, too. They came over every weekend to check our progress. One afternoon Ethelyne handed me a bucket full of hosta. "We saw these plants growing on a lot where a house used to be. I thought they would be pretty in the V where your new walks meet." Hosta was exactly what I had wanted to put there.

The only fly in my peanut butter was that they always asked, as they left, "Do you mind if we pick a little something from your garden?" Either they were picking more than a little or I had creative rabbits. Still, I found Verna out weeding my beans one morning, so they weren't all take and no give.

When I stopped by the trailer to pick up my June rent check, though, Verna came to the door twisting her wedding ring. "Ethelyne's not well, honey. Could you come back tomorrow?"

The next afternoon, Ethelyne answered before I knocked. "Verna's caught whatever I had. Can you come back tomorrow?"

When I went by the next day, they were out and didn't come home until past my bedtime.

The following day I moseyed over after work and found Verna sitting in their front yard, drinking tea. She twisted her ring. "Your check! It's ready." She hurried in and came out with it.

It was for two weeks' rent. "I only agreed to credit Ethelyne for one week," I pointed out.

"I forgot and I'm plumb out of checks. I'll get you the rest when my new ones come."

I deposited the check the next day. It bounced.

After Luke helped me put up the shutters the following Saturday, I joked, "Do you do collections? I can't seem to get my rent from the lovely ladies next door."

"Let me run them through our computer."

"They aren't criminals. They're just slow in paying rent."

"Maybe so, but it never hurts to check. I'll get back to you. Now let's go get a good view of the house." He draped his arm around my shoulders and led me out to the edge of the yard.

"Are you happy with it now that we're done?" Luke seemed to have forgotten that he had his arm on my shoulders. I pretended not to notice.

"I love it. Franklin was right—the shutters do give it class."

Luke's arm still rested on my shoulders. I kept talking, hoping he wouldn't remember it was there. "When I get more plants put in beside the walks, I'll call *Southern Living*. I really appreciate all you've done."

"You were helping me, too, don't forget. Painting and watching Chellie has kept the kids out of trouble. Mama is changing her schedule after Fourth of July, so she won't be working weekends anymore."

"That's good." But the idea of not seeing Luke on weekends made me sadder than a Georgia husky in August. Looked like I'd be dependent on Bethany's news bulletins for the rest of the summer.

"Is it?" He took my chin in his hand and tilted it so I was looking up at him. "I'm gonna miss working over here every week. It's kind of gotten to be a habit."

I felt that same thing I'd felt in the trailer, the sizzling between us. It still scared me enough to make me take a step back.

Luke took away his arm. My shoulders felt bare. "I promised to run Franklin over to Wal-Mart tonight, so I guess we ought to be going. Don't forget we still have a swim date. I guess Fourth of July weekend would be too crowded at the lake. What do you think?"

What I was thinking was that I needed a new bathing suit and to lose a few pounds before I went swimming with Luke. What I said was, "The next weekend would probably be better."

"Suits me. It's a date?"

"Sounds great."

As he drove away, I found myself humming. Unless you've lived with nothing to look forward to, you don't know what a gift that can be.

I WENT TO BED THAT night with a book—my usual Saturday night riotous entertainment—but I mostly lay there thinking about Luke. Did he feel the tremors I felt when we looked at each other? Did he like me? Or to him was I still a little freshman who needed picking up off the floor? Could he be coming over because he felt sorry for me?

That idea disturbed me so much I had to get up for a bowl of chocolate ice cream. *Way to go, Billie! You'll lose a lot of pounds that way.*

It took me a long time to fall asleep, even tired as I was, and it seemed like I'd just dozed off when somebody pounded on my door. "Billie? Billie! Let me in! Please! Let me in!" My bedside clock read one a.m.

I stumbled through the living room, which was lit only by a night-light I burned outside the bathroom door. Aware that I wasn't dressed for company in the raggedy tank top and shorts I slept in, I flicked on the porch light.

Margaret stood there, her cheeks wet with tears. A long scratch on her cheek oozed blood. Her left hand clutched the front of a green sun-dress that was lovely once, with tiny brown leaves falling down the bod-ice. Now it was ripped to the waist. She wore only one shoe.

I flung open the door. "What the dickens happened to you?" She looked so pitiful I reached out to hold her—as I would any friend. She backed away, her eyes enormous. I helped her hobble in instead. She shiv-ered like it was December, so I snatched an afghan from the back of the couch and draped it over her. She clutched it and sank onto the couch, whimpering. I hurried to close Chellie's door. "We'll have to keep our voices down. My walls are like rice paper." I flicked off the front porch light and reached for the floor lamp.

"Don't!" She turned her face away. "I couldn't bear it!" She shook like peanuts in a blender.

If she was cold in my living room in June, she was in shock. I had moved both fans to the bedrooms, so the air was hot and fuggy with the smell of our supper bacon.

"Let me get you some hot tea."

While the water boiled, I fetched a damp washcloth and antibiotic ointment. I put three spoonfuls of sugar in the tea and carried every-thing to the living room.

Margaret poked a hand out of the afghan to grab the mug, but she shook too much to hold it. "Here." I held it to her lips. "Drink." That was the first order I had ever given my sister that she obeyed. After sev-eral swallows, her shaking slowed.

"Can you hold the tea now? I need to clean up your cheek." I could barely see to wash the scratch and cover it with ointment. "It's pretty deep, but I don't think it needs stitches." It felt odd to be taking care of Margaret, like I was eight and practicing for a first-aid badge in Brownies. *You are grown-up, Billie. Focus on Margaret.*

I perched on the chair across from her. While she finished her tea, I rubbed my shirt between my breasts to stop a trickle of sweat. "Are you warm enough yet? Could I open a window?" She nodded but didn't let go of the afghan.

I raised the blind a foot and shoved up the window. There wasn't a whisper of breeze. I fluttered my tank to cool myself while Margaret, still wrapped in the afghan, stared into the darkness. I saw the glint of tears on her cheeks. She seemed not to notice. I took a tissue from a box on the coffee table and blotted her tears. She didn't notice that, either. "Did you have a wreck?" I asked. "Do you need to go to the hospital?"

"No!" She shrank back against the couch.

With her face turned toward the dim light, I saw that the dark spot on her other cheekbone wasn't blusher; it was a bruise. She had another on her chin. "You really got banged up."

She closed her eyes. "Thanks for taking me in. I didn't know where else to go. I didn't want Daddy to see me like this, and I was afraid he'd be waiting up like he used to."

"He always waited for me, too, sitting in his recliner. I'd better call him."

"Don't tell him . . ." I didn't hear the rest. I was in the kitchen punching buttons.

"Yeah?" Daddy answered the phone like he was trying out for Grumpy in *Snow White*. He was waiting downstairs, all right. He wouldn't put a phone in his bedroom. Said he didn't want it to wake him up.

"Hey. This is Billie. Look, I'm sorry to be calling so late, but Maggie and I got to talking, and the time got away from us. Yeah, she stopped by here on her way home from supper. She may stay here tonight. Can you give Andy his breakfast? Yeah, she'll be back in time to get ready for church. What? Okay, Chellie and I'll come if you can help me carry her chair up the steps. Go on to bed, now. I'm real sorry we forgot to call earlier."

I went back to the living room and sat across from Margaret, my hands clasped between my knees. "Okay. I have waked up for you, anointed your wounds, made you tea, lied to Daddy for you, and promised to go to church. Do you feel up to telling me what happened?"

I figured she had missed a curve and hit a power pole. The way our county road winds through the hills, even people who are used to it occasionally miscalculate in the dark. I never had, but I knew one person who had gotten real smashed up.

Margaret went to the window, trailing the afghan like a royal robe. She peered out so long, she made me nervous. Was she looking for something—or somebody—out there?

The heat finally penetrated her bones, and she tossed the afghan to the couch.

I stood behind her and held her gently by the shoulders. "Margaret! Tell me!"

She spoke without turning around. "I nearly got raped."

That took the gelatin out of my Jell-O. "What? *Who?*"

"Rick Landiss." She buried her face in her hands. Her body shook with sobs.

"That sleazeball!" I grabbed a throw pillow from the couch and gave it several savage punches. "Do you want me to call the police?"

"No, I'm okay. I was just a fool. I am so ashamed!" Tears trickled between her fingers.

"*You* are ashamed? It wasn't your fault."

"Well, I . . . Maybe I . . . I might have . . ."

I grabbed her shoulders again and shook her none too gently. "Margaret! It wasn't your fault. No matter what you said or did, he had no right to try to rape you—or to hit you. He did hit you, didn't he?"

She pulled away from me and grabbed a tissue to dab her eyes. "Could I have a glass of water, please?"

When I got back with the water, she had replaced the afghan over the back of the couch and sat down, taking deep breaths. Princess Margaret regaining composure. Not quite as composed as she thought—her dress gapped, showing an expanse of lacy white bra. I rummaged on my closet shelf for the first thing I touched—a faded navy T-shirt. "This won't do much for your style, but it will cover you up."

She pulled it over her head and looked down in distaste. "You need some decent clothes."

"Do you want to discuss my wardrobe, or tell me what Rick did to you? I warn you, if you say 'wardrobe,' I'm going back to bed."

She picked up the glass. As she drank she darted little looks at me over the rim, like she didn't know what to say now that she had invited me into her mess.

Mama was always good at getting us to tell her anything that was bothering us. Did she really know exactly what to say, or did she play it by ear? I was definitely playing by ear, so I tried to think like Mama. *Sit down and speak calmly. Slide into the story slowly.*

I sat back in my chair like we had all night to chat. "What were you doing with Rick tonight? You don't work Saturdays, do you?"

She had no trouble answering that. "No, he asked me out to dinner."

"Does he take out all his employees, even the married ones?"

"I doubt it, but we've known each other for years. His wife was on my tennis team, and he gives Ben a lot of work."

All my good intentions flew out the open window. I even forgot to keep my voice down. "Why didn't you say that when I first called about finding Porter? Or when I found Rick's card at Daddy's? No wonder you and he looked so cozy in his office. I thought you were awfully good at making friends fast."

She looked down at her lap, where her hands pleated her skirt. "I should have told you."

"You certainly should have." I glared.

She threw me a look from under tear-damp lashes. In dim light, wearing my old T-shirt with her cheek cut and her face tear-splotched, she looked nothing like my perfect older sister. She looked like a miserable woman who had just been through a terrifying experience. My anger fizzled into pity. "Don't worry about it. Skip from going out to dinner to when he got rough."

"He drove me to the office. I'd met him there because I didn't want Daddy hassling him if Rick came to pick me up. When we got back, he. . ." She squeezed her eyes shut but could not hold back tears. "He asked me to come back to his office. He said we had things to discuss. I thought it was business, Billie. Really I did." She angrily swiped tears off her cheeks. "I cannot believe I was that dumb. When we got there, his sofa had been made up as a queen-sized bed."

"Definitely pointing to dishonorable intentions."

Margaret gave me a sharp look, like she was shocked by her baby sister's knowledge of the seamy side of life. I maintained my best poker face. Even those of us who get most of our experience from romance novels know better than to go into a man's office when it has a bed in it. In some ways Margaret was more naive than me.

She showed that in her next sentence. "He said he'd made it up before we went out because he thought we might be late coming in—he sleeps there on nights when he doesn't drive back to Marietta. I told him I'd prefer to talk in the front office but he said, 'There are no blinds. We'll look like we're on a stage. I've got chairs back here. We'll be all right.' *All right?*" Her voice grew shrill.

"Shhh," I reminded her.

She lowered her voice. "Like a fool, I agreed. At first it was okay. He poured drinks. We talked. Finally I got up to go home. That's when he grabbed me and started kissing me. I couldn't get away. He told me to relax, we were two lonely adults who could comfort each other. I tried to pull away from him, but he shoved me down on the bed and—you know."

I didn't know. No man had ever tried to seduce me, not even Porter. If I'd been a little wiser—or older—I'd have suspected long before our wedding night that we might have a problem in that area. But I didn't need to be thinking about Porter. I needed to be comforting Margaret.

Some comfort I was. I blurted the first thing that came to mind. "Does Mr. Landiss seduce all his employees' wives?"

"I'm—Ben—he's—" Margaret seemed to be having trouble forming a complete sentence. "Ben isn't his employee. Rick subcontracts the landscaping, so Ben's his own boss."

"Pardon me? This makes a difference? The man knows Ben, right? He knows you are married to Ben, right? So where does he come off trying to seduce you?" I was as furious with Rick Landiss as Margaret was.

Or so I thought.

"He's not usually like that. Not around me, at least. He can be very sweet and funny. He's been lonely since Louise left."

"Don't defend that scumbag! His wife probably left for a very good reason. Maybe he knocked her around, too."

Margaret picked up her purse from the coffee table. "I shouldn't have come."

I was smaller but faster. I beat her to the front door and pressed my back against it. "Maggie! What's there to understand? The man hit you! Right?"

She looked at me for a long minute like she was thinking that over. "Yeah. He hit me."

"He was wrong to hurt and scare you. You do know that, don't you?"

Her face was in shadow, but I saw the gleam of her eyes as she nodded. Her knees crumpled. I caught her just before she hit the floor.

I half-carried, half-dragged her to the couch and made her lie down. I sat beside her at her waist. She was shaking so hard that I covered her with the afghan and tucked it in. "Look, you don't have to tell me the rest, but if you want to, I'm here."

She didn't open her eyes, and she hesitated so long I thought she'd decided not to speak. Once she did, words poured out. "I hit him. I was hysterical, you see. He was lying on top of me, and when I tried to push him off, he was so strong! He pulled my dress up. I tried to knee him in the groin. . . ."

"Good for you."

"No. I missed and it made him furious. He slapped me again and again. He called me names like 'tease' and 'cheat.' I hadn't *meant* to lead him on. Honest, I hadn't."

"Of course you hadn't."

She opened her eyes. They were pools of misery. "Maybe I did. I shouldn't have gone out with him. He probably thought I owed him something for dinner."

"That's prehistoric. But slapping you wouldn't cut your cheek. How did that happen?"

She touched the scratch and winced. "He had on a ring. Sometimes"— her voice caught—"sometimes he used the back of his hand." Her head swung from side to side at the memory. "Oh, Billie! He kept hitting me and hitting me, saying cruel things, like it was no wonder . . ." She pressed a hand to her mouth.

"No wonder what?"

"I don't remember." She breathed heavily, as if sucking in courage with air.

"How did you tear your dress?"

"I rolled out from under him and tried to get up. He grabbed my dress."

"He must have grabbed hard. What did you do then?"

"I started screaming at him. I told him I didn't pay for dinner with sex and he was no gentleman."

"That must have made a big impression, considering the way he was acting."

"Oddly it did. At least it stopped him long enough for me to jump up and run across the office, but there's no door in that end. When he came for me again, I—I—" She drew a long, shuddering breath. "I think I killed him!"

My breath took a hike.

When I could breathe again, I demanded, "You've been in my house over half an hour, and you only just decided to mention this?"

"I forgot. Truly I did. It was only as I was telling you about the—the rest that I remembered. I—" She rolled over on her side and sobbed into the arm of my couch.

"Wait." I got up. "We both need a drink before you say another word. I bought a bottle of wine this week to have on hand for a special occasion. This isn't the occasion I had in mind, but I think we both need a glass."

She lay and sobbed while I fetched the wine. When I brought it in, she struggled to sit up. She curled in one corner of the couch with her feet tucked under her, like she didn't want any extraneous parts lying around that could get hurt.

After we'd taken a few sips, I asked, "Okay, so what did you do to him?" I tried to keep my voice steady. Nothing else in our world was.

"When he came toward me, I grabbed that awful statue on his desk—you know, the silver woman? I grabbed her by the head and I hit him, hard. Blood spurted everywhere." She held out her skirt. "Some even spattered on me."

Those weren't tiny brown leaves; they were splashes of blood.

"He fell and was real still, but I don't know if I killed him. I couldn't bear to touch him, so I ran. I didn't know where else to go but here. What should I do?"

She started sobbing again.

I put down my wine and went to hold her. While she cried, I tried to think.

Only later would I see the irony in the situation: my sister had to kill a man before she asked my advice?

"We really ought to call the police," I said when Margaret calmed down. "Now, while you're still all messed up. You need to report Mr. Landiss for attempted rape."

She drew away from me in horror. "I couldn't tell Tee!"

She had a point. Tee Hodson was a chauvinist to the tips of his splayed fingers. If he found Margaret sitting on my couch blubbering, "I didn't mean to lead him on. Maybe it *was* my fault," he would no doubt agree that it certainly was.

Once he had heard her complete story, he'd call Daddy. Daddy would come over and read Margaret the riot act for going out with that developer fellow in the first place while Tee—and maybe Luke—went to Rick's office and found Rick's body. After that, I'd be raising Margaret's kids, taking them to prison on visiting days.

I thought as furiously as it was possible for me to think in the middle of the night after my sister had arrived on my doorstep all beat up and confessed to a possible homicide.

"Call Rick's office." I nudged her toward the kitchen. "See if he's there."

"What if he's dead?"

"If he's dead, he won't answer. We'll go to plan B."

"What will I say if he answers?"

"Nothing. Hang up. You'll know he's alive. That's what we are trying to find out. Do you know the number?" When she nodded, I pulled her toward the phone.

"He isn't answering," she whispered a minute later.

I sighed. "Then we're on to plan B. We have to go see if he's really dead."

She shrank back against the counter. "I can't."

"Of course you can't. I'll go. You stay here with Chellie. Do you have an office key?"

"I didn't lock the door when I left. But I don't want you to go. I'll go."

I was already on my way to the bedroom for jeans and a fresh T-shirt. "What if you get stopped by a cop? You don't want anybody to see you looking like that."

I meant with her face bruised and cut and her eyes red from crying.

Margaret, being Margaret, stared down at my faded T-shirt. "No, I sure don't."

I left her huddled on my couch looking terrified.

THE SOLACE CITY COUNCIL HAD never seen a need for streetlights outside the downtown area and didn't waste tax dollars on downtown lights after midnight. It was eerie to drive through the darkness, past familiar houses, and know they were full of sleeping people. We are so vulnerable when we sleep, as helpless as infants. It's amazing that most of us do it almost every night.

On Main Street the buildings were dead, waiting for daylight to resuscitate them. *Think, Billie. What are you going to do when you get to the office?*

I wasn't going to leave fingerprints. Or hair. I knew that much from watching television. I had gloves and a cap in the truck. When I parked, I pulled on the gloves, tucked my hair up under the cap, and took a flashlight so I wouldn't need to turn on lights.

As I eased through the unlocked front door, I saw a thin ribbon of yellow around Mr. Landiss's closed door. Whoever had remodeled the place hadn't done a real good job.

I tiptoed to the door and listened. I didn't hear a thing.

I turned the handle slowly and peered in.

He was lying on the sofa bed holding a wad of wet paper towels to his nose.

I couldn't decide if the surge of energy I felt was relief that he was alive or fury at what he'd done to my sister. I slammed the door against the wall. "Remember me? I'm Margaret's sister. She sent me to see if you're all right."

"Bidge. She boke by dode." He spat out the words from beneath his towels.

I needed a few seconds to translate.

"She's not a bitch, and you deserve a broken nose. You were a bastard."

"She broke my nose!" He flexed his right fist. "And hurt my hand. I was just getting over breaking it."

Either he was speaking clearer, or I was getting better at understanding what he said.

"You hurt your own hand, hitting her. I've seen her. You ought to be locked up!"

"She asked for it. She—"

In one step I stood over him, glaring down. "Don't give me that. No woman asks to be attacked. I ought to—" I actually drew back a fist before I had a saner thought. "It's a bad idea, Mr. Landiss, hitting a woman. You ruined her dress, too, and caused her considerable mental distress. Our family has lived around here a long time. I'd suggest you leave Solace and take your development plans somewhere else."

If that sorry evening could run Rick Landiss out of town, it wouldn't be a total waste.

He sat up, glaring. "I don't quit that easy, hon. Tell Mags I understand Ben better now. I'll say so if she spreads stories around here, and I will ruin Ben's business if she so much as mentions tonight to any of our friends in Marietta. Oh—and tell her she's fired."

"As if she'd ever want to see you again. But you'd better send her a paycheck and some severance pay. You owe her, big-time."

On my way through the office, I picked up Margaret's shoe.

"Is he dead?" she asked as she opened the door. "I kept waiting for you to call."

"I didn't want to wake Chellie." I didn't mention that I didn't have a cell phone. That wouldn't have occurred to Margaret. "Here's your shoe. And I'm sorry to disappoint you, but Rick is fine except for a broken nose and dented pride."

She let out a breath I suspected she'd been holding since I left.

She had been a busy little bee, though. She had washed her face, combed her hair, and put on lipstick. She had also put my nicest summer blouse over her dress.

I bit back the objection that sprang to mind and went to the kitchen to pour us each another glass of wine. We sat side by side on the couch while I told her everything that had happened on my trip, from putting on the gloves and baseball cap to how ridiculous Rick looked holding wet paper towels to his nose. By our third glass we were mellow enough to giggle at Margaret hitting him with a nude to prevent a rape.

"Oh, I nearly forgot. Rick says you're fired."

She said a word I didn't know she knew, adding, "And I was so looking forward to working with him some more."

"He also said he'll ruin Ben's business if you mention this to any of your mutual friends. He is a real nice man."

"It's okay. I sure don't want to talk about it again."

"There was something else—something about understanding Ben, and he'll say so if you talk about this around here. Do you know what that was about?"

She bent to pick up her purse. "I have no idea."

"He said it like you'd know."

"I don't." She stood. "I'd better be going. Oh—while I was rummaging in your closet, I found something else." She went into my bedroom and brought back the outfit she gave me for Christmas, the one I had ripped chasing Franklin down the hill.

I flinched. "I'm real sorry about that. I fell and tore it. It was the prettiest thing I ever owned, and it broke my heart to ruin it."

"I may be able to fix it. But we really do need to do something about your wardrobe. This blouse was the best thing I could find. Can I wear it to Daddy's and get it back to you later?"

"I'd rather you didn't. It's the only thing I have that's decent enough to wear to church tomorrow."

She shook it off and pulled on the faded navy T with visible reluctance.

"It's only a mile up the road," I reminded her.

"Let's just hope a cop doesn't stop me. Honestly, Billie—"

I held up my hand to stop her. "I'll get up for you at one a.m. I'll listen to all your problems. I'll even drive ten miles to see if you killed a man. But I will not stand here at this hour and listen to comments about my wardrobe. Save it!"

She huffed and glared. We were back on our old footing. Then her face seemed to melt. She reached out and held me so close I could feel her heartbeat. Her cheek was soft and damp against mine. "Thanks for everything," she whispered. "I am so glad you were here." She drew back as if embarrassed at having showed so much emotion. "I hope I can remember how to creep up the stairs so Daddy doesn't hear me."

"Don't forget the third step creaks unless you step real far over to the left."

"How on earth did you learn that?"

"From watching you sneak down and back up again."

At the foot of the porch steps, she turned. "I am so glad you were here."

"Me, too. By the way, take a bath when you get home. You smell sweaty."

"Horses sweat, men perspire, women glow," she reminded me.

"You're glowing something terrible."

I watched until her taillights disappeared around the curve. Margaret had said she didn't understand what Rick Landiss meant about understanding Ben, but she was a lousy liar.

MARGARET DIDN'T COME TO CHURCH the next morning. I invited Daddy and Andy to come back to our place and share a roast I'd put in the oven before I left, but Daddy said, "Margaret fell on your drive last night leaving your place in the dark, and banged up her face real bad. I think we ought to go home and keep her company."

Hey, if she could fool Daddy, maybe she was a better liar than I thought.

Twenty-two

S peaking of liars, the following Wednesday, Luke dropped by the garage.

I backed out from under the hood of a Honda. "Which law have I broken now?"

"None that I know of." He used his thumb to wipe my chin. "You got your motor-oil blusher a little low this morning."

I wiped my hands on a rag so he wouldn't notice they were trembling. "You came by to give me a makeover? I could really use a manicure."

"I came by because I want to talk to you. What time does Chellie go to bed?"

A butterfly fluttered in my solar plexus. What could he want to talk about that she couldn't hear? I hoped my voice was steady as I said, "Around eight."

"Good. I'll be there around eight thirty."

I dressed in new white shorts with a yellow tank I'd bought at Wal-Mart after Margaret's stinging comments about my closet, and I twisted my hair up in a style I'd been trying out. I couldn't believe it when Luke arrived in white shorts and a yellow shirt, too.

"You got the memo!" I greeted him.

"Sure did. Hey, you clean up real good."

Blushing, I picked up a tray I had fixed with brownies and tea. "Let's sit on the porch."

My house was hotter than Hades, but my yard looked pretty under a sky painted magenta, gold, and lavender. In a little while, lightning bugs would flicker across the grass. I always think there is something magical about dusk lit up by lightning bugs.

I set the tray on a table between the rockers and handed him a can of repellant. "We will be completing our matching ensembles with eau de bug spray. As the guest, you can go first."

After he sprayed himself, he pointed the can at me. "Shall I?" When I nodded, he sprayed my arms, legs, and bare feet. When he sprayed his hand and gently wiped my face and neck, I got goose bumps. The way we were looking into each other's eyes, I expected him to slide his arms around me and kiss me. He looked down at his hands. "I'd better wash before I eat."

I sat on the swing in case he wanted to join me and pick up where we'd left off, but when he returned, he took the nearest rocker and reached for a brownie. "These look good. Thanks. I came to talk about your tenants."

He had come all that way on a gorgeous evening to talk about my tenants? So much for sunset and lightning bugs. I kick-started the swing instead of kicking him.

He washed down a chunk of brownie with a swallow of tea. "Those lovely sisters have played housing roulette for two years or more. They tell a sob story, move in a place, pay a month's rent, and then string the landlord along with more stories until they get kicked out."

I was in no mood to listen to him bad-mouthing ladies who kept Chellie and brought me hostas. "You've got the wrong people. My ladies are nice folks."

"Did they tell you their mother died recently, their half brother sold her house, and Verna can't get along with her daughter-in-law?"

He could read the answer on my face.

He took another bite of brownie and finished it before he went on.

"Their mother died three years ago, I can't find confirmation that they have a brother, and Verna has never been married. She doesn't have a son, either, that I can find."

"She's got on a wedding ring."

"You've got on a wedding ring."

"Because I'm married."

"Like I said."

I chose to ignore that. "Her son moved them over. She gave me his phone number, too, as a reference."

"Did you ever call to check it?"

"No." I couldn't even remember what I'd done with the sheet of paper Verna had written the numbers on.

"Their last landlord moved them over. I found him because Ethelyne hasn't changed the address on her driver's license. He said he let them stay four months after they stopped paying because his wife felt sorry for them, but his son is getting married and he needs the apartment. That fellow was so glad to get rid of them, he moved them for free."

"Those poor old women. They must be pretty desperate."

"Don't waste your pity. After their mother's death, her property—which was over by the interstate—sold for a hotel. Your ladies' names are both on the sales contract, and they got a bundle. Yet for the past two years, these lovelies have been mooching off landlords."

That was too much information too fast. "I don't believe it. Why should they?"

"I have no idea, but I found records of three evictions." He heaved himself out of the rocker. "I think we ought to go over and tell them their stay at Chez Waits is over."

"Where will they go?"

"That's not your problem."

"What if they really don't have any money? Maybe they made bad investments. Or somebody cheated them out of what they got for the land. Or—"

"Even if that is all true, you can't support them on what you make."

"You have no idea what I make."

"I know it's not enough to support you and Chellie plus a couple of deadbeats."

"They may not be deadbeats. They could be two old women the world has treated badly. Maybe you've never been destitute. I have. And while I may not have much now, I can give them a place to live. The trailer isn't costing me anything except a little electricity."

"It could be bringing in money to save in case you lose your job."

He was right, of course. The comfort of no longer living on the edge of the precipice had lulled me into forgetting I had only moved a couple of steps away.

Luke offered me a hand. "Come over with me. Let's see what they say."

I took his hand as if I needed it to get out of the swing. "I won't have you browbeating them."

"You can do most of the talking. But remember—if I'm right, these are highly successful con artists, not sweet little old ladies." He licked his forefinger and touched one of the brownies. "Note that I'm claiming that brownie right there—the one with the most nuts."

"Nuts for the nutty." I set a good pace across the yard.

He tugged my hand to slow me down. "Hey! We aren't running a marathon here. Do you know what you plan to say?"

"Sure. I'm going to ask why two filthy rich women are taking advantage of a poor single mom and whether they think I'm made of money. Of course, it is possible they figure I've got a house with land plus a job, which is more than they may have."

"Or it's possible they know you have a real soft heart they can take advantage of."

I was glad when we reached the trailer. I wanted to get this interview over with and send Luke home so I could go pound a tree.

LIGHTS WERE ON IN EVERY room. We could hear a television. "They sure don't mind using your electricity." Luke motioned for me to knock.

"Who's there?" Verna quavered.

"Billie. I need to talk to you."

She opened the door, but when she saw Luke, she started to close it again.

I put in a knee. "We need to talk."

"Oh, dear." She looked over her shoulder. "Ethylene is . . ." The sound of a flushing toilet finished her sentence.

"Who was at the door?" Ethelyne called, coming through the kitchen.

Luke took advantage of the moment when Verna turned to answer to push me ahead of him into the living room.

"We've come to talk to you about the rent." If I sounded a little breathless, it was because of the impact of Luke's broad hand on my back. "Verna's check bounced."

Ethelyne lumbered to the recliner and sat down without a word.

Verna started toward a pocketbook on the counter. "I'm sorry. I'll write you another one. My new ones came."

"That won't do any good if there's no money in the account," Luke pointed out. He sat on the couch and motioned for me to join him.

It was the first time I'd been in the trailer since they had moved in. Their furniture looked not simply old but valuable. I told myself it was probably stuff they had inherited from their mother.

Ethelyne used the remote to turn off the TV. Verna perched on the edge of a small rocker like an anxious chickadee at a feeder glimpsing a person through a window.

Luke cleared his throat. "I understand you ladies have had several landlords in the past few years."

"We've moved some," Ethylene admitted easily. She peered at him through thick glasses. "Aren't you that new policeman Tee Hobson's got working with him? The one some say will replace Tee when he retires?" She gave him a wide smile of admiration.

"I don't know about replacing Tee, but I'm working with him. Right now, though, I'm here in an unofficial capacity to discuss your failure to pay rent." Luke sat with his hands resting on his thighs like any minute he might jump up and arrest them.

I leaned forward to seem friendlier and less threatening. "We need to talk about why your check bounced. Are you having financial problems? Maybe we can make arrangements. I mean, it's not like I'm rich or anything—I count on your rent to clothe my child and pay her school expenses next year—but if you are having a cash flow problem . . ."

I let the sentence trail off to give them a chance to reply.

Verna brightened like we'd discovered a mutual acquaintance. "Will Chellie go to Solace Elementary? I taught first grade there for years—until those children made me so nervous I simply couldn't take it any longer."

"Miss Jackson!" She hadn't taught me, but I remembered her.

She peered at me as if trying to see the child I had been. "You are one of the Anderson girls. Your father told us when he stopped by to visit one evening. I don't remember you, but I do remember your sister. Beautiful little thing. Smart as a whip, too."

That took the sugar out of my cake. I was glad Luke spoke before I could say something I might regret. "So you are getting a teacher's pension and Social Security?"

"Not a lot," Verna insisted. "Just enough to buy a few groceries."

"What about you?" I asked Ethylene. "Did you work before your mother got sick?"

"I was at the mill a while, but I couldn't stand the pressure. They set real high quotas, and somebody was always yelling at you if you didn't meet them."

I'd had women like that on my line. "Delicate flowers," Mamie used to call them. Always wanting us to ease up on their quotas because they were too fragile to work hard, even though most of them looked like they could stop a truck if need be. They seldom lasted long.

"We did all right so long as Mama was alive," Ethelyne lamented. "She had a little money coming in. Daddy's pension, Social Security—enough to make ends meet."

"We'd still be all right if Roy hadn't sold the house." Verna sounded ready to cry. "That was cruel, selling the only home Ethelyne had!"

"I appreciate your predicament, but I have a child to support." I decided to test one of Luke's so-called lies. "What about your son? Can't he help you?"

"No. His wife won't let him."

"You don't have a son," Luke said bluntly. "You never married."

"How did you find that out?" Ethylene sounded downright proud of him. "We neither one ever married, to tell the truth. Daddy was real particular about the company we kept, and after he died— Well, Mama was sick and nobody we fancied came around."

Verna twisted her ring. What I had thought was a plain gold band was set with a large ruby on the other side. "We say I was married because some people think funny things about two women living together." I thought funnier things about women who wore rubies and tried to cheat a single mother out of rent.

Before I could say so, Luke said, "Your last landlord says you strung him along for four months with one fantastic story after another—"

"Ethelyne ought to write for television!" Verna crowed in admiration. "Some of the things she thinks up!"

"But we really are hard-up," Ethelyne assured us. "Daddy's pension died with Mama."

I looked around. "You have some nice antiques here. Have you considered selling any?"

"They were Mama's!" Verna objected. "We couldn't sell Mama's things."

"Besides, we'd have to buy other furniture," Ethelyne pointed out. "It don't make sense to sell what you got and go buy more."

I sighed. "I appreciate that you've had difficulties. I've had some, too. But—"

"But you're young and strong." Ethelyne stretched out in her recliner like she was waiting for the undertaker. "And you got a good job. What if you were old and feeble and knew that for the rest of your life, there wasn't going to be any more income than you was already getting? A little bit of Social Security and Verna's piddly little pension—that's all we got to feed and clothe ourselves. It's not much. I can tell you that."

"What happened to the money you got for your mother's land?" Luke slid the question in as smooth as glass.

Ethelyne's sizable bosom fell in a sigh. "The real estate fellah cheated us; then our stockbroker cheated us. It's a hard world for women alone."

I could identify with that. I began to feel sorry for them again. "What about your church?"

"They hit every church in the county, in rotation," Luke said softly without moving his mouth. "They take food from church pantries, and they show up at church suppers and *claim* to have forgotten their wallets."

"They may be hungry," I said, also without moving my mouth. If we got good, maybe we could take our show on the road.

I remembered my own trips to church pantries. Luke had never known that kind of humiliation. Maybe I ought to check their pantry like Mamie had checked mine. They might need me to bring them something.

"I think I will get a glass of water, if you don't mind." I got up and sauntered to the kitchen.

When I opened the fridge, the shelves practically groaned. I saw a thick steak, a carton of mushrooms, the remains of a casserole, a bottle of wine, and a crisper full of vegetables that looked suspiciously like they had come from my garden. I distinctly remembered one tomato shaped like Lucky's head. The freezer was full of meat, frozen vegetables, and the priciest of frozen dinners. Through the open bedroom door, I saw a pile of bulging bags from the nearest outlet mall. On the counter was a brochure for a Caribbean cruise. A letter on the shipping line's letterhead began, "We are happy you are interested . . ."

Every kindly feeling I had toward those two women vanished in a red haze. I wanted to smack them upside the head with that brochure. I waved it, paced, and stormed. I have no idea what I said, but Luke said I was astonishing. I do remember I wished I had a long tail like Lucky's so I could swish from side to side. And I remember shouting at the end, "I am not running a charity here!"

"Why, honey, we just wrote off for that brochure to give us something to dream about," Ethelyne said, sweet as ever, "and that food is some things our church brought by in a box."

"Churches don't give out steak. I know that from personal experience."

Verna twisted her hands in her lap. Ethelyne shrugged. "Maybe a friend brought that. My memory's getting bad, the older I get. I can't remember half of what I ought to."

"Can't remember half the lies you've told, more likely," said Luke. "Can't remember that you got enough for your mother's property to keep you the rest of your lives. I'll bet if I got a warrant to look at your financial records—" Ethelyne didn't flinch, but Verna did.

"Can you remember I've got a disabled child to support?" I demanded. "Can you remember you owe me rent? What are my options for getting them out, Luke?"

"We can ask the ladies to voluntarily quit the premises, or you can file official eviction papers. I'll be happy to serve them."

Verna wrung her hands. "Where will we go? What will we do?"

"Oh, shut up." Ethelyne hauled herself to her feet. "I told you this couldn't last forever." She reached for the brochure I still held. "Maybe we oughta take this cruise. I hear they's nice men on senior cruises."

I stomped out, too angry to speak. Luke followed, but he paused at the door. "As a gesture of goodwill, would you leave Mrs. Waits a check for the rent you owe her?"

"And would you tell me why you do it?" I cried from the steps. "The truth?"

"It's fun," said Ethylene. "Making up stories good enough that people believe them. It brightens our lives some. Besides, as Mama always said, why spend money you don't have to?"

"But if you have money, why did your check bounce?"

"We keep an account to pay rent out of. It sometimes gets overdrawn."

"Don't use that one for Mrs. Waits's check," Luke warned.

"Tomorrow," I stormed. "By sundown tomorrow I want you out of here. And don't expect your deposit back. You stole half my vegetables."

I STOMPED TOWARD HOME WITHOUT waiting to see if Luke came or not. He caught me halfway across the orchard. "Are you all right?"

I turned my back to him and swiped my eyes. I didn't want him to see me cry. "How could I be dumb enough to believe them? Even after we got there, I believed them, off and on."

"That's because you are a nice person and they aren't." He pulled me to him. My eyes came exactly to his heart. It thudded as loud as mine. When he starting rubbing my back in circles like Mama used to, I bawled. I bawled so long and hard, I soaked his yellow shirt through to the skin.

I only stopped crying because he had begun to kiss my hair, my forehead, and my sorry, wet eyes. A warm, lovely sweetness spread through me. I wanted to stand there forever.

Yet I couldn't forget the ladies and how they had used me.

"I must be the stupidest, dumbest—" I stopped talking. Luke was kissing my lips.

We sure weren't teenagers anymore.

"Oh, Mina," he groaned when we finally came up for air.

I hated to bring it up, but, "I'm getting a crick in my neck."

"Here." He picked me up so I could wrap my legs around his waist. "Better?"

"Much." We resumed where we had left off. I forgot the lovely ladies in my trailer.

But then I remembered Chellie, asleep and alone in the house. To complete the happy family portrait, Porter's ghost climbed in between us. I pulled back and would have fallen if Luke hadn't caught me.

He held me close. "I always seem to have that effect on you. What happened?"

I slid down to the ground. "I can't do this, Luke. I really am married."

He was still holding my arms. He shook me gently. "He's been gone—what? Five years? He hasn't been back a single time. I've been asking around."

I jerked away from him. "Don't talk about me with other people! Besides, nobody in this town liked Porter."

"You've got that right." He stood there with his arms slightly curved. They looked real empty without me in them.

"Whatever they told you, he is still my husband. We never got a divorce. And he sends checks every month."

"Not lately he hasn't. Face it: Porter is gone. You need to get on with your life." Thank goodness Luke wasn't a dragon. The way he was breathing, he'd have burned down my orchard. He caught my arm again, his long fingers digging into the skin, and tried to pull me to him.

I stood my ground. "Stop. You're hurting me."

He dropped his hand and went over to the nearest peach tree. He gave the truck three solid whacks with one fist. Pounding things when we were mad was something else we had in common, apparently.

He rested his head against the branch. "I think you and I have a chance at something special. Don't you?" His voice was gruff.

I wanted to fling my arms around him and say, "Oh, yes! Yes! Yes!" but one of us had to keep a tenuous hold on reality. "I'm not free, Luke. I have a legal husband out there somewhere, and I have a seriously handicapped child. She is going to need me all her life. How can I give time or energy to anybody else? I can't. I just can't!" I fell to my knees in the grass, fighting tears. If I started crying, I might sob all night.

He knelt beside me. "I can take care of you and Chellie. Will you let me?"

I was so tempted. But we were having that conversation on the wrong night. I had not only made a mistake in choosing a husband—I'd made two mistakes choosing tenants. I was terrible at sizing up people, as the past hour had shown. "I can't." It came out a whisper.

Moonlight striped him in black and gold, like he was behind prison bars. Or maybe it was me in prison. We looked at each other for a very long time. The electricity between us was still there, but this time it hurt.

Luke stood up first. "I'd better be getting home."

I climbed to my feet and brushed twigs off my knees. "You want to eat your brownie?"

"I'm not hungry. But you let me know when you're tired of pretending to be married—you hear me? Because you and I both know that's a crock."

I raised my hand to stop him, but he strode to his truck and slammed the door. As his taillights disappeared, a train wailed in the distance. I wanted to wail, too.

For the next hour I sat in my swing. First I cried. I cried for what Luke and I couldn't have and for the stupid mistake I'd made marrying Porter. I cried for Chellie, and what she would never be. I cried because I was so pitiful that I had nobody in my life and had to cry alone.

But gradually the magic of the evening soothed me. A warm breeze dried my tears. Lightning bugs flickered across my lawn. Clouds floated overhead, light against the dark sky, constantly changing shapes.

My life was changing shape, too. I finally accepted it. Those last few months had been the birth pangs of a new Billie. I thought about Porter and the five years we'd had together. For the first time I admitted something I'd kept even from myself. When I read Porter's note on the counter saying he was leaving me and our newborn child? What I'd mostly felt was relief. In the hospital I had held Michelle and wondered how I was going to cope with her handicaps *and* her daddy. Porter's note came as the answer to a prayer I hadn't dared to pray.

I tugged off my wedding ring and carried it back to my jewelry box. Maybe someday I'd get desperate enough to sell it for food. Or maybe Chellie would want it. I would never wear it again. I did not wish Porter any harm. I truly did not. But whatever happened or didn't happen with Luke Braswell, I wasn't going to pretend any longer that I wanted Porter back.

Twenty-three

I didn't see Luke for nearly two weeks, but I thought about him every day. Feeling like I was still fourteen lurking in halls, I drove slow by the police station on my way home each afternoon in case he was going in or coming out. I never caught a glimpse of him.

Even so, he was changing my life in good ways. Ever since he'd announced my hair was the color of apricots, I'd been looking at myself differently in the mirror. I treated myself to more new clothes and chose colors that went with apricot hair. I bought lipstick and nail polish that went with apricot hair. I painted my fingernails and my toenails. And I decided to use some of the lovely ladies' deposit money and give myself and Chellie a trip to the beauty parlor. I needed a good haircut. Chellie's brown curls deserved one, too.

As I held Chellie for her cut, the stylist said in a careless manner, "Maggie is so sweet. I hated we couldn't take her on. But we're in the same fix as everybody else—trying to make enough to keep the people we already have."

"Margaret applied for a job here?"

"Yeah, yesterday."

She had said she worked for Rick because she was bored. Exactly how bored was she?

When I stopped by the grocery store, the cashier mentioned that my "real sweet sister" had filled out an application there, too. I decided to run by Daddy's on my way home. I hadn't spoken with Margaret since Saturday night, so I could use the excuse of wanting to see how she was.

I had another motive, of course. I wanted to show off our haircuts. Chellie looked like a pixie, and the stylist had cut mine chin level, parted it in the center, and put a relaxer on it so that gentle curls fell on both sides of my face. I loved it, and my head felt a pound lighter. I wanted somebody to admire us while we were still beauty parlor fresh.

It was close to sunset when we drove in. Margaret came onto the porch carrying a dishpan of water. Since my truck was in the shade and the window was down, Chellie would be fine for a little while. "Back in a minute," I told her. I hurried toward the porch, wanting to talk before Margaret went back inside. I raised my voice to reach her. "That's a great ramp." I figured a little chitchat might ease us into other topics.

Since I'd been there, Daddy had built a long wooden incline with railings to the left of the back porch steps. Where it ended, he had laid a new cement walk to the drive in one direction and another down past the henhouse and pigsty to the barns. I walked up the ramp instead of using the steps. "This is great! I'll bet Andy could push Chellie up it. I can't believe Daddy did all this for her."

"He says he's getting ready for his old age." Margaret carefully poured dishwater onto a bush in a pot by the steps. It looked like a tomato, but the fruit wasn't bigger than cherries. She said, "I am determined he is going to live." She shook the last few drops of water from the dishpan into the pot.

"He?"

"Yeah. I figure anything that stands there waiting to be served has to be a he."

She lifted her face to smile. Her bruises had faded but her cheek had a long scab. I wondered if she'd have a permanent scar.

I tossed my head. "What do you think about my new haircut?"

She studied it for several seconds. "It's nice."

I couldn't tell if she liked it or not. "Don't jump up and down or get excited."

"No, it's great. You look glamorous."

I wondered why Margaret hadn't gotten a trim while she was applying for a job. She was getting shaggy around the edges. Maybe she didn't trust anybody except her expensive stylist back in Marietta.

"Chellie got a new style, too. She looks adorable."

Margaret hurried to the truck. I got there in time to hear her say, "You look beautiful, honey." Chellie preened.

"That's more than you said about me," I pointed out.

"Chellie! Chellie!" Andy bounded toward us, Jimbo pounding along beside him. I hadn't realized that old dog could run. "Come see! Papa gave me a calf. I've named her Milky. She has a stall in the hay barn."

The hay barn was a tall, open structure with stalls along each side for new calves or ailing cows. The rest of the space was used for storing hay for winter use.

As soon as I had Chellie in her chair, Andy grabbed the handles and started for the barn at a clip.

"Don't go too fast," I yelled.

"I'm not." He hurtled on. Chellie's laugh floated back.

I smiled as I watched them go, then joined Margaret at the steps. "Daddy still milking?"

"Or cleaning up."

It was as good a time as any to ask Margaret what I wanted to know. "When I was at the beauty parlor, they said you'd been in there looking for work. They said the same thing in the grocery store."

Her nostrils flared. "You can't breathe in this town without everybody talking about it. You want to come in and stay for supper? I'll be making spaghetti when Daddy's done."

"We stopped by Hardee's, thanks." I followed her. "Why are you looking for work?"

She thumped the dishpan against her leg. "I told you, I get bored around here."

"Clerking in a grocery store isn't an antidote to boredom. Run into Marietta one day a week and meet Katrinka for tennis and lunch. Daddy wouldn't mind keeping Andy. You don't need to get a job. Other people need work a lot worse than you do."

Margaret jerked open the screen door. "I thought it would be fun to work a little, okay? It's no big deal." She obviously didn't want to talk about it. "Don't let in flies," she added as I came in behind her.

I shooed a fly out before I shut the door and did something I never did: looked in the mirror Mama had hung by the back door. I almost didn't recognize myself, but I gave the reflection a smile.

"You want a glass of tea?" Margaret knew the answer. She was already filling a glass with ice. She poured in tea, squirted in juice from a yellow plastic lemon, and set it on the table.

I took a swallow before I asked, "So what have you been doing besides applying for jobs?"

"Hey, I just asked a few places if they were hiring." Margaret seemed determined to convince me—or was it herself? "I've also been trying to get a start on clearing out this place." She went into the dining room and picked up a stack of magazines from the table. "You wouldn't believe the stuff Daddy's been keeping. Some of these magazines are older than you. And our bedroom was awful. Both the drawers and the closet were crammed full."

"That stuff was mine. You didn't throw it out, did you?"

"I should have, but no, I boxed it up and put it in the attic. Why leave your stuff here when you have a place of your own?"

"Never needed it, I guess."

"I can't imagine why you ever would. High school basketball uniforms and trophies?"

"I might put the trophies on a shelf in my bedroom. You know—shore up the old ego when it needs it."

"I hope you've got something better to shore up your ego than high school trophies, but if you ever do want them, you'll find them in the attic in boxes labeled 'Billie's high school junk.'"

"It isn't junk. It's my illustrious past."

"Of course." She moved around the dining room adding magazines to the stack in her arms. "This whole house needs clearing out, but this week I'm concentrating on this room and on getting the sewing room ready for Jason. Did I tell you? He's coming Saturday to stay through the Fourth of July." She sounded happier than she had since she first arrived at Daddy's.

"I thought Daddy fixed up the sewing room for you."

"He did, but I've been sharing with Andy so I could sew a little. Besides, Jason doesn't like to share."

"Just like somebody else we know."

She wrinkled her nose. "Be nice to me. I've got you a present." She dumped the magazines on the kitchen table and went upstairs. She came back holding a gorgeous yellow sundress. "Try this on. It still has to be hemmed, but it's almost done."

I held the dress against me. "You made this for me?"

"Yeah. I told you, I'm bored, and Mama left a trunk full of fabric and patterns. That color suits you, don't you think?"

"It's fantastic!" I stepped into the dining room, stripped down, and pulled on the dress. "Absolutely perfect." I pirouetted to show it off.

"What do you all do with old papers and magazines?" she called from the kitchen.

"Let them accumulate until they fill up a room; then we torch it." I paused a second for her exasperated huff. She didn't disappoint me. "We aren't in the boonies, you know. We recycle like everybody else. Let me change back to my jeans, and I'll dump the magazines in the back of my truck. I've got to take a load to the recycling center this weekend anyway."

I thumbed through a copy of *Southern Farm Equipment*. "This is older than either one of us. We ought to donate it to a museum. You're sure Daddy doesn't want any of these?"

"He said not."

I went back to the den to change. She followed and sat in Daddy's recliner. "Jason's been so miserable this summer. He calls every day complaining about something. So I want to make his visit a happy one. Who knows? Maybe he'll stay more than a week. Summer school is over. I had to clear out the closet in that room, though. It was full of Mama's winter clothes."

My breath caught in my throat. "You didn't give them away, did you?"

"No, I put them in boxes with mothballs." We shared a long moment of silence. Even after a year, Mama's loss was a raw grief for us both. Margaret spoke first. "Do you realize Daddy hasn't gotten rid of any of her things? We ought to go through them and figure out what to do with all of it."

"Did Daddy tell you to do that?"

"No, but it's been a long time."

"I think we ought to wait until he's ready." I didn't want to admit to my practical sister that I wasn't ready.

Margaret pulled the lever to make the chair recline and closed her eyes.

"You look plumb worn-out," I told her. "You aren't killing yourself out here, are you? Although it's hard to believe anything you'd do here would be more strenuous than running every committee in Marietta and taking care of your house."

She didn't open her eyes. "I've been doing a lot of thinking. That wears me out."

"I can see how it might." She didn't rise to the bait. "What are you thinking about?"

"Life. How I got from here to there and back again."

I thought back to a day when I was eight and found Margaret sobbing in our bedroom. "Are you sick?" I had asked, worried. If Maggie was sick, I'd have to do her chores.

"Sick and tired of this hick town, but Daddy says he won't pay for college unless I stay at home my first two years. I am getting out of here if I have to sell my soul!"

I had sat on the bank in front of our house to ponder how Maggie could sell her soul. If everybody had one, who would buy it? Could she live without hers?

In the next weeks Maggie went to her sewing machine and earned sewing awards that got her a college scholarship.

"Sheer determination is how you got from here to there," I reminded her. "You told me when you were sixteen that you were getting out of Solace if you had to sell your soul to do it, and you set a goal and achieved it. What's there to think about?"

"Whether it was the right goal."

"It's a bit late to ask now, isn't it? I mean, you've got Ben, Jason, Andy, the house, and all the rest of it. You aren't considering running away to join a circus, are you?"

She still didn't open her eyes. "I might. I could become a bareback rider in pink sequins. When I was little, I wanted a dress with pink sequins. Mama made me a green jumper instead."

"From what I've heard about your riding skills, you'd better become a trapeze artist."

She fumbled for Jimbo's rawhide beside the recliner and threw it at me. Margaret's big failure in life—which happened about the time I was born—was when Daddy bought her a pony. She could not stay on its back.

"You know why Daddy got me that pony, don't you?" she said, eyes still closed.

"Because you told him you'd rather have a pony than a sister. I guess he decided to give you both. Pity you couldn't ride."

"We should have kept the pony and sold you at auction."

"Don't you wish."

We'd had that conversation many times before. That was the first time it made us smile.

I went back to the mirror to check out my new haircut. It was as soft and shiny as hair in a shampoo commercial. Would Luke like it?

Margaret called after me, "I wish I could replace that old bed and chest Daddy's got in that room. Have you seen them? He must have gotten them from Goodwill. They might not be bad if we refinished them, but there's no time. I wonder if he'd let me paint them—or if they'd dry before Jason gets here?"

I might have said some awful things about that bed and chest when I had them, but it made me mad for her to insult them. I satisfied my urge to smack her by making faces at my reflection.

"Speaking of painting," she added, "I love what you've done with your house. It's adorable, like a little English cottage."

That description did a lot to dissolve my annoyance. "Thanks. I really like the way it turned out." Would Luke remember we had a date for the week after the Fourth of July? After our final scene in the orchard, would he still want to come?

Those questions occupied me as I carried one load of magazines out to my truck and came back for another. Margaret was at the fridge getting herself some tea. "Is Ben bringing Jason?" I asked. "Can he stay, too?"

"No, I'll drive in and pick Jase up. This is a busy season for Ben." She sat at the table.

I refilled my glass and joined her. "Is Daddy working Andy to death?"

"He's working him hard, but Andy seems to love it. He always enjoyed working in the yard. When he was a toddler, I called him Farmer Andy. I never imagined he'd take to farming like he has, though. If he's not out with Daddy on the tractor, he's pulling weeds in the garden or checking out the livestock. He knows the names of all the cows and he's made friends with King George, Daddy's current hog. Do you reckon Daddy names hogs after royalty because he thinks they are regal beasts or because he has a low opinion of government?"

"I'd suspect the latter."

"Me, too. Anyway, I was about to say if I hadn't been there for Andy's birth, I'd swear he was yours instead of mine."

I blew on my nails and buffed them on my shirt. "Good genes will tell. Of course, he is the spitting image of Ben."

"Yeah."

"That wasn't exactly an enthusiastic agreement."

She drew circles with water drops left by her chilly glass on the table-top. "We're having a few problems right now. Nothing serious, but that's part of what's got Jason upset."

"Want to talk about it?"

"No, thanks."

"Were you wise to come out here? Shouldn't you be there?"

"No, I needed to get away. And I told you, Andy's been a little puny this past winter."

I could understand if she didn't want Daddy knowing she and Ben were having trouble. I'd certainly concealed things from our parents during my marriage.

"Well, I'd better tear Chellie away from the barn and get her home to bed." I was at the screen door before I remembered something I wanted to ask. "Would you be upset if I went to see Mr. Landiss again? To see if he's found out anything about Porter?"

"Why can't you admit Porter has left you? You aren't likely to get him back."

"I don't think he has—left me, I mean. It isn't like him. But I don't want to find him to get him back. I want to find him because I want a divorce."

There! I had said it out loud and in public, and the sky didn't fall.

I tensed for Margaret's next words. I knew what they'd be: "It's about time."

She said nothing.

I went ahead and gave her the arguments I'd been giving myself since I sat on the porch watching fireflies. "I'm still young, with a life to live. I don't want to spend the rest of it tethered like a goat by an invisible chain."

She sat drawing in water drops on the table like she was trying for the perfect circle—or waiting for me to turn into a woman as perfect as herself.

I plunged on. "Okay, you've known it all along, but I've finally realized we got married too young. I didn't know who I was or what I was going to become. I've changed since then. What I wanted and needed then isn't what I want or need now. I'd be willing to bet that's true for him, too. Divorce would be best for us both."

Margaret shoved back her chair, eyes blazing. "Who are you to decide what is best for Porter? It takes two people to make a marriage. It ought to take two to end one. You can't make an arbitrary decision like that. Maybe he *hasn't* changed. Maybe, in spite of all the evidence to the contrary, he still loves you very much!" She ran from the kitchen and up the stairs.

I stood there bewildered. Why should Margaret take Porter's side?

I FINISHED MY TEA WHILE I waited for Margaret to return. When she didn't, I figured I might as well fetch Chellie and go home.

I was diverted by the sight of two people limping down the road toward the house. The setting sun at their backs turned them into black paper cutouts against a vibrant orange sky. Both were slight and wore pants, but one wore a straw hat with a narrow brim. As they got closer, I saw that the one with the hat was a man, the other a woman. The way they put one foot in front of the other, I got the feeling they had to will themselves to take each step.

I crossed the yard and waved. "Hey! Can I help you?"

As they turned in the drive, the woman stumbled. I saw that both of them were carrying heavy backpacks. The man caught her elbow with a gesture so loving that for a second I envied her, miserable as she looked.

They came into the yard and pulled off their packs. They dropped them to the ground and stood hand in hand like children. "Our truck broke up on the road." The man spoke in a thick accent I was getting used to as more and more Mexicans poured into Georgia.

"Broke down," the woman corrected him gently. "The truck broke down up the road." She also spoke with an accent, but I had no trouble understanding her.

Even exhausted, she was beautiful, with straight dark hair falling over her shoulders like a shawl, a pure pale complexion, and brows like delicate wings. The man was rugged rather than handsome, with the defeated slump of someone who has reached his last extremity. Both of them wore faded jeans and T-shirts that could use a wash.

Jimbo came running from the hay barn and gave a warning bark. "It's okay, Jimbo," I reassured him. He sniffed the newcomers. When the woman scratched behind his ears, his tail wagged.

I put out a hand. "Hey. I'm Billie Waits."

The man backed up a wary step, like a stray who has met with too much abuse to know how to deal with unexpected kindness. The woman lifted her chin and said, "I am Emerita Gomez." So might a queen of Spain have announced, "I am Isabella."

"Hey, Emerita."

"This is my husband, José."

I gave him a quick smile. "Hello, José. How far away is your truck? One mile? Two?"

Again, she answered. "I do not know—far. May we sit down?" She gestured toward an old picnic table in the shade of an oak. Daddy had built that table when I was small. We used to eat lunch and dinner out there every summer, but I wondered how long it had been since anybody had sat at it. I hoped the seats hadn't rotted.

Apparently not, for it bore their weight. Emerita gave a sigh of relief. "It seems far when you are walking."

"I'll be glad to look at your truck. I'm a mechanic. But first, let me get you something to drink. Iced tea? Water?"

"Water," Emerita said gratefully. She looked around at the shaded yard and the house. "You live here?"

"No, my father does. I live down the road a piece." I went to the kitchen and brought out two glasses of water with ice. José was sitting beside her at the table. They reached for the glasses with remarkable restraint, considering the way they drained them as soon as I turned my back. I went inside and filled a half-gallon plastic jug. Then I got a tray and rummaged in the fridge. I found the end of a ham, so I filled a tray with sliced tomatoes, lettuce leaves, ham slices, and half a loaf of bread. I didn't know if they liked mustard and mayo, but I added those, along with a knife, plates, and paper napkins. Chances were they hadn't eaten if they'd been walking. A gleam in their eyes when they saw the food told me I'd been right.

They didn't need me watching them eat. "You have a bite to eat, and I'll go tell my father you are here."

I started toward the milking barn, but Chellie called from the hay barn. "Mama! Come see Milky!" I made my way through the soft fragrance of hay and cows to a pen at the back of the barn, where the children were petting a small tan heifer. "This is Milky," Chellie informed me.

I took a second to give Milky the admiration she deserved before I joined Daddy. It had been years since I'd been in the milking barn. I had forgotten how compact it was. I passed through the room filled with a huge gleaming milk tank and into the second room, where Daddy was cleaning equipment in a sunken well in the center. Along each side of the room ran two aisles, where twice each day twelve cows at a time stood patiently in a herringbone pattern while they were milked. Small doors at one end let the cows in to their stations and one at the far end let them back out to the pasture. "Sorry to bother you while you are cleaning up, but some Mexicans have showed up saying their truck broke down up the road."

"I don't have any farmwork this year."

"I know, but can I leave Chellie here while I take a look at their truck?"

"Sure." He reached for a towel to wipe his hands. "Don't you kids go into the milking barn—you hear me?" he called into the hay barn as we passed. "I've got to go up to the house a minute. I'll be right back."

The newcomers watched our approach with an expression like

Chellie's when I took her into a new place—hopeful and anxious at the same time. The food was all gone.

"Daddy, meet Emerita and José Gomez."

"Good evening. I'm Bill Anderson. Billie here says you've had trouble with your truck."

"It broke up down the road," the man said carefully. The woman and I shared a smile.

"Would you like to ride with me and show me where?" I asked.

They both stood.

"You don't have to go," I told Emerita.

"We will go together."

They had walked quite a distance in the heat. I drove four miles before the man pointed to the most derelict truck I ever saw outside a junkyard—an eighty-two Dodge Ram that had been badly mistreated. The body was more rust than paint, the interior squalid. They had spread a serape across the seat, but springs made lumps under it like a mole had been burrowing. The floorboard on the passenger side was almost nonexistent. If what was under the hood looked as bad as what I could see, I doubted I could more than resuscitate it temporarily.

The man muttered in Spanish as I lifted the hood.

"What is he saying?" I asked Emerita.

"He says it is junk. It spills oil on the road, and the—" She stopped and asked the man a question in Spanish. He pointed to the radiator.

"That part also leaks," she informed me.

The man's assessment was correct. A dark black circle of oil had seeped into red dust under the engine, and the radiator was empty when I opened it. I checked the hoses, but I'd need more time than we had before dark to make a good diagnosis.

"It needs work," I agreed, "but I should be able to get it running."

The woman asked a question in Spanish, her voice anxious.

"*No.*" The man burst into another spate of Spanish and pulled out both pockets. They held only a few bills and coins.

"We cannot pay," she translated. "First we must find work." She contemplated the engine with angry eyes.

"Green cards." José pulled out his wallet and showed them to me. "We can work."

I fetched a chain and hook from my truck. "Let's tow your truck to Daddy's for the time being. I'll look at it tomorrow and see what all it needs."

The man helped me secure the chain between the trucks. I motioned him to his cab. "It will not go," Emerita reminded me, puzzled.

The man and I exchanged a look of perfect comprehension without saying a word. He climbed into his truck, put it in neutral, and motioned for me to drive on.

Emerita decided to ride with me. "Here we go," I said. I eased onto the road and felt the chain pull taut. I sounded a lot more cheerful than I felt. José hadn't turned on his lights, so they must not work. I wasn't crazy about towing an unlit truck down the road with dark coming on.

Still, it was a beautiful evening—very like the evening when I'd waited for Luke. To keep from thinking about him, I asked the woman beside me, "How long have you been in America?"

"We came Monday before Easter."

"You speak very good English."

"My father worked in the fields in California when he was small. He vowed his children would not work in fields, so when he married, he and my mother went to Mexico City and worked in a hotel so my brother and I could go to a good school. *Papí* insisted we learn English."

If she'd gone to a good school, what was she doing riding around in a broken-down truck looking for work to get it repaired? I rejected several questions before I settled on, "What have you been doing since you got to America?"

Her laugh was bitter. "Working in fields. And in restaurants. It is because of that old truck. We sent money to a man to buy a good truck so we could drive to Georgia and work with José's brother Humberto in a chicken plant in Dalton. The man got us that old thing instead. It only lasted one day before it needed repairs. We went to my father's cousin in San Antonio and washed dishes in his restaurant one month—one whole month"—she held up a finger in case I misunderstood how long that had been—"to earn money for all the repairs it needed before we could start for Georgia." She turned and glared over her shoulder at the truck behind us. "But again and again something has broken. We have worked two more months from Texas to Georgia, and most of our money has gone to fix that truck. Someday, when we are settled, I will write the man who cheated us and tell him how angry I am."

I wished I could offer them a bed and food for a few days so they could rest. But even though Ethylene and Verna had moved out like they were supposed to, I didn't have a stick of furniture in the trailer.

Daddy already had a plan when we got to his place. "Billie, don't you still have a sleeping bag and air mattress upstairs?"

"I used to before Margaret cleaned out the closet."

"Go ask her where they are. She's been sharing with Andy anyway, so we'll give them the sewing room. Emerita can have the bed and José can sleep on the floor."

That was going to be real popular with my sister after she'd been fixing the room up for Jason. "They could both sleep in the living room," I suggested. "She could have Mama's daybed and he could use the floor."

"No reason for them to have to run upstairs to the bathroom." Daddy's tone made it clear he didn't want an argument.

I found Margaret sitting at the kitchen table with a glass of tea. She had on more makeup than she'd worn earlier, like she'd been crying and tried to repair the damage. She didn't mention our recent conversation, so neither did I.

"Daddy wants to know where my old sleeping bag and air mattress are. He's inviting some people to spend the night. The man will need to sleep on the floor."

"Who on earth?"

"A couple of Mexicans whose truck broke down up the road—or, as the man told me, 'broke up down the road.'"

I didn't get the smile I expected. Instead she gave a huff of impatience and went to peer out the screen door. Daddy and the newcomers were sitting at the picnic table. Daddy and Emerita were doing most of the talking. José sat with slumped shoulders, the picture of a man whose dream has failed.

"They look like migrant workers," she said.

"They are migrant workers, sort of. They came to work in a chicken plant up in Dalton, but they've had to do farmwork all the way from Texas to keep their truck repaired. Their names are José and Emerita Gomez."

"I don't give a turkey feather what their names are—Daddy shouldn't be inviting them in to spend the night. We don't know those people. We could be murdered in our beds."

"They seem nice enough, just down on their luck. I told them I'll take a look at their truck tomorrow and see what it needs, but I suspect it isn't worth fixing. The poor old thing has been abused far too long."

"Trust you to be worrying about a truck when I've got to cope with two strangers. I am utterly exhausted. I don't have energy for this. Do they even speak English?"

"She does, real good. His is a bit iffy."

"Well."

"Well what?"

"She speaks English *well*. You talk sometimes like you never finished school."

"Maybe I skipped that particular lesson. Or maybe I didn't learn it very *well*. Or maybe I don't give a— Anyway, Daddy wants you to find my sleeping bag and air mattress so he can let the Gomez family have the sewing room."

"The sewing room? They can sleep down here."

"Daddy said they're to have the sewing room."

"Where is Jason supposed to sleep? He comes tomorrow, you know."

"Maybe they'll be gone before he gets here—if I can get their truck up and running. If not, he can use the daybed."

"He'd have to go all the way upstairs to use the bathroom."

"He's a track star, isn't he?"

"I still don't like it. I wish those people would stay in Mexico, where they belong. We don't have room or resources in this country to take in every peasant who wants to cross the—"

"Maggie!" Daddy spoke through the screen. He came into the kitchen and let the door slam behind him. I hadn't seen him look so stern since he had blessed me out for wanting to marry Porter. He glared at Margaret for several seconds. Then he asked, "Do you remember a house bank you got in Sunday school when you were little? Pink cardboard, I believe, with a red tiled roof and a slot for pennies and nickels?"

Margaret looked as bewildered as I felt. "Sort of. Didn't it have cactus on one side of the door and red flowers on the other? Oh! And it had a black cat sleeping beneath the back window. I loved that bank."

"You deviled me to death wanting change to put in that thing, and you carried it to church proud as punch on Missions Sunday."

"And I cried when they wanted me to leave it on the communion table. Didn't you go back to the kitchen for a bowl so we kids could dump our money in it and take our banks home?"

"Yeah. Better that than you wailing through the sermon. Do you remember what was printed on the roof of that bank?"

"I don't remember it having words."

"I don't remember it at all," I said.

They both looked at me like I was crazy. "You weren't alive," Margaret said. "I wasn't but—what?—four at the time?"

"Something like that," Daddy agreed.

I hated it when Margaret and my parents talked about having a life before I was born. It made me feel less a part of the family.

"What the bank said," Daddy went on, "was BECAUSE GOD LOVES THEM AND WE LOVE THEM. It was a collection for a Mexican mission project." He scratched his chin and we heard the whisper of whiskers. "I can't send them messages that God loves them and I love them and then turn them away when they show up at my front door. I can't do it. Find that sleeping bag and air mattress, will you?"

Margaret set her lips in a tight line and didn't say a word.

Twenty-four

On my way in to work the next morning, I stopped by Daddy's. The old truck was gone.

Mamie pulled in right behind me. "Hey, Mamie!" I called as I swung down from my cab.

Mamie fanned the air in front of her face as she got out. "Hot as blazes already and barely eight o'clock. But who is this? Looks like a grown-up Billie Waits."

"You like it?" I turned so she could get the full effect of my new haircut. It still looked good. I had discovered that spending a few minutes in front of the mirror did wonders for my appearance.

"Shoulda done it years ago. Fools folks into thinking you're a grown-up."

"Some of us take longer to grow up than others." I looked toward the house. "I guess the Mexicans have gone."

"What Mexicans?"

"A couple whose truck died on them yesterday afternoon. I helped them tow it here, and when I left, Daddy was offering them a bed for the night."

Margaret came out the back door wearing white shorts and a lime green top. She carried a basket of wet laundry.

"Did José and Emerita leave?" I called.

She came nearer so she didn't have to shout. "No, unfortunately. He helped Daddy with the milking, and they are still cleaning up."

"Where's their truck?"

"I told Daddy to tow it behind the barn. It looked tacky sitting out here."

"What difference does that make? The fashion police seldom come out this far."

She gave me what I call the Big Sister Look—utter disbelief that our parents didn't smother me at birth. "We don't need to live like white trash." She darted a look at the screen door and lowered her voice. "Are there any other places they could stay? If they aren't gone by tonight, Jason will have to sleep on the daybed, and I really am worried they aren't legal. Any minute Tee Hobson could show up and haul us all to jail."

"I doubt Tee would take Daddy. Just you and Andy."

She didn't crack a smile.

"Are they here illegally?" A worried frown puckered Mamie's forehead.

"She said they have green cards," I said.

"You'd better check those cards," Mamie warned. "We had a man at the mill who loaned out his cards to three different men."

Margaret shifted the basket of clothes on her hip. I saw it was delicate things she probably wished she could dry on the gentle cycle, low heat. "To what do we owe the honor of your appearance?" she asked me.

"I came by to ask them something."

"Emerita's in the kitchen washing dishes while I hang out a few clothes." She went toward the line in back of the house. Mamie trudged slowly toward the ramp. I went faster, since I had to get to work.

Emerita was up to her elbows in soapy water. When I called her name, she turned but she did not smile. "*¿Sí?*"

"Does José know enough about cars to work on them? I work at a garage. My boss might let him work for a few days in exchange for parts."

"No. He can repair farm equipment, but not a truck."

"Okay. It was just an idea. I'll come over this afternoon and look at it."

When I got to the back porch, Mamie had finally reached the top of the ramp. I asked her, "Isn't there a place downtown where day laborers wait to be hired?"

"Yeah, but there was a line as I drove by a minute ago. Nobody's hiring right now."

"I guess we're lucky to have jobs ourselves."

As if prompted by an evil angel, Margaret came back. "Oh, Mamie? I meant to call you and I forgot. We won't need you while Emerita is here. She can do the cleaning."

We heard her say to Emerita as she went inside, "Today we'll clean out the pantry. Heaven only knows the last time that was done."

Mamie stared at me. "Did I just get fired?"

"Sounded like it."

We made our way slowly down the ramp.

Mamie huffed in exasperation. "What's gotten into Margaret? She was the sweetest little girl, but she's turned into Miss Sourpuss. Mopes around here like somebody broke her favorite doll baby and doesn't have a nice word to say to anybody. She perked up a little after she got that job, but since she had that bad fall last Saturday night and had to give up the job, she's been a pill again." She gave me a sharp look. "You know anything about that fall?"

I answered carefully. Mamie could spot a lie faster than a buzzard can spot roadkill. "Only what she told me. She was pretty nice yesterday until I told her I'm planning to divorce Porter."

"You are? Why, child, I am proud of you. As a rule I don't hold with divorce, but if there was ever a wife who deserved one, it is you. I am delighted with that news."

I glanced toward the screen door. "I thought Margaret would be delighted, too, but she wasn't. Since then, it's been like somebody swapped her for her evil twin."

"I wish they'd bring her back, then." Mamie took her keys from her purse. "Like I said, she was the sweetest little girl I ever saw."

"Hey—you saw me."

"Honey, you were many things growing up, but sweet was seldom one of them." Her smile took the sting out of the words. She and I both knew I'd been the kind of child whom fond parents call curious and others call a pain in the neck.

"Will you be all right if you aren't working?" I asked.

"All right? You mean for money? I'm fine. My house and car are paid for, Social Security pays my bills, and if I get sick, Medicare takes care of that. It's possible I'm a whole lot better off in the money department than you are."

"I'm doing all right, finally," I assured her.

Somebody once said, *Life is uncertain—eat dessert first.* I didn't get around to dessert that day. As soon as I got to the garage, Stamps called me into his office. "I've got a little problem. That mechanic you replaced? His mother-in-law died, and he's back, wanting his job. I have to take him on, Billie. He's been with me fifteen years, and his customers are real loyal. But I can keep you on mornings. Maybe things will pick up."

Stamps looked so embarrassed that I felt sorry for him, but he deserved the truth. "I really need full-time work, with my little girl and all, but I thank you for mornings until I can find something else. And hey"—I put on my Happy Face and hoped I could hold it for a sentence or two—"don't feel bad about it. Okay?"

"It's not okay, Billie. It's just what I gotta do."

"Can I bring in an old truck late this afternoon and use your tools to work on it? It's not for pay—the couple doesn't have any money."

Stamps was not only a good mechanic—he was a good man. "Absolutely. And if you find other folks who want you to work on their cars and can't afford my prices, bring them in any Saturday afternoon. How about this: you use my tools and buy supplies at cost, and give me ten percent of what you make. Be sure to set your prices high enough, now."

I TOWED JOSÉ'S TRUCK IN to the garage that evening and checked it out. As I'd expected, it needed a lot of work. "I can get it running," I reported to Emerita, José, and Daddy, who were standing by for the verdict, "but I can't guarantee it will still be running in a few days. It's really not worth fixing. Even if we replaced the engine, the body is so rusted it could fall out any minute. Maybe I ought to just drive you up to Dalton on Sunday. It's not far."

Emerita translated for José. He shook his head and said something in Spanish. "We will need a truck in Dalton," she reported. "How soon can you repair it? And how much will it cost?"

"It won't cost too much, but I can't work on it tomorrow or Sunday." Franklin was coming Saturday to help me get the trailer ready to rent again, and Daddy expected Chellie and me to go to church with him Sunday. To my surprise, I had enjoyed being back. Folks seemed real glad to see us, and Chellie loved sitting with Andy.

"I'll have to work on it several evenings next week," I told them.

"You'll be fine at my place until then," Daddy said. "I got some chores José can do, and I know Margaret can use some help around the house. Besides, you both look like you can use a few days' rest."

I suspected Margaret was not going to be fine when she got back with Jason, but that was Daddy's lookout, not mine.

MY LADIES HAD LEFT THE trailer very clean, and a month's rent on the kitchen counter. Ethelyne had even left a note: *We like your spunk.*

Franklin and I spent Saturday morning tidying the yard. I wondered who would rent it. I didn't have any furniture. I also didn't have any confidence in my ability to pick tenants.

In lieu of payment, I took Franklin, Bethany, and Chellie to a county pool that afternoon. Chellie loved to move her limbs in water. Bethany took time out from diving to chat with us. As much as I hated to, I explained that I would pay her for the following week, but couldn't use her after that. "I can't ask you to come all that way for half a day's work and I can't pay you for full-time."

"This might be God's gift to me!" she exclaimed. "My best friend works at the coolest clothing store in the mall, and she said last night they have an opening for somebody to work from two to nine. They'd even give me a discount on clothes for college. So if I could work for you until one, I could do both jobs."

As she went for one last dive, I wondered why God gave her two jobs and me a half.

MONDAY MORNING ON MY WAY to work, I saw Margaret pouring water on her precious grape tomato plant beside the steps. I was still early, so I stopped by. If Jason was up, I could welcome him.

"Even if the whole state of Georgia dries up and dies—which is highly likely—I am determined this thing will survive." Margaret picked a tiny red ball. "Try one. Sweetest tomato in God's green creation." I tasted one. It was good, but no better than tomatoes in my garden.

Daddy echoed my thoughts through the screen door. "What you fooling with that yuppie food for? We got Better Boys in the garden bigger than two fists."

Margaret ate another. "I prefer these. They're like eating candy."

He lifted his John Deere cap so he could smooth his hair. "Morning, Billie." He peered upward. "Gonna be another sizzler. Not a puff of white in sight."

We all contemplated the sky. A flat, heavy blue, it seemed to sit on the earth like the lid of a pot.

"I feel smothered," Margaret said, "like a huge blue dome is shutting out all the air." She swiped unruly curls off her forehead with the back of one hand. "I still don't understand why you never put in air-conditioning."

Back in Marietta her friends were probably having a second cup of coffee in air-conditioned breakfast rooms before an arduous day of shopping, lunching with friends, or getting highlights in their hair. I wondered why she didn't go back there and be comfortable.

I shoved up the back of my hair, faintly wishing it were still long enough to pull up where air could get to my neck. Most of the summer we'd had hot, clear mornings followed by late-afternoon clouds that built to towering heights and made all kinds of rumbling promises, but passed overhead at sunset as sterile as a herd of mules. Everywhere you looked, the red earth was cracked and parched. Daddy's pastures were brown, and he was talking about having to buy hay if his crop didn't make enough. Fields of brittle crops stood next to forests spotted with brown trees that had given up the ghost. "Drought quickly culls the weak," was one of his favorite sayings lately.

"Garden's looking pretty good," I said, trying for a positive note.

Daddy shrugged. "Only fair to middling."

From the way she scowled, Margaret took that personally. "It looks better than it would if I didn't go out there and give it every blessed drop of bathwater and laundry water we use."

I couldn't believe my ears. "You're carrying bathwater downstairs?"

Daddy clumped down the back steps in his worn brown boots. "Don't be fooled by her whining. She's not carrying water. She's standing in the garden holding a hose. I rigged up some pipe so the bathtub and washing machine drain into a barrel behind the house. All she has to do is turn on the spigot. A hose does the rest."

I went to examine the barrel. I expected to find an old oil drum, but Daddy had actually invested in a plastic rain barrel with a tight-fitting lid to keep out mosquitoes. It had a spigot at the bottom, where he could attach his hose. "That's great!" I said as I rejoined them. "Could you rig me up something like that?"

"Not today. José and I have a couple of calves on their way. Maggie, I got the boys up and told them to bring you a bushel of tomatoes before they eat breakfast. That'll get you started on the canning. They are to pick another bushel before they even think about playing those silly games Jason brought. That ought to keep you women busy. Blueberries look like they'll be ready by the end of the week."

Margaret gave a little grunt of disgust. "Why waste time canning blueberries when we can freeze them faster?"

Daddy took off his cap and scratched his curls. "Why pay for electricity to keep something frozen when you can process it for thirty minutes in boiling water and keep it on a shelf for years without paying another cent?"

I gave her a "don't you remember having this conversation before?" look, but she ignored me. "Why waste time canning anything when you could buy it at a store? You aren't going to eat all that food."

"Never said I would. But canning preserves the present for the future. I've still got beans and tomatoes in there that your mother put up. Every time I open one of those jars—" He stopped. "Don't you let those boys off easy, now."

Margaret shaded her eyes and looked toward the garden. "I'll bet Jason loved being sent out to pick tomatoes before breakfast."

"It doesn't matter what he loves. You got to get that boy working. It's past time. Oh, and, Billie, we're having a cookout July Fourth evening, right after milking. Hamburgers on the grill. You and Chellie plan to be here." He strode off toward his day's work—a long, lean man with grizzled curls and a deceptive dimple in each of his tanned cheeks. Jimbo padded behind him.

"Bossy as ever," Margaret muttered.

"Heaven forbid he'd ever let a feeling show. But he's still a handsome cuss, isn't he?"

"And Jason looks more and more like him."

I joined her on the porch so I could get a better view of the garden. All I could see of Jason was slim jeans and a white T-shirt working its way down a row. The way he snatched fruit off the vine, he was seething with rage. "Where's Andy?" He was so short the vines would be over his head.

"Chasing butterflies. Andy!" Margaret called. "Help your brother pick tomatoes!" She lowered her voice to my range. "He's been slacking off since Jason arrived with a new laptop and computer games, but Daddy's right. I never did make them work, and they need to learn. Life isn't going to coddle them." This was Margaret speaking? The "I do it all for you, dear" wife and mother?

"You're a lot like him, you know." I told her.

"Who? Jason?"

"No, Daddy."

"That's a nasty thing to say. We may look alike, but I'm not like him. He's hard."

"Firm. You can be, too. But you are both kind, too. You spend a lot of time working on committees, and he gives away a lot of what his garden grows. Did you know that? The church food pantry is full of canned fruits and vegetables with Mama's labels on them. You and Daddy both see things that need to be done and figure out how to do it, too. And you can both do just about anything."

She sighed. "If you only knew how wrong you are about me." She strode toward the clothesline, where a basket of wash waited to be hung out. My wash was already on the line. Anybody raised by Mama knew Monday was your major wash day.

"I don't know why Daddy doesn't get a dryer," Margaret grumbled as I joined her. "Everybody else in the world has one."

I threw a sheet over the line and pinned it. "I don't. Daddy and I are in the forefront of the green revolution. We use solar power to dry our clothes. It releases moisture into the air, which you will agree is badly needed at the moment. Ultraviolet rays kill germs in the clothes, which a dryer doesn't. Hanging up clothes provides a few moments of peace and quiet out in nature for the person hanging up the clothes, and when you bring them in, the clothes smell wonderful. Haven't you noticed how all the commercials for fabric softeners tell you the clothes smell like the outdoors? Mine and Daddy's really do."

"Did you stop by for anything except to give a lecture?"

"Mostly to say hello to Jason, but I'll come back for that later. He'd bite my head off if I went to the garden right now. Oh—I also wondered if you could watch Chellie afternoons, now that you are used to her. I've been cut back to mornings, and Bethany's been offered an afternoon job at a clothing store up at the mall, where she can get a discount on college clothes. If you could watch Chellie, I might be able to find an afternoon job."

Margaret cast a Big Sister eye at my cutoffs and faded T-shirt. "If you aren't working in a garage, you'll need better clothes than that."

"I've actually bought a few, so there." I cast a Little Sister eye at her yellow Oxford cloth shirt that had faded to cream. "You aren't exactly dressed for the Junior League. I didn't know you kept anything that worn-out."

"It was Mama's. You heard Daddy—we're starting to can today. I didn't bring anything I could can in, but I found this in Daddy's closet."

I stroked her sleeve. "I remember Mama wearing this."

"We really do have to go through her stuff."

"You won't sneak and do it without me, will you?"

"No." She drew out the word and emphasized it until it was an entire sentence—something along the lines of *I won't go against your precious wishes, little sister.*

"Good. About watching Chellie. It would only be afternoons. Maybe Emerita can help."

Margaret pinned up the last pillowcase. "Sorry, but I have enough on my plate right now without taking on Michelle. Jason's not happy to be here. Andy's whining. Daddy's—same old Daddy. And I've got to spend the week canning with a Mexican woman who resents anything I ask her to do."

Mamie's PT Cruiser bounced up Daddy's gravel drive. A plump

brown arm waved through the passenger window. Margaret raised her own arm in a reluctant wave. "Did I mention that Daddy called Mamie and asked her to come back?" She fanned herself with one hand. "*And* told me in no uncertain terms that I have to apologize for letting her go?"

"Why is he hiring her back with Emerita here?" It had hurt me the way Margaret had dismissed Mamie—like a servant, not a friend—but I had to admit they didn't really need Mamie and Emerita both.

"Because I have forgotten anything I ever knew about canning. Mamie is here as our expert consultant."

"With all three of you here, couldn't you please keep Chellie? She won't be any trouble. She can watch Andy and Jason play computer games."

"In case you missed it the first time, Andy and Jason are going to be working their heads off. You heard Daddy. And we are going to be canning, not lolling around eating bonbons."

As Mamie labored up the walk, Emerita appeared at the back door. "What do you want us to do today?" Her voice was haughty.

Margaret was curt. "Can."

"Pardon?" She clearly thought Margaret was making a joke at her expense.

"They're canning tomatoes. Putting them in jars for winter," I explained.

"And now that Mamie's here, we'd better get started." Margaret stalked past Emerita and went inside.

Emerita came out and said to me in a puzzled voice, "I still do not understand what she wants me to do."

Before I could reply, Mamie pulled herself up the steps. "Hey, Billie. Who's this?"

It took me a second to realize Mamie had left Friday before they had met. "Emerita Gomez, meet Mamie Fountain. She'll explain canning better than I could."

Mamie took Emerita by one elbow. Her words came in gasps with wheezes between them. "Glad to meet you, honey. By the time this day is over, you will understand more about canning than you ever wanted to know."

"I might come over and help this afternoon," I told them. I suspected I'd better be there to keep them all from killing one another. "Stamps cut me back to mornings," I added to Mamie.

Mamie shook her head and peered up at the cloudless sky. "Dear God, what are you doing to us? We need mercy down here, Jesus. We surely do."

On my way to work, I did think of a couple of cockeyed blessings God had given me: I wasn't working afternoons and José was a Mexican. Instead of payment for my labor on the truck, I would ask him to drive with me to Marietta one afternoon to talk with the men Porter had worked with. They'd be a lot more likely to talk to him than to me.

Twenty-five

Walking into Daddy's kitchen that afternoon was a journey into the interior of a boiling kettle. Steam rose from a blue-and-white-speckled canner waiting to be filled. Steam rose from a pot of boiling water into which Emerita was lowering tomatoes to split their skins. A big oscillating fan sent waves of hot, damp air around the room to smack us like unwelcome kisses.

Beyond Emerita, Mamie took tomatoes from the cooling bath, slipped off their skins, and slid them into a waiting jar. Deftly she pressed down on the jar's contents to release juice to fill the spaces, then added lemon juice and salt. Without a pause, she reached for the next jar. Margaret was at the dining room table, setting the most recent batch of processed tomatoes on a towel to cool. All the women were barefoot. Margaret had tied the tails of Mama's shirt beneath her breasts.

"Looks like you've got an assembly line here," I greeted them.

Mamie didn't waste time on chitchat. "Come get the air out of these jars and put lids on. We need to get them into that canner. The boys are bringing in another basket any minute."

I moved over beside her and slid a spatula down the sides of the nearest jar to release the air. "Where's José?" I wiped the mouth of the jar with the damp cloth Mamie handed me. "I came over to talk about his truck." I put on a sealing lid, tightened the ring, and put the jar in the canner.

"Out in the field," Emerita said.

"Where's Chellie?" Mamie asked. "You shouldn't leave that child out in this heat."

"Andy dragged her off to see his calf."

"You have a daughter?" Emerita asked with a strange, eager look I could not interpret.

When we heard the kids laughing on the walk, she ran to the screen door. I expected her to flinch when she saw Michelle. Instead she broke into a spate of Spanish as soft and gentle as a rippling stream and held the door for Andy to maneuver the wheelchair through. Andy wore a cap, but he was flushed, his lip beaded with sweat. Chellie was pale from the heat.

Emerita bent and touched Michelle's arm. "I am Emerita. Em-er-ee-ta." She had such a hungry look in her face that Chellie pulled away. Emerita knelt beside the wheelchair. "What is your name?"

"Michelle," I said when it became apparent Chellie wasn't going to answer. "I call her Chellie." I moved over behind the wheelchair and put a reassuring arm on Chellie's shoulder.

Emerita seemed to realize that the child was wary of her, because she moved back and smiled. "Hello, Chellie. Do you want something to drink?"

Before Chellie could reply, Jason shouted from the yard. "Andy, get your butt out here!" He stood at the edge of the garden, shading his eyes. A bushel of tomatoes sat at his feet. "I can't bring these in by myself."

Andy heaved a martyr's sigh. "I'm coming."

Together they carried the basket toward the porch. Andy's face was beet red, and he struggled with the weight. "I can't go so fast, Jase. It's heavy. Slow down."

Jason was dark and handsome, with ropy muscles in his arms and a mop of black curls, but his eyes smoldered and his mouth was sulky.

"I'm not doing all the work around here. You have to carry your share, brat."

Emerita handed me a glass of juice she had poured for Chellie and went to meet the boys. "Let me help. I can carry Andy's half."

"You can carry the whole thing." Jason dropped the basket to the ground with a thud guaranteed to bruise the fruit. As he loped past me without a greeting, he muttered, "I didn't come here to work like a Mexican." Emerita's eyes narrowed.

I helped her carry the basket in and set it on the kitchen table.

"She likes children," Mamie told me.

"No a todos," Emerita muttered under her breath.

I knew enough Spanish to translate that: *Not all of them.*

As THE WEEK PROGRESSED AND the canning kettle boiled on and on, tempers frayed. Andy and Jason argued in the dining room where they played computer games. Chellie watched and begged for a turn. By the time Thursday arrived, she and Andy were whining while Jason sulked and monopolized the game. Margaret had pulled out more of Mama's oldest shirts. The white one she wore Thursday was so damp with sweat that it was practically transparent. "I hope we don't get company," I joked.

Margaret didn't smile. "Emerita, why don't you start washing up? Billie can dry and put things away, and Mamie—"

"Don't boss us, General." I circled the dining room table pressing down the tops of jars with a fingertip to be sure the seals were tight. "We know what we are doing."

"I was trying to help us not get in one another's way. Mamie, are you all right?"

Mamie had sunk into one of the kitchen chairs and dropped her head into her hands. "Having a spell of dizziness from the heat. It'll pass."

"Go on home," I told her. "We can do blueberries tomorrow."

"Them blueberries won't take long. He didn't get many this year."

"At least go in the living room and put your feet up. I'll bring you some tea."

"I'm fine. Just let me catch my breath."

"Mama, Michelle wants to go to the bathroom," Andy called from the dining room.

"How can you tell?" Jason snarled. "All she says is, 'uh-uh-uh.' "

As I went to get Chellie, I heard Margaret say, "I wish Daddy would put in a downstairs bathroom like a civilized person."

"I wish he'd get air-conditioning and an Internet connection," Jason snapped. "This heat is ruining my computer."

"It's not your computer. It's our computer, isn't it, Mama? Daddy sent it to both of us. And Jason's had it too long. Make him give me a turn."

"Jason—"

They wrangled the whole time I carried Chellie upstairs.

When we got back down, I saw Margaret put a warning hand on Jason's shoulder. He shoved back his chair. "Don't touch me!" He stormed through the kitchen, shouting, "Take the dumb game. What kind of stupid people don't have Internet?" He slammed the door behind him. "I wish I hadn't come."

Margaret stared after him with stricken eyes.

"Let him be," Mamie advised. "He's at a tough age."

"He's a brat," I said bluntly. "What's happened? He used to be such a sweet boy." I set Michelle in her chair. "How about juice and a movie?" I asked the children. "I don't like to use the TV as a babysitter, but there are exceptions," I added to Margaret as I poured grape juice.

"My whole life is an exception right now. Does everybody want tea?" She poured four glasses from a gallon jug in the refrigerator and picked up two of them. "I've got yours, Mamie. Let's go out on the porch. Maybe there's a breeze."

She and I shared the swing. Emerita and Mamie sat in rockers. I pushed with one toe to keep us gently rocking. Nobody said a word for nearly ten minutes.

Margaret took a deep breath of summer air. "It's peaceful out here in the country when you aren't working yourself to death."

"Sure is," Mamie agreed. "I don't know why you don't come to Solace more often. You girls ought to be ashamed for the way you neglect your daddy."

"I don't neglect him," Margaret protested. "I'm busy. Besides, he never acts like he cares whether I come or not. And remember how he treated us growing up? Like little slaves. I had my first row in the garden by the time I was five."

Mamie stopped rocking and gave her a look we had learned to dread as children. "There were no 'little slaves' around here. He was strict, that's all. He's a particular man, wanting things done just right."

"By which he means his way."

"Like somebody else we know. But he loves you girls more than life itself."

"If he does, he has a funny way of showing it. You don't see him coming to Marietta to visit me, do you? The road runs both ways."

"Don't fuss," I begged. "We're all tired. Let's rest and enjoy what little breeze there is."

We had a few more minutes of blessed silence until Margaret said, "I feel like I've taken a bath in sweat. How did we all wind up in that god-awful kitchen canning in this heat? Why did I decide to spend the summer with Daddy?"

"Why did our truck break down *here*?" Emerita muttered softly.

I held my sweaty shirt out and fluttered it to make a breeze. "Even if I had the misfortune to be laid off afternoons, why was I stupid enough to come over here?"

Mamie made a sound like a hundred bees. "*Hmmm-hmmm.* We're here because we're supposed to be. God's weaving a tapestry, and we're all part of it. It's hard to see the pattern at the moment, but one day we will. Dark threads and light threads—"

I'd heard her say that, one way or another, all my life. I no longer believed it. Since I couldn't—or wouldn't—flat-out say, "Mamie, you are wrong," I asked instead, "You think God makes bad things happen just so they'll fit in a tapestry? Things like trucks breaking down and people losing jobs?"

And kids like Michelle getting born?

Mamie pressed her chilly glass to the side of her throat. "He doesn't make most bad things happen. Some things we think are bad, of course, we later see were for our own good, but most bad things happen because of things people either do or don't do. Everything that happens, though, God uses as threads to weave his tapestries. When he's done, our little tapestries—which are all part of one great big tapestry—will be beautiful."

Margaret stopped the swing so abruptly that I spilled tea down my already-damp shirt. "Nonsense! Look at that." She gestured toward the fields stretching parched in all directions. "Would a good God let that happen to Daddy after all the years he's put into this farm? Look at—look at Billie, and Chellie, and how they have suffered! What has God ever done for them?"

"Give God credit, honey," Mamie chided. "I'll bet if Billie thought about it a minute, she could think of all sorts of things God has done for her."

I fluttered my shirt to dry it and tried to think of a tactful way to say, "Actually, he hasn't." Instead I found myself thinking of Chellie's sunny spirit, which warmed my life. Of Porter who, unlike a lot of absent fathers, had sent a check every month until March. Of my six acres of good land—one of the best presents a person who loves to dig in the dirt could get. Of Mamie showing up with pudding the night our pantry was at its lowest. Of Bethany being available the month after Porter's checks stopped coming. God had been blessing me—I just hadn't given him credit.

Before I could say so, Margaret gave an angry little kick to set the swing going again. "I still don't believe in any tapestry. We are four unfortunate women stuck together in a hot kitchen on a sweltering day.

That's all there is to it. If there is a God, he's not in Solace. He's sitting beside a pool with a tall drink and a good book—which is where I'd like to be."

A train whistled in the distance. Its wail felt like a match striking my temper. "Life has always been so simple for you, hasn't it? If you wanted to sit by a pool, you sat by a pool. If you wanted to drop in on Daddy for the summer, you dropped in for the summer. All your life you've gotten exactly what you wanted, until now. Even right this minute, if you really wanted to, you could drive straight back to your air-conditioned house, where tomatoes come in cans. You have no call to whine just because you're getting a little taste of how hard life is for the rest of us."

Before Margaret could answer, Emerita leaned forward so she had a clear view of me. "You think your life is hard? You have a house and land. You have a child. You are strong, so you can work, and you have a job. Your child can go to school. You get sick, there is a doctor. You don't have any idea what a hard life really is!"

In front of my eyes floated pictures I'd seen on Missions Sundays at church—children with swollen bellies, children playing on garbage heaps, mothers weeping over dead children.

"I'm sorry," I apologized. "You are right. I have no idea how hard your life has been."

"My life has not been hard—not all of it. I worked at a hospital. José worked on a farm. We had a house and food on our table. We even saved a little, because José dreams of buying a farm one day. But my mother got ill and could not buy medicine. My sister is raising her child alone, so she cannot help our mother. José's father died last winter, and his mother has two small daughters. We did not come here because our life was hard. We came to help them because their lives are impossible."

Margaret untied her shirt and bent to wipe sweat off her forehead with her shirttail. "I don't care how hard things are. Americans can't take in everybody in the world with a tough life. Even with all God has blessed us with, there's not enough here for that."

Emerita's eyes flashed. "You know nothing about the blessing of

God! You think God's blessing comes like little gifts dropped in your lap. A house. A car. Money in the bank. Those are nothing! They can be taken away like that!" She snapped her fingers. With a haughty tilt of her chin, she gave Margaret a smoldering glare. "The poor know the true blessing of God—that he is with us, no matter what we face. No one can take that away." Her face softened. "When you know that, nothing else matters and you will truly know God."

Mamie slapped her thigh. "Preach it, sister. But God has spared you and Margaret your husbands. Thank him for that. I miss my Earl every day."

Margaret went to stand by the railing, looking over the farm. Something about the slump of her shoulders aroused my pity. She couldn't help it that she had a good husband with a thriving business, a pretty house, two healthy sons. We shouldn't be blaming her for that—or that she found it difficult to live as we did. I might find it difficult to live as she did (although I'd be willing to try for a week or two).

"Let's don't fuss anymore," I said again. "It's the weather. Doesn't that sky look like a blue slab that could crush us any minute?" I rotated my shoulders, which were stiff and sore. "I read somewhere that the Chinese have a proverb: 'Women hold up half the sky.' Today it feels like we're holding up more than our share."

Margaret spoke without turning around. "Atlas held up the sky, but when Hercules came by to ask a favor, Atlas shifted it to him."

"Who's Hercules and Atlas?" Mamie demanded.

"Heroes in Andy's book of Greek myths."

"Did Hercules have to hold it up forever after that?" I didn't know that story.

"No, he tricked Atlas into taking it back." Over her shoulder, she gave me a lopsided smile. "Know anybody we could trick into holding it up for us awhile?"

"I sure don't." Mamie hauled herself with difficulty to her feet. "And right now, except for Bill and José, I don't see any men around helping out, do you? So we'd better get back in there and finish what we started."

PART FOUR

Hold Up the Sky

"A woman is like a tea bag—you never know how strong she is until she gets in hot water."

—Eleanor Roosevelt

Twenty-six

Males outnumbered females seven to five at Daddy's Fourth of July cookout. Margaret had invited Katrinka and Hal Smith for the afternoon. Daddy had invited Luke's whole family—in spite of Margaret's fear that Luke would arrest Emerita and José and drag all of us off to jail. Bethany had other plans and their mother had to work, but Luke and Franklin came.

I wore my new yellow sundress and wondered if I'd find a time to talk with Luke privately. I wanted to tell him about my decision to divorce Porter if I could find him.

I felt real pretty until I saw Katrinka and Margaret. Katrinka wore white slacks with a wild silk shirt and matching multicolored sandals. Margaret wore a blue denim dress exactly the color of her eyes, with little flags appliquéd on the collar and a red, white, and blue belt. With it, she wore red flats. I would never look as stylish as those two.

"Do you get much wear out of that dress?" I asked Margaret.

"I wear it Memorial Day, Fourth of July, and to political barbecues."

Katrinka laughed. "Trust Margaret to have a dress for political barbecues."

Daddy must have had brownie points with the weather angel, because a strong breeze came in puffs out of the northwest, announcing itself in rustling treetops before it touched the ground. It turned leaves as if it carried rain, but none of us believed those lies anymore. Still, it felt good as I assembled a serving table from two sawhorses and planks Daddy kept in a shed. When Luke climbed down from his truck, I was wrestling a red cloth over the table. I hoped he'd attribute my pink face to a glow from the cloth and not to my thinking about events before he stomped out of my orchard.

I also wondered if he would like my haircut or notice my new sundress.

He didn't even notice me. He went straight to the grill, where Daddy and Hal were cooking burgers. They talked baseball. Jason and Franklin eyed each other warily, talked a little, then disappeared around the barn.

Daddy sent José and Andy to the garden to choose sweet watermelons. I pushed Chellie to the edge of the garden so she could offer her opinion, and went to the kitchen. "Has Daddy said where we're going to eat?" I asked Margaret, who was taking potato salad from the fridge.

"I guess he'll put out all the lawn chairs."

Emerita was stirring black beans at the stove. "You wait. Bill and José have a surprise." She lifted the lid on a big pot of rice. "These are done. They can go to the table."

I looked over the food on the table ready to be carried out. "I guess we aren't having corn on the cob this year."

"You got that right." Margaret's voice was sharp. "Daddy didn't grow any corn, and he wouldn't let me buy some from the grocery store. Said we didn't need to be eating Yankee corn."

After I added my deviled eggs and fresh sliced tomatoes to the other food, and Luke surprised us with a churn of homemade peach ice cream, we had a feast.

When the burgers were ready, Daddy sent Andy to ring the big dinner bell to call Jason and Franklin while he and José carried out a second, longer picnic table they had built in the past week. Daddy waved away our compliments as they set it near the old one. "Family's gotten too big for one table." When I heard the pleasure in his voice, I realized how lonely he must have been those past months. I mentally kicked myself for being so wrapped up in my life that I hadn't noticed his.

Jason and Franklin appeared, looking as pleased as if they'd successfully planned a revolution. "What have you been up to?" I asked.

"Nothing," they replied in unison. I was relieved to see Luke eyeing them. He'd been a boy. He'd know what to watch for.

Daddy gave the orders, as usual. "Children at the little table, grownups at the big one. Jason, you sit with the children." Jason accepted with more grace than I expected. He and Franklin sat across from each other and exchanged looks like they were up to something. Andy climbed onto the bench beside Franklin. I positioned Chellie at the end of the table in her chair. "Eat what you can, and I'll feed you more later," I whispered.

"I'll be fine," she told me with so much irritation you'd have thought she'd been taking care of herself for years. Only five and my child was developing an attitude?

Daddy, Hal, and Katrinka climbed in on one side of the new table before anybody sat on the other. The table promptly tilted.

Luke and I flung ourselves in unison across it and kept it stable. He grinned at me. "Good save." That broke the ice. I think we'd have had a great meal together if his phone hadn't rung.

He sprinted for his truck. "Bad wreck up near the interstate. I'll be back when I can. Mina, can you keep an eye on Franklin until I get back?"

"Sure. No problem."

The food was delicious and the watermelon at the peak of sweetness. After dinner we women put away food while José dismantled the serving table. Daddy told Jason, "Get the hose and douse the fire." Jason turned it on full-blast like a television fireman. "Just a trickle," Daddy yelled. "We don't want sparks flying around here, dry as everything is. The whole place could go up in flames. Andy, you and Franklin fetch lawn chairs from the shed so the grown-ups can digest their food and watch the sun go down. Looks like we're getting a spectacular sunset." The sky was burning in shades from red to palest pink, streaked with gold and lavender.

Katrinka and Hal gathered up their things to leave. When Katrinka gave Margaret a hug and whispered something in her ear, Margaret looked ready to cry. I wanted to say, "If you want to go back to Marietta, go."

Jason finished dousing the fire and jerked his head toward the barn. "Come on, Franklin."

Andy ran after them. "I'm coming, too."

"No, you aren't, brat. You stay here. Play with Chellie." Jason's tone was so sarcastic I wanted to smack him. Andy's shoulders slumped as he trudged back toward us.

"Don't you fellahs run off and leave your little cousins," Daddy ordered. "Stay up here near the house and play."

"We're too old to play." Jason pushed Andy away and headed toward the barn, followed by Franklin.

"That boy needs a whipping," Daddy told Margaret.

"He's had a rough time lately. He'll be all right." But her eyes were worried.

"Andy, take Chellie down to see how Milky is doing," I suggested. With a huff to show how put-upon he was, he seized Michelle's chair and started for the barn. I cut across the grass to reach the other two. "Jason?"

He paused midstride, a proof of guilt if I ever saw one.

"What are you guys up to? Where are you going?"

"Down to that old pond."

Daddy had a pasture behind the hay barn that used to have a good-sized cattle pond. Because the drought had dried up the pond to a knee-deep puddle, he didn't keep cows in that pasture at the moment. Between the pasture and the hay barn was an old unpainted barn my great-granddaddy had built, where Daddy kept his tractor, its attachments, and derelict farm equipment he couldn't bear to throw away.

"You aren't going to try and drive the tractor, are you?" I asked. They shook their heads. "Then what are you going to do down there?"

"We're looking at frogs," Franklin explained with a shade too much frankness. "There's a million frogs down there."

"And two million mosquitoes and probably a hundred snakes. Still, go if you want to, but come back before it gets dark, okay? And don't do anything you know you shouldn't." That sounded lame, but I didn't know what else to say. I wasn't used to boys.

"Okay." They moved through the dry weeds like men on a mission.

I reminded myself how much I used to hate having grown-ups dog my steps at their ages, and that most of the private activities I zealously guarded from grown-ups were harmless. Maybe Jason had stolen cigarettes, and they were trying them out. I hoped he didn't have anything stronger, like marijuana. Luke would kill Franklin and me both.

I stopped by the hay barn long enough to satisfy myself that Andy and Chellie were occupied feeding wisps to the calf. After that, I went back to my lawn chair. It felt good to relax with grown-ups for a while, even if Luke hadn't gotten back. I rubbed the place where my wedding ring used to be and wondered if he'd noticed it was gone.

IT WAS NEARLY DARK WHEN a bang sounded in the distance. Emerita dropped her head to her lap and covered it with her arms. José leaped to his feet and looked wildly about. "Gun?"

Daddy lay stretched out full-length on an aluminum chaise he had claimed as the oldest person there. "Probably a firecracker." He was visibly not worried. José and Emerita relaxed.

"Firecrackers are illegal in Georgia," I reminded him.

"Yeah, but you know kids. They like to set off a couple on the Fourth of July."

"How could they be close enough to hear?" Margaret asked as another bang echoed across the garden. Daddy's nearest neighbor lived a mile away.

"Jamieson sold some pasture for a subdivision. It was probably kids who live there."

We resumed our contemplation of the sky. I tried to figure out where peach sky left off and lilac sky began, but the sky-painting angel was so skillful, they blended seamlessly. A frisky breeze traveled over the garden.

"Nice breeze," Daddy said lazily. "We ought to sit out like this more often."

Nobody reminded him that Margaret lived fifty miles away and that José and Emerita would be leaving Tuesday. I'd fixed everything I could on that old truck. José was going with me Monday afternoon to Porter's former work site to talk with the workers.

We were so deep in lazy, none of us noticed the first cries. What caught my attention was a scent on the breeze. "Do I smell smoke?" In that same instant, I heard, "Help! Help! Fire! Fire!" I realized I'd been hearing the cries without registering them for some time.

I looked over one shoulder and saw haze and smoke over the pasture and a curl of smoke rising above the tractor barn. "The pasture's on fire!"

Margaret and I both jumped to our feet. "Jason!" "Franklin!" we yelled in unison and started running. I heard Daddy swearing as he disentangled himself from his chaise.

He caught me and shouted, "Call nine-one-one!" He pushed me toward the kitchen.

My rational mind knew I was the logical one to call, but it took every ounce of willpower I possessed to go. My child was in the hay barn, and it was in the path of the fire.

As soon as fire trucks were on their way, I dashed outside. Margaret and Emerita stood near the edge of the garden watching flames creep in living tongues. Margaret seemed rooted to the earth, turning to shout "Jason!" toward the pond and "Andy!" at the barn.

In the near corner of the pasture, snakes of fire slithered across dry grass past the milking barn, toward the hay barn's timber wall. Margaret ran and tried to stomp them out, but she couldn't keep up with them. Emerita ran into the garden, which bordered the burning pasture.

I headed toward the hay barn. "Chellie! Oh, God, get her out of that barn. Andy, bring Chellie! Daddy! God! Oh, Chellie!" Blinded by tears of terror, I prayed for anybody who might be inside.

By the time I reached the cool dark doorway, billows of smoke rose from the back wall, the one nearest the pasture. I doubled over, coughing. "Chellie! Chellie!" I covered my mouth and nose with one hand as I plunged inside. I bumped into José, pushing Chellie in her chair.

I grabbed her and pushed her to safety. José ran beside me long enough to gulp air, then turned back to the barn. Chellie flailed her arms and screamed out words I could not understand. José came out again, dragging Jimbo by the collar and Andy under one arm. Andy pulled back, trying to get free. "Milky! Milky!" he screamed. As soon as they were clear of the barn, José let go of Jimbo and half-carried, half-dragged Andy to where Chellie and I were. Jimbo looked around for Daddy, then barked and streaked toward the tractor barn. José had to forcibly restrain Andy to keep him from running back to Milky. The children were covered with soot. Their hair was singed. Both were screaming—Chellie from panic and Andy for his little calf. Their screams were punctuated by paroxysms of coughing.

Margaret hobbled over to us. Her face was sooty, her red flats scorched to an ugly brown. "You're okay?" she asked Andy, pulling him close.

He tried to yank away. "Milky's . . . Milky's in there!"

"Stay with Billie. I have to find Jason." She thrust him toward me and José and hobbled rapidly toward the garden.

Gray clouds billowed from both barns. The air was full of the snap, crackle, and pop of burning wood. Sparks flew overhead and landed around us. "We have to get farther back!" I pushed Chellie's chair. José dragged Andy, who was again bucking and screaming.

As several volunteer fire departments began to arrive, a crowd gathered out at the road.

"Where's Daddy?" I asked as soon as we reached air I could breathe.

José kept his arms tight around Andy. His voice came in gasps. "Getting tractor. He say, 'Get the kids and dog! I get tractor.'" His eyes raked the crowd. "Where is Emerita?"

"She went down through the garden. Keep the kids here. I'm going to find Daddy." I pulled my skirt over my face and tried to breathe as little as possible as I ran toward the tractor barn, but smoke overpowered me. Choking and sobbing, I had to retreat.

Over the roar of flames, I heard a heavenly clatter. Through smoke billowing from the wide doors came a ghostly green tractor with Daddy on the seat. Jimbo lay limp across his knees. They were almost through the door when the whole wall caved in with a sound like thunder.

Burning chunks of wood flew past me. Hot sparks stung my bare arms and shoulders.

"Daddy!" I ran, but others were ahead of me. José and several men ran to the inferno.

It took all my willpower to retreat to the children. Andy jumped up and down and pointed at me. "Your hair's on fire! Your hair's on fire!" I grabbed my head in both hands and massaged furiously to put out sparks. Another fire truck wailed down the road.

I dared not leave the children, hysterical as they were, but I could not breathe. Daddy had been knocked off the tractor, and he lay beneath a burning beam. I had heard of people who had superhuman strength in emergencies, but I had never seen it. José lifted that beam with his bare hands while others dragged Daddy from beneath it. Daddy's clothes were in flames. José lay down on him and rolled with him in the dirt until the fire was out.

Another man, meanwhile, had climbed onto the tractor and driven it to safety under a tree. I saw it was Rick Landiss. "Thank you!" I called. He waved as he climbed down.

I crept close enough to be sure Daddy was breathing. He was in good hands. One of the men working on him was a doctor. I returned to the children.

Andy crouched on the ground, arms covering his head, but I knew the pictures were still in his mind. "Jimbo's dead. Milky is burning up. She's burning up." He and Chellie both wailed.

The wails of the children were echoed by the wails of yet another fire truck coming up the drive. Solace didn't have a paid fire department, but almost every man in the area belonged to one of the volunteer fire departments that dotted the county. Looked like they had all turned out that night.

"We can't stay here," I told Andy. "I have to get you and Chellie out of the way. Can you walk?"

The house was far enough from the barns to be out of harm's way unless the wind shifted. "We'll go to the kitchen," I told the children.

Andy climbed to his feet and—hiccuping and sobbing—lurched after me as I pushed Chellie up the ramp. Once we got inside, how long did I spend calming two small children? It seemed an eternity. I made them each drink water. I rubbed aloe on their burns, grateful that Daddy had kept Mama's plant alive. I gave them sweet tea for shock. I smoothed their singed hair. I assured them that firemen would put out the fire before it reached the house. I prayed that was true.

I closed the door and windows, but smoke already filled air dotted with specks of soot. I not only smelled smoke—I could taste it.

My heart lifted at a blessed sound. "Where's Franklin?" Luke stood in the door, his voice taut.

God, forgive me. I forgot all about Franklin.

"I don't know," I admitted. "He and Jason were down at the cattle pond and must have had firecrackers."

"They started this?"

I didn't need to answer. He had already vanished into the strange night that was dark around the edges but murky with steam and smoke at its dreadful center.

Even the cinder block milk barn was ablaze by then, its wooden joists and ceiling burning merrily like the rest.

A few minutes later I heard a shout in the yard and went to the kitchen door, which had a glass pane at the top. Through the garden, which Margaret's faithful watering had protected against the worst of the fire, she hobbled with one arm around Jason. It was hard to tell who supported whom. Emerita—bent over and limping—came with her arm around Franklin. Like monstrous multiarmed creatures they stumbled into the yard, heads down.

I ran to meet them. Both boys were shirtless. Trails of tears snailed down Franklin's sooty cheeks. Jason's eyes were sapphire chips surrounded by a blackened face. Their hands and arms were burned and raw. Emerita's shoes were scorched, her pants burned to the knee, her legs blistering. "Water, please. Water." She collapsed onto the back steps, grimacing with pain.

Andy flew down the ramp. "Jason! Oh, Jason! I thought you were dead!" He clung to his brother's waist, sobbing. "I thought you were dead. Milky's dead."

Jason shoved him away, threw off his mother's arm, and went into the kitchen. When I went to fetch water for the others, I found him sitting at the table with his elbows on his knees and his head bowed. I put a hand on his shoulder and touched his lips with a glass of water. "Drink." He shook his head. "Drink," I commanded. When he lifted his head, his cheeks were wet with tears. He took the glass from me, and I saw that while the backs of his hands were covered with huge blisters and burns; his palms were burn free.

"How did you keep from burning your palms?" I asked.

"I tried to beat the fire out with a wet shirt." He gulped down the water and set the glass carefully on the table. Moving his fingers even that little bit must have been agony. I was tempted to tell him we all knew it was an accident and nobody blamed him, but I don't believe in lying to children, and Jason would have to face the consequences of what he'd done. I gave his shoulder a gentle squeeze and left him to do his own suffering.

Luke ran around a fire truck. "Is Franklin— There you are! What have you done? What fool thing—"

I held up a warning hand. "Not now. We need to get everybody to the hospital. We've all inhaled smoke, and several folks have burns. Isn't there an ambulance?" Everybody else in the county seemed to have turned out for the Anderson Fire Show.

"Ambulance take *Señor* Bill," José informed me.

For the first time in my life, I appreciated Margaret's organizational skills. She said, "Why don't I take Jason, Andy, José, and Emerita? Luke, you use Daddy's car to take Billie, Franklin, and Chellie. Billie, Daddy's keys and wallet are in his top desk drawer, as usual."

I grabbed the keys and wallet and took time to dash upstairs and bring down two of Jason's shirts for him and Franklin. Luke was on his phone to his mother, telling her what had happened and asking her to meet him at the hospital with Franklin's insurance card.

I checked with our fire chief—another of Daddy's poker buddies— to be sure none of us needed to stay, but he assured me, "You all go get everybody checked out, shug. We'll be here a while, but the fire's under control."

Nothing else was. Chellie was hysterical. Franklin and Jason couldn't use their hands and weren't speaking to anybody. Andy was sobbing for Milky and Jimbo. Emerita clung to José, in obvious pain. Margaret limped. I was shaking so hard, I could hardly stand. And the barns were still burning, smoke mingling with steam rising above them. From the furious look Luke gave Franklin, he had a pretty good head of steam building, too.

Twenty-seven

"Front or back?" I asked Franklin at the car, handing him one of Jason's shirts.

He pulled it on, wincing with pain. "Who's driving?"

"Luke. I'm in no shape to drive."

He cast a nervous look at Luke the Angry Dragon. "Back."

"Roll down the windows so we can breathe," I told Luke. Not only did we smell smoky, but Chellie must have wet her pants. I couldn't do a thing about it at the moment. Good thing Daddy had leather upholstery.

Once we reached the highway, Luke looked over his shoulder like he was ready to speak to his brother. I put a hand on his arm. "Not now," I said softly.

"Okay. But he's in for it later." He reached over and stroked my cheek. "You've got soot on your face."

"It's the latest thing in makeup. Better than motor oil for the complexion."

"Did the fire burn off all your hair?"

"A few patches. I had the rest cut. I wondered if you'd notice."

"I noticed. Looks cute. But we still need to talk."

"Yeah, we do, but not now." I looked over my shoulder. Franklin had his head out the window, taking in great gulps of fresh air. Chellie was asleep. I took Luke's right hand from the wheel and cradled it between mine. My bare finger was in plain view. He steered with his knees long enough to use his free hand to rub the spot. "Does that mean something?"

"Yeah." The same old thing sizzled between us in the dim light. "But watch the road."

I smiled. He smiled back. We didn't speak again, but we smiled all the way to the hospital.

ARE EMERGENCY ROOMS THE SAME everywhere? We had to drive forty minutes to the county hospital, and the first thing the woman at the desk wanted to know was not "What is the matter with you? How can we help?" but "What insurance do you have?"

Daddy was already in a treatment room, but they wanted his information before they would discuss my child. "I'll stay with Chellie," Luke said. "You do what you have to."

At a second window, Margaret pulled out an insurance card and Jason got registered. Franklin's mother pulled out a card and he got registered. I only got a glimpse of her because I was trying to get Daddy squared away. Once Daddy was registered, I pulled out my card and prayed Porter's benefits hadn't been canceled. Apparently the card went through, for the woman started registering Chellie. While I was answering more questions, I heard a ruckus at the next window.

In the tone of one repeating something for the second or third time, a clerk was saying, "I am sorry, but we are no longer able to treat the uninsured. You must go to Grady in Atlanta."

José stood with tears running down his cheeks while Emerita's shoulders shook with sobs. "Please! Oh, please help me."

"Do something!" I called to Margaret across the room, waving toward Emerita and José.

"What can I do?" She lifted both hands in a gesture of helplessness. Margaret helpless?

I went over there. I didn't want the whole place hearing our business. "They won't treat them without proof of payment. Offer to pay the bill of the family who saved your kids."

"I can't. I—I can't." She bit her lip and turned away.

It was all I could do not to grab her by the shoulders and shake her, but Emerita and José needed me more. I joined them and stormed at the clerk, "These people have saved several lives. Doesn't that count for something?"

"I am sorry, but we are no longer able to treat the uninsured." She spoke like a robot.

"Do you wake up saying that in your sleep?" I demanded.

Luke laid a hand on my shoulder. "How much would it cost to treat them?" he asked. The two clerks looked at each other like he was speaking a foreign language.

"My father and I will cover their bills," I said. We might have to mortgage both our houses to pay for one evening in the emergency room, but dang it! Emerita and José had saved all three of Daddy's grandchildren and his own life.

Emerita's clerk looked uncertain, but the one who had taken Daddy's information said, "I know these people. Her daddy owns a big farm down near Solace. He'll be good for it." I was glad to see she looked sorry to be working for a system that turned hurting people away.

EMERITA AND JOSÉ TOOK CHAIRS closest to the desk. Luke's family and Chellie sat on the other end of the room from Margaret, Andy, and Jason. Franklin and Jason, I noticed, looked anywhere in the room except at each other. Margaret stared at Jason's burned hands.

I went to Luke's end of the room. "You must be Bethany and Franklin's mother," I said to the woman sitting with them. She looked like Luke—the same auburn curls, blue eyes, and nice strong chin. "I had begun to think you were a myth."

She smiled. "I know you aren't. The three of them talk about you all the time."

"Mom!" wailed Franklin. Even Luke looked embarrassed, but I was too tired to preen. I felt like somebody had hung me from a pine branch and beat me with a stick.

Emerita had the worst burns, so they took her to a treatment room first. I hated to bring up a subject that might make Luke mad again, but I wanted to know. "How did Emerita get so burned?" I asked Franklin.

He chewed his lower lip.

"Mina asked you a question." Luke sounded so stern that I put a hand on his arm to calm him. That felt so good, I left it there.

Franklin chewed his lip some more.

"Franklin?" his mother prompted.

"She came to get us. We were lighting firecrackers—I know we weren't supposed to," he answered Luke's glare. "But Jason had a box of 'em and we were real careful. We stood in the water and stuck the firecrackers in the mud at the edge. We even dropped the matches into the pond. Only a couple of the firecrackers were any good anyway. Jason said they were old. Most fizzled out. One of the fizzlers, though, it"—he spiraled his hand to show us the trajectory—"came down in a clump of tall grass. Nothing happened at first, but then the wind picked up, and the whole clump burst into flames."

"You've seen that in Scouts," Luke reminded him, "lighting fires with flint and lint. First you get a spark and a tiny glow, but when you blow on it, it blazes."

"It was exactly like that! One little breeze and *whoosh*! Fire started going everywhere! We stomped and stomped, but we couldn't stop it. We wet our shirts and beat it and beat it, but—" His eyes were wide with remembered terror.

I put a hand on his arm. "What did Emerita do?"

"She came through the garden and saw us. By then the pond was surrounded by fire. Not high"—he measured a few inches above his ankle—"but we couldn't walk through it. Jason scooped water all over his pants and tried running, but the fire steamed them and made them too hot. He had to come back." He hung his head. "I was so scared I peed in my pants."

I was glad I hadn't said anything to Chellie.

"Emerita brought a big bucket and ran through that fire like Super Woman. Her pants caught fire but she kept on running. When she got to the pond, she put out the fire on her clothes and told us to fill the bucket and pour it on the grass, to make a wet path from the pond to the garden. Jason and I took turns, but his hands were burned worse, so I did most of it." Franklin permitted himself one short moment of pride. "We finally made a path about yay wide." His hands measured two feet. "I was never so glad to get on good red dirt in my life."

The nurse called for him to go into a treatment room. Margaret and Jason were called at the same time. Franklin's mother went in with him, but Margaret limped out soon. We could hear Jason's yells of pain from where we sat. Margaret clutched Andy and winced with each yell.

"I wonder why she didn't go in with him," I said to Luke as Franklin and his mother came out. His hands were wrapped in bandages.

"He wouldn't let her," Franklin said.

I felt pity as I looked at Margaret, whose gaze was fixed on the door to the examining area. How would I feel if Chellie refused to let me be with her in that much pain? I reached over and gave my child such a tight hug that she struggled to get free.

Eventually Chellie, Andy, and José were treated for minor burns, and we were all treated for smoke inhalation and told we could go home. I wanted to wait for news about Daddy. José was still waiting for news of Emerita.

I expected Luke and his family to leave, but they stayed with me. We didn't talk much, but Luke held my hand the whole time. Every time I looked up at him, he was smiling down at me.

————

Nobody had to stay overnight except Daddy, but Jason came out with his hands bandaged to the elbows and Emerita rode out in a wheelchair, bandaged to her knees. Margaret and I didn't want to leave until we'd seen Daddy even though our children needed to get to bed. "Why don't Margaret and I drive everybody home except you?" Luke suggested. "If Margaret wants to come back later, she can."

"What about Franklin?"

"Mom can take Franklin."

Franklin agreed gladly. I could tell he'd been dreading riding alone with his brother.

"Emerita can't climb the stairs with burned feet," I said. "Take the Gomezes to my house and let them sleep in my bed. I changed the sheets this morning, and I doubt I'll get home in time to sleep anyway. I'll keep Chellie here. She can doze in her chair. But Margaret can't come back. I don't think she'd leave her boys in a house alone under the best of circumstances—"

"Why don't Chellie and your sister's boys come home with Franklin and me?" Luke's mother suggested. "Bethany and Franklin each have two beds in their rooms, and I've got a fold-out bed in the den one of the boys can use. I'm a nurse, so if Jason needs pain meds, I can give them to him. I've probably even got clothes to fit all of them."

"She's probably got every stitch any of us ever wore," Luke said out of the side of his mouth, obviously intending his mother to hear. "She's never thrown a thing away in her life."

"And isn't that fortunate tonight?" she retorted. "Go talk to Margaret and the boys to see if they'd like to come home with us. Mina and her sister don't need to be worrying about their kids when they're worrying about their daddy." She knelt beside Chellie's chair. "Michelle, would you like to come have a sleepover with Bethany?"

I expected an anxious protest. Chellie and I had never spent a night apart. Instead she looked at me with eager eyes. "Can I have a sleepover with Bethany?"

Margaret's boys got up and followed Franklin before she even gave permission. As Franklin's mother pushed Chellie out the door, my child didn't look back. I felt utterly forlorn.

Luke had gone to speak to Emerita and José. They listened, nodded, and threw me a thankful glance. He loped back to me. "Give me your daddy's keys. I'll get them settled, then come back. See you in a little while."

I felt considerably less forlorn.

I AMBLED OVER TO MARGARET and sat in the chair Andy had vacated. Margaret buried her nose in a magazine. I curled my legs under me and leaned close. "Do you want to explain why you refused to help Emerita?"

She shook her head and continued to read.

I put my hand over the columns of type. "You and I both know you aren't interested in an article on ectopic pregnancy. Talk to me. I've loved you, hated you, admired you, and sometimes envied you, but I have never been ashamed of you until this evening. Why wouldn't you help?"

She lifted the magazine out of my reach. "I told you, we can't afford it."

I snatched the magazine and hurled it into a vacant chair. "Come off it. You have more money than Daddy and me put together, and she saved your son!"

She stood. "Let's go outside. I do not want to have this conversation in public."

Folks around us did seem to be interested, entertainment in emergency rooms being chiefly of the voyeur variety.

I followed her into the simmering night. We sat on opposite ends of a bench. At that hour few lights burned, so stars were bright overhead.

Margaret didn't say a word.

I pointed to the Big Dipper. "Remember how sailors used to steer by the North Star? Up until tonight, you've been my North Star. I knew I'd never be as talented as you, or as pretty as you, or even as competent as you, but you pointed the way toward adulthood. So what happened? That's all I want to know."

Margaret's voice was low and desperate. "I couldn't help her! I can't!"

Her passion scared me. "Have you lost the business?"

Her laugh was harsh. "No, but I've lost my husband, my house, most of my money, and one of my sons. Ben divorced me."

Seeing that she had rendered me speechless, she plunged on. "Remember that big storm we had back in April? The next morning he took a swig of breakfast coffee and said, 'I want a divorce.' He gave me the same song and dance you gave about Porter—'We were young when we got married. We didn't know who we were. Now that I've grown up I want different things.'"

"But Porter. . . ."

"You were right about Porter. It was just hard to listen to again. Ben found an apartment that afternoon and moved out. He filed for divorce later that week."

"What did you do?"

"What could I do? I tried to get him to change his mind, but his reply was, 'I want to have fun while I'm still young enough to enjoy it.' Last I knew he was running around with a twenty-six-year-old member of my tennis team." Her voice was bleak.

"Do you still love him?"

"I wish I didn't, but yes, I do." She tried a smile but it flopped. "Habit, I guess."

We sat for several minutes in silence while I rethought every conversation we'd had that spring and summer. No wonder she had sounded like she was on drugs and had been impatient with people. No wonder she killed flies with such vigor. "Why didn't you fight it?"

"You can't. The law says any unhappy partner can end a marriage. All there is to discuss is who gets what. The way we've been living right up to the edge of our income these past few years, there was precious little 'what' to share."

"So what's been bugging Jason is you all splitting up?"

"Yeah. He got so upset that the weekend before I came out here, he vandalized one of the properties Ben landscaped. He got sent before a juvenile judge, and because Ben had told him it was my fault he'd left, Jason blamed me for the whole mess his family was in. He asked to live with his dad."

"Whew! That's pretty heavy."

"It was the worst day of my life. A lot worse than bringing him into the world."

Remembering how much it hurt me just to leave Chellie with a sitter, I could not imagine the pain of having my daughter turn her back on me. I put an arm around Margaret and drew her close. "I am so sorry. I don't know how you stood it."

She rested her head against mine. "The only thing that made it bearable was that Jason already had to go to summer school. I figured he could live with Ben that long, then maybe he'd want to come out here for the rest of the summer."

"Do you think he will stay—after the fire and all?"

She shook her head. "He wouldn't have stayed even if he hadn't started the fire. He is still furious with me for the divorce. But he's turning some of that fury toward his dad, too. Before Jason got here, Ben called almost every night to beg, 'Help me out here, Margaret. Talk to Jason. He's unruly—won't listen to a thing I say.'" Margaret's voice grew rich with anger. "Ben even wants me to come back now—to Marietta, not to him—so I can find a job, oversee both boys, and advise him about the business."

"Why should he expect you to do all that?"

"Because I've always solved his problems. You know what I did wrong in my marriage? I wasn't a person. I was a reflection. I shaped myself into anything Ben wanted or needed—lover, servant, nanny, business partner, and problem solver. All he had to do with any problem was dump it in my lap. So while it took me a while to accept it, some of this *is* my fault. Not that we got the divorce, but that he is nearly forty and hasn't grown up. I loved him so much, I asked him for nothing. That's exactly what I got."

I was no marriage counselor. The safest thing was to return to the subject of my nephews. "Maybe the fire will turn Jason around. He used to be a real sweet kid. I can't believe he blames you for Ben leaving."

"I can't believe both boys are gullible enough to believe whatever Ben tells them. And he tells them a lot, apparently—that I wasn't sympathetic enough or available enough, I don't know what all. Now Jason . . . he's . . ." Her voice trembled. "He isn't unruly. He's brokenhearted, like his mo-o-ther." Her last word was a wail.

I sketched circles around her shoulder blades as if she was Chellie. She shuddered under my hand. "Shhh," I whispered. Gradually she calmed enough to sit up. I didn't have a tissue to offer, but I held up the hem of my skirt. "Here. It's ruined anyway. I always seem to destroy clothes you make for me."

She blew her nose on my skirt and shrugged. "I can always make you more."

"What about the house? What did you mean you lost it? Is Ben living there?"

"We sold it." Her voice was bleak.

"You sold your *house*? You love that house!"

"Oh, yes. But the business has hit a rough patch—which Ben didn't mention until things got so bad that we either had to sell the house or lose the business. Since the house wasn't bringing in money and the business does, most of the time . . ." She gave an unhappy little shrug. "After we paid off the mortgage and a home-equity loan, the sister you envy so much has a houseful of furniture she is paying to store, a few thousand dollars in equity from the house, half interest in a struggling business, and one year's alimony. No job skills and very little work experience. For the past two months, I have squeezed pennies so hard, they bleed. You want to know something really sick?"

"I suppose so."

"I took Mamie home one day when her car was being serviced. Did you know she owns a brick house that is completely paid for and she gets Social Security every month? I sat in my car and envied her with all my heart. Our maid is better off than I am."

"Mamie's not a maid. She's a friend."

"Whatever, she's better off than me. And Ben is already trying to weasel out of paying alimony. He keeps grousing about how poorly the business is doing and how hard it is for him to find money to send me. But I suspect he's still taking his bimbo all over town."

I ignored the last remark. Ben and his bimbo were not my business. My sister was. "So you went to work for Rick Landiss because you needed money?"

"And to have something to put on a résumé."

"And you tried to get jobs downtown for the same reason?"

"Yeah, but nobody would hire me."

"Why didn't you at least tell me you were having money troubles? Were you broke when you offered to send me that check?"

"No, it happened after that—the very next morning, in fact."

"So that's why you sounded funny when I called back to ask if you'd talked to Porter. I thought you might be on a prescription drug or something."

"It was definitely 'or something.'"

"Does Katrinka know about all this?"

"Yes. I told her during the garage sale. She's been wonderful."

I tried not to feel jealous that Margaret would tell Katrinka what she wouldn't tell me.

"Does Daddy know?"

"No, and please don't tell him. I don't want him saying, 'I told you so. You ought to have finished college. Now look at you—no skills, no job experience, no husband, and nowhere else to go, so you come back here like a whipped dog with its tail between its legs.'"

"He wouldn't say that."

She looked at me in the moonlight.

"Okay, he might. He's said similar things to me a few times. But if you're planning on staying here permanently, you'll have to tell him."

She got up and began to pace. "I don't know what I'm going to do. At first I wanted to come for the summer so I'd have breathing space to figure out what to do next, but we've been so busy with the garden, canning, and carrying water, my mind goes round and round like a hamster on a wheel. Some nights I dream I am carrying water to pour over tomato plants."

I sat and let her pace. She needed time to recover from her tears, and I needed time to take in all she had told me. After a few minutes, I said, "I wish you had told me sooner about the divorce."

Her voice was a whisper. "I couldn't. I just couldn't. Not after all the nasty things I've said about Porter leaving you. Besides, you have always expected so much of me. How could I let you down? And—" She stopped and flopped down beside me.

"And?"

"I keep thinking Ben may come back. He's not really a swing-all-over-town guy. He likes to come home at night and chill in front of sports on TV. He likes to roughhouse with the boys. He likes going places as a family. Up until recently, he liked being with me. He calls me almost every night, and not just to complain. He wants to talk about what's happened in his day."

Anger rose in me. "He's using you just like he always did. A convenient sounding board for his triumphs and his troubles. I can't believe you take his calls. After the way he treated you—the divorce is final, right?"

"Yes, but I keep hoping . . ."

"You can't go back to where you were. The marriage is dissolved, your house is gone, and so are the people you all used to be."

"I know that. I don't even want what we had before. But maybe"—her voice was wistful—"maybe when Ben finds out who he is and what he wants, and I find out who I am and what I want, we will discover we still want to be together. I know"—she held up a hand to stop what I was about to say—"it may never happen. But because it might, I didn't want you all to know."

Not everybody gets happy endings, and happy endings are not always what we want them to be. I thought she was silly for holding on to a notion that Ben would come to his senses, drive out to Solace, and take her back to another lovely house with contented kids. But she was so sad, and we had already been so far toward hell and back that day, I couldn't say anything to hurt her. I tried for a lighter touch.

"Well, you're down on my level now, the 'I hope I have enough to make it to next month' level. It's not such a bad place to be when you've got a sister to share it with."

She sat back down on the bench and touched my nose lightly with her finger. "You are my favorite baby sister."

I took her hand and kissed it. "You are my favorite big sister." We sat sharing a closeness we'd never had.

A nurse came out looking for us. "Your father needs to have his leg set, but refuses to let us give him anesthesia until he's talked with you."

Twenty-eight

Daddy had second-degree burns, a broken femur, a broken collarbone, and one broken rib. Considering that he was lucky to be alive, that didn't seem too bad, but to him it was a disaster. He lay on the operating room gurney, his eyes squinted with pain, and demanded, "Who's gonna do my milking?"

I had not given one thought to those fifty cows out in Daddy's pasture expecting to be milked in the morning. Daddy, in spite of his pain, thought of nothing else.

"Did the milking barn make it through the fire?" he asked.

"No, sir, I'm afraid not," I told him. "When we left for the emergency room, I saw flames coming from all the windows. By now the roof will have caved in, I expect."

"Get to a phone and call Jamieson, Wilburn, and Casey. They're the only other dairy farmers left in the county. See if they'll each take some of my cows until I'm outta here."

"They're all at the fire. I'll call them in the morning."

"Call right after they finish milking. Try Jamieson first. He's sold off some of his stock. He'll have room. You'll have to tell them which cows have been treated, though. You'll find my record books in my desk in the dining room."

It is against the law to sell milk from cows that are receiving antibiotics, so dairymen have to keep careful records of that.

"You still using electrical tape on their tails to mark them?" I asked.

"Yeah. Red and yellow. Oh—Merrylegs calved night before last. Tell Jamieson I was watching her for milk fever. Somebody's gonna have to go after the insurance company, too, to get me new barns. You're too soft, Billie. Can you handle that, Maggie? You'll have to ride them hard."

"I can do that," Margaret said crisply. "I'll take care of the insurance and the garden."

He sighed. "I guess we'll have to let the hay go unmowed. Too bad. It's likely to be the only crop I get this year." He looked at us to see if either of his daughters was going to volunteer to mow fifteen acres of hayfield and roll the hay. I hadn't done that for ten years and had a job and a child. I doubted that Margaret had ever mowed. She had mostly worked in the garden and kitchen with Mama. While he eyed us, Daddy gave an involuntary groan.

"We really need to get him to surgery," the orderly told us.

"Why don't we invite José and Emerita to stay on and pay them?" I suggested. "He managed a farm in Mexico and they're trying to earn enough to help their mothers back home. Can you afford to pay them?"

"Yeah, I can. While your mother was sick, I took out insurance good for anything I'd have to spend in case I got laid up. I wanted to make sure I could pay for nurses for her. But I kept up the policy, thinking it was good to have in case I got sick during harvest some year. It ought to cover wages for both José and Emerita. If he knows how to mow and roll hay, tell them to move into my room. I'm not going to need it for a while."

He closed his eyes. "Did Jimbo get out when the roof fell in?"

Margaret and I took a silent ballot. I won that awful election. "No, sir, he didn't."

Daddy pleated the sheet with his uninjured hand. A tear rolled past his shut lid. His voice was a husky whisper. "He was a good old dog. When they find him in the rubble, I'd like him buried in the front yard with a little stone."

"I'll tell the men who take down the barn."

"Thanks. Okay, fellah. You can give me that needle now."

Margaret and I held hands tightly as they wheeled him through the double doors toward surgery. But as soon as he was out of sight, she turned on me in fury. "You should have asked me before you offered to let José and Emerita stay. You're not the one who has to sleep in the house with them. How do we know we can trust them?"

After all José and Emerita had done for us that night, I was so annoyed by her question that I stomped back to the waiting room without a word. Luke was there. "How's he doing?"

"Headed to surgery to set a broken femur; then they'll take him to a room. It's going to be a very long night."

"Why don't you let Luke take you home? I'll stay with Daddy," Margaret offered.

I started to protest, but why? After what she'd said about Emerita and José, I didn't want to spend the night with her. Besides, I would get enough hospital visiting time before Daddy was released.

"You want to go to your house or your Daddy's?" Luke asked when we reached the highway.

What I wanted was to go somewhere far, far away and forget the whole blessed mess my life was turning out to be, but that wasn't one of the options he'd offered.

"Daddy's, I guess. I don't like to bother José and Emerita. I wish I'd thought to tell him to sleep in Chellie's bed if Emerita needs more space."

"I told him. But the smoke is still bad at your Dad's. I could hardly breathe when I stopped to swap out his car for my truck."

"Let's see how it smells now. Maybe it's not so bad inside."

Daddy's yard was empty and dark, but there was enough light to see the mess where his barns had been. Smoke and the odor of smoke were still thick and heavy. "You can't stay here," Luke said when we rolled down our windows. "How about your trailer?"

"That could work. Let me get my sleeping bag and air mattress from upstairs. José's been using them."

"I'll get them. You rest." He sprinted across the yard and up the stairs before I had time to object.

He came back with a rolled-up sleeping bag and a flat air mattress. "I don't think he's been using these. There were two pillows on the bed. Can you get in the trailer?"

"I've got a key on my ring. After Kyle and Mo got arrested, I decided to keep one in case I wanted to make an emergency visit."

"That's good. Let's get out of here before we asphyxiate."

As we pulled out of Daddy's drive, he said in the tone of one making casual conversation, "Actually, I was going to ask if I could stay at the trailer tonight. The extra bed in Franklin's room that Mama offered Andy is mine. Does the trailer have two bedrooms?"

I tried to match his tone. "Yeah, but I don't have two sleeping bags."

"No problem. I keep a sleeping bag and change of clothes in my truck at all times."

"Oh, yeah?"

"Yeah. I was once a Boy Scout."

We didn't say anything else on the short drive. I didn't know what Luke was thinking, but from the looks he kept darting my way whenever I darted one his way, he was thinking the same thing I was. Big empty trailer. No kids around. I was so nervous, I trembled.

We carefully did not touch each other as we got the sleeping bags, my air mattress, and his duffel from the truck. We did not touch as we walked up the path to the front door. But as I fumbled for my keys, I bumped his arm. I looked up to apologize, and in an instant, we were back to where we'd left off in the orchard—with one exception. There was no room between us for Porter's ghost.

I do not remember who unlocked the door or closed it behind us. I do remember that we never made it to a bedroom. We shed clothes like water. Luke spread out our sleeping bags on the living room carpet. And in the next hours, while cicadas sang hallelujahs in high shrill voices through our open windows, I learned more about the possibilities for bodily pleasure than I had learned in five years of marriage. I learned about shooting stars, and I learned about incredible tenderness. Afterward, I slept like one dead, curled against my love.

I WOKE WITH SUN SLANTING into my eyes through the open blind. For one drowsy minute, I felt nothing but pleasure—until I glanced at my watch. I shot straight up. I had badly overslept. "It's seven thirty and I've got fifty cows standing in the pasture bawling to be milked! I need to call some other farms to see if they can help us out."

"Can I help?" Luke spoke without opening his eyes.

"Do you have a milking barn and a pasture?"

"No."

"Then you can't help." I pulled on the sooty clothes I'd worn the night before. "I'll need to go down to Daddy's to call, because I need his record books."

He reached for his clothes. "I can at least come to keep you company."

Luke later claimed I pulled the truck to the farm by leaning forward in the seat. "You look like an old pointer I used to have," he teased.

When we pulled in, I gasped. The yard was full of cow trailers, farmers, and farmers' sons and daughters. They were leading Daddy's cows to the trailers. There must have been six or seven families there. Some of them had been out of the dairy business for years. Their trailers were old and rusty. Every one of those farmers had been up since five working, and they still had a long day ahead. But they had taken time to come help Daddy because he needed it.

We climbed down and started that way. Luke took a couple of exploratory sniffs. "The air's finally breathable, but I'd guess you'll be smelling smoke until the debris is removed."

I couldn't answer. I was too choked up with gratitude.

Mr. Jamieson, our nearest neighbor, ambled over to meet us. "We're moving Bill's cows. I'm taking thirty, and Casey and Wilburn are taking ten each. Do you know where your daddy's record books are? We'll handle his herd while he's out of commission, and reimburse him at the end of the month." He looked embarrassed. "Maybe you know that I sold off half my herd and some of my land for a subdivision. Times are hard for everybody, aren't they?"

All I could do was nod. If I'd opened my mouth, I'd have bawled.

He put his arms around me and gave me a squeeze. "You know Bill would do the same for any of us, shug. Folks can't get along unless they can depend on one another."

I fetched the record books, then took the time to thank each one of the folks, although I couldn't get anything past the lump in my throat except, "Thanks. We really appreciate this."

They asked how Daddy was. I was still on the verge of tears, so I let Luke describe Daddy's injuries. "He'll be in rehab after the hospital. I know he'd love to see you," I added.

Mr. Jamison gave me another hug. "We'll visit the old cuss. And don't worry about the cows. Tell Bill we've got him covered as long as he needs us."

ON OUR WAY BACK TO my place Luke loaned me his cell phone to call the hospital. Daddy had been anxious about his cows all night, Margaret reported. Once he'd come out of anesthesia, he had hardly slept.

"Put him on." When he came on, I reported, "The cows are taken care of. Every farmer in this part of the county who owns a cow trailer showed up to help move them. Jamieson's got twenty and Wilburn and Casey took ten each."

"That's good. Did you give them the record books?"

"Of course."

Margaret came back on the line. "He just slumped over fast asleep."

"You ready for me to come in, or can I eat breakfast first?"

"Eat and then come."

Luke dropped me off at my house and went back to the trailer to shower.

Emerita sat at my kitchen table with José, eating a bowl of cereal.

"Is okay we eat?" he asked, anxious.

"Absolutely. How are you feeling, Emerita?" I peered at her legs, bandaged to the knee.

"Not too bad." Her gaze was vague and unfocused.

"She take pills for pain," José explained.

"We are so grateful for what you did," I told her. "You must have run like a rabbit, or skimmed the fire like a duck over a pond."

"My shoes and jeans protected me—and the Mother of God." She crossed herself reverently.

"But to run across the fire—Jason tried. He couldn't do it, and he's a track star."

"I was running toward the water, so I had hope."

"Now we need to go back to the house and take care of things for Mr. Bill," said José.

When Luke arrived, showered and fresh, he offered, "I'll drive them over while you shower and change. You aren't fit to go out in public." His smile kept those words from stinging. "Waffle House suit you?"

Before I showered, I called to check on Chellie. She could hardly take time from eating her breakfast to tell me she was fine.

I also called Mamie. "I heard you all had a fire," she said. "Lurleen passed there last evening, and she said it was real bad."

"She's speaking to you again?"

"No, she had Skeeter call. What happened?"

"The barns are gone, and Daddy will be laid up for a while, but the house is fine except for soot and smoke. Emerita got burned, too."

The whole time I described the fire and their injuries, Mamie murmured, "Lord, Lord, Lord." I knew she wasn't swearing; she was praying. "Who's taking care of his cows?" When I'd answered that, she asked, "Have folks started bringing food by yet?"

I hadn't given a second's thought to the inevitable procession of women laden with food that would begin to arrive at the house very soon. "No, and Margaret's been up all night at the hospital, Emerita's on pain pills, and I've got to go be with Daddy. Could you or Lurleen possibly go over to the house until Margaret gets up? The air's pretty breathable by now."

"One of us will go. Is the back door locked?"

"I think I forgot to lock it this morning when I left, but if it is, you know where we keep the key." The whole county knew where we kept the key—the same place they did: under a rock at the foot of the back stairs.

If you don't know about Waffle House, you are not from the South. Their little buildings with big plate-glass faces dot every highway. Any town of decent size has at least one with a sign spelling out the name in yellow-and-black squares. In cities, they're about a mile apart. They are famous for waffles, good coffee, and staying open twenty-four hours. Teenagers drop by late at night to keep from going home. Retired men meet in groups for breakfast. I've heard that Waffle House was started by two men, but I'd be willing to bet their mothers came up with the idea to get their fathers out of the house.

There's not much space and no privacy in a Waffle House, but as we sat across from each other in a booth, Luke reached across the table to cover both my hands with his. The way he was grinning made my whole body turn inside out.

"You look mighty happy for somebody whose house burned down," the waitress said as she sauntered over to take our order. The other thing you can usually count on at Waffle House is a friendly waitress who is swift with the coffeepot. This one wasn't going to last long. She had attitude written all over her and no coffeepot in her hand.

"It wasn't my house. It was my daddy's barn."

"Whatever." She smacked her gum and bent over to give Luke a good view of her freckled bosom. "You want coffee, hon?" She wasn't talking to me.

Luke nodded.

"I want coffee, too," I said.

She marked it on her pad, but her attention was all on Luke. "Black or with cream and sugar?" The way she said "sugar" made it sound like an invitation.

"Black, with waffles and bacon," Luke replied. She wrote down his order like it was a love note. She still hadn't looked at me.

"I'll have waffles and bacon, too," I said. "And cream with my coffee." When she didn't move her pencil, I asked, "Shall I write that down for you?"

"I got it." She flounced off to fetch the coffee.

"So," Luke said when he had let go of my hands long enough for each of us to lift a mug. "What are we going to do about Porter?"

"I'm gonna find him and divorce him. Tomorrow afternoon I'd planned on taking José to the site where Porter last worked so he could talk to some of the workers and find out what they know. We'll have to postpone that for a little while, but after that, I'll take it from there."

"Good plan, but can I suggest one alteration? You and Margaret are going to be busy these next weeks visiting your dad, dealing with the barns, and taking care of kids."

I groaned. "Not to mention canning beans and peas."

"Let me take José to the work site. The fellahs might be more relaxed around two guys, anyway."

"I think I ought to go myself." I wasn't sure José's green card could stand up to police scrutiny, and I didn't want Luke deporting him.

He sipped his coffee and considered me. "If you're worried that José might not be in the country legally, I'm not with immigration, you know. We'll go on my day off and take my truck, not a cruiser, so I'll just be Luke Braswell, private citizen. So, if that's what's worrying you, don't let it. I'm not going to send José and Emerita home when you all need them so badly. Besides, I like them. I hope they make it here."

The man could read my mind. How cool was that? I slipped off my shoe and snaked my toe up his calf. "Thanks."

"If José doesn't find out anything," he went on, grabbing my foot under the table and giving it a squeeze, "I think we ought to advertise. If that doesn't produce results— We'll cross that ravine if we have to. But I'm not waiting around for seven years to declare Porter dead."

The longing in his eyes sent such a shock through me that I spilled coffee all over the table.

Our waitress—who hadn't bothered to heat up our coffee in all that time—looked our way, but was too engrossed with a trucker to come help. I mopped up the table with a wad of paper napkins. As I finished, I smiled at Luke and said, "Me, neither."

"Beg your pardon?" The waitress sashayed up to the table once I'd dealt with the disaster.

I handed her the soggy napkins. "I said I don't know, either, who spilled that coffee. You must have ghosts in here." I wiped up one more spot and added another wet napkin to the mess she held. "Are our waffles and bacon nearly up? I'm about to start chewing off your arm."

"You will never be allowed back in here," Luke warned as the waitress flounced away for the second time.

On our way to the hospital I called Luke's mother to say I'd come get the kids as soon as I could. She insisted on keeping them for the rest of the day. "You need to be with your father. Besides, you've had Franklin and Bethany so many weekends."

"They were painting my house and watching my child."

"Even so, let me keep the kids today. I've changed the boys' dressings, and right now they are playing video games. Bethany has taken the younger children to a park."

"You are both angels. I hope you know that."

She laughed. "Only on our best days."

Luke and I went to the hospital after we dropped off José and Emerita. Margaret—beautiful even with tousled hair and dark circles under her eyes—went home gladly to sleep.

"When this is over," she announced as she left, "I'm going to hog-tie the hospital purchasing agent and make him spend a night in that chair." She probably would.

"Don't forget my pants, now," Daddy told her.

"I won't. But let me get some sleep first."

I settled in for the rest of the day, and Luke perched on a straight chair for a short chat. After ten minutes Daddy told us, "You all go on home, now."

"Luke can go. I'll sit here and read. You won't have to talk to me."

"No, you both go. They've got me so doped up, all I want to do is sleep, and if I need to groan, I want to do it in private. Go home and come back this evening. I don't want anybody hovering over me."

I don't think our parents meant to give Luke and me their blessing, but they did give us one blessed afternoon to ourselves. I felt a little guilty that I wasn't over at Daddy's house helping Mamie or Lurleen greet folks and take in food. I felt a little guilty that I hadn't insisted that Luke's mom bring back the kids. Luke said he didn't mind a little guilt so long as it didn't get in the way of pleasure. It didn't.

Twenty-nine

D addy insisted he didn't want anybody spending the night, so Sunday evening Chellie and I went together for a short visit. Chellie was wide-eyed at his injuries. "You can borrow my wheelchair if you need it, Papa," she promised.

His fingers played with her soft curls. "Thanks, baby. I'll keep that in mind." Margaret had sent a plastic grocery bag holding three pairs of boxer shorts. I didn't think they'd be much use to him with one leg in traction, but he brought them out with a shout of pleasure. "Good old Maggie!"

"You can't get those on right now," I pointed out.

"Sure I can. See what she's rigged up? She said this ought to work."

She had slit and hemmed the outer seams and attached Velcro strips along the edges. "The hospital offered me paper diapers, but I don't want diapers. I want underwear. Send a nurse in here and leave us a minute so I can get decent."

After he was dressed, as he called it, we visited for half an hour. As I prepared to leave, I tidied his covers. "I'll come by tomorrow after work."

"Don't bother. Come in the evening. I prefer to be alone all day to suffer."

"You old liar. The nurse already told me you had a poker game in here all afternoon. If you prefer poker buddies to your daughters—" I took a brush from my purse and started smoothing his curls.

He swatted me away. "Poker buddies don't mess with my cover or my hair. Now get outta here and let me sleep. I gotta rest up for tomorrow's game."

AFTER WORK ON MONDAY, I stopped by Rick Landiss's office. The new woman at the front desk looked about fourteen and her skirt was little more than a ruffle attached to a waistband, but she didn't give me a hard time about seeing her boss. When I asked, she nodded me back to the office without even calling him first.

Mr. Landiss looked a lot more professional behind his desk than he had lying on his hide-a-bed, holding wet towels to a bloody nose. He still had some green across the bridge, though. Margaret had given him a serious whack.

I stood in the doorway, not planning to stay long. "I stopped by to thank you for what you did Saturday night—saving Daddy's tractor. We really appreciate it."

He gave me his wolf's smile, showing too many teeth. "Glad I could do it."

"How'd you learn to drive a tractor? Did you grow up on a farm?"

"No, I'm a city kid. But back when I was in high school, my dad said, 'Son, if you're ever gonna sit in the driver's seat of this business, you need to know how to run the equipment. We got a wetland to clear of stumps this summer, and I want you on the tractor.'" Rick's mouth twisted in a bitter smile. "The old man is eighty and still hasn't let go of the steering wheel, but at least I've graduated from tractors."

"My daddy says you never learn something you won't need later. I don't suppose you've learned anything about Porter Waits, did you?" I thought that was a neat segue. Maybe I could save Luke and José a trip.

"No. No, I haven't." He looked down at the papers on his desk to let me know he had important work to do.

"Well, thanks again for saving Daddy's tractor."

"Don't mention it. But if your daddy ever wants to sell some of his land—"

"That's not gonna happen."

"You can't fault a man for asking."

CHELLIE AND I WENT TO Daddy's for the afternoon so I could help get soot and the smell of smoke out of the house.

Margaret was hanging out sheets when I arrived.

"A bit late with the wash, aren't you?" I asked, reaching for a sheet to pin to the line.

"This is the third load. I did bedspreads and blankets already, and tomorrow we'll start on our clothes. Every fabric in the house smells like smoke. Heaven only knows how we'll get the stink out of the upholstery."

"How's Jason?" He was nowhere to be seen.

"Sore, but sobered. Luke Braswell came by this morning and took him and Franklin over to see Daddy. I wasn't sure that was a good idea—you know how hard Daddy can be on people who make mistakes—but they both came back looking relieved. Franklin told me, 'All Mr. Anderson wants us to do to make up for burning down the barns is come work on the farm for a month next summer.'" Margaret laughed at my expression. "Right. He has no clue how hard that month is going to be."

"Where is Jase now?" I asked.

"Digging a grave for Jimbo and Milky."

"With his sore hands?"

"His palms are okay, and he insisted. He said he promised Daddy he'd bury the animals. The clean-up crew found them this morning."

"How's Andy?"

"Teary. I'm cooking only chicken for the next few days—although I don't think he's made the connection between Milky and beef."

"Should we have a little service after Jason finishes digging the grave?"

"I think so. After that, I'm taking Jason back to Ben. We had a good talk after Jase got back from seeing Daddy, and we decided together that he'll go back to Marietta for the rest of the summer. He has things he wants and needs to do there. But he's more like the Jason we used to know and love. Should we stop by to see Daddy on our way to town?"

"Not unless you want to be thrown out of the county's hottest poker game."

"I'll wait until tonight, then. I also need to tell him that the insurance adjuster says he can have a whole new hay barn and a new milking barn, but the tractor barn wasn't insured."

I wondered if the adjuster knew it was Daddy's grandson who set the fire. He wouldn't hear it from me.

Inside the house, the fans whirred in the kitchen. Mamie was wiping soot off furniture while Emerita, perched on a stool to spare her legs, washed dishes. "Every dish in this house is dirty," she informed me.

When Jason came in and announced the graves were ready, we women and the three kids met in the front yard and buried two garbage sacks into which the barn-clearing crew had put what remained of Jimbo the dog and Milky the calf. Mamie talked briefly about how God makes animals, cares for them, and knows how we hurt when we lose one we love. Each of us shared a memory or two. Chellie said, "Jimbo loved Papa, and Milky licked my fingers." I said a prayer, and Andy and Jason shoveled dirt into the grave. Chellie threw in handfuls from a bowl I had set in her lap. Chellie and Andy cried as he placed a jar of daisies on the grave. None of the rest of us was dry-eyed, either.

While Margaret went to shower, Emerita went to lie down. I could tell her burns were paining her, even if she wouldn't admit it. Jason offered, "I'll go look for a big rock to mark the grave until Papa can get a real stone."

"Don't try to carry it," I told him. "You've used those sore hands enough for one day. I'll bring it in if you tell me where to find it."

"Thanks." He loped out the door.

Mamie took Andy and Chellie out on the front porch for juice and cookies while I washed more dishes.

Fifteen minutes later I went out to see if the kids and Mamie needed juice refills. I paused at the open living room windows for a chance to look at my child when she didn't know I was watching. Mamie had propped her in a rocker with pillows all around her and a belt to anchor her. Chellie happily rocked by thrusting her head back and forth. Andy sat on Mamie's lap in another rocker. While I was watching, he started telling a story.

"Once upon a time there was a mother named Margaret, a daddy named Ben, a big brother named Jason, and a little brother named Andy." Through the screen I saw him pause, settle his head more firmly against Mamie's large breasts.

"They all lived in a big brick house near a forest, with a brave little dog named MacTavish. They were very happy." When she didn't speak, he insisted, "They *were*!"

Her arms tightened around him. "Of course they were, honey." Her voice was as deep and gold as honey.

He heaved a sigh too big for his years. "But the daddy went to live in another place called a 'partment, and the big brother went to live there, too, and the mommy and the boy named Andy went to live on a farm." The rocker checked. He kicked her leg with one bare heel. "Don't stop rocking."

"I'll rock. You keep on telling your story." Now her voice was troubled. "They went to live on a farm?"

"Yes, so they didn't live happily ever after. And they couldn't take the dog because the farm already had a dog, so he went to live with the daddy. Do you know why?"

"Why the dog went to live with the daddy?"

"No, why they didn't live happily ever after." He sounded impatient, as if she should have kept up with the plot.

"No, I don't. Do you?"

He heaved another deep sigh. "God only knows." He sounded very like his mother.

A thumb crept into his mouth. I was glad Mamie let the thumb stay. Andy had worries enough to earn him a thumb suck when his mama wasn't looking.

ANDY DECIDED TO RIDE WITH Margaret to take Jason to Ben's. To my amazement, Margaret invited Chellie to ride along, too. "Don't count on us for supper. We'll stop for something on our way back, and swing by the hospital."

I was about to ask if she was sure she could manage Chellie, but I didn't. Chellie could make her needs known. I didn't have to be with her every minute.

That was such a startling thought that I had to sit down at the table with a fresh glass of tea.

Mamie waited until they had gone before joining me. "You heard Andy's story? I felt you listening behind the curtains."

I poured her a glass of tea while I answered. "Yeah, I heard."

"What you know about all that?"

I took a second to think what to say. "Margaret said she and Ben have been having a little trouble, so they thought it would be better for everybody if she came out here for the summer."

"Better for whom? Not better for those boys. I can tell you that. Jason sulking around here mean as a snake. Andy needing to be with some grown-up every minute of the day. You've seen the way he sticks to his granddaddy, like he's afraid to let him out of his sight. Margaret isn't improving much since she came, either, is she? So who is it better for? I ask you." She fixed me with the stare I used to get when cookies were missing from the pantry. "Is Ben Baxter tomcatting around on her?"

I rose and went to stand at the screen door while I finished my tea, so I didn't have to look at her. "Margaret doesn't tell me everything."

"Humph." Mamie hauled herself with difficulty to her feet. "I never thought you wanted me here killing myself just so Bill would have tomatoes come winter, but dear Lord, I never expected this kind of mess." Mamie wasn't talking to me any longer.

From the way the PT Cruiser shot out of Daddy's drive a few minutes later, I figured the conversation was far from over.

LUKE HAD TO WORK THAT night, but he called around nine thirty to ask if he could stop by on his break. I waited on the porch, my heart as light and playful as the evening. The sky was full of scudding clouds playing peekaboo with the stars. A hot breeze rustled the shrubbery like ghosts were playing hide-and-seek in the bushes. Lightning bugs flirted across the lawn. A hawk swooped from the sky and buzzed my grass.

I felt like I could float away on a bubble of happiness when Luke climbed down from his truck. On his way to the porch, he picked up my basketball and made a perfect arc shot as he came up the walk. I leaped down the steps, caught the ball on the rebound, and shot one of my own. For a few minutes, we played. So magical was that evening that every shot went in. Finally he let the ball slide from his hands, took me in his arms, and kissed me thoroughly. "I've wanted to do that all day." He stepped back and cupped my face in his hands. "Marry me. As soon as we get this thing with Porter settled. Promise?"

I opened my mouth to say, "Absolutely." Instead, I said nothing. Life had been in such turmoil lately, I didn't know my own mind.

Luke misunderstood my silence. "You don't want to marry me?" He sounded baffled.

"Come here." I took his hand and led him up the steps. When we were seated in the swing, I pulled his arm around me and laid my head on his shoulder. I wanted him close while I figured out what to say. But I found it impossible to begin while we sat bathed in moonlight and he rubbed his cheek on my hair. I gave myself over to the joy of the moment.

A mosquito bit my leg. A nudge from God, Mamie might call it. When I reached down to smack it, Luke murmured, "So are you going to marry me once we get Porter out of the way?"

"I hope so." I settled against him again and worked my way through tangled emotions. "I think I want to marry you. I can't imagine anything I'd rather do—but first I need to find out who the heck I am. Back in high school, all I wanted was to be somebody's wife. I want more than that now. I know I'm not having a lot of success yet in running my life, but I keep thinking I might become somebody if I put a little effort into it and get a few breaks. Not somebody famous or anything, but somebody I can be proud of—and proud not because I'm somebody's wife but because I am me. Does that make any sense?"

He nuzzled my hair. "Not really, but I'm probably not listening as clearly as I might be if I weren't sitting here wanting to sling you over my shoulder and take you back to the trailer."

"We can't, Luke! That's another thing!" I didn't mean for it to come out a wail, but I wanted him as much as he wanted me. It took superhuman effort to haul myself out of that swing and lean against the porch railing beyond his reach. In the yard, fireflies were still courting. How simple to be a firefly and have nothing to worry about but flashing at your mate.

I took a deep breath of courage. "Yesterday was the most beautiful day of my life. You were glorious. We were glorious. But I don't want to get so sidetracked by wanting you that I rush into another marriage. And I don't want the glory we have to become something furtive and sordid. I don't want us sneaking into my room or down to the trailer while Chellie is asleep. If we have something as precious as I hope we do, I want to save it until we can stand up before God and everybody and state how we feel about each other out loud and in public." I looked over my shoulder. "Am I making any sense?"

Luke's eyes shone in the moonlight, but if eyes are the windows of the soul, he had his shutters up. "Not much. Are you saying you do want to marry me or you don't?"

"Oh, I do. But I built one marriage on hormones and fantasies. I don't want to make that mistake again. I want to sort out who I am before I think about—you know—the other thing."

"Marrying me? Sleeping with me? What?"

"All of the above." Just looking at him made me so happy, I smiled. In the moonlight I saw the ice in his face melt until he was smiling, too.

"Okay. You need some time, take some time. But I warn you, I am not a real patient man." He took my hand and drew me back down beside him. The swing rocked gently as we sat in moonlight and happiness.

A cloud drifted over the moon.

"You need to do some thinking, too," I warned. "Chellie's— She isn't like other kids. She isn't going to grow up and leave the nest. You and I wouldn't be able to do a lot of things other couples do, like go away for long trips alone or have nights in our house while she's away at a sleepover. And caring for her takes a lot of time."

"I know that."

"You don't know diddly-squat! Getting her up and dressed in the morning can take an hour. Bathing takes another hour. Feeding, toileting—she's a full-time job in herself."

"She'll start school in the fall."

"I haven't decided to send her yet. I may homeschool."

"You can't keep her isolated. She needs to be with other kids."

"You can't tell me what to do with my child!" Already he didn't understand.

"Somebody has to tell you. Bethany says there are all sorts of programs that could help Chellie. She can learn to take care of herself some, and to talk plainer. She can even go to college and prepare for a job. But she needs people with training to teach her. She also needs friends her own age. Look how much she enjoys Andy and Franklin."

"Other kids might make fun of her."

"Andy and Franklin didn't. Besides, kids make fun of everybody. Didn't they ever make fun of you?"

"Not more than once. I whipped them good."

A chuckle rumbled from deep in his chest. "I'll bet you did."

"Chellie can't do that."

"So we'll have to be sensitive to whether she's having a rough time and come up with ways to deal with that. I'm not marrying only you. I'm marrying Chellie, too. I want to help take care of her while she grows up. I want to see how independent she can become, what she wants to do with her life. If you want to become somebody you can be proud of, don't you think Chellie will want that, too?"

That thought had never crossed my mind. Chellie becoming somebody? Leaving home and taking care of herself? Finding a way to use her fine mind? Laughing and joking with people when I wasn't around? The cloud drifted away from the moon. I could see clear to forever.

I laughed for the sheer happiness of possibilities. "At the moment she wants to become a farmer."

"Maybe Bill will leave her the farm. She'll get software programs to help her manage it, hire workers, and next thing you know we'll have the Braswell Agribusiness in Solace."

"Braswell? She's not a Braswell. She's a Waits."

"She'll be a Braswell if you'll let me adopt her. Will you?"

He was so far ahead of me it took my breath away. "I—we—we'll have to see what Porter says about that, once we find him. I can't imagine him objecting, since he hasn't seen her but once since she was born, but Porter can be—well, a little difficult at times."

"So can I, honey. So can I. Can we forget Porter for a while and think about you and me?"

"Yeah, but I have to warn you. Thinking about a long-range future is hard for me. I haven't thought more than a couple of days ahead for a very long time."

"Not since Chellie was born, right?"

His voice was so full of understanding that tears clogged my throat. "Right. It's been all I could do—"

He reached up and laid his finger on my lips. "It's over. As soon as you figure out what you want to do to become somebody you can be proud of, we are going to add your problems to my problems and take care of them together. Okay?"

I was so happy, I couldn't say a word, but I managed to give him an answer anyway. The next few minutes belonged to nobody but us.

After a while, he gave a husky laugh. "You know something? I actually thought about you sometimes all these years—wondered whatever happened to that little reader I knocked down in the hall. I figured you became a professor or something. Sometimes I even wished you hadn't been so young, or that I had ignored how young you were and asked you out anyway."

I snuggled up to him. "I wrote your name all over my class notes."

"Are you serious?" When I nodded, he gave me a squeeze. "We were so dumb. If—"

"No. We were too young. We had to go through what we did to get here, and this is where we needed to be before we really got together."

"I still think we were dumb. I give you fair warning. I'm gonna spend our whole married life trying to make up for lost time."

Thirty

D addy progressed faster than the doctors expected, his spirits buoyed by winning hands at poker. When he was able to get up and about, Margaret fixed some of his work pants so the inner seams snapped like a toddler's. The first time he put on a pair of pants after the accident we heard his little "*Ummm*" of pleasure again.

José turned out to be a good farm manager. He hired several other Mexicans to help carry away barn debris, and under his supervision, they made a quick job of it. They also mowed Daddy's hayfield, leaving the hay in fat big rolls like shredded wheat at the end of the field. In the evening, José and the other workers sat under the trees strumming my old guitar and singing while Emerita served Mexican food—which, fortunately, was heavy on tomatoes. We had tomatoes.

Andy and Chellie sat outside most afternoons and watched the men haul away the charred debris, or played with Andy's dog, MacTavish. Margaret had brought Mac back with her from Marietta. That little mop of white fur with bright black eyes did a lot to console the children for the loss of Milky and Jimbo.

Out in the garden, vines withered in the heat, and tomatoes began to look like wizened faces, but beans and peas were in, and Margaret was determined that not one pod the drought had spared would die on the vine. She got up early to give those rows all the gray water in Daddy's rain barrel, and she and Emerita picked while the mornings were cooler. When I teased that she was getting browner than José, she said, "I run out to pick another bucket of something, and only when I'm halfway through do I think about sunblock, long sleeves, and a hat."

Afternoons were awful. Except for being on a desert island with only one attractive man, there is nothing less likely to bring peace and tranquillity to a group of women than standing in a steamy kitchen in ninety-five-degree heat, doing the same old tasks over and over.

Margaret was surly and sharp. I knew from the sidelong glances she gave Mamie that she resented her financial security and from the way she watched Emerita that she still distrusted the visitors from Mexico.

Emerita had no love for Margaret, either. Whenever Margaret spoke to her, Emerita lifted her chin, flared her nostrils, and gave her the Queen Isabella face I'd seen the day they arrived. Several times I heard her mutter under her breath, "Soft, rich bitch."

Mamie came every afternoon now, but to me she looked grayer and grayer. She grew short-tempered with our various failings or any of our attempts to get her to sit down or go home. After giving us girls orders all our lives, Mamie wasn't in a mood to take orders from us. Margaret got real impatient with what she called Mamie's "hardheadedness."

Yet, in spite of our squabbles, after five years of solitude with Michelle, I craved those women's company like an addict craves drugs. At the library one evening, I read about a study on stress. The researchers were studying fight and flight—which were considered the only human responses to stress—when they discovered something odd. When the study team itself got stressed, the men either quarreled or went to their offices, but the women went to the coffee room together. The team did more research and discovered that if a stressed woman seeks out other women or spends time with children, those activities release a hormone in her brain that serves as a mood regulator.

That's as good an explanation as any of why every afternoon I sought out the company of those ornery women. Canning with them helped me forget, for a time, how desperate my finances were. Business at the garage was still slow, so Stamps couldn't increase my hours. I could pay the phone bill and buy a few groceries, but that was about it. The few peaches I had managed to salvage from my orchard barely paid one month's electric bill. Nobody had answered my ads to rent the trailer, and nobody was hiring. Thank goodness we had plenty of food, but I had no idea how I'd clothe Chellie for school.

So many hulls passed through our fingers one week that one night I dreamed I was sitting in a chair with piles of them all around me, like the princess in Rumpelstiltskin who sat surrounded by straw she had to spin into gold.

"What would it take for you and Emerita to be pleasant to each other?" I demanded in a rare moment when Margaret and I were alone in the kitchen. "You act like she ought to be bootlicking grateful for a bed and days full of hot, sweaty work."

"There's not a grateful bone in her body. She thinks we owe her because we have so much. If she only knew how little any of us has at the moment!"

"Tell her, then. Tell her you're as poor as she is."

"I can't, Billie. I have my pride."

"You'd be a whole lot lighter without it."

Margaret went to wash out a perfectly clean sink. "I'll make you a promise. I'll be nice to Emerita when she's nice to me. Some days I want to smack her."

"Some days I want to smack you both."

I also wanted to shake Mamie. She trudged up the ramp every afternoon on ankles so heavy she could hardly lift them, and as we worked, she gasped in the hot, humid air. But when I begged her, "Go home and rest. We've got this under control," she would leave a little early, but she'd be back the following afternoon. She wouldn't even take pay.

I was so worried about Mamie one evening that I called Lurleen to demand, "Tell me straight what's the matter with your mother. She's not just a little tired or stressed. I want to know how bad off she is and what we can do about it."

Lurleen took her own sweet time answering. "There's nothing anybody can do. The doctor says she's got congestive heart failure. Fluid has built up around her heart and in her lungs, and the pills he gave her to help drain it aren't working because her kidneys are failing."

I forgot how to breathe. "You mean she's dying?" A world without Mamie was unthinkable.

"I'm afraid so. Of course, if she'd take it easy, she might last longer."

"Can't she have an operation?"

"Not that would help."

"Are you and she speaking again?"

Lurleen huffed. "What's the point? I can't talk sense into her, and when I think what she's doing to herself, I get so mad at her, I could spit. She knows good and well the shape she's in, but she won't stop going over to your daddy's and killing herself. I've sent Skeeter by her place time and time again to beg her to let us take care of her, but she keeps telling him she has stuff to do over there, that you all need her."

"We do need her. She keeps Margaret and Emerita from killing each other every day until I get there. But I'll see if she'll listen to me."

"Don't you tell her I told you about how bad her heart is. She made me promise not to tell a soul except Skeeter, and if she thought I'd told you, she'd skin us both and nail our hides to your daddy's— I nearly said his barn, but I guess she'd have to nail them to his house. Anyway, promise not to tell her I told you how bad she is."

"I promise." I hung up with my own heart so heavy, it felt like lead.

I TOOK CHELLIE OVER TO Daddy's for lunch the next day, trying to figure out how I could get Mamie off to myself for a few minutes and suggest she quit work. I would come up with a reason when I needed it.

They were already at the table. Margaret had made herself a salad of lettuce, cucumbers, green pepper, a boiled egg, and some of those grape tomatoes she was so fond of. The others were having beefsteak tomato sandwiches on white bread. We might be sick of canning tomatoes, but I don't know anybody who gets tired of eating them right off the vine.

I wheeled Chellie out to the table under the tree so she, Andy, and MacTavish could have a picnic, and I slid into a kitchen chair in time for Margaret's blessing. "Dear God, bless this food to the nourishment of our bodies and us to thy service. Bless those we love in every place, and send us a sign of hope that this drought will soon be ended. Amen."

Emerita said, contempt in her voice, "You do not pray. You simply give God a list of things to do. I think you believe God is your errand boy."

"I do not. I simply tell God what I need. I believe he wants the best for us."

Mamie reached for the bread plate. "The best as defined by who?"

"If you all can pray better, do it then." Margaret's voice was as sharp as the knife Emerita was using to peel a tomato.

Emerita laid her knife on the plate, clenched her hands together so hard the knuckles turned white, bowed her head, and began to cry out in a loud voice, "Mother of God! O Mother of God! You know how hard things can be for people on earth, how hard things are here today. Thank you for your presence with us. Thank you that you speak for us to your Son. Thank you for this food, which you give us every day. Thank you for this house, which protects us. Thank you that Bill is better at the hospital, that the rest of us were not badly hurt. Thank you that we have health and strength for what we must do. Thank you that José and the men are harvesting the hay you have sent to Bill. You know we could use rain. We beg you to intercede with your blessed Son on our behalf. We . . ." She lapsed into Spanish so fervent and impassioned that tears stung my eyes. I had no idea what she was saying, and I didn't think God or God's mother needed to be shouted at, but I had no doubt whatsoever that Emerita's spirit knelt at the throne of heaven to pour out its longings and love. When she had finished, she straightened up in her chair. "That is how I pray."

Margaret shoved back her chair. "We forgot the tea." She jerked one of Daddy's plastic ice-cube trays from the freezer and demanded, "Why doesn't Daddy get a fridge with an ice maker?"

"We can't all be rich," I snapped. "It doesn't hurt you to twist out ice cubes now and then."

Mamie slathered mayo on two slices of bread. She placed peeled tomato slices between her bread and took a bite. "We may not have a lot of variety to eat around here, but what we got is truly blessed."

I could tell she was trying to calm the rest of us down before our tempers boiled over, but I had a question for Emerita. "How come you pray to Mary instead of to Jesus?"

"A woman understands how a woman feels. A man cannot understand."

"God isn't a man," Margaret objected, twisting the ice-cube tray like she'd rather be wringing a neck. "Both men and women are made in God's image."

Mamie chewed her sandwich thoughtfully. "The Bible says we're supposed to pray to Jesus or in His name."

"A man cannot understand," Emerita insisted. "I pray to the mother of Jesus. She knows how I have suffered."

"He suffered, too, baby. He understands suffering. You can talk straight to Him."

"You think you are the only one who has suffered?" Margaret demanded. "We have all suffered. This year has been so bad, I feel like those fields out there, parched and dry."

"They's lessons to be learned from drought and scarcity," mused Mamie, apparently still hoping she could turn down the heat under our tempers. "They pare us down. Make us choose what we're willing to give up."

Margaret set glasses at each place like she was flinging down a gauntlet. "Sometimes we don't get a choice." I suspected she was thinking of Jason, Ben, and her house.

Emerita's eyes lashed her. "What have you suffered? Have you lost a brother who was as close as a twin? Did death then snatch away your father and your dreams in one night and force you to move to a village because your mother could not support two daughters in the city? Did you marry a man who beat you, abused you, and murdered your babies? You think *you* have suffered? Pah!" She stood and hurled her plate into the sink so hard it shattered.

"Not José!" I was shocked.

Emerita pressed one hand over her eyes and flapped the other behind her. "No. José is a good man."

Mamie thrust a tissue into her hand. "Sit down, honey, and tell us about it. I'd a whole lot rather listen to you than snap those beans over yonder in the sink."

"I do not speak of it."

"You already did," Margaret muttered.

Mamie waved her to silence. "You said you worked in a hospital. Don't you know you can't heal a boil until you lance it and let all the nasty stuff out?" She patted the vacant chair with one hand. "Sit down, now, and tell us about yourself."

Emerita sat. She looked down at the place mat before her as if its shiny blue surface were a crystal ball showing her past. "My parents moved to Mexico City when they married so their children could have opportunities they never had. They worked in a hotel to send my brother and me to school. He was to become a lawyer. I was to be a nurse. But Carlos was killed by a drunk driver a month before he was to enter university. *Papí* died from a heart attack the next year. *Mamí* could not support me and my baby sister, so she took us to her home village. Instead of training to become a nurse, I worked as an aide in a hospital run by nuns."

She fell silent and took several deep breaths, like a diver preparing to go off a very high board. Then she moved in choppy sentences through the rapids of her past. "The mayor from a nearby town got sick. I helped take care of him. He had a son, Bernardo. Bernardo was handsome. His family was wealthy. He wanted to marry me. He gave me presents. He said he loved me." She looked around the table, tears in her eyes. "He promised if I married him, he would give *Mamí* a house and send Victoria away to school."

She pounded the table with both fists. "Lies! All lies! He did not give *Mamí* a house or send Victoria to school. He worked for his uncle, who lived in Mexico City, and he said he was not making as much as he expected. But he traveled for his work, and sometimes I traveled with him. On trips, he had money for good hotels and nice dinners. Only at home did he pinch pesos. Another thing. He said he was a salesman, but he sold nothing. He took me to hotels and left me there while he went out 'to work.'" She sketched quotation marks. "I was not permitted to leave the hotel. I was—how do you say it?—clothes in the window to make people think we were a respectable couple."

"Window dressing?" I suggested.

"Yes, Window dressing. He was not respectable. He was a pig! When he drank—and he drank every night—he beat me and"—her voice faltered and grew bitter—"he made me do shaming things."

She looked around the table as if warning us about what was to come. "Even when I got pregnant, he beat me. One night he knocked me across the room. I fell against the corner of a chest. Our first child, a son, was born two days later, dead. I got pregnant again. Still Bernardo beat me. Our second child, also a son, was born three months early and lived an hour. I begged God to stop Bernardo's violence. God did nothing. I begged the mother of God for a child who would live. When I got pregnant again, my sister got sick. *Mi mamá* needed me to care for Victoria while she worked, so I asked Bernardo to let me stay with *mi mamá* until the baby came. Because his father wanted a grandson, he persuaded Bernardo to agree."

Again Emerita took several high-dive breaths. Her fists clenched on the table. She wiped away tears that threatened to spill.

"My daughter, Gabriella, was so beautiful. Her skin was soft as silk. Her hair curled over my fingers, so." She reached up and rolled one of Margaret's curls over her forefinger. "I begged to stay with *Mamí* in the village, but Bernardo came to get me. He had hired a nurse for the baby, and he said a wife belongs with her husband. I cried and begged to stay. His father came and ordered me to go home. We all went back to that house where there was no love." Her voice became bleak. "Gabriella had gas in her stomach, so she cried. Or perhaps she knew how unhappy her mother was. Every night I walked her for hours. But I loved her so much." Her voice dropped to a whisper. "So much."

Emerita paused, looking not at the place mat but beyond it into the past. She was silent for so long, I could not stand it. "What happened?"

"When Gabriella was three months old, *Mamí* sent a message one evening that Victoria was ill again. She asked me to come help her decide if they needed to go to the hospital. She could not afford the hospital. She hoped I would bring money—but I had none to bring. Bernardo paid our bills, but he never gave me a peso of my own. I could have taken the baby with me, but there was flu in the village, so I left her with the nurse. Only two hours I was gone! But when I got back . . ." Emerita was no longer with us. Her voice came from far away. "Gabriella lay dead in her crib. The nurse said she heard nothing, but I smelled alcohol on her breath. I called the doctor, but he could not save my child. He said she died of death in her bed."

"Crib death."

"Yes. She died in her crib. I wept for days. But when Bernardo came to bed the night after she died, he scratched his belly and said, 'Ah, a night without a baby crying.' And I knew. He killed her! I saw it in his cruel smile. I do not know how he did it, but I know! I know!" Again she beat a tattoo on the table. Tears flowed down her cheeks.

Mamie gathered her into her arms and held her until she grew calmer.

"So you left him." I didn't bother to make it a question.

"I could not. I discovered how Bernardo's family grew so rich. They all worked for a drug cartel." She nodded at our shocked expressions. "Yes. Bernardo was what they call 'a fixer'—someone who takes care of men who displease the bosses." She made her fingers into a pistol and pretended to shoot. "I could not leave him. He would have killed me. So I stayed—hating him, hating myself, begging God to end my suffering but not brave enough to end my life. I lived in fear every month that I would become pregnant again. At last I went to the Mother Superior at the hospital where I had worked. I told my story. I hoped she would help me safely leave my husband. She—she said marriage is a sacrament, and we cannot choose to end it. But she told me to go to the chapel and pray to the *Madre de Dios* for help. In the chapel, I got a miracle. A doctor came also to pray, a compassionate man. He saw me weeping and spoke to me. I told him my story and he—he offered to fix me so no more babies would come. No more would suffer. No more would die. The Mother of God helped me when the Father and Son would not."

"Sounds like the Mother Superior helped you," Margaret said. "I'll bet she sent that doctor to you."

"She would not do such a thing!" But behind her indignation, uncertainty flickered.

Mamie reached for her tea. "Prayers are answered in strange ways sometimes."

Emerita nodded. "I was saved from killing Bernardo. For six years, I promised myself I would as soon as I got the courage, and I prayed for courage. But before I found my courage, Bernardo went to 'fix' someone in Durango, and the other man fixed him first. After ten years, I was free. I could help my mother and my sister. Or so I thought. When the time came to read Bernardo's will, another woman came. She said she was his wife. She had a paper to prove it. Bernardo never married me—he only pretended to to please his father. For all those years of pain, I got nothing." She stopped like a hot, dry day winding down to dusk.

Mamie gave a short grunt. "That was one man who needed killing."

"He was not a man. He was a beast. You cannot know how it hurts me even now, to think of my babies."

"Oh, I know, honey," Mamie said. "I lost a baby, too—my little sister, Emmaline. I wasn't but five, but she was like my own child. I took care of her and loved her so much. When she died, she wasn't but six months old, sleeping in a box in my room. We had a storm and a rafter fell on her."

Emerita clutched Mamie's hand. "How long did you suffer? When did it stop?"

Mamie shook her head. "It never stops. I've carried the pain of losing her all my life. The guilt, too. It was my fault, you see. Mama told me to let the baby sleep with me, but sometimes she wet the bed, and I didn't want a wet bed. I put her to sleep in that box." Mamie laid her face down on her forearms and wept.

Before I could think how to comfort her, Emerita wailed, "I left Gabriella at home. Mother of God, have pity on us! We killed our babies!"

"Jesus, forgive us!"

They held each other, tears mingling cheek to cheek.

I gave Margaret a "do something" look—she was the big sister, after all. But she seemed paralyzed.

I tried putting an arm around each of the sobbing women's shoulders, but they didn't seem to notice I was there. After what seemed like an hour (but was ten minutes by Daddy's kitchen clock), Mamie reached for a dish towel hanging on the oven door and gently wiped Emerita's face. Emerita took the towel and wiped Mamie's. It was as sweet and simple as love. I sat back in my chair.

Mamie said, "What we crying and carrying on like this for? We know God forgives us, whatever we've done, if we are truly sorry. And, honey, God knows we are both truly sorry."

"Truly, truly sorry." Emerita wiped tears from the tabletop.

"Then that is that. Whooee, I feel better! I never told that story to anybody in my whole life, not even Earl. But I feel a whole lot better for telling you all."

"I do, as well."

"Plumb purged." Mamie picked up her sandwich and took a bite like she hadn't been watering the place with tears a minute before.

Emerita fetched herself another plate and made a sandwich. "You really think the Father and the Son love us as much as the Mother of God?"

Mamie licked mayonnaise off one finger. "I think God's love is like kudzu, honey. You know kudzu?"

Emerita nodded as she reached for a bowl of sliced onions and cucumbers in vinegar. "Bill calls it a pesky vine."

"He's got that right. Well, the love of God is a pesky vine, too. Just like kudzu, it's got only one thing on its mind: to cover the world with lovely new life. It creeps, one tendril at a time, over bad places and good places, over bad people, good people, and folks like us who are a little bit of both. Now most folks don't want kudzu around. Some folks don't want the love of God, either. They try to cut God's love off, or chop it out of their lives, or confine it to one little plot. But you know what? Nobody ever confined kudzu yet, and I don't reckon anybody ever will. And when the cutters and choppers and folks who try to put the love of God into little boxes are gone from the earth? That love's still gonna be here. You don't need to worry about Jesus understanding when you cry out to His mama. He understands every sorrow we got, and He plumb covers it with His love."

They sat there talking about God over tomato sandwiches like two nuns at lunch. I sat there feeling like I'd stood in a safe valley and had an avalanche sweep over me. From Margaret's expression, she felt the same.

I JERKED MY HEAD TOWARD the front of the house. "Let's go out on the porch awhile."

I doubt that Mamie and Emerita knew we'd left.

"Whew!" Margaret settled onto one end of the swing and offered me the other. For a second I was a preschooler—delighted to be invited to sit with my sister, who was tall enough to reach the floor. To reassure myself that I was an adult, I gave the first push.

"You sure can't tell about people from looking at them, can you?" she said.

"You sure can't. Imagine Emerita having all that in her past. And Mamie! The only problem I ever guessed from her past was that she must have had Lurleen when she was seventeen. But why didn't you tell them about Ben?"

"I'm not real comfortable discussing my private life with the help. Not even Mamie, after all these years away from her. I don't need to pour my guts out to them. What I do need is to get this canning done and Daddy back home so Emerita and José can go on their way and Mamie can go home and get her health back."

I nearly said, "That's not going to happen," but I didn't. If Margaret didn't want to discuss her private affairs with Mamie, I wouldn't share Mamie's private affairs with her.

I was surprised at the question that came out of my mouth instead. "Do you need me?"

She let the swing go back and forth several times before she answered. "I do—which is odd, considering how much I've resented you most of your life."

"Resented me? I resented *you*. You were the one who got everything. Looks, talent, praise from teachers. I cannot tell you how tired I got of having a teacher tell me, 'I taught your sister, Margaret. She was a wonderful student.'"

"I cannot tell you how tired I got of having you tag along with Daddy and me. Before you were born, we went everywhere together. He used to call me Princess Margaret. Did you know that?"

"No. I thought I made up that name. I must have heard him call you that."

"He said it a lot sweeter than you ever did. But after you came, I had to share him. He took you wherever we went. I hated it."

"That's pretty Freudian."

"Maybe so, but Daddy and I never fought until you were born."

"You blame me because you and Daddy can't get along?"

"Utterly. The fact that we are both hardheaded, opinionated cusses has nothing to do with it." She picked up one of my hands and squeezed it. "I cannot believe how I resented you, even after we grew up. Every time I called Mama, she was full of what you were doing. You even got to be with her when she died."

"You were here the week before she died, and I lived here, silly. She saw me nearly every day. And she was always telling me about you and what your family was doing, too."

"You got the daughter. There is something wrong with a universe where a woman who loves to sew gets only boys. But you didn't need to resent me. You were our parents' favorite."

"Oh, sure. That's why I was the servant around here after you left."

"I was the servant before you were born."

"You were little most of that time. I was only half grown when you left, so I had to work harder and longer. Besides, I had to put up with all those nasty remarks."

"What nasty remarks?"

"You know. 'Who's that?' 'That's Maggie Anderson's little sister.' 'She can't be! Maggie was such a *beautiful* child. And so *talented*. Look at all those awards she won for sewing.' In the I Resented My Sister competition, I win."

"Call it even." Margaret kept the swing moving. "But sewing isn't a talent—it's a skill. I worked hard to learn to sew."

"Yeah, but knowing how to design clothes—that was talent."

"Fat lot of good it's done me."

We swung gently for a while, our elbows touching.

"Speaking of sewing," I said, "how broke were you when I called and begged you to make clothes for Chellie?"

"Scraping the bottom of the barrel."

"You should have told me. We'd have gotten by somehow. Did you buy fabric?"

She gave a little snort to suppress a giggle. "If you promise not to tell, I'll confess."

That was when she told me how she had cut up Ben's clothes.

"Chellie is wearing Ben's wardrobe?" I couldn't believe it.

"Only part of it. He has more clothes than any man needs. And I loved every snip and slash. Am I awful?"

I grinned. "Perfectly dreadful. What did he do when he found out?"

"Roared down the stairs, asking where his clothes were. I put on a sweet dumb-wife face and said, 'I don't wear your clothes.' He knew I must have done something with them, but he couldn't prove it."

"Let's make sure he doesn't run into Chellie if he comes out here this summer. But where did you get the material for that little peach sundress? It is gorgeous."

She let the swing go back and forth several times before she answered. "I cut up a dress of my own. I didn't wear it often. And the last time I did— It was a really bad memory. I thought I could redeem it by cutting the memories and the dress up into smaller pieces and making a little girl happy."

"Want to tell me about it?"

"The Friday after Ben left, he invited me to dinner." Her voice went on and on, pouring out the shaming, awful events of that evening. When she was done, we swung quietly for a few minutes. There wasn't a thing I knew to say except, "I'm sorry," and it was inadequate. I reached over and held her hand. She did not take it back.

"You really are talented," I told her after a while. "Could you sew to make money?"

"I tried. I made five bridesmaid dresses in May."

I nearly said, "Want to make mine when I marry Luke?" but I didn't. He came over almost every night, and I loved him more every time I saw him, but I wasn't ready to share my feelings with the world. They were a private joy I wanted to hug to myself for a while.

I came back to earth to find Margaret still talking about those bridesmaids' dresses. ". . . girls didn't show up for fittings, gained weight after I'd measured them—it was a nightmare. I swore I'd never do that again. I might, though. The sewing part was fun."

"I wish you'd design a line of clothes for kids like Chellie—things that are easier to get on. Or for folks who have injuries, like Daddy. But listen to me, thinking I can solve your problems when I can't even solve my own."

"Have you had any news about Porter?"

"No. Luke and José plan to go visit his old work site next week on Luke's day off. If they don't learn anything, do you know whether, if I advertise for him and he doesn't show up, I can go ahead and divorce him? Or do I have to wait seven years or something to declare him dead?"

"How should I know?"

"You're the big sister. You're supposed to know everything."

"Get rid of that illusion. You'd have to ask a lawyer that question. But what's your hurry after all these years?"

All my good intentions to keep my feelings to myself flew over the banister. "Luke and I want to get married, but we can't as long as I'm married to Porter."

"You and Luke? I didn't even know you were dating."

"We aren't—we haven't. But we've seen a lot of each other while painting my house, cleaning a carpet, taking folks to the hospital, and sitting on my porch after Chellie's in bed." I didn't mention the day we'd seen a lot more of each other. That didn't count as a date, either.

She took a minute to let that sink in. "Wow. You are really serious?"

"Absolutely."

"So you *have* to find Porter."

"Which means I need to talk to Rick. If he hasn't learned anything, I'll call a lawyer, but I hate to pay a lawyer if I don't have to. You don't have to see Rick, though."

She winced. "If I never see him again, it will be too soon."

"Hey—does Rick know about your divorce? Is that what he was talking about when he told me he understood Ben and would tell folks around here if you said he had hit you?"

"Yeah. At dinner, I had made him promise not to tell any of you."

"He was willing to use that to blackmail you into keeping quiet about what he did? Scumbag! I still need to talk to him, though. Maybe if I tell him how important this is to me—"

"You plan to appeal to Rick's beautiful nature?" Skepticism oozed from every word.

I stood. "No, I plan to ask nicely and then, if necessary, to hit him again with his unbeautiful statue. I'm hoping it won't get that far. I'm going to call him. Wish me luck."

"Good luck. If he's in Solace today, I'll keep Chellie while you run into town."

Rick Landiss wasn't in Solace. "He's taking a Baltic cruise," I reported. "He won't be back until late August. Must be nice."

"Must be. But even if we can't do anything about Rick at the moment, I can help you another way. Pick an evening to go to dinner and a movie with Luke, and I'll bring Andy over to sit with Chellie. Nobody ought to get married without having a single date."

Thirty-one

On Luke's next afternoon off, he and José drove to Porter's old work site in Marietta to see what they could learn. I wasn't crazy about Andy and Chellie being around when they came back to report, so I suggested to Margaret, "Why don't you take the kids to that movie they've been pestering us about?" Andy had seen previews on TV and started campaigning to see it. Chellie—who had never been to a theater in her life—had developed a passion to see it, too.

"What do you suggest I use for money?" Margaret asked. "Movies cost a fortune, and the kids are sure to want popcorn and a drink."

"Take it out of Daddy's bank account. Didn't he give you power of attorney to write checks for household expenses? Keeping the children happy is a legitimate household expense."

Margaret and two delighted children drove out around two. At the same time Mamie went home, gray and exhausted. Emerita and I finished the last canner of beans, then went out on the porch to wait for the men. I settled in the swing and set it moving gently. "How are you feeling? Do your burns still hurt?"

"Not so much. When they do, I take a pill the doctor gave me for pain. Then I feel"—she waved her hands in a loop over her head—"very happy."

"You look better than Mamie. Did she seem grayer than usual today?"

Emerita pressed her glass to her forehead to cool herself. "I have seen women look like that before. She is a very sick woman."

"She told you that?" I was annoyed that Mamie would discuss her condition with a stranger and not with me, but it was fear that made me sharp.

"Yes. Because I once worked in a hospital."

"Should she be working? Especially with all this smoke still around?"

"No, but she says God wants her here. She has something to do."

"I can't think God wants her killing herself canning."

"No."

Beyond the porch, lightning flickered in tall clouds that had doubled and darkened in the past hour. When it was clear Emerita would say no more, I asked, "You reckon those clouds signal rain?"

She fluttered the tail of her T-shirt. "They never do."

I gave the swing another push with my toe, trying to create a breeze. Whatever the clouds brought, they hadn't brought any wind.

We watched them approach over the drought-ridden landscape. Poplars were already turning yellow, though it was only July. Dead pines stood brown and ugly against green brothers beyond the pasture. The ground beside the road was dusty red powder that passing traffic trailed like rusty clouds. Daddy had been buying hay for several weeks before he got hurt, the pastures were so dry. If rain didn't come soon, he would need to sell some cows to keep the rest from starving. Even the kudzu in the ditch by the road looked discouraged, and it takes a lot to discourage kudzu.

"Is it this dry in Mexico?" I asked.

"Parts of it. The desert. But we also have beautiful mountains, lovely beaches, and good farmland. Many kinds of geography, like the United States."

"Have you seen much of your country?" I asked.

"I saw many places when I traveled with Bernardo, but I do not like to remember that time." The subject was closed.

Freshening air stirred the hair at my neck. "Hey, there's a breeze. Maybe we *will* get rain." Distant thunder rumbled like hollow laughter. The day grew dark as dusk. I smelled sulfur on the wind. I hoped for rain any second.

Instead, the clouds dropped hail. Chunks of ice like marbles, then golf balls, then tennis balls pounded Daddy's tin roof and bounced off the hard, dry ground.

Emerita pointed down the road. "Here they come!"

Luke's truck crept along the icy asphalt, pummeled by ice. As they passed the porch, I saw a chunk the size of a softball bounce off the cab roof, leaving a dent. It was not the first. He slowed to turn and slid on the ice. My heart thudded as I watched the truck execute two complete turns and slide into the ditch across the road, nose down and tail up. Luke leaned out the driver's window to survey the situation. We heard him yowl as hail hit his head.

"Wait right there," I yelled. "I'll bring help."

By the time I fetched buckets to cover their heads, the hail had stopped. Luke and José minced across the road like flamingos, avoiding chunks of ice. Luke was rubbing his head.

"Hail, the conquering hero comes!" I shouted.

"You want a whipping?" he called back.

"Not today, thanks." I swept the porch and steps before they got there. It seemed odd to see ice all over the grass when the temperature on Daddy's thermometer read eighty-five. I wanted to rake it up before it melted and pour it on the garden, but by the time I got a rake, most of it would be gone.

I poured tea for the men, and we joined Emerita on the porch. José took the rocker beside his wife. Luke joined me on the swing.

I saw no reason to make small talk. "So, what did you find out?"

José looked at the pasture across the road. Luke studied the tea in his glass like it was some exotic drink.

"Did you find Luis? Did you talk to him?"

José waited for Luke to answer. When he didn't, José said, "We find. We wait and we talk. He say—" José stopped and gestured to Luke.

Luke gave the sigh of a man who has decided to get the worst over with fast. "He said Porter's dead. He and another man got into a fight, the other man knocked Porter down, and he hit his head on a concrete curb."

Porter was dead? Hearing my worst fears stated as fact sucked out all my air. When I could catch my breath, I wasn't grieving, I was mad. "Why didn't somebody call me? Why didn't the office know?"

Luke and José exchanged a look I couldn't interpret.

"What? What aren't you telling me?"

Luke rubbed the back of my hand with his forefinger, like he was writing the story there. "It happened after the men had gone home for the day. Luis had forgotten his hammer and went back to the site to fetch it. That's when he saw Porter and the other man arguing. Right, José?"

"*Sí.*" José took up the tale, his hands supplying words he omitted. "Porter say work not good, need do over. Man get angry, knock Porter down. He die."

Luke picked up the story. "Luis was apparently hidden by the foreman's trailer. He said that when the other man realized Porter was dead, he started up a backhoe, dug a hole, and buried Porter on the site."

"Buried Porter on the site?" I tried to take that in. "And Luis didn't tell anybody?"

"Luis scared," José explained. "He no want to get—" He wiggled his hands in the air.

Luke supplied the missing word. "Involved. He's still scared and he still doesn't want to get involved. My guess is he isn't here legally and fears being deported."

"But didn't the men notice anything the next morning?"

"No. The landscaper had started preparing the site for planting and the backhoe was there to dig trenches for the irrigation system, which was almost complete. The man dug a grave where sod was going to be laid and smoothed the ground over."

José nodded. "He do good job. Luis say nobody see when they come."

I remembered spongy sod underfoot. Had I walked over Porter's unmarked grave? My stomach gave a lurch. I ran for the stairs.

I think I threw up my entire married life in the next five minutes. I certainly threw up anything I had eaten in the past day. I was kneeling beside the toilet when I felt a cool wet washcloth pressed against the back of my neck. "This will help," Emerita said. "Did you love Porter very much?"

I tried to summon the energy to perpetuate the lie, but I couldn't. "No. He was a teenage crush, and I was a foolish girl. Still, he should not have ended up buried in an office park." I felt woozy as I climbed to my feet. "Porter did have possibilities."

"Bernardo had possibilities, too. But he let evil into his life, and it consumed him."

Emerita refreshed the washcloth and wrung it as if she were wringing the neck of the evil that had possessed and diminished our husbands. She handed me the cloth to wipe my mouth. "Men who share our life and our bed—we always grieve for what they do not become."

I closed my eyes and saw Porter handing me a tiny bedraggled black kitten. In that moment I had seen him as he could have been: a person with principles who wanted to make the world a better place. The waste of his life swept over me like desolation. I swayed. Emerita caught and held me. We sobbed together the tears of irretrievable dreams.

When our tears were spent, we backed away from each other and scrubbed our cheeks. Our soggy gazes met in the mirror. Emerita chuckled. "José and Luke will think we are dying up here. We should go down, no?" We washed our faces, and she shared her brush and powder for my shiny nose. Refreshed, we went back downstairs, but I carried the weight of Porter's death on my shoulders.

José and Luke sat looking out over the fields, trying to pretend they hadn't heard wails and cries coming from upstairs.

"We are fine now," Emerita said, taking José's hand as she sat beside him. "For women, tears are sometimes as necessary as a shower."

I sat by Luke and took his hand, too. "Who killed Porter? Did Luis say?"

"No." Luke's voice was full of frustration. "José asked and asked, but Luis flat-out refused to tell."

"Say he get *mucho* trouble," José added. "He no need trouble. He have wife and five *hijos*."

"But he showed us exactly where Porter is buried. I've already talked to the Marietta PD. They aren't happy about asking a judge for permission to dig up an expanse of sod on the report of an unidentified eyewitness, but I think I finally convinced them."

"So what do we do now?"

He covered both my hands with his. "We do the only thing we can. We wait."

It took effort, but I managed a smile. They had gone to a lot of trouble for me that afternoon. "Hey—that's my name: Billie Waits."

When Margaret got home, Chellie and Andy had to give me a scene-by-scene report on the film. I thought we'd never arrive at the moment when I could settle the children at the kitchen table with Andy's cars while Emerita cooked supper and I could take Margaret out on the porch to report.

I gave it to her in short sentences. "José talked to Luis, one of the men from the site. He saw Porter and another man get into a fight. Porter fell and hit his head on a concrete curb. He—he died."

She sat very still, taking it in. "Porter is actually dead?"

"Yeah. I kept telling people he wouldn't run out on me."

"Yeah, you did." I could see she had never believed it. "This Luis saw it happen?"

"He said so. He went back after work for a hammer and saw the fight."

"Good old Porter. Always good for a brawl. Why didn't somebody notify you?"

"Because the man who fought him dug a hole with a backhoe they had on the site and buried Porter where sod would be laid the next day." I felt a chill that had nothing to do with the temperature. "Did Ben landscape that site?"

"He could have. He does a lot of work for Rick. But I know the man who drives Ben's equipment. I wouldn't trust him on his bulldozer around trees I wanted to save, but he wouldn't fight anybody. Except on earthmoving equipment, he's a sweetie."

"Luis wouldn't have any reason to be afraid of exposing him, anyway. Who else can drive the backhoe?" I wondered how long it would take Margaret to figure out what was worrying me.

"Nobody that I know of, except— Wait a minute! You don't— That's ridiculous! Ben wouldn't quarrel with Porter."

"Anybody would quarrel with Porter. Porter's stance toward the world was 'I'm right and you're wrong, so let's straighten you out.' Remember? Luis said he was on his high horse about something that wasn't being done right—the irrigation system, maybe? Ben might not have known who he was. They didn't see each other more than two or three times."

"Ben wouldn't kill anybody."

"He might have hit Porter if Porter made him mad enough. Porter had talents along those lines."

"Ben wouldn't! Besides, why would Luis be afraid of telling on Ben?"

She had a point. "Who *would* Luis be afraid of?"

"That pig of a man—Caesar."

"His name wasn't Caesar. Caesar was Daddy's pig. You mean the site foreman."

"Yeah. He could have authorized short cuts and Porter found out."

I set the swing moving again. "I wonder if there's any way we could get him to confess."

"Let the police handle it, Billie."

But finding and burying Porter hit an immediate snag. When the Marietta police asked a judge for permission to excavate the site, Rick Landiss's lawyer contacted him on his cruise, and Rick went ballistic. Next he went to court. His lawyer pointed out that the office park was ready for tenants, and Rick couldn't expect to get tenants if police were digging for bodies on the premises. He asked for a sworn statement from the eyewitness that there was a body buried on the site before digging began.

Even I had to admit he had a point, but Luis had melted away like a snow cone in July. After talking with José, he had worked the rest of the week, collected his pay, and disappeared. Luke and José spoke to every worker on the site, but none could—or would—say where he had gone. Heaven only knew if Porter would ever be laid to rest in a real cemetery.

It was a shame Porter didn't know how bizarre things were. He'd have gotten a kick out of giving people so much trouble.

Thirty-two

As July slid toward August I found a plastic swimming pool at a garage sale and set it under Daddy's big oak. I filled it with the hose every afternoon, drought or no drought, so Chellie and Andy could splash around in cool water. Lucky kids. Sometimes I looked out the kitchen window and was tempted to join them.

"One of the fans died," Margaret announced when I arrived one day. "We're drowning in our own sweat." She was at the stove, taking peaches from boiling water. Daddy hadn't gotten many from his trees, but he had instructed us to put them up for winter.

"People all over the world live without fans," Emerita snapped. "They do not die in their sweat. You are soft." She was at the sink, slipping the peeling from hot peaches.

"I'm not soft. I'm hot!" Margaret raged. "Stop criticizing everything I say."

"Sorry. It's just that you have so much, you don't know how to live like the rest of us."

"Like the rest of you?" Margaret's face was white. "Like Mamie, there, who has a house and a pension? Like Billie, who has a house and a job? Like you and José, who are getting paid for your work? I have nothing! I get paid nothing! Don't tell me I don't know how to live like the rest of you. And don't criticize me when I say I'm hot. I am hot. And I'm sick and tired of . . . of . . . of everything!" She stumbled to a chair and wept in great, gusty sobs.

Emerita and Mamie stared.

Andy appeared at the back door. "What's the matter with Mama?"

I hustled him back out to the yard. "Your mama is very tired today. You kids stay in the pool."

Margaret was still sobbing when I returned. I put my arms around her and spoke over her head. "Her husband divorced her last April. They had to sell their house and didn't get much for it, and Jason moved in with his dad. So she lost her husband, her home, and her son all in a few weeks. She has never worked, and she doesn't know what she can do."

Margaret's sobs grew louder.

"Oh, baby!" Mamie shoved me out of the way, pulled up a chair, and enveloped Margaret in her arms. "My poor baby," she crooned. "My poor little baby." I was ashamed of how jealous I felt. After all, Mamie had rocked and cuddled Margaret long before she rocked and cuddled me.

"I am so sorry!" Emerita pulled a chair to Margaret's other side. "I did not know." She stroked Margaret's hair and twined one black curl around her finger. She reached into her pocket and pulled out a crucifix. "Here." She thrust it into Margaret's hand.

Margaret shoved it back at her. "I can't bear to look at it. He looks exactly like I feel—beaten and betrayed."

"He knows what suffering is," Mamie reminded her. She started to sing. "'What a friend we have in Jesus, all our sins and griefs . . .'"

"Don't Mamie." Margaret held up one hand. "I hurt too much. I don't know how long I can hang on."

"We're here to help, honey. Trust us. We'll see you through." She held Margaret for a long time.

When Margaret finally sat up and wiped her eyes, Mamie said, "Long as we're having confession this afternoon, I got something I need to confess, too. Something I oughta told you weeks ago. The doctor—" Her voice faltered. I put my hands on her shoulders and gave her an encouraging squeeze. She covered one of my hands with one of hers and her voice grew stronger. "The doctor says my old heart is plumb wore-out. I don't have much time left. I know I'm not much use hanging around here every afternoon, but I—I take comfort in being here with you all. I'm ashamed to admit it, but I find I'm scared to die."

Margaret's face went white. "We can't lose *you*!" She clutched Mamie again. I knew how she felt. I had cried myself to sleep the night after I'd talked with Lurleen and several nights since, thinking how empty the world would be without Mamie. But hearing Margaret's selfish cry, I realized I hadn't spent one minute looking at Mamie's death from her point of view.

As Margaret and Mamie held each other and sobbed, I leaned down and embraced them both. Emerita put her arms around us all. We cried and cried and cried. If anybody had come in, we'd have made a curious sight.

When our sobs ceased, we sat sniffing. Mamie looked around the table. "If I look half as pitiful as the rest of you, I need a bag over my head."

I fetched paper napkins for everybody to wipe their eyes. "Let's declare a holiday. Daddy's got enough peaches put up for the winter. We can put the rest in the freezer and eat them before he gets home. How about tea on the porch for everybody?"

I brought down glasses and twisted an ice-cube tray over a bowl. Emerita poured tea while Mamie and Margaret stroked and petted each other.

Mamie pulled herself heavily to her feet. "Let's get out of this sweltering kitchen." She grabbed a glass and led the way.

That afternoon, she took the swing like she used to when I was little. I started in that direction, but she waved me away. "Join me, Maggie. I haven't swung with you for years."

A little hurt, I took the rocker beside Emerita. But as I watched Margaret lean into Mamie and hold her hand, I knew there was enough love in Mamie to share.

Silence is the best healer after cathartic tears. We sat silent for a very long time, the only sounds the soft thud of rockers on the porch floor, the creak of the swing, and the muted sounds of children laughing under the tree. Birds had deserted us for wetter climes.

Emerita kept darting looks at Margaret like she wanted to say something, but she didn't. Margaret held Mamie's hand and looked over the pasture like she was drinking it in. Mamie had her eyes closed. I wondered if she was praying. I was looking at Mamie, trying to memorize every line for when she wasn't there.

As if she felt my gaze, Mamie opened her eyes. "What you thinking? You miffed that I wanted to sit in the swing with Maggie instead of you?"

I couldn't bear to tell her what I had been thinking. "No, but you did used to swing with me."

Margaret squeezed Mamie's hand. "Mamie and I swung for years before you were born."

Mamie chuckled. "Maggie wasn't pleased to have a sister, neither. Did you know that?"

"Oh, yeah. She'd rather have had a pony."

Emerita laughed, so of course, Margaret had to tell her that story.

"She tried to trade you for a dog, too, once," Mamie informed me. "Did you ever hear about that?" When I shook my head, she commanded, "Go on. Tell her, Maggie."

Margaret gave me a rueful smile. "You must have been about six months old. I was pushing your stroller up and down the sidewalk while Daddy was in the bank, when a woman came by with a darling cocker spaniel. She said I was so lucky to have a cute baby sister—that she wanted a baby, but hadn't had one yet. I offered to trade you for her dog. I even offered to throw in the stroller. But she decided not to trade. I was crushed."

Mamie and Margaret both laughed. I felt hurt for about three seconds; then I saw the funny side of the story. "Can't you see Daddy's face if he got back in the truck and saw you'd swapped me for a dog?"

"Not to mention Grace," Mamie added. "She never was fond of dogs. She sure wouldn't have wanted one instead of her baby girl."

Next thing we knew, the four of us were laughing as hard as we had cried.

When we finally calmed down, Emerita leaned toward Margaret. "I think maybe Billie is a little hurt by that story, though. I have a niece, Juanita, who is not quite two. My sister is not married, so she and the baby live with my mother. One of their neighbors has a son who is six and he calls Juanita *gordo*, which means fat. It makes Juanita cry. But one day Juanita will grow up to be beautiful, and the boy will be sorry he made fun of her. I think now that Billie has grown up, you are sorry, too."

Margaret leaned over and put her hand on my knee. "I am sorry, Billie. I wouldn't trade you for all the puppies in the world. Not unless they were really cute puppies."

Mamie propped her hands on her thighs, and I suspected we were in for a little sermon. "You know what's good about this afternoon? We've admitted we are down at the bottom of life, which means we are truly blessed." She smiled at each of us in turn. "You don't believe me, but it's a fact. There's something I read once that was so true, I tried to memorize it. Let's see how it goes, now. Something like, 'The best spiritual blessing is knowing we are utterly destitute. Until we get there, God is powerless. He can do nothing if we think we are sufficient to ourselves.' That's not quite it, but very like. I don't see how any of us could get much more destitute, do you? I'm dying. Maggie's been betrayed and abandoned. Billie—well, Billie's been down so long she wouldn't know up if it slapped her in the face, and I suspect you have, too, Emerita. Maggie and I been clinging to our pride. We didn't want you all to know how bad off we are. Now that we've admitted it, maybe God can bless us all."

The phone rang. "That must be him," I joked. "I'll get it. If it's not God, it's Daddy, checking to be sure we're doing everything his way."

———

IT WASN'T. IT WAS SOMEBODY shouting in Spanish. "Emerita? I think it's for you."

She came back to the porch with her eyes huge, her face pale. "*Mamí* and Victoria, my sister—they are dead!" She fell to her knees on the porch, screaming and crying. She wept so hard, I was afraid she would make herself sick.

I knelt beside her. "What happened?"

"Victoria—she was wild. Went with men, liked parties. She was stabbed in a bar last night. When *Mamí* heard, her heart stopped." She sobbed and sobbed.

"Who was on the phone?" I tried to calm her by making her think.

"The priest. He said a neighbor took little Juanita, but I must go to her. How frightened she must be! And Victoria . . . *Mamí!*" She burst into Spanish and began to scream again.

Accustomed to more reserved grief, we were paralyzed by the violence of her weeping. We tried to calm her, but she would not be comforted. Leaving her with Margaret and Mamie, I hurried to my truck and went to find José. He was supervising the men who were roofing Daddy's new barn. When I explained what had happened, he pelted for the back door. By the time I got back to the house, he and Emerita were upstairs. We could all hear her screaming and José trying to calm her. Spanish rippled like water overhead.

"Don't you say one word about God's tapestry," Margaret warned Mamie.

"It's just more dark threads," Mamie insisted. "Don't you say one word about 'How could a good God let this happen?' God didn't take Victoria into that bar."

"He gave Emerita's mama a bad heart."

"You don't know that, and I don't know it. That's between her and God. But dying isn't the worst thing that can happen to us. It's the best." She added so low I almost didn't hear, "I need to remember that."

"'To die is different from what anyone supposed, and luckier,'"

I quoted. They looked at me curiously. "Walt Whitman, *Leaves of Grass*."

"Should we be getting them plane tickets?" Margaret asked.

I was touched by her generosity. Two tickets to Mexico would take a major bite out of both our budgets. "I'll go up and ask."

In their room, Emerita huddled on the bed while José sat beside her, holding her. I asked softly from the doorway, "Would you all like to fly home? I can call about tickets."

They exchanged a look of fear. "No, no," he said. "No plane."

"It's a lot faster than anything else, and the little girl needs you. We'll be glad to buy the tickets."

Emerita fell across her lap, weeping. José murmured something and came to join me. His dark eyes watched for my reaction as he said, "We do not have documents for America. We cannot go through customs."

"You have green cards."

"They are forged." Emerita's voice was bitter. "I told him we should not come that way. I told him!"

"It was the only way," he said over his shoulder. I could tell it was an old argument between them.

I wasn't as shocked as I might have been if I hadn't suspected it all along.

"We will think what to do," he told me. He went back to their room and closed the door.

I found Mamie and Margaret back on the porch in the swing. "You were right—they don't have visas," I reported, "and undocumented immigrants can't use a plane."

I expected Margaret to at least say, "I told you so." Instead, she puckered her forehead in worry. "Then how are they going to get back across the border?"

Mamie gently pushed the swing. "Best thing we can do right now is pray. She'll be down when she's ready."

"I don't know what to pray," Margaret said.

"You know hurting, honey. That's all you need to know to pray for somebody else." Mamie began to speak in a low voice, as if to herself. "The night of that big storm back in April, I had something you could call a dream or you might call a vision. I was lying in my bed, remembering Emmaline and that terrible night the roof blew off our house, when all of a sudden, right above my bed, I felt a broad, deep stream made up of all the sorrows of the world. As it rushed along over my head"—she put her hand up as if to touch it—"my own sorrow flowed up and joined it. I realized it had always been there, but I had never noticed. My grief joined me to all who suffer. I felt it as clearly as I feel you now." She put a hand on Margaret's arm. Margaret covered it with her other hand.

Mamie's voice rumbled on. "Flowing with that stream, I could hardly breathe, much less pray. All I could do was feel my pain and theirs. But then I saw that we were gliding toward a bright and golden light. I heard a voice saying, 'God himself will be with you. He will wipe every tear from your eyes. And death shall be no more. Nor shall there be mourning or crying or pain anymore.' As soon as that voice stopped, the storm stopped, too, quick as it came up. But ever since that night I have felt that stream. It's up there." She pointed to the pale green beaded boards of the porch ceiling.

"Excuse me, please?" José stood in the doorway, looking miserable. "Emerita say we go home. Juanita have nobody else. But I say, 'How I can leave the farm? Bill need me.' We don't know what to do." He waited for us to offer a workable solution.

"With the cows gone and the hay mowed, there's not a lot you have to do," I reminded him. "I think you should both go."

"There is still a barn to build, but I suppose I must go." I could see his dreams evaporating like sweat on that hot porch. No money to care for his mother. No farm of his own.

"What if one of us drove Emerita and brought her back? Could we get her across the border?" I asked.

"Oh, no, *señora*! Border police would stop you. We have to find a way is not watched. That is why I go with her."

"Can you go back the same way you came across?"

"No. That *coyote* was the man I gave money for the truck. He cheated us much. I would not trust him."

"He owes us!" Emerita spoke from the doorway. "I have his phone number. I will call and ask him to help us."

José scowled. "Who knows what he will do? He cheated us."

"I will ask." Emerita started for the phone.

"If he wants money, we'll find it somehow." That was the Margaret I used to know.

We sat in silence while Emerita placed her call. I didn't understand a word she said, but her tones were unmistakable. She hung up, smoldering. "He is away in his truck. I spoke with his wife. She says her husband never cheated anybody, that he is an honorable man. She says he helps people across the border in memory of his brother, who died when a bad *coyote* put too many people in a truck with bad air. She will call him and have him call me."

While we waited, we tried out different plans. If they both went and stayed in Mexico, how could they support José's mother there and eventually buy a farm? "We cannot," Emerita said flatly.

"And I do not like to leave *Señor* Bill," José insisted. "He is good to us. Now he need me. I must build him a new barn."

Emerita could go back to their village while José stayed in America to earn the money they needed, but they clearly did not like that plan.

Mamie rested her elbow on the arm of the swing, her chin in her palm. "Looks to me like Emerita needs to go home and bring that baby back."

Emerita and José looked at each other. "How?" she asked. But I heard hope rising in her.

The phone rang. We let her answer it.

First she was firm and angry. Next she was uncertain. She was apologetic. Finally she burst into tears. *"Gracias. Gracias. Gracias."* We heard a pencil scribbling in the kitchen. *"Gracias."*

"The *coyote* is very angry with the *gringo* about the truck," she reported. "He says he gave him our money for a good truck. He will speak to the *gringo* about getting some of our money back. He will also get me into Mexico without charge and bring me and Juanita back again!"

José barked out a question, his hands moving like birds. The only word I really caught was *coyote*, but the way José's eyes flashed, he clearly still did not trust the man.

Emerita replied in Spanish and did not translate everything. All she told us was, "He said I am to meet him at the place where he left us before. I am to call him when I know when I can be there."

Margaret was invaluable in the next hour. She ordered Emerita's bus tickets. She set Mamie and me to packing food for the trip. She washed Emerita's dirty clothes and drove them to a self-service laundry to dry them faster than they could dry on the line. I suspected it was the first time she'd been in one of those places since college.

Once the plans were in place, Emerita's grief returned. She sat and stared into space, tears rolling down her cheeks. Each of us who passed her at the kitchen table stopped to give her a hug. "You are so good to me," she murmured over and over. "You are so good to me."

"That's what friends are for," Mamie told her. "We're all linked up, honey. It is only together that we can hold up the sky."

José drove Emerita to catch a six o'clock bus. When we sat down to supper, Margaret ended her prayer, "Dear God, we thank you for our friend Emerita. You know all she means to us. Please keep her safe on her journey and bring her back safely to us with little Juanita. Amen."

She opened her eyes and saw me staring at her. "What? What's that look on your face?"

"Who would have ever thought Margaret Baxter would pray for an illegal immigrant to sneak back safely into the country?"

"This isn't about laws. It's about Emerita."

Thirty-three

Emerita called when she arrived in her village. She said she and little Juanita were going to stay with José's mother and sisters while she sold her mother's house and waited for the *coyote*'s call that he was making another run to the United States. José purchased international phone cards and called her every few days, but the *coyote* did not call. José wandered around the farm like a man who had lost a limb, his eyes so sad we could have drowned in unshed tears.

I carried around some unshed tears, too. Knowing Porter was lying under the sod of an office park in Marietta made me sad. Knowing I couldn't marry Luke until we could dig Porter up and bury him decently made me crazy. I called Rick Landiss's lawyer several times to ask him to please let somebody look for Porter, but he said he would not discuss it further until Mr. Landiss got home near the end of August.

August was hot, the air so thick you could cut it and spread it on bread. Gardens and yards shriveled. Only veins remained of leaves. We had nothing left to can, but Mamie and I still went to Daddy's every afternoon—afternoons as breathless as the air. We all knew we were keeping vigil on Mamie's life.

The plastic pool out in the yard grew too limp to support Chellie's back, and watching the new barn go up lost its charm for the children.

They, too, felt an instinct to herd close to the family; Chellie and Andy moved into the dining room. I turned the air conditioner on high, found Daddy's old Monopoly game, and taught them the rules. They took to it like budding entrepreneurs. To hear them chortle, Donald Trump should prepare for a takeover. Watching Chellie shake the dice and set houses on her properties, I was astonished at how much dexterity she was developing from working with Bethany each morning and playing with Andy in the afternoons. As much as I hated to admit it, trained teachers could be better for her development at that stage than a loving mom.

Sometimes we women sat on the porch. Sometimes we played canasta at the kitchen table like we used to when I was small. Margaret gave Mamie a sharp look in one canasta game after she had thrown down a card I needed to pick up a big pile. "You don't have to let the baby win. She's all grown-up now." Mamie looked real embarrassed. She won the next hand.

We passed precious afternoons reminiscing about our childhoods, Mama, and good times Mamie and I had had at the mill. As children, Margaret and I had told Mamie everything. We fell into that pattern again. Margaret told all about Ben—his betrayal, her dreadful month of May. I talked about Porter and our years together. I admitted I had been too immature to know what marriage was when I walked down the aisle, but I still didn't say anything bad about Porter. I felt it would be wrong, now that he was dead; besides, part of me was afraid if I did, God wouldn't ever let me dig him up and marry Luke. Margaret and I talked about how worried we were for the future—how we would support ourselves and our children, and Mamie told us to trust God. I learned more about my sister in those afternoons than I learned about Mamie. Mamie was getting noticeably shorter of breath.

ONE AFTERNOON WHILE WE PLAYED cards, Mamie got to talking about God's tapestry again. "Just look at how God took dark things that happened to all of us—you two, me, Emerita—and wove them together to get us all on this farm this summer. Now he's adding a few light threads. We get to play cards and laugh together. Emerita is back with little Juanita. When God finishes with this tapestry, it's gonna be beautiful! And I'll have the best view of any of us, up in heaven."

"Don't talk like that," I begged.

Mamie pointed to her pile of canastas. "Black cards are as much a part of the game as red ones, child. And death is as much a part of the tapestry as life is. You know that. I forgot it for a little while, but I'm remembering again."

Margaret slid me a sideways look. "If Porter hadn't died, you wouldn't be mooning around here planning to marry Luke."

"Sure I would. I'd have divorced Porter. I refuse to lay Porter's death on God!"

But was that true? If Porter's checks had kept coming, would I have drifted on month after month, content with Chellie in our cocoon? Would I have looked twice at Luke as long as Porter supported his little girl? I hadn't looked at any man before. Would I have gotten a job and let Bethany keep Chellie? Probably not for another year or so. I was willing to admit that Porter's failure to send checks gave me a shove I needed—for Chellie's sake as well as for my own. But the idea that God would *kill* Porter to free me was monstrous.

"You don't think God had a hand in Porter's death, do you, Mamie? A *man* killed him!"

Mamie laid down her cards and spoke slowly, as if she was thinking it over as she spoke. "Given the kind of man Porter was, I think it was certain he would one day die by violence, and God has a hand in all deaths. He decides every single instant whether any of us will live or die. So while I don't know exactly how God handles things, maybe God just decided to let Porter die in a fight timed to fit in with God's plans for you."

"Yeah. Porter could have just gotten a bump on his head that night." Margaret was clearly more enamored of Mamie's idea than I was.

"God did not kill Porter! That's a terrible thing to say!"

Mamie shrugged. "I don't know all the answers, honey. I just know God uses threads of violence and death as well as love and goodness to weave purposes of which we are only dimly aware. The Bible says, 'All things work together for good to them that love the Lord,' and I've lived long enough to believe it. I also know our life and our death are in his hands. I am so blessed God let me know I was gonna die. I get to say good-bye to the people I care about before I go."

Tears stung my eyes. I didn't feel real blessed when I thought of Mamie's death.

As usual, Margaret said the right thing. She leaned her forehead against Mamie's. "We are blessed to share this summer with you. I would not have missed this time with you for anything."

"Me, neither," I managed over a frog in my throat. "Have I ever told you I love you? You have always been my second mom."

"Mine, too," said Margaret.

Mamie's eyes filled with tears. "You have always been my precious girls."

That reminded me of something I'd been meaning to ask. I sniffed to clear my passages. "Have you and Lurleen made things right between you?"

Mamie picked up her cards and studied them like we were playing for money.

"Have you?" Anxiety made my voice sharp.

"Not yet, honey. She's still mad at me for coming over here to work and not going into that old folks' home. I been thinking maybe I ought to move in there, just to please her. What do you think?"

I headed for the phone. "I think you ought to at least talk to her." Lurleen's cell number was posted on the wall next to Daddy's phone.

She answered on the first ring and must have recognized Daddy's number. "Has something happened to Mama?"

"Sure has," I said cheerfully. "She has decided she wants to talk to your sorry self. How soon can you get over here?"

"She's not—she's okay?"

"Ornery as ever. Come on over as soon as you finish your route. I'll pour you some tea."

We tried to finish our game before Lurleen arrived, but Mamie was so distracted she kept discarding cards she needed to complete canastas. She jumped at the knock on the back door.

Lurleen came into the kitchen with wary eyes. "You wanted to see me?" Her voice was as stiff as her face.

Mamie gave her a long look. "Been wanting to see you every day of your life. Wasn't me decided to march out of here."

"You made me so mad, Mama! You know you had no business working in this heat." Lurleen was shaking all over, and she was pale.

"I told you, God had something—"

"Whoa!" I held up two hands between them like a referee with angry players. "You are not going to fight in this kitchen. Sit down, Lurleen. Your tea is waiting. Mamie, I think you said you had something to discuss with Lurleen. Margaret, shall we go out on the porch?"

We left them sitting at the table staring at each other like boxers about to enter the ring.

"You think we did the right thing leaving them alone?" Margaret whispered. "Maybe—"

A storm of boo-hooing drowned out what she was saying. "I think they'll work it out," I said.

After that, Lurleen dropped by every afternoon when she finished her route. Sometimes we played canasta. Sometimes we talked. Lurleen and Skeeter decided to move Mamie in with them to spend the nights. She spent her mornings in her own house, her afternoons with us, and her evenings with them. She seemed happy with that arrangement.

ONE AFTERNOON WHEN I ARRIVED, Margaret pointed to a pile of beans on the kitchen table. "Would you look at that? I went down to the garden this morning to see if there might be a ripe tomato or two for lunch, and way in the very back, where the ground holds more moisture, I found vines still bearing. We can put up a few more quarts."

Mamie found us snapping beans. She did her share, but worked slowly. Around three, I noticed she was gasping like somebody was rationing oxygen. I found myself breathing in short gasps, too, willing her to breathe while my own lungs were paralyzed by fear.

I moved to the phone. "You don't look good. I'm calling an ambulance to take you to the hospital."

"No!" She got that word out. After a few more gasps for air she managed, "No hospital. Please. Lurleen."

As before, Lurleen answered her cell on the first ring. "Is it Mama?"

"Yeah. She's looking bad, but she says not to call an ambulance. She doesn't want to go to a hospital."

"Get her to lie down. I'll be there as soon as I can."

Between us, Margaret and I got Mamie to the daybed in the living room and propped her up on a couple of pillows to ease her breathing. She closed her eyes with a grateful, "Thanks."

When Lurleen arrived a few minutes later, Mamie's eyes fluttered open. She reached for Lurleen's hand and held it. "I need you, baby. I need you bad."

"I'm right here, Mama. I'm not going anywhere."

"Could I have a drink?" Mamie asked.

I shoved a chair behind Lurleen's knees and went for water. Mamie managed a few swallows before she collapsed against the pillows, her eyes closed. "You sure you don't want me to call an ambulance to take you to the hospital?" I asked.

Mamie and Lurleen both shook their heads.

"She made me promise she wouldn't have to go to the hospital," Lurleen said quietly, still holding Mamie's hand. "There's nothing they can do, and she doesn't want a lot of tests."

Mamie gave a faint nod.

Lurleen bent and spoke loudly, as if she thought Mamie was going far away. "But we need to get you home, Mama. That's where an ambulance will take you. Okay?"

Mamie groaned.

"Can't she stay here?" Margaret asked behind me. "Do you have to move her? You can stay, too, Lurleen. If José moves in with Andy, Daddy's room will be free. We can take turns looking after her."

"I would appreciate that, until she's well enough to move." Lurleen's cheeks shone with tears. I wondered if she feared, as I did, that Mamie would never get well enough to move.

I became aware of silence in the dining room, where cutthroat Monopoly should have been going on. I tiptoed to the doorway and saw the children staring at me with eyes as big as headlights. Even MacTavish looked worried.

"Mamie's sick," I told them. "Go on with your game."

"Is she dying?" Andy's voice was high and scared. MacTavish growled.

"She may be. Would you all like to go down to my place and let me call somebody to come stay with you?"

Two small heads shook in unison.

"You will need to be very quiet. Okay? I'll let you know if anything happens. Would you like some cherry Kool-Aid?" Two nods. I brought them each a glass. "Remember. Quiet as mice. Okay?"

Two more nods. I had never seen them that solemn. "You are good kids." I gave them each a hug.

When I got back to the living room, Mamie's eyes were open. "Are the children worried?"

I nodded. "A little."

She motioned weakly with one hand. "Bring them here."

I wheeled Chellie up beside her. Andy stood at Mamie's head. She looked up at them. "What you grieving for? You know how excited you are about going to kindergarten?" she asked Chellie. "And you about going to second grade?" she asked Andy.

They gave her puzzled nods.

"I've finished all the classes I need down here. I'm graduating to the next level. That's all I'm doing. I'm graduating to glory. So don't you be worrying, now. God's got my diploma all ready."

I could see in their faces that they were processing that.

"But we'll miss you!" Andy cried.

"I'll miss you, too, baby. But you keep on keeping on, and you'll graduate someday, too."

Chellie reached up and gave Mamie an awkward pat with her grimace grin. "Bye, Mamie. Have fun in heaven."

"I sure will, honey."

She was visibly weaker. I took the children back to the dining room and settled them to Monopoly. Lurleen sat holding Mamie's hand.

Skeeter arrived and Lurleen gave him her place by the bed. He patted Mamie's shoulder. "You gonna be all right, Mama. You gonna be fine."

Mamie gave him a broad smile. "You got that right, Skeeter. I am gonna be *fine*." But her voice was little more than a whisper.

She looked up at Margaret and me. "Take . . . care. . . Bill." She struggled with every word. "Needs you."

"We will," I promised. "Don't try to talk."

Mamie's hand plucked at the afghan. Margaret and I reached for it at the same time. She lifted each of our hands toward the ceiling. "We hold up . . ." She was seized by a coughing fit and could not finish.

"Hush," said Margaret. "We know." Tears ran down her cheeks.

I bent and whispered, "Say hello to Mama for us."

"Soon as I . . . hug Earl and . . . Emmaline."

"Who's Emmaline?" Lurleen asked.

Margaret laid her free hand on Lurleen's shoulder. "We'll tell you."

Mamie nodded. She let go of our hands and reached out to Lurleen and Skeeter. "Precious to me. So precious." Her breathing became more and more labored. Her voice was barely a whisper. "No more tears. No more crying."

After that, she did not speak. Lurleen and Skeeter sat beside her bed. Margaret and I went back to the kitchen.

Tears streaming down her face, Margaret reached for the small pile of remaining beans.

"We aren't going to can beans today," I chided her.

"We can put them in the fridge and freeze them later."

I stood looking down at the bowl of beans at Mamie's place, the last beans Mamie would ever snap. I wanted to bronze them like Mama did our baby shoes. "We . . . we can't just can those like they were ordinary. They . . . She . . ."

Through blurred vision I saw Mamie all over that kitchen. She had lifted me in soft, plump arms onto chairs to help her stir cookie dough. Shelled peas while I told rambling stories. Laughed when I blew soap bubbles to catch in her hair. Rumbled a bass hum as she rocked me to sleep. Margaret must have been having similar memories, because she picked up a bean and held it reverently.

"Do this in remembrance of me," she murmured.

For the first time I understood how something so small could hold so much meaning. Wordlessly, she and I picked up raw beans and ate them as tiny sacraments.

I collapsed into a chair, laid my head on my arms, and wept. Margaret moved her chair close and put her arms around me. We clung to each other. "She didn't only take care of us," I said between sobs. "She shaped who we are. But we'll never be that good."

"We have to try," said Margaret. "We owe it to her."

Thirty-four

Mamie Butler Fountain was buried on August thirteenth from the Holy Comfort and Praise Baptist Church. She would have adored her going-away party.

The small packed sanctuary was so hot that paper fans from the pews were about as effective as small plastic spoons in pound cake batter. I heard sniffs and muffled sobs all over the congregation. I contributed a few.

The preacher didn't use one of the familiar texts. Instead, he preached on the story of two blind men who came to Jesus. "They did not ask for money or power," the preacher said. "They simply asked to be like other men. Most of us try so hard to be different. We want to be better than, richer than, or more powerful than everybody else. These men only wanted to see clearly. They wanted to see Jesus. They remind me of Sister Mamie. She never wanted to be better than or richer than or more important than anybody else. She only wanted to see Jesus."

When he finished, he surprised us. "Sister Mamie and I talked about this service a few weeks ago. You know she couldn't die without leaving a few instructions." Laughter rippled through the sanctuary. "She told me, 'When you're done with whatever you're gonna say, call on Bill Anderson to say a few words.' Mr. Anderson, will you come up front?"

Margaret and I had fetched Daddy to the funeral from the rehab center. We had been braced for him to pitch a fit about having to go in a wheelchair, but while he grumbled a little for show, he seemed glad to come. I wondered if he had known all along he'd be called on to speak.

He spoke some very moving words about Mamie, ending with, "She was one of those people who know what Christianity is all about. G. K. Chesterton once said that Christianity hasn't been tried and found wanting—it has been found difficult and not tried. But no matter how difficult it was, Mamie not only practiced it—she taught it to the rest of us. Mamie?" He looked up and gave a little salute. "You've passed us the torch. We'll do our best not to drop it."

Knowing Mamie, I figured she had given instructions about the weather as well as the funeral. The church was hot because of all the people, but the day outside was cool for August, with a refreshing breeze—perfect for her burial in the little cemetery next to the church. Afterward, the whole crowd was invited to stay for an old-fashioned dinner on the grounds. Mamie had requested that, too. Long tables were spread and covered with white paper, and it looked to me like every woman in town had brought something to eat. Margaret and I set one of Daddy's hams on a long table loaded with fried chicken, potato salad, deviled eggs, green beans, corn on the cob, corn and beans, crowder peas, fried okra, sliced red tomatoes, iced tea, lemonade, and more pies than I could count.

Once people started telling Mamie stories, nobody went home for hours.

Daddy must also have told the story about his fire some fifty times. You'd have thought half of Georgia had burned.

I ran into friends from the mill I hadn't seen in years. We were sitting together on a blanket eating dessert and talking about Mamie back at the mill when one of them asked me, "You still read all the time? I remember on break you always had your nose in a book."

"I still read some," I admitted.

Another teased, "You oughta be a librarian. You love books better than food." She said to the others, "Billie was always telling me about books I ought to read because I'd love them."

A third piped up, "Me, too, and as much as I hate to admit it, she was usually right. You may not know it, hon, but you made a reader out of me."

"That's what you remember me for?" I demanded. "Reading on breaks? Not for all the times I was patient with your mistakes and covered your behinds when you came in late? You'd better be nice, or I won't invite you to my wedding."

Oops! As their eyes widened, I realized what I'd said. "I mean if I ever get married again. I'm not planning to at the moment, but—"

On cue from some devil in hell, Luke walked up and put his hand on my head like it belonged there. "Why don't I take Chellie to your dad's, hon, so you can stick around a while? We can play Monopoly until you get there."

Solace has no secrets. In two days it would be all over town that I was marrying Luke.

I followed him out to his truck. "Do you reckon we could go ahead and get married without waiting to dig up Porter? He hasn't been around for a long time, and everybody thinks we're divorced."

He gave me a quizzical look. "Everybody except the police chief and your daddy. I'd say those are two pretty big obstacles to bigamy, wouldn't you?"

"How about if we pretend we dug him up and go ahead and hold a memorial service? We can invite Tee and Daddy, and I'll be a widow."

"A widow with no death certificate. I appreciate your sudden eagerness, but what's got you so worked up?"

Feeling like a fool, I admitted what I'd let slip. He nuzzled my neck and kissed me, but wouldn't help. "It's your foot in your mouth. I'd advise you to chew and swallow."

AFTER MAMIE'S PARTY, AS MARGARET and I took Daddy back to the rehab center, I told him how touched I'd been by what he said about Mamie.

"That's well and good," he said from the backseat, "but don't try to sweet-talk me, now. I'm coming home in a few weeks, so you girls better be fixing any damage you've done to my farm."

"We've got it running so well, you'll have to retire," Margaret retorted.

"Don't get sassy, missy. I'm not close to retiring yet. But by the way, I've got a builder coming out this week to see about adding a toilet and lavatory behind the dining room. They tell me I can come home the first of September, but I can't run up and down those stairs every time I need to pee."

I was afraid Margaret was about to say something like, "Why didn't you do that when Mama needed it?"—something that would cause his temper to flare, so I said quickly, "That's good. Why don't you put in a walk-in shower while you're at it? It wouldn't cost much more. Then you can stay in the house even when you're old."

Margaret gave me a thumbs-up down where he couldn't see it. I held my breath.

We heard the scrape of whiskers as he rubbed one cheek. "I'll think about it."

As Margaret helped him out of the car, I remembered something Mama used to do.

I climbed out of the car and circled them both with my arms. "Family hug time."

I expected them to draw back, but maybe they were remembering Mama, too. Or maybe they felt, as I did, that with both Mama and Mamie gone, we had to be the glue to hold our family together.

I tried to pretend I wasn't crying, but I heard Margaret sniff and saw Daddy wipe his eye. "A speck of dust," he muttered. But he gave us one more squeeze. "I don't know what I'd do without the two of you, and that's a fact. Now get me in that danged chair before I fall on my rear right here on the sidewalk."

THE DAY AFTER MAMIE'S FUNERAL, Margaret greeted me with a little dress over her arm. "Take this home and see if it's easier to get on Chellie." It opened all the way down the back so I could put it on her like a smock, then wrap it around and tie a cute little sash in front.

"I can already tell it's gonna be easier to put on than dresses with zippers or buttons. Did you design it?"

"I've been playing with some ideas. Daddy's problems with traction and his cast and Michelle's problems getting dressed have made me aware there must be a lot of people who could use some creative clothing. I'm thinking about taking courses at the college of art and design in Atlanta to learn what I don't know about clothing design and marketing. After that, I may become the Coco Chanel of the handicapped world."

"Sounds good to me."

"In the meantime, would you mind terribly if I gave away Mama's things? I know I upset you when I asked before, but if Andy and I stay over the winter, I'll need to bring more of our stuff out here, and we'll need more space."

"You're thinking of staying all winter?" Three months ago that would have sounded like a threat. Now it shimmered like a promise. "Go ahead and give away her clothes, then. I heard Lurleen at the funeral today inviting Mamie's friends to come over tomorrow to take her things. She said Mamie said not to let them hang in closets when somebody could be getting use out of them. And remember what Daddy used to say about Mama? That if he'd let her—"

"—she'd give people the shirt off his back."

It felt wonderful to laugh with my sister at a joke nobody but us would appreciate.

ONE AFTERNOON WHEN I GOT to the farm, Margaret was dressed nicer than usual. "We need to go register our kids at Solace Elementary. I called, and they are open until three."

"You've definitely decided to stay?"

"For the coming year, at least. Andy really loves it out here."

She loved it, too. I saw it in the way her eyes roved over the fields and pasture. If she had bartered her soul to leave Solace, she had gotten it back when she returned.

"I'll go with you," I agreed. "But I'm giving you fair warning. If one person identifies me as Maggie Baxter's little sister, both your life and theirs are in jeopardy."

Chellie and Andy were delighted at the idea of going to the same school. I was relieved Chellie would have a champion there.

The special-education teacher evaluated her and reported back to me, "We'll put her in a special class part of the day, but she will be in a regular class most of the time." She went on to tell me about specific training she had had for working with children with cerebral palsy and showed me equipment—computers, even special pencils and silverware Chellie could use. I left confident that my child would be in good hands.

WHAT THE WOMEN FROM THE mill had said kept running through my head. I'd look up from a page I was reading and realize I didn't remember a word. When Luke came over one evening, after we'd had a little snuggle in the swing, I asked, "Do you think I could become a librarian?"

"Why not? You have your nose in a book most of the time."

"Yeah, but a librarian? I mean, I love books. Not simply reading them, but smelling them, holding them, how one of them leads you to another. And I love telling people about something I've read that I think they'll like, too, but—"

"Sounds like a librarian to me. So now that you know what you want to become, can you marry me?"

"Not until I get a job. And don't forget Porter."

He groaned. "How could I ever forget Porter?"

"Don't be rude. You owe Porter a lot. It was because he didn't send money that I went to the church food pantry, and it was because Franklin saw Chellie's chair at the church that you and I met again." I could hear Mamie in my head: *God's tapestry.*

I was glad to think Porter's threads weren't all dark. He deserved to be remembered for doing something good.

THE NEXT DAY I WENT to the library and asked at the desk, "Do you have to have a library degree to work here?"

"Not to work here, only to be a director or a reference librarian. If you're interested, we've got a vacancy coming up. One of the clerks is moving to Texas in a couple of weeks."

I went straight to the office and applied. I also talked to the librarian about what I'd need to do to become one. When she told me, I despaired.

"She said I'd need a master's degree in library science," I told Luke. "That would take years if I do it while working. It could take six years even if I don't work while I go to school."

"Look at it this way: what will you be doing six years from now if you *don't* get a library science degree? I'd say, go for it. I can support us while you're in school."

I loved that man more than he would ever know.

BECAUSE MARGARET ORGANIZED THE PROCESS, the new bathroom took shape in record time. She chose a color scheme, consulted with Daddy about tile and fixtures, and persuaded him to go ahead and install the walk-in shower and a door wide enough to accommodate a wheelchair.

One afternoon when I went over so Andy and Chellie could finish a Monopoly game they'd started the day before, Margaret whispered, "Get the kids started and meet me in the new bathroom. Bring two of Mama's crystal goblets."

She sounded so mysterious, I felt like a cat burglar as I turned my back on the kids and sneaked goblets from the china cabinet.

Margaret pulled me into the new bathroom and shut the door behind us. "Voilà! A working sink, toilet, and shower! And see what I found when I was cleaning out the pantry?" She held up a bottle of Mama's scuppernong wine. Those big bronze grapes have the sweetest taste God ever made. I quickly rinsed the goblets in the new sink while she pulled out the cork.

I looked at the bottle doubtfully. "Just give me a little. I remember how potent that stuff can be."

Margaret poured me an inch and herself half a glass.

"To you, new bathroom. May you ever flush." Margaret lifted her glass and touched it to mine with the sweet ring of crystal. We drained our glasses.

I had forgotten how good that wine tasted. "Yum." I reached for the bottle. "Another toast to us for putting up with one bathroom for so many years." Again I poured myself an inch. Margaret took the bottle from me and poured herself half a glass.

"To us." We touched rims and drank.

She filled both goblets. "To Mama and Mamie, who would have loved this new bathroom and found life a lot easier if they'd had it."

I drained the bottle into our glasses. "And to Daddy, who has proved a person can change—"

"—even if he is an old curmudgeon, set in his ways."

Solemnly Margaret raised the bottle over her head. I think she would have brought it down across the back of the toilet if I hadn't grabbed her arm. "Don't! Those things are porcelain! You're more likely to break the toilet than the bottle."

Andy knocked on the door. "What are you all doing in there? I need to go!"

Thus was the new bathroom launched.

Thirty-five

As we went back to the kitchen, my eye fell on Daddy's wall calendar. "Rick Landiss got back yesterday. I guess I'd better wait to tackle him until tomorrow, though."

"Why?" Margaret peered at the calendar. "I have lots more courage now."

"You're coming?"

"Yeah. I feel like a fight. Let's go."

"I don't want Luke picking me up for DUI."

"You didn't drink more than half a glass." She nodded toward the sink. "Can you walk a straight line?" I walked four feet along a pattern in the vinyl. "That's good enough. Call and see if Rick is there."

His secretary said he was out, but would be back in half an hour. Margaret grabbed her purse. "Let's go."

"We can't leave the kids here alone."

"Where's José?"

I found him scratching the back of the current boar, a bristly black-and-white monster. "If Margaret and I run into town for an hour, can you keep an ear out for the children?" I asked. "They're playing Monopoly and shouldn't need anything, but save them in case of fire."

He smiled. "I do it before. I do it again."

I clapped him fondly on one arm. As we headed toward the drive-way, I said softly to Margaret, "Do you realize you just left your worldly possessions, including your younger son, in the hands of an illegal immigrant?"

She hiccuped. "Even a crusty old curmudgeon can change. Take my car. I'm too clean to ride in your truck." She was stylish, as usual—khaki slacks, a smart peach top, and expensive yellow-and-peach san-dals. I was wearing my working shoes and the shorts and T-shirt I'd worn under my coveralls all morning. Not to mention that I could have used a shower and shampoo.

"I'm not clean. I'm in no shape to ask favors from Rick Landiss. You're gonna have to go in by yourself. Do you have the courage for that?"

She made fists and pretended to box. "I have the courage of a lion. I'll tell him he *has* to let you dig up Porter so you can get married."

"That's the story," I agreed. "Tell him it's really important to my future. And tell him we can try to arrange to do it late at night so none of his tenants need know."

Parking is seldom a problem in downtown Solace, but I still consid-ered a parking space right in front a good sign.

Margaret climbed down. I gave her a salute. "Good luck! And don't forget to tell him we think the foreman did it," I called after her.

"Stuff it, Billie. I'm not senile."

I sat there with the window rolled down, waiting. I hoped Margaret could stay dignified. I hoped he wouldn't make a pass at her. I hoped she wouldn't brain him with his statue again. He'd already had a broken nose and a broken hand that year.

A broken hand? Broken back in April, Maggie had said. Around the time Porter disappeared.

Rick was a violent man when angered. Margaret and I could testify to that.

And he could operate a backhoe. He'd told me his daddy insisted he learn to operate all the equipment.

I remembered the way he had stopped writing when I mentioned Porter's name. He'd covered it pretty well, asking which was the last name, but now that I thought about it, I was pretty sure I had shaken him some, coming out with the name like that.

I started to tremble. How dumb could I be, sending Margaret into his office all by herself? I wished I had a cell phone.

I opened the door, uncertain whether to barge in on them or go find Luke. Luke won. I might be dumb, but I wasn't a fool. I drove as fast as I could to the police station. "Luke!" I cried as I stumbled in the door. "Luke!"

Tee jogged from the back office, patting air in front of him to calm me down. "Hold on now, Billie. What's the matter?"

"Margaret. She's gone into the office of somebody I think killed my husband. We've got to get her out of there. Now!"

He sniffed. "Have you been drinking?"

"Not enough to make any difference. Margaret's in danger!"

Tee shook his head. "Things are never as desperate as they seem, hon. We haven't had any reports that Porter was even killed, and certainly not that he was killed out here." He reached for a piece of paper. "Give me the details—"

"By then Margaret could be dead. Where's Luke?"

"Gone down to the pharmacy to get something for his mama."

"Thanks."

I hurried to the pharmacy, praying all the way. "Please, Lord, please, Lord, please."

Luke was climbing into his cruiser. "Margaret's gone to see Rick Landiss, and I think he's the killer," I called as I pulled up beside him.

He blinked. "Come again?"

I leaned out my window. "Margaret has gone to ask Rick Landiss for permission to dig up Porter as a favor to me, so we can get married, but after she went in, I got to thinking. Rick broke his hand sometime in April. It was still tender the first time I met him. He beat the fire out of Margaret when she made him mad one night. He drove Daddy's tractor out of the fire and told me his daddy made him learn how to use all their equipment. And he recognized Porter's name—I swear he did. When I asked him to ask around and see if anybody knew where Porter Waits had gone, he recognized the name. I think he's the killer, Luke!"

Like Tee, he sniffed the air. "Have you been drinking?"

"A little scuppernong wine, but I'm stone sober. Come on, Luke, Margaret could be—"

"I'll meet you there. But act casual and let me do the talking. In case you're wrong, we don't want to charge in like the cavalry."

He headed up Main Street. No point in using his siren. It was only two blocks. My parking space was gone. Luke parked half a block down the street, and I had to park around the corner. Bad omen.

I reached the corner in time to see him strolling casually into the office.

I raced after him, but stopped before I reached their window long enough to smooth my hair and calm my breathing.

"He has someone with him," the child at the desk was saying as I went in the door.

"It's my sister." I hoped I sounded casual enough. "She won't mind if we join them."

The secretary shrugged. "If you say so."

Luke was already halfway to the office. The door was closed. He knocked. "Mr. Landiss?"

He got no response.

He knocked again. "Margaret's sister, Billie, is here. She'd like to speak with you while Margaret is there."

Still no response.

Luke turned the knob. It was locked.

"Mr. Landiss. Please open this door."

"Luke!" somebody called from inside.

"Open it!" I cried. "That was Margaret."

"I don't have a warrant."

"By the time you get a warrant . . ."

We heard Margaret cry out.

Luke put his shoulder to the door and it popped open like a jack-in-the-box. Like I said before, whoever did the work on that project did a lousy job. I wondered if Rick's own people had done it. If so, no wonder Porter criticized him for cutting corners.

Rick leveled a gun at the two of us.

"Breaking and entering, Officer? I was about to call the police and ask them to arrest Margaret here for trespassing. I came in and found her at my desk. Now that you've broken my door, I'm going to sue the nice citizens of Solace for a bundle. Put your hands up, please."

Luke raised his hands over his head. Under his arm I saw Margaret sitting on the couch. She was pale and shaking.

Rick called loudly, "Tiffany? Please call the police and tell them to send another officer to arrest this one—and Margaret Baxter, too. On the double!"

I heard her punching the numbers behind me.

Luke stood between me and Rick. Was it possible Rick hadn't seen me?

I took Luke by the back of the shirt and tugged sideways. He eased over and leaned against the doorjamb, blocking the crack that would have exposed me if I moved.

I glanced toward the secretary. She was on the phone. She didn't strike me as somebody who could do two things at once—like make a call and watch the office door.

I slid down the hall. The next door was a bathroom. It had a door into Rick's office.

I looked around for a weapon, but Rick didn't keep weapons in his bathroom. All I saw was an extra roll of paper on the back of the toilet.

I eased the door open a crack. He had his back to me. I eased the door open a little wider and made a three-point shot. The roll hit his head as squarely as if he had been circled by a net.

Rick whirled. I slammed the door.

"Duck!" Luke yelled.

I fell to my knees, covering my head with my arms. A bullet whizzed overhead and hit the far wall. I heard a scuffle on the other side of the door, then another shot. I cowered on the floor and prayed Luke and Margaret were safe. I waited for Rick to kill me.

"You can come out now, Billie," Margaret called. "It's all over."

Luke was gripping Rick with his hands behind his back. The gun lay on the floor near the desk. I reached for it, but Luke said, "Leave it. It's got his prints on it."

Tee felt no compunction about using his siren for short drives. We heard him barging into the front office. "What's going on?"

"In here, Tee," Luke called.

Tee arrived looking like thunder. "Why are you holding that man, Luke?"

"Because he threatened me with a gun, sir."

Rick started right up about how he had been protecting himself because Margaret had been trespassing and Luke had busted his door and I had inflicted grievous bodily harm on his person, but Tee held up one beefy hand. "Wait a minute. Wait a dadgum minute. I've known these young women all their lives. Maggie has never been a snoop, and Billie here never hurt anybody with anything other than a basketball, and that was fair and square. So why don't we all sit down and sort this out?"

"Chief, I am Rick Landiss of Landiss Construction Company. I refuse to speak without my attorney present."

"Sit down, man. You can call your attorney in a little while if you want to, but for now sit down."

Tee can be real impressive when he wants to. Rick sat. He was getting an inkling of how justice worked in Solace. It wasn't based on who you were but on who you knew.

"You might secure his gun, sir." Luke nodded to where it lay by the desk. Tee fumbled in his pockets and came up with a handkerchief. He lifted the gun gingerly and set it on the desk.

Luke held out a plastic evidence bag. "Shall I put it in this?"

"Good."

Luke secured the gun. Tee motioned for everybody to sit. "Suppose you all tell me what this is about. Maybe we can settle it between us."

"He killed Porter," I said, "and he buried him with a backhoe in one of his office parks, but he won't let us dig him up for a proper burial."

"I am not a murderer," Rick insisted.

"Nobody's mentioned murder," Margaret said. "Everybody knows Porter would quarrel with a cow."

"That right, Billie?" Tee asked, although he had had his own run-ins with Porter over the years.

"I never actually saw him quarrel with a cow, but I did catch him yelling at squirrels a few times. When they chattered back, he yelled louder."

"We don't even want to know what you quarreled about," Luke said in the voice of somebody trying to instill a little dignity in the proceedings. "All we ask is permission for Porter to be dug up and given a proper burial so I can marry Mina."

Rick's eyes flicked over Luke and me like we were dirt.

"Who's Mina?" Tee asked.

"Me," I said.

"Well, well. Isn't that nice!" Tee beamed like he was about to shake everybody's hand and go back to his office.

"We know exactly where the body is buried," I said, bringing him back on track.

Rick began to look a little green around the gills.

"Is it around here?" Tee asked. He had gotten green around the gills, too—probably thinking about all the work he was going to have to do before this was over.

"No, sir, it's in a Marietta office park." That was Luke. "I have the word of a witness to the crime. He is not available, but he showed me exactly where the body is buried. I left a marker there so I could find it again."

Tee looked relieved. "Oh, in Marietta." You'd have thought that was beyond Siberia.

"But Mr. Landiss here has been refusing to let the police look for the body," Luke continued. "He has even taken the case to court."

I opened my mouth to say, "Because he killed him," but Luke moved smoothly on. "What we need is for him to agree to let his place be dug up in hopes of finding Porter's body."

Tee studied Rick Landiss like he was an interesting specimen of humanity.

"When we got here, he had Margaret locked with him in this office. He also had a gun in his hand when Luke opened the door," I said.

"Is that right?" Tee studied Rick some more. "Maggie, you want to charge this man with false imprisonment and intent to commit bodily harm?"

Margaret thought it over. I suspected she was thinking of Ben, and how her charging Rick could put a real dent in how much work he did for Rick Landiss.

Rick made the mistake of smirking. "I do," she said more firmly than any bride. "He nearly scared me to death, locking the door and waving that gun around."

Rick flushed, indignant. "I never waved it!"

"Waving it," she repeated. "He could have shot me any minute. Why, he—"

Margaret was getting talkative, which meant Tee would realize any minute that she had drunk too much wine. I figured we ought to keep court advantage while we had it. "He took a shot at me while I was in his bathroom. You can see the bullet hole in the door"—I pointed—"and the bullet's in the wall. He could have killed me."

Tee heaved himself to his feet and inspected the door and the wall. "Looks like you're gonna have to come down to the station with me," he told Rick. "You can call your lawyer from there."

RICK LANDISS'S LAWYER CALLED ME the next morning. "Your sister is dropping all charges against Mr. Landiss for yesterday's regrettable incident. We are asking you to do the same. Mr. Landiss contends that the firearm went off accidentally."

"It did not!"

He ignored me. "However, Mr. Landis has authorized me. . ." He proceeded with a lot of legal jargon, the gist of which was that Rick was willing to pay me a comfortable sum not to go to court.

I needed that money so bad I could taste it, but I needed something else worse.

I spoke with as much dignity as I could muster, sitting in my living room in cutoffs and bare feet. "Tell Mr. Landiss to permit them to dig up my husband's body, and we will discuss this further. If he won't, I will see you both in court." I didn't have money to take anybody to court, but Daddy hadn't taught me the art of bluffing for nothing.

The lawyer gave me a curt good-bye. I didn't take an easy breath until he called back in an hour. "Mr. Landiss will authorize a search for your husband's body based on information received if you will agree to drop all charges against him."

"There were two eyewitnesses that he intentionally shot at me," I reminded him. "Tell Mr. Landiss thank you for letting them look for Porter, and I'll be glad to discuss the other matter when that is finished."

THE NIGHT THEY DUG FOR Porter's body, we got one of our few useless drizzles of the summer. The parking lot lights at the office park created a misty glow. Around to one side of the property, where Luke led the small band of people charged with the sorry task, the property was poorly lit. They set up their own lights, which formed a harsh glow over the top of a privacy barricade they erected.

I had insisted on being there, even though I had no desire to watch the process. I stayed in Luke's truck a while, but I got restless, so I climbed out and stood under an umbrella, straining to hear and see. I was too far away to distinguish words. All I saw were the tops of heads moving around behind the barricade. I tried not to picture what they might be finding.

Why was I there? They could identify Porter from his dental records. He'd had a lot of work done. But I felt Porter ought to have at least one member of his family present for the event, and I was the only nominee.

I shifted and stepped directly into a stream of water running toward a drain. My feet got soaked, my sandals ruined. "Why didn't Mrs. Waits have eight kids?" I demanded.

Luke came from the site, head down against the drizzle. "They found him. Looks like he has a skull fracture consistent with hitting his head on a curb, just like Luis said. They'll have to do an autopsy, of course. You ready to go?"

"Not yet." I offered him half my umbrella, which meant we both got wet.

We stood there until two men walked by carrying a black plastic bag between them. I felt as heavy as Porter looked. "Nobody deserves to be bagged up like garbage!"

Luke put an arm around me. "Especially not somebody you once knew. Let's go find some hot coffee."

THE VERDICT AFTER AN AUTOPSY was accidental death. Rick's lawyer sounded smug when he called me.

"But an accident at his work site," I pointed out. "I am willing to drop my charges against Rick for trying to shoot me if Landiss Construction agrees to compensate my little girl for the loss of her daddy on a Landiss work site. I want his last paycheck, too."

Mr. Landiss and his lawyer conferred. They agreed to give me the paycheck and Chellie a sum that would provide therapy she needed and help pay for college, but they made me sign a document that I would use the money only for Chellie, not for myself. I had no problem with that. I spent most of my money on Chellie, anyway. Besides, I was working at the library. It didn't bring in a lot, but it met our needs.

I spent Porter's last paycheck burying him next to his mother. I knew that would have pleased them both. I told Chellie he died from an accident at work but left money for her to go to college. She wept during the funeral like she'd known him all her life. Watching her weep, I cried, too, for the daddy she had never had.

Nobody came to the burial except my family and Luke, but it was a sweet graveside service. I vowed to save up enough for a little gravestone.

As it turned out, I didn't have to. As Porter's legal widow, I got not only his last paycheck from Landiss Construction; I got the address of where he'd been living. Margaret and I went to his place—a rented room in an old house—to pick up his things. "I boxed everything up and stored it," the landlady told me. "You owe me storage charges."

I hated to spend the money, considering I would be taking everything to the Salvation Army on our way out of town, but Margaret advised, "Take it all home and go through the boxes. You might find something you want to keep." She came by the house to give me moral support while I examined Porter's stuff.

As usual, Margaret was right. Among the clothes—clean and dirty—and several novels I'd burn rather than give to anybody, I found Porter's wedding ring and my graduation picture from high school—the only good picture I'd ever had made. Chellie might want those someday. I also found a few sheets of paper in a large white envelope. When I read the top sheet, I squealed. "Look at this! Porter took out life insurance for us. A hundred thousand dollars' worth, with double indemnity if he died by accident!"

Margaret said what I never would: "Porter's worth more to you dead than he was alive."

I was so glad I had never said anything nasty about Porter to anybody else. He had his faults, like the rest of us, but he would pay for me to get a library science degree. Like he'd promised, he took care of his own.

Thirty-six

The first of September Margaret brought Daddy home while the children were at school. I went over on my lunch hour and found him inspecting his new hay barn. José and his crew were now working on a shed for the tractor. The milking barn stood without a roof, milking equipment, or tank. José said Daddy had told him to wait until he got home to do anything about that.

"Hay barn doesn't look too bad," Daddy said.

I punched him lightly on the arm. "It's wonderful. Admit it. Better than the old one."

"There were years left in that old barn." But his face was pleased as he noted the steel girders holding up the roof.

He let us help him up the ramp for a rest, but nothing could keep Daddy indoors for long. He and José spent the rest of the afternoon riding around in Daddy's truck, looking over the farm and visiting his cows at other farms.

"Checking every hair on the cows and every blade of grass in the pastures?" I teased when they got back.

"Nope. Arranging to sell my cows."

We stared. "You're giving up farming?" I could not believe it.

"Who said anything about giving up farming? I've decided to go into beef instead of dairy, that's all. Don't need to keep as many animals and don't have to milk them, so I won't need to replace the milking barn. I won't have to work so hard, either, and I won't need as much pasturage, so I can lease about fifty acres to horse people. Lots of people wanting places to keep their horses."

Margaret frowned. "You'll kill yourself looking after horses." I could tell she was picturing herself currying horses and mucking out stables come winter.

"Didn't say anything about looking after horses. I'll just rent them the pasture. The owners can take care of the animals themselves."

After the meal, at my urging, Margaret took him out on the porch while I did dishes and got the kids started on Monopoly. While they were alone, she told him about her divorce.

I joined them in time to hear him saying, as if he were talking about the weather, "Ben's a good man, but if I told you once, I told you a hundred times, he never had much staying power. Surprises me he stuck around as long as he did."

"He may come back." I heard anger and a glimmer of hope in her voice.

He laid his hand over hers. "Don't pin your hopes on it, shug. But you'll be all right, once you get your bearings."

"We've sold our house, and I got almost nothing from it. Can Andy and I live here until I find work and another place to go?"

"Why not? This is your home."

Tears flowed down Margaret's cheeks.

"No waterworks," he grumbled. "Didn't you say there was peach cobbler for dessert?"

EMERITA CALLED ON THE FRIDAY before Labor Day. "They in Texas!" José reported in sentences that shot out like fireworks. "Emerita get bus tonight! She be home tomorrow! Seven o'clock in evening! And *coyote* get money from gringo for new truck!"

Margaret joked that we ought to tie José down to keep him from floating away.

The next morning she gave Daddy's room the cleaning of its life and hung new curtains she had made for the occasion. I carried over Chellie's crib from my shed, and Luke and I struggled to put it together.

"I had no earthly reason to save this thing, but aren't we glad I did?" I asked.

He circled my waist with his arms. "I sure am. We may need it ourselves one of these days."

I gave him a little kiss that turned into a long one.

"Stop smooching and put on the sheet," Margaret said sharply. But she gave me a wink.

DADDY INSISTED THAT JOSÉ TAKE his car to the station. He left at four on Saturday. "I wait there. Perhaps they be early."

"It's more likely the bus will be late," Luke cautioned. "It's a holiday. Lots of traffic."

"No matter. I wait. I no want to be late."

After supper, we went out on the porch, even the children. Chellie's chair was close to Daddy's rocker. Andy sat on the floor with his back to a banister. Since Luke was there, Margaret took the other rocker and left us the swing.

Once again the evening sky was thick with gray clouds. Occasional lightning flickered in them and around the edges. As they drew closer, the sky darkened to early dusk.

"Dratted thunder," Daddy said in disgust. "Never amounts to a danged thing."

Luke put his arm around my shoulders and squeezed. "You ready to tell him?" he asked softly.

I replied equally softly. "Yeah." An hour of thunder and lightning seemed appropriate to the occasion, given Daddy's reaction the last two times his daughters had announced a marriage.

Luke cleared his throat. "Mina and I hope you folks are free Thanksgiving Day. She has agreed to marry me then."

"Thanksgiving?" Daddy exploded. "What about—?"

"We're having it in the morning," I told him. "It won't get in the way of dinner *or* your football game." Football is the second-largest religion in Georgia.

He rocked a couple of minutes, looking at us without saying a word. I braced myself.

"I reckon that'll be all right, then. Do I have to wear a penguin suit?"

Luke sounded as relieved as I felt. "No, sir. Coat and tie is all. But we'd like you to give Mina away."

He did some more ruminating. "Didn't give either one of the girls away the first time, and they both came back. This time I'll do it right. Maybe I'll get rid of one of them for good."

"I get to be the flower girl," Chellie boasted. We had already told her.

"That's nice." Daddy rumpled her hair. Margaret shot me a questioning look. Chellie's spastic muscles tended to freeze, so I knew she was wondering how Chellie would manage.

"She's going to carry a basket of flowers on her lap," I explained. "We aren't going to try tossing petals."

Andy scowled. "I'm not carrying rings on a dumb pillow."

"Of course not," said Luke. "I thought you and Franklin would usher, if that's all right."

Andy lit up like a candle. "Sure!"

"You'll be my matron of honor?" I asked Margaret. "I'm going to ask Bethany and Emerita to be bridesmaids."

"Am I supposed to make your dress, Chellie's, and our three?"

"If you will. After that, you can hang out your shingle."

Before she could reply, lightning lit up the entire sky.

"Wow!" Andy yelled. "Did you see that? It was green and purple and yellow—"

A clap of thunder nearly deafened us.

"Let's get inside," I ordered. "Chellie's chair is metal."

In the living room the lightning was so bright, nobody bothered to turn on a light.

"We might get another hay crop in the fall," Daddy said. Farmers live on hope.

"I could plant collards and turnips," said Margaret.

Again the thunder rolled.

"The angels are bowling," Andy exclaimed.

"Bowling." Chellie bounced in her chair as if she knew what bowling was.

The thunder and lightning slacked off, but the early twilight continued. I looked around at the faces in the dim light. How dear each of them had become to me in the past few months. How had I ever lived without them?

Luke came in from the kitchen. "I think they are here."

"Emerita! Emerita!" Chellie bounced again.

I scanned the sky for lightning. Seeing none, I pushed her down the ramp. Margaret followed at my heels. Luke and Andy slowed their steps to Daddy's walker.

José pulled into the yard. Emerita tumbled out of the car. From a child seat in the back, she retrieved a brown toddler with hair as black as licorice. Under long bangs, the child's eyes were like malted milk balls.

"You darling!" Margaret flew to take the child from Emerita. Juanita laughed, showing little white teeth. As she looked around at the new faces, she squirmed to be put down. "Chellie!" She toddled over to Chellie's chair. "Chellie!" She patted my daughter's knee.

"Her first American friend." Emerita hugged me while rain pattered around us.

Margaret joined us in a three-way hug.

Thunder sounded overhead.

"Rain!" Chellie yelled. Sure enough, fat drops were pelting us.

"Yes!" Margaret pumped air with both fists.

I started singing the first bars of the "Hallelujah Chorus."

Chellie jerked her arms and swayed in her chair. "Hallelujah!"

Juanita jumped up and down squealing, even if she had no idea what the excitement was about.

Emerita reached for my hand and Margaret's. "Dance!" She began singing a high, fast tune. Margaret reached for my other hand and we circled the children, heads back and mouths open to receive the blessed rain.

José stepped into the circle between Emerita and me and joined in Emerita's song. Luke slipped in on my other side, taking my hand and Margaret's. As if pulled by invisible strings, we all lifted our hands in the air and danced to the music for nothing but joy.

Andy dodged under our arms and lifted Chellie's hands. "Hallelujah!" he shouted.

The rain ended as quickly as it had begun, leaving us barely damp. A bit self-conscious, we dropped hands and stepped out of the circle.

Daddy barked from the walk. "What do you fools think you are doing?"

Emerita ran to give him a hug. "We are not foolish, *Señor* Bill. We are holding up the sky."

Thirty-seven

The leaves refused to die that year, or perhaps the trees had no strength to let them go. They hung on the branches well into November, turning more and more brilliant. Daddy's sugar maples glowed gold, frosted with rose. Mama's dwarf maple was such a deep red it was almost black. Oaks turned yellow, then brown—except for a young one near the house, which remained a determined green. Dogwood berries glowed red beneath multicolored leaves of pink, burgundy, and brown.

Every day Daddy craned his neck at the yard and said, "No point in blowing leaves yet. Still a lot to fall." I suspected he left them because Andy and Juanita loved to roll in leaves with MacTavish. I even put Chellie down with them sometimes so she could jerk her arms and legs and hear dead leaves rustle all around her.

Once José was certain Daddy could handle raising beef, he announced it was time they moved to Dalton. We weren't surprised—they could make more there than we could pay them—but I felt as if a piece of me was being cut away. All of us were sorry to see them go. Even Margaret.

"We will be back for Thanksgiving," they promised. Margaret finished Emerita's bridesmaid dress while she was still around for fittings.

Having had one unsuccessful white wedding, I had vetoed another. I was going to wear soft green crepe in a short style I could wear later for special occasions. The other women would wear peach, which looked good on all of them and would be stunning with bouquets of bronze and golden mums from my yard. Chellie would wear dark green and carry a basket of tiny yellow mums.

Margaret, being Margaret, was not only doing most of the work for my wedding; she was planning an elaborate Thanksgiving dinner in lieu of a reception. Luke and I had decided to invite only family and close friends to the wedding, so Margaret insisted that everybody should come back to Daddy's house for dinner. She agreed to let other women bring a few dishes, but mostly she was doing the cooking herself.

"Would you mind if I invited Jason out that weekend?" she asked one night while I was trying on my wedding dress.

"I'd love it. He can't stay away forever. Everybody has forgiven him for the fire." Jason hadn't been back to the farm since July.

"He's not avoiding us because of the fire. He's boycotting me because I decided to stay here for the winter. Neither he nor Ben was pleased. Jason misses Andy, and I think having a teenager around all the time crimps Ben's style."

"Tell Jason he can usher if he will come. Katrina and Hal can bring him."

Another afternoon we sat together in the swing while thunder rumbled in the distance. It was one of those warm fall days that make it so pleasant to live in Georgia. The yard was bare and brown, but Margaret had planted collards and turnips in the garden, which she kept watered with Daddy's barrel. I picked up one of her hands. She hadn't gotten a professional manicure for months, but being Margaret, she kept her nails filed and polished. "Sisters make good friends," I told her.

She gave my hand a squeeze. "I need a friend right now. Jason turned me down. His other grandparents and all the rest of their family are going on a cruise for Thanksgiving, but Ben can't afford to go, and

Jason won't leave his dad on his own. He said they'll go to a restaurant for dinner." She kept her smile in place, but her eyes were bleak.

"Invite Ben out here, too," I suggested.

"Absolutely not. I'll be over my head between your wedding and dinner. I couldn't cope with Ben as well."

"What's to cope with? The man comes to the wedding, eats dinner, and goes home. No big deal."

"That's what you think. We haven't said a civil word to each other in weeks."

"Then it's time you did. You have two kids who need civil parents. Call him, Maggie. See what he says."

She huffed, but went to the kitchen phone. I heard her say, "Hey. Billie and I've been talking, and she really wants Jason out here for the wedding and Thanksgiving dinner. Why don't you come, too? Andy would love to see you. What? Okay."

She came back with a stunned look on her face. "He said yes. I think he was surprised into accepting."

"Is your heart all aflutter?"

"No. Ben and I are growing so far apart, I don't think we'll ever get back together. Oddly, I'm all right with that. But you are right, too—we need to do the best we can for our boys."

THAT WAS LAST WEEK. THIS morning I woke early, wanting to run into the morning and pull the day toward me until I reached the hour when I would marry Luke. But time doesn't work like that. It gets woven into the tapestry one hour at a time, one day at a time, one life at a time. Now we see only in part. Someday perhaps we shall see the whole pattern. It will be amazing.

Meanwhile, I have come into my pantry to touch the jars. Scarlet tomatoes, golden peaches, emerald beans, and blueberries the color of my sister's eyes. They rekindle memories: Emerita standing by Daddy's stove smoldering with anger; Margaret sobbing at the kitchen table, exhausted by grief; Mamie snapping beans her last afternoon of life; one afternoon after a long day canning when we laughed until we cried and vowed life would never get that bad again.

We did not like one another when we began. Four strong women, we were fiercely independent. But as we shared our stories, we discovered that the story of one was the story of all. As we filled jars with fruit and vegetables, we created touchstones to preserve what is honest, strong, and true.

The food in the jars is preserved for a season, but I can preserve the lessons they contain for years to come. I want my daughter and all daughters to know that true strength comes not from independence but from interdependence. The differences between us are so much smaller than what we share.

"Mama!" Chellie yells from her room. "What the Sam Hill are you doing? I need to put on my wedding dress!"

"Sorry, honey." I hurry to help her.

After she is dressed, we need to go down to Daddy's so I can put on my own dress. Margaret was obstinate about that. "You are not wearing that dress in your filthy truck."

I dress Chellie in her dark green dress and brush her curls until they shine. Before we head to the truck, I catch her hands and lift them high. "Remind me to teach you someday to hold up the sky."

Author's Thanks

Posthumous thanks are due to our dear friend Gerard Van Lier, who listened to members of a Wednesday night prayer group air struggles and personal griefs during a year of severe drought, and said, in his quiet way, "I think we're all suffering a drought of the spirit." That was the impetus I needed to begin this book. I grabbed a pen, went to a roll of paper by his telephone, and began to write notes for the story—from the bottom of the paper up.

Twenty years of writing mysteries intervened while the story ripened. Many people contributed wisdom and experiences that became a part of it. Susan Williams, who plays for ALTA, was my "tennis consultant." Dr. Warren Weber helped me with symptoms and treatment for congestive heart failure. Dr. Robert Lowery, retired agriculture professor from the University of Georgia, steered me to retired dairy farmer James Casey, who introduced me to the process of dairy and beef farming and also to his delightful family and their dogs. Thank you, James, for all you taught me, and for insights into Bill Anderson's probable decision about his future once he got home from the hospital.

Thanks also to Priscilla Apodaca and Miriam Machida, first readers who caught errors I hadn't seen. Enormous thanks to my husband, Bob, and our housemate, Jaleh Riehn, for not killing me during the months I was consumed by this story.

The real soldiers behind this manuscript were the invisible ones: agent Nancy Yost and editor Ellen Edwards, who unfailingly saw what was wrong and helped put it right. I appreciate you both more than you can ever know.

Finally, many thanks to you, the reader, whose thirst for more books keeps me going.

Patricia Sprinkle is the author of two previous novels, *The Remember Box* and *Carley's Song*, as well as bestselling mysteries and several nonfiction books. Sprinkle writes novels drawn from her own Southern roots, chronicling the lives of women in the contemporary South. In addition to writing, she is active in organizations that serve neglected, deprived, and abused children. She and her husband have two grown sons and live in Smyrna, Georgia, where she enjoys reading, gardening, and doing nothing. Visit her at www.patricia sprinkle.com.

Hold Up the Sky

PATRICIA SPRINKLE

This Conversation Guide is intended to enrich the
individual reading experience, as well as encourage us
to explore these topics together—because books,
and life, are meant for sharing.

A CONVERSATION
WITH PATRICIA SPRINKLE

Q. In recent years you've been writing mysteries. What made you want to move away from them and write Hold Up the Sky?

A. My feeling about some books is that they mature like infants in the womb until they are finally ready to be born.

This book was conceived one night in 1986 at a Japanese steak house. My husband and I shared our table with a party of three strangers—a couple and a woman whom they had obviously not seen in a while. As they got reacquainted, I overheard her say, "My life is my house, my family, and tennis." Something in me wanted to hand her my card and say, "Honey, when you crash, give me a call." I knew those things were not enough—that they could all be taken away and leave her with no life at all.

She and women like her, who place all their faith in things they can lose, haunted me for weeks. Meanwhile Georgia was experiencing a major drought. One night during a small prayer group, members recounted fruitless struggles they were going through. Our host said, "Sounds like we're all having a drought of the spirit."

I knew immediately that my character's name was Margaret Baxter and that she would experience her own drought of the spirit during a year of Georgia drought. She sprang to life that evening—her name, how she looked, how she lived, the fact that she had a sister with a disabled child—and I went to a roll of paper beside my host's telephone and started writing notes for this book. I even wrote a couple of chapters later that week.

However, I had already written two unpublished mysteries and felt I ought to give them a chance. When they succeeded and readers asked for more, I put Margaret on the shelf for twenty years while I wrote twenty mysteries. I loved writing the mysteries until 2006, when I found I didn't love writing them anymore. I wanted to write about Margaret. Her birthing time had come.

Q. The novel's title comes from a proverb: "Women hold up half the sky." Can you explain what it means and where you came across it?

A. It is also attributed to the Chinese, but I first heard it as an *African* proverb probably during the 1970s when most of my energy went into educating people about world hunger. In those years, nowhere was there more hunger than in Ethiopia and the Sahel of Africa. As a result, I read everything I could about Africa. When I found that proverb, I used it to illustrate the fact that women farmers grow most of Africa's food, yet receive very little assistance from government or nongovernment organizations.

As I worked through themes for this book, I realized that theme also applied to the four women in this story. They were doing more than half the work, yet receiving very little recognition or assistance.

Q. What is the main message that you hope readers will take away after reading Hold Up the Sky?

A. I would hope women will take away a couple of messages. Billie speaks one of them at the end: women's strength comes not from independence, but from interdependence. Each of our stories is the story of us all, and we are linked by our stories, our joys, and our sufferings.

While revising one of my nonfiction books, *Women Who Do Too Much*, I found the article Billie refers to, about UCLA researchers who discovered that women's natural response to stress is not fight or flight, like the male response, but rather to seek out other women or to spend time with children. This literally releases chemicals in our brains that reduce stress. So one primary message of this book is, "If you're going through a tough time, call your girlfriends."

Another message is that we need to put our trust and our faith in what cannot be taken away from us, and that we need to know we are not accidents here on earth; we are part of a larger plan and we are each one loved.

Q. In Hold Up the Sky *you create a complex, believable world in the small town of Solace, Georgia. Despite the assumption we sometimes have that life in a small town is quiet and simple, here each character is dealing with major challenges, problems that test their ingenuity and resilience. Is that true of your experience of small-town life?*

A. While ten of my mysteries and all three of my general novels have been set in small towns, I have not lived in a small town since I was five, except for seven months soon after college that I spent in a village of five hundred people in the Scottish Highlands. In those months, however, I saw how a small town is a microcosm of the world. Since then, I have enjoyed spending time in small towns and getting to know people who live there. I think in small towns people experience the same challenges, struggles between good and evil, and possibilities for joy that people in cities do, but they have a harder time hiding their lives because people know one another so well. I also wanted to show how the world, in the form of immigrants, is impinging even on small towns.

Q. The novel explores in some detail Billie's efforts to support herself once her husband's checks stop coming. She encounters many catch-22s along the way from a system that often functions illogically, denies the very help it's intended to offer, and treats poor people as outcasts who don't deserve kindness or respect. Would you like to share personal thoughts and experiences about how poor people are treated in this country—a subject that becomes more relevant during hard economic times?

A. Once for six months our family lived with no income and no health insurance. It was scary. We watched our savings dwindle to nothing.

We looked for work, but found none. We had no mortgage, no car payments, and no credit card debt, so we were much luckier than some, but like Billie and Margaret, we squeezed every penny until it screamed. We delayed every purchase until necessary. We lived the deception of not letting other people know how badly off we were. And we, too, saw how once in a while we needed some good ice cream or even a steak to prove to ourselves that we were still part of the human race. Never again have I criticized a poor person in a grocery line for buying some small luxury.

But we were not as desperate as Billie. Those six months for us were a lab in which we learned greater empathy for the poor, but since my husband's degree is in urban ministry, we have spent a good bit of our lives working with and sometimes living with those who are truly poor. We have seen how demeaning programs ostensibly designed to "help" the poor can be. I often say that laws concerning the poor would look very different if lawmakers actually lived poor for a year. Instead, bailouts for the rich come in billions and are considered "necessary" and even "deserved," but a hue and cry goes up at the suggestion that the minimum wage ought to be high enough to actually support a parent and her children. Public transportation is put on back burners because "everybody" has cars. Laws are passed that ensure that children with disabilities get a chance at an education, but nobody can find money to provide enough buses so those children don't have longer days than other children. Welfare is, reluctantly, made available, but the hoops that have to be jumped through are so many and so difficult that it is no wonder many people try to "beat" the system. It is exhausting to sit with a small child all day in a food-stamp office only to be told you have to come back another day with another piece of documentation.

Once when trying to get help for a single mom who was working at a minimum-wage job, could not find another job, and could not feed her two kids on what she earned, much less afford health insurance, I exclaimed, "We need a car here, and the system offers a steering wheel."

I was not trying to write a diatribe in this novel, but I did want to give an accurate picture of what a woman in Billie's situation goes through.

Q. You've been a writer all your adult life, and you have tackled a wide variety of writing projects. What has given you the most satisfaction?

A. The most satisfaction comes from getting a book as nearly right as I can make it. Right up next to that is hearing from readers who have been touched by a character, a plot, or a situation. Learning that one of my books got somebody through a tough time, or gave them a new insight, or even made them laugh is an enormous reward.

Q. When did you first know you wanted to be a writer?

A. In ninth grade. A teacher assigned the class to do reports on various careers, and I missed class the day of the assignment. By the time I got back, all the careers I was interested in were taken, so she sent me to a box in the corner to use booklets I found there to choose something. There were three books left: farmer, mortician, and writer. I was a voracious reader, but had never realized writers might be living people. All the writers we read in school were dead, so if I had thought about it at all, I'd have thought people wrote books and died and somebody else published them. When I read what a writer did, my immediate sense was not "I want to be a writer," but "I am a writer!" I never looked back after that.

Q. As a young woman just out of college, you spent time in Scotland writing, as a test of your calling as a writer. In a few words, why did you choose this experience, what was it like for you, and what did you learn about yourself?

A. The hardest part of writing is sitting down with an idea and staying in that chair long enough to birth it into something you recognize.

After college I needed to know if I wanted to write badly enough to do it without a professor assigning a topic and setting a deadline. I chose Scotland because I had read a lot about it and wanted to see it, and because, in those days, it was cheap. I worked for one year after college and saved enough to spend seven months in a Scottish village away from everything that was familiar to me.

I learned I could write. That was a relief. I actually published a poem, an article, and a short story there and wrote a short play I sold when I got back home. I learned I loved to write—that it was what I wanted to do above all other things. I learned how to be alone and live through loneliness, which is an important lesson for a writer, who spends most of her time alone. I learned I could cope with life, with a little help from new friends. I learned about living in a small village, and that I could happily live in one all my life (although later I married an *urban* minister). I learned how much love there is in people all over the world, if you are open to receive it. And I learned that I not only needed the people in my village, but that winter they also needed me. A friend got badly burned and required a temporary dishwasher. The children's Sunday school teacher emigrated to New Zealand. The organist in our tiny kirk was often ill. An elderly woman lost her "wee doggie" and went temporarily insane. My extra pair of hands came in useful that winter, and I saw that my being in that village that particular winter was not just for me, but part of a larger plan or tapestry. Maybe that's when I first decided to write a book about God's tapestry.

QUESTIONS
FOR DISCUSSION

1. This book is largely about four very different women. What part does each play, and why was she necessary to the "tapestry" of the book?

2. Billie and Margaret experience two very different kinds of poverty. What are some differences between the two poverties, and how are they alike? Which of the sisters do you most identify with, and why?

3. Mamie in this story is unashamedly Christian. How does her presence enrich or diminish the story for you? How might the story have been different if Mamie had not been included as one of the characters?

4. Emerita's arrival raises questions for Margaret about illegal immigrants in this country. When she prays for Emerita's safety, she says, "This is not about immigration laws; it's about Emerita." How can knowing a person rather than a situation sometimes change our perspective?

5. In the novel, people often feel uncomfortable around Chellie until they get to know her. Have you had an opportunity to get to know a disabled person? Has that experience changed how you see and behave toward other disabled people?

6. Many of the characters in the novel have contributed to their own troubles because of choices they made in the past. Discuss in particular how Billie, Margaret, Bill, and Mamie made or are still making their situation more difficult for themselves and others.

7. This story is partly about a family and the glue that holds families together. What issues surface and have to be resolved after Grace's

death? What precipitates various changes in this family structure? What do Billie, Margaret, and Bill learn?

8. Discuss the relationship between Billie and Margaret. How does it compare to your relationship with your own sisters or between other sisters you know?

9. Billie and Margaret both see their dad as hard and unsupportive of their marriages. Can you think of instances in which Bill actually helped his daughters, but they didn't notice? Why do you think they didn't notice?

10. A writer uses "what if?" to change the direction a story takes. Can you think of places in this story where, if something had happened differently, the entire story would have changed? For example, what if Porter's checks had continued to come? How would that have changed the story?

11. When Billie is desperately in need of money, a job, and assistance with her daughter, she has a hard time getting help. When Bill is laid up in the hospital, neighboring farmers immediately pitch in to help milk the cows. What was your reaction to both situations? Is this sexism at work in a small town? Or is it simply easier to meet one need than the other?

12. Toward the end of the novel, the women join together to harvest and can the vegetables they've been growing all summer. Despite the hard work, they get a lot of satisfaction out of it. How does canning come to symbolize the entire summer for Billie?

13. Canning is largely a lost art. How do you feel about that? What have we perhaps gained and lost as we've moved away from growing and preserving our own food?